THE
PRIEST

GERARD O'DONOVAN

SPHERE

First published in Great Britain in 2010 by Sphere as a paperback orginal

Copyright © Gerard O'Donovan 2010

The moral right of the author has been asserted.

A CIP catalogue record for this book
is available from the British Library.

ISBN 978-0-7515-4485-5

Typeset in Plantin by M Rules
Printed and bound in Great Britain by
Clays Ltd, St Ives plc

Papers used by Sphere are natural, renewable and
recyclable products sourced from well-managed forests and certified
in accordance with the rules of the Forest Stewardship Council.

Mixed Sources
Product group from well-managed
forests and other controlled sources
www.fsc.org Cert no. SGS-COC-004081
© 1996 Forest Stewardship Council

FSC

Sphere
An imprint of
Little, Brown Book Group
100 Victoria Embankment
London EC4Y 0DY

An Hachette UK Company
www.hachette.co.uk

www.littlebrown.co.uk

Gerard O'Donovan was born in Cork and raised in Dublin. After a brief career in the Irish civil service, he travelled widely, working as a barman, bookseller, gherkin-bottler, philosophy tutor and English teacher before settling down to make a living as a journalist and critic for, among others, *The Sunday Times* and the *Daily Telegraph*. In 2007 he was short-listed for the Crime Writers' Association's prestigious Debut Dagger competition.

Visit his website at www.gerard-odonovan.com.

for Muds and Angela

Henceforth let no man be troublesome to me, for I bear the marks of the Lord Jesus on my body.

St Paul, Letter to the Galatians, 6:17

Prologue

Was it luck, really? Some might call it fate. Others the manifest presence of God's guiding hand. He almost missed her. Between the dark and the trees and the cars parked up on the grass verge, his headlights caught a flash of white top and the gleam of something gold. He'd never have seen her if he hadn't been in the van, sitting high up. By the time it hit him full on, he'd driven past. But he knew the road well, the quiet residential estates behind laid out in a grid. He took the next left, then three rights, and he was back out on the main road again – behind her now, taking it slowly.

She'd got barely thirty yards further, sauntering along like all of them did, like there was no tomorrow. He glanced in the rear-view mirror. Nothing. Scanned ahead. Not a ghost in sight but her. No need even to stop and ask. As he passed her again, he tried to get a better look but a lamp post was in the way and he only caught a glimpse. It was enough, though. He gave it fifty yards or so, then pulled up on the verge, nice and easy, cut the engine and lights. Then it was just a matter of slipping into the back, checking the gauge on the cylinder and making sure everything was in place.

Watching her through the square tinted windows at the back, he could tell she hadn't noticed him stopping. Wasn't noticing much by the look of it. Excitement gripped his breath as each step brought her closer, slowly, until he got his first clear look at her. Dark hair, shoulder-length and glossy, a white crop top flattening out her chest, a slash of bare belly, a tiny slip of skirt only just covering her. The gleam of precious metal on her neck. Typical.

He struggled to keep his breathing slow, forced himself to relax using the technique the doctor taught him. Concentrating, making sure he got it right this time. He'd practised it over and over in his head but experience had taught him to make allowances for the unpredictable in these matters and be prepared to react accordingly. Only the last few yards now. He closed his eyes, blessed himself and began counting down. It was easier that way. Left hand holding the sack, right hand gripping the handle of the side panel door. He'd spent hours getting the sliding action smooth. Then he was out, landing perfectly, just a couple of feet in front of her, and his right hand was a fist now, flying like a missile straight at her face, so startled she didn't have time to take a step back – or even be frightened.

1

'**E**xcuse me?' The receptionist in Emergency frowned at Mulcahy and leaned forward a fraction.

'Mul-cah-hee,' he repeated, drawing out the syllables, each a fraction longer than the last. Automatic. Forgot for a minute where he was. That surname had been the bane of his life while he was abroad, every conceivable pronunciation except the right one. But here in Dublin? The woman scowled like she thought he was winding her up. He fished in his jacket pocket and flipped open his Garda warrant card for her.

'*Inspector* Mulcahy,' he emphasised. 'I was told I'd find Inspector Brogan here.'

'Oh,' she said. As people so often did, transfixed by the card. 'Right, Inspector, just a second.'

While she was on the phone Mulcahy checked out the shabby reception area. Very quiet. A few disconsolate patients scattered here and there on the ranks of orange plastic chairs. A pair of pensioners, grey, enfeebled, resigned to waiting. A pregnant woman in the front row, her milk-faced husband leaning into her, one arm around her shoulders, the other hand stroking the rotund mass of her belly, whispering. All the rest looked to be the usual sport and DIY crowd, hobbling around in unlaced football boots or cradling nail-gunned fingers. A typical summer Sunday at St Vincent's Hospital, he reckoned, annoyed he had to be there to witness it.

In the car, on the way over to the hospital, he'd glared up at the fine blue sky, cursing Superintendent Brendan Healy for calling him in on his day off. It wasn't so much that he was having trouble taking orders after being, more or less, his own boss for so long over in Spain. He was a cop, orders came with the territory. And though deference never came naturally to him, he'd developed over the years his own ways of dealing with hierarchy – chiefly by doing everything in his power to move up in it. But he was finding it hard settling back in Dublin. Everyone he'd known from before seemed to be swamped in kids and other lives now. So the prospect of an afternoon's hard sailing with a bunch of lads from the boat club in Dun Laoghaire, getting the tang of salt air in his lungs, working the knots out of his muscles, having a laugh over a few beers in the bar afterwards ... Bollocks, just another fifteen minutes and they'd have been away.

'It's not like you're being given an option here, Mike,' Healy had spat down the phone at him when he questioned his suitability for the task. 'The Minister's having a fit about it already. If we're in a position to do something to cover our arses, then we're sure as hell going to do it.'

Bloody politicians.

'Well,' the receptionist said, putting down the phone. 'Your colleagues *were* up in St Catherine's Ward but there's no sign of them there now.'

He was about to ask her for directions to the ward anyway when he spotted two figures, a man and a woman, standing by the vending machines at the far end of the waiting area. Sipping from plastic cups, hawk-eyed over the rims, something unmistakably hard and reserved in their features. Apart from the old couple, they were the only ones wearing coats. Cops, for sure.

'That's okay,' he said. 'I think that might be them over there.'

As he headed towards them he tried to figure out which was more likely to be the ranking officer. Healy had only said 'Brogan will brief you when you get there.' Of the two it was the woman who had the air of authority about her. She was taller by at least a couple of inches – younger and better turned out, too. Ambitious, definitely. Her wavy red hair was tied back in some kind of complicated plait and her face was attractive, helped by a tint of warm colour on her lips.

Apart from his height, which must have only just scraped five-nine, the guy was more your stereotype plain-clothes man: squat, muscular, watchful, with a flat, flushed bogman's face, the black hair cropped short and flecked with grey. Under his tan car coat was a crumpled grey suit that, together with the creased cream shirt and brown tie, didn't

5

show much in the way of aspiration. What settled it for Mulcahy was that it was the guy, not the woman, who clocked his approach and coughed her a heads-up. Clearly, she was the one who had more important things to think about.

'Inspector Brogan?' Mulcahy asked.

The woman turned towards him and looked him up and down before replying. Up close, he could see now that she was much the younger of the two. Early thirties, tops. And her green eyes full of intelligence. A fast-tracker, most likely. Degrees up to her eyeballs but short on the hard stuff, the street stuff – maybe.

'Inspector Mulcahy?' she said, her tone flat, an echo of somewhere southern in the accent. Waterford, at a guess.

'That's me,' he said, nodding once. Wouldn't want her to think he was pleased to be here. Still, he added 'Mike' for good measure while extending his hand.

'Claire Brogan.' Her smile was as tight and professional as her handshake. 'And this is Detective Sergeant Andy Cassidy.'

The sergeant acknowledged him with a jut of his chin, an ingrained sullenness in his expression.

'Superintendent Healy said you needed some help?' Mulcahy began.

'Well, a translator anyway,' Brogan replied. 'Our usual woman's sick and her backup's buggered off for the week-end. Uncontactable. Healy said you were our best bet, in the circs.'

'Is that right?' Mulcahy wondered at the prickliness in her voice. 'Well, I'm no translator but I am reasonably fluent. I'll give it a go if it's as urgent as Healy says.'

'He said you were in Spain with Europol. Drugs, was it?'

'Until recently, yeah,' Mulcahy said. 'With the Narcotics Intelligence Unit in Madrid. Until they moved the main operation over to Lisbon, when they set up the Maritime Analysis and Operations Centre last September.'

'And they didn't move you with it?'

Again he thought he caught a hint of aggression in the question. But maybe she'd just put it badly. There was no way she could know anything about his personal circumstances and he was damned if he was going to discuss the ups and downs of his career with her.

'Other fish to fry,' he said, half smiling, not giving anything away.

Her eyes showed interest but the corners of her mouth stayed turned down, as if she was determined not to indulge her curiosity.

'Madrid's nice,' she said. 'I was over there myself for a few days last year, doing a course. Europol information exchange on paedophiles – it was good.'

'Speaking of which . . .' he said, recalling now that Healy had said something about her being with Sex Crimes. He glanced meaningfully around the waiting room. 'Shouldn't we be getting on with it? It's an assault, on a Spanish kid, right?'

'A girl, yeah, but not . . .' Brogan paused. 'Is that *all* Healy told you?'

7

'He didn't go into it. Said you'd brief me yourself. Is there a problem?'

'Not at all.' She broke off again and turned to Cassidy. 'Andy, run up to the ward, will you, and make sure they're ready. We'll be along as soon as I've brought the inspector here up to speed.'

Cassidy grunted, threw his empty coffee cup on top of an already overflowing bin and headed towards the double doors. Brogan waited until they whumped shut behind him.

'Okay, Inspector, you'd better—'

'Just Mike will do,' he interrupted.

She looked at him, eyes narrowed. 'Right, uh, Mike,' she continued. 'You'd better be aware that this is a bit of a tricky one. A serious assault on a teenage girl, sixteen years old, with really nasty elements of sexual violence. But there are other factors in play – which is what Healy's up in a heap about.'

'What factors?' Mulcahy asked, his curiosity aroused instinctively.

'Christ, he really didn't tell you, did he?'

Mulcahy shook his head, wishing she'd get on with it. 'He mentioned something about the Minister taking an interest but I assumed that was just to get me over here quicker.'

'Oh, the Minister's taking an interest alright, yeah.' Her laugh betrayed more nervousness than humour. 'A *keen* interest. The victim's the daughter of a Spanish politician.'

'Oh?' That would explain the urgency in Healy's voice, the Minister's supposed panic. Mulcahy felt the curiosity like a cold spring welling up inside him. 'Which politician would that be, then?'

Brogan drew her breath in sharply. 'Does it matter?'

He watched her high cheekbones take on a faint bloom of red, wondering if she was being arsy or just naive. The latter seemed unlikely.

'I'd say it probably does,' he said finally. 'To the Minister, at least. But, look, I've only just been pulled in on this, so I really can't say. All I know is that, generally, if there's any kind of politics involved, it's as well to know exactly what we're dealing with. Right?'

She held his gaze. He could see her thinking it through. Then she nodded.

'I don't know the details but he's in the Spanish government and this thing's really rattled the brass. Not enough for any of them to come down and handle it themselves, of course.'

'No chance,' Mulcahy agreed. 'They'll all steer clear for as long as they can. Or at least until they know which way the wind is blowing.'

She didn't respond to that, didn't need to.

'So how's the girl?' he asked. 'Well enough to be interviewed, anyway?'

'Hard to say. She's out of immediate danger, according to the doctors. Whether she's really up to questioning is another matter. Healy says to push it, if we can. Got to have something for the Minister.'

She looked away and tucked a loose strand of hair back in line behind her ear, a flicker of uncertainty on her face now.

'Her name is Jesica – with just the one S, they said. Doesn't sound very Spanish, does it?'

Mulcahy shrugged. He'd heard the name occasionally in Madrid, the distinctive pronunciation of the J making it sound as natural in Spanish as in English. He thought Brogan was going to leave it at that but then she pulled out a notebook from her coat pocket.

'Family name's Me-laddo Salsa, or something like that,' she said, leafing through the pages. 'I've got a note of it here somewhere.'

Me-laddo Salsa? What the hell sort of name was that? Then it hit him.

'Me*ll*ado?' he blurted, pronouncing it halfway between a J and a Y, as the Spanish would. Now the name was instantly recognisable. His heart thumped hard in his chest. 'Are you saying her father's name is Mellado Salazar?'

'That sounds about right,' Brogan said, frowning at him like she thought he was being a smart-arse correcting her pronunciation. 'You know it?'

'It'd be hard not to, where I was working,' he said, trying to keep the alarm out of his voice. 'Alfonso Mellado Salazar is the Spanish Interior Minister.'

El Juez, they called him. The Judge. A notorious hardliner – zero tolerance, Spanish style. A throwback to the old regime. Jesus, if it was his daughter there would be trouble for certain.

'Let's just say it was immediately obvious she'd been seriously sexually assaulted.'

10

Brogan was showing Mulcahy up to the ward now, explaining how the girl had been spotted on the Lower Kilmacud Road in the early hours, half naked and in terrible distress, by a motorist who stopped and rang for the Gardai and an ambulance. 'It took them a bit longer to figure out she was Spanish. She was in an awful state, completely incoherent. Meanwhile, Dundrum Garda Station took a call from a couple worrying because the sixteen-year-old Spanish student lodging with them hadn't come home from a night out. It was only later they thought to mention whose daughter she was.'

She looked at him closely, letting him put it together for himself. 'It took a while for the pieces to fall into place but, once they did, it didn't take long for panic to break out in the Park.'

Mulcahy nodded sympathetically. Few if any from the upper echelons of the force would have been on duty at the Garda Siochana headquarters in the Phoenix Park on such a sunny Sunday morning. He could imagine the riptide of career anxiety that must have washed out along the phone lines to Dublin's fancier suburbs. Healy had called him from his home out in Foxrock. How many other Sunday lunches would this news have spoiled?

'Have the press got hold of it yet?' Mulcahy asked.

'No,' she said. 'And Healy's determined to keep it that way.'

'He can't seriously think he'll be able to do that?'

Brogan shrugged. 'Well, nobody here in the hospital

11

knows whose daughter she is. Whatever English she had, it's been knocked out of her. So, beyond the brass and us, it's only the Dundrum lads who know. Healy's made it quite clear it's a one-way trip to the sticks for anyone who breathes a word.'

Mulcahy thought about it. Being transferred out of Dublin to man some godforsaken small-town station would be a fate worse than death for most guards. But he doubted it was Garda tongues wagging that Healy needed to worry about. Hospitals are big places, and Healy could never control that side of things.

'Of course, the Spanish embassy's been informed as well. But they're not very likely to go blabbing to the papers.'

'Have they not been down here yet?' He was surprised about that. When it came to protecting one of their own, diplomats were usually even quicker off the mark than cops.

'On their way, I'm told. Probably not many of *them* around on a Sunday, either.' Brogan checked her watch again. 'Which is why we need to get cracking, or they'll be trying to tie us up in red tape before we can get anything out of her.'

As they pushed through a door leading on to the ward, Brogan put a hand out, stopping him. 'Before we get into this, I need you to know that I'm the one who's directing the interview, not you.'

'Fine with me,' he said. Territoriality was part and parcel of life in the Garda Siochana, everybody guarding their own patches like chained dogs. 'It's your bag,' he added. 'And by the sounds of it you're welcome to it. I might need a minute or two to build a rapport with the girl, y'know, but otherwise she's all yours. Like you said, I'm only the translator.'

'Good.' A brief smile lit up Brogan's face, only for it to darken again. 'Look, there are a couple of ground rules I need to go through with you before we go in. But first I've got to warn you. I'm sure you've been in the job for years, Mike, and you're a hard man and all. But I'm telling you, this guy did a right job on the poor kid.'

2

Siobhan Fallon waited outside her apartment while the delivery guy clattered down the stairs. Only when she heard the downstairs door slam shut did she go back in and close hers behind her. As far as she knew, there'd never been any actual intruders discovered in Ballsbridge Court. It was much too nice a block for that. But the busybodies in the residents' association would be on her back about 'security' if she didn't toe the line. And the last thing she needed was to rock the boat in this, the one place she could retreat to for a bit of peace and quiet. Hampered by the huge basket of flowers in her arms – pink and white roses, starburst lilies, and God knows what else – she gingerly made her way over to the small pine dining table by the living-room window. Setting it down beside the newspaper already laid out there, she thought about getting her camera to record the moment, then noticed the envelope taped to the basket. No one but Harry Heffernan, her editor, could have organised a Sunday delivery. Still, she wanted to see it for herself in black and white.

As it was, the card was a bit of a let-down: 'To our very own top striker! Love and appreciation – Harry.' How lame was that? It was worse than his duff headlines.

Siobhan stared down at the copy of the *Sunday Herald* spread out on the table. A classic paparazzi shot took up most of the tabloid front page, the colours washed out by the flare of a flashgun in the night: soccer international Gary Maloney frozen in time, exiting an elegant Georgian doorway, his dyed-blond hair tousled like a sleepy six-year-old's, his eyes rimmed red with excess of one sort or another – or quite possibly more. But, from a news point of view, all the magic was in the background where, peering out, caught in the act of blowing a kiss, could be seen the easily recognisable, blonde-haloed face of Suzy Lenihan. As in the celebrity, ex-model wife of Maloney's boss, the Republic of Ireland team manager Marty Lenihan. Which might have been fine, even quite charming, had it not been for those two perfectly lit curves of shoulder and hip also jutting out from behind the door, attesting to the fact that Suzy was buck naked. In the circumstances, the blaring headline – splashed in reversed-out 72-point white down the left side of the picture: MALONEY SCORES WITH MANAGER'S MISSUS – was pretty much surplus to requirements.

All the other words on that page were Siobhan's. She looked them over, if not exactly with pride, then at least with a heartfelt sense of satisfaction. In particular, she liked the four words picked out in bold at the head of the story: *Siobhan Fallon, Chief Reporter*. It had taken a heck of a lot to win that title, and all too often it was only when, as now, she saw it in print that she felt it was worth it. Every element of the story was down to her. She'd sniffed it out from one of her best sources, tracked down the lovers, told Franny the snapper where to meet her. All he had to do was sit in the car with her and wait until Maloney came out. Flash, whirr, flash – pics in the bag. And then she'd dived in with the voice recorder. No hassle, no fists, no abuse. Maloney was too startled, or too coked out of his tree. And when she asked him for a comment, the dim hunk gave her one to die for. 'Did the wife send you?' he'd asked. Christ, you couldn't make it up. If she was the editor, that would have been the headline.

Not that it mattered. It was the biggest scoop of the day by a long shot. Siobhan grinned to herself, ran her eye over the page again, and went to fetch her camera from her bag. The story had been picked up by every newsdesk in the country and it was one of the lead items on RTE radio's *Ireland on Sunday*, to which she'd contributed by phone earlier. After which, it was prominent on every other radio and TV bulletin she'd seen and heard. Even made it as high as the number-three item on Sky News at one point. And still Harry thought he could palm her off with a bunch of flowers?

She tried to hold out against the thought, didn't want to spoil the moment. She looked again at the profusion of blooms in the basket. Flowers were all well and good but they wouldn't pay any bills. She wondered what Heffernan would have sent one of her male colleagues in the same circumstances. Tickets for a big match, probably. At least you could flog those on eBay. But she pushed the idea away impatiently. It wasn't about that. It was about getting her due. That long-promised pay rise, she thought, as the frustration began to build again.

She flopped on to the sofa, feeling suddenly defeated. Around the room, newspapers and magazines, most weeks out of date, were strewn everywhere. The few sticks of furniture she possessed were buried under stacks of unironed clothes, half-read books and discarded packaging from things she mostly couldn't recall buying. It was worse in the bedroom, where stuff got dumped and left for weeks on end before being washed or else picked up, brushed down and re-worn after a decent interval. Every moment she had, she gave to her job. There never seemed to be time for all the other bits and pieces.

Siobhan stared up at the white, uncluttered ceiling. The only trapping of success that would mean anything to her right now was a cleaner. If only for one or two mornings a week, just to tidy up, do some ironing, take a tiny bit of the burden of living from her. But the mortgage payments, even on this shoebox, were already crippling. She'd bought at the height of the boom and, even if she wanted to, wouldn't have a hope in hell of getting rid of it now without losing out big time. If she were chief reporter on the *Irish Times* or *Irish Independent* her finances would be very different. But on the piddling, cash-strapped *Sunday Herald* . . .? Dream on, Siobhan, dream on.

*

Brogan hadn't been exaggerating.

Mulcahy stopped by the metal bed-end and drew his breath in sharply on seeing the mottled mass of bruising, clotted blood and stitches that was Jesica Mellado Salazar's face. The dark, purpling flesh around her eyelids was so swollen, he couldn't tell if she was awake or asleep. The nurse sent in to supervise the interview, a thin, careworn but kindly looking woman, went over to the far side of the bed, smoothing her pale blue uniform under narrow hips as she sat down. The plastic name tag on her chest said, simply, Sorenson.

'Dr Baggot said to remind you to keep this short, Inspector,' she warned Brogan. 'Jesica's not really well enough.'

Brogan muttered something about the need to act fast and that she'd keep it as brief as possible. Then she took a chair and placed it in a position by the bed where she could be in the girl's eyeline. She drew another over beside it, for Mulcahy. Cassidy remained standing by the door. As Mulcahy sat down, he felt a momentary flicker of uncertainty. His Spanish was fine for most situations. He'd lived in Madrid for seven years, worked, socialised, and even romanced in the language. But could he be subtle enough for the delicate handling this situation would require? He'd just have to keep it simple. By the look of her, the girl wouldn't be able to say much anyway. He could always shut the interview down if it wasn't going well.

Mulcahy looked up to make sure Brogan hadn't spotted

his hesitation, but she was busy asking Nurse Sorenson to wake up Jesica.

The nurse nodded and touched her patient gently on the shoulder. 'Jesica, love, some people are here to see you.'

A low moan came from somewhere deep inside the girl, but she didn't move. Mulcahy coughed gently, to clear his throat. The narrow adolescent body beneath the sheets stiffened visibly, and the girl's head jerked round on the pillow. One puffed eyelid flickered open fractionally, then the other, fixing on Brogan who was first in her sightline.

'Hello, Jesica,' Brogan began. Calm, soft and steady. She smiled at the girl. What little white was left in Jesica's eyes shone with anxiety as they flicked from Brogan's face to Mulcahy's.

'*Buenos días, Jesica,*' Mulcahy said, trying to keep his voice low and reassuring. Even so, she flinched when she heard his voice.

'*Tranquilo, niña,*' he said, as softly as he could. '*No te preocupes. Somos policías. Queremos ayudarte.*'

Don't worry. We're police. We want to help you.

The girl trembled at every word he spoke. Instinct urged him to reach out and take her hand, to try to comfort her with something other than words. But Brogan had been very specific, and he knew it himself, from long experience: no physical contact. Words would have to do.

It took a while for him to know for sure that she understood him. At first she wouldn't reply in any way, evading even his eyes by closing her own and keeping them that way.

19

So he asked her to nod if she agreed that her name was Jesica . . . that she was from Madrid . . . that she was sixteen years old. With each question that followed, her head moved a touch more surely on the pillow. Then, when he asked her to confirm her father's name, her eyes flickered open again, narrowly, tears welling along the lids, and she mouthed her first words. So indistinct, so full of fear, that he could barely catch them.

'*Dónde está . . . dónde está mi padre?*'

A little girl looking for her daddy.

Mulcahy didn't want to destroy what little trust he'd built up, so he said he was sure her father was on his way. That seemed to reassure her. He then looked over at Brogan, whose expression left no doubt of her frustration at being left out of the loop. He nodded encouragingly at her, but said nothing. He wanted to broach the main issue with Jesica without breaking the mood. So he turned back to the girl and asked what had happened to her.

'*Fuiste asaltada?*' Had someone attacked her?

She turned away, her swollen eyelids blinking as rapidly as they could, as if trying to fend off some terrible thought. Then she nodded. It was a tiny movement, replete with emotion.

'What're you saying to her?' Brogan whispered, plucking at his sleeve. He mouthed at her to wait a second, then turned back to face Jesica. The girl looked more uncertain than ever, glancing up, then the tears started to flow.

'*Un hombre me golpeó . . . No sé que pasó.*'

Beside him, Brogan wouldn't remain patient.

'What's she saying?' she hissed at him, beneath her breath.

'A man hit her. She doesn't know what happened.'

'Ask her did she know the man?'

Mulcahy turned back to Jesica. '*Este hombre, lo conoces?*'

'*No vi nada . . .*' She didn't see anything, Jesica replied, as haltingly as before. The blow had come from nowhere. Straight in her face. So hard, so unexpected, that she fell to the ground.

'What did he look like?'

Mulcahy translated Brogan's question.

'*No, no sé,*' the girl insisted, the tears now in full flow.

'She doesn't know.'

'Did he say anything to her?'

Mulcahy's heart took a dive as he watched Jesica's swollen features seize up with fear again.

'*Todo se puso oscuro,*' she said, her facial muscles contracting until the tendons in her neck stood out like cables under the effort of voicing her fear.

'Everything went dark, she says. The man threw something over her, and dragged her somewhere inside. He kept punching her, over and over again.'

Mulcahy stopped as Jesica subsided into a long coughing fit, grasping for a bowl on the cabinet beside her as the terror within tried to work its way out, though nothing emerged but a long dribble of blood-streaked saliva. The nurse helped her up, then wiped her lips gently with a tissue

21

as the girl lay back against the pillows, each heave of her chest a fraction shallower as she slowly found calm again.

'She shouldn't be having to be put through this now,' the nurse complained. 'Can't it wait until she's a bit stronger?'

'I don't think the bastard who did this to her should be on the streets for a second longer than necessary, do you?' Brogan snapped at her.

The nurse flushed and looked like she was going to say something back. Instead she tutted to herself and turned to Jesica, stroking her forehead and holding out a beaker for her to sip from.

'Okay,' Brogan whispered to Mulcahy. 'Steer away from the attack or she'll get too upset. Ask her what she was doing just before? We'll go for detail again in a minute.'

'Are you sure about this?' Mulcahy asked her. Bugger Healy. Bugger the bloody Minister, for that matter. This girl was in no condition to be interviewed.

'Just ask the question,' Brogan insisted. 'It could be the only shot we get for days.'

He held her gaze, turning things over in his mind. She was the sex crimes expert. She had to know what she was doing. How would he feel if some shoe-in tried to tell him how to operate? He turned back to Jesica and asked. But they didn't get much more from her. She said she'd been to a club, but didn't know where. When they asked her if she'd left on her own, she became distressed.

'*Me golpeó*' – he punched me – '*me golpeó*,' was all she would say, over and over. Then something new and even

22

more terrible seized her, and her eyes rolled and she whimpered something Mulcahy could only just make out: about hellfire, a flaming sword and the vengeance of God. Could that be right, though? Mulcahy repeated the words in his head, and was certain he'd heard correctly.

But, even as he did so, the girl cried out and curled herself into a ball, rocking and sobbing in the nurse's arms.

Mulcahy turned to Brogan again. 'What the hell did he do to her?'

Brogan met his eye with a fierce glare. 'He tortured her, the sick fucker. Burned her, or branded her more like, all across her stomach and genitals. We don't know what with, yet, maybe a knife and a blowtorch. Whatever it was, he absolutely destroyed her.'

'Jesus wept,' Mulcahy said, struggling to hold back the shock.

'You're really going to have to leave it at that now,' Nurse Sorenson insisted to Brogan. 'She's too upset. She badly needs to rest.'

Brogan nodded in agreement, but wasn't done yet.

'Okay, yeah. Just one more thing.' She plucked at Mulcahy's sleeve again. 'Tell her it would really help us if she could remember one small detail, anything at all, about the guy who did this. About his clothes, his hair, his shoes – or where they went to. Anything.'

Mulcahy spoke as gently as he could but, almost instantly, panic rose in the girl again – as if his words were smashing through all the barriers of analgesia she'd been given, worming out the pain, sharp as the first time. He cursed quietly and stood up, unable to imagine what she was reliving and unwilling to provoke it any further. Quickly he told the girl it was okay, he wouldn't ask her any more questions. Then he pushed past Brogan towards the door. He'd had enough.

'Where're you going?' Brogan was staring at him like he was crazy.

'Okay, that's it,' the nurse said. 'Out now, all of you. No arguments.' But even as she was standing up to shoo them out, Jesica erupted. Like a burst dam it came, flooding out, a torrent of tears, snot and terror. The nurse struggled to control her, to stop her tearing at herself beneath the sheets. Mulcahy's first thought was to step in, too, but Brogan was there before him, lunging to restrain the girl's flailing limbs. He stepped away, mesmerised by the ferocity of emotion.

Just as he did so, a small, elegantly dressed man swept into the room. In his late thirties, jet-black hair slicked back, he took one look at the distressed girl, another at the scrum around her and launched straight into a heavily accented diatribe against both Brogan and the nurse.

Having encountered a few excitable Spanish diplomats in his time, Mulcahy instantly recognised the type. Detective Sergeant Cassidy, however, was not so subtle. Rounding on the newcomer, shoulders hunched, palms raised to block his approach, he warned him to step out of the room. When the Spaniard became only more incensed, and tried to push past, there was a blur of brown, a groan of pain, and in an instant

24

the man was on his knees, bent over, his right arm twisted and locked upright behind him. The look of agony on his face mirrored the one of flushed triumph on Cassidy's.

Beside them, it was alarm that was now paralysing Brogan's features.

'Jesus, Andy! Let him go, for God's sake. He's from the embassy.'

By now even Jesica had been startled into silence by the scuffle at her bedside. She looked on uncomprehendingly as Brogan and Cassidy helped the man to his feet, dusting him down. Meanwhile the nurse, flushed and outraged, was forcing all three towards the door, demanding they take their appalling behaviour elsewhere.

Mulcahy dragged his disbelieving gaze away from them and found it connecting with Jesica's. He shook his head, smiling as reassuringly as he could. But she appeared to have forgotten the ruckus already and made no response other than to hold his gaze intently as she touched a red weal on her neck, anxiously checking for something, a look of pleading in her injured eyes.

She whimpered to him that her cross and chain was missing.

'*Quizás lo tienen las enfermeras*,' Mulcahy suggested. Maybe the nurses had it. But looking at the severity of the injury on her neck, he guessed it was more likely it had been torn off during the attack. She wasn't really listening to him, anyway, just staring at him, playing something out inside her head.

'*Recuerdo una cosa*,' she said, her voice so fragile he could

25

see her fighting hard to stay in control. She remembered something.

'*Hizo la señal del Cristo.*' she said, almost too low for him to hear it, the voices of the others raised again now they were outside the room.

'*La señal del Cristo?*' he repeated, making sure he'd heard her correctly.

'*Sí, claro,*' she said, choking back tears. '*Como un cura.*'

But before he could say anything else the nurse was back in the room, taking him by the elbow, insisting that he leave. He took a look back as he went, wanting to say goodbye, but Jesica had forgotten him already, another spasm of tears testimony that her focus was back again on the horror replaying itself inside her.

'Like a priest!' Brogan exclaimed. They were standing by the main hospital entrance. Mulcahy took a deep drag on his cigarette, relieved to be outdoors again.

'That's what she said to me,' Mulcahy said. 'Her exact words were: "He made the sign of the cross. Like a priest."'

It was a good half-hour since he'd left Jesica's room. Down the corridor he'd found Brogan still trying to calm the indignant Spanish diplomat but clearly getting nowhere. Mulcahy introduced himself to the man, then asked Brogan if she minded him having a word with the guy in Spanish. Maybe it was surprise at being addressed in his own language, or maybe it was just Mulcahy's equable presence towering over him, but First Secretary Ibañez calmed down rapidly after

26

that. A couple of minutes later, he cracked a smile when Mulcahy alluded to a legendary Spanish joke about a doltish member of the Guardia Civil, while apologising for Cassidy's short fuse. Ibañez even seemed to have forgotten the ache in his right arm by the time he shook Mulcahy's hand and headed back towards the ward, an assurance having been brokered that no attempt would be made to interview Jesica again without an embassy official present.

It wasn't until they were outside, waiting for Cassidy to bring the car around, that Mulcahy got to tell Brogan what Jesica had said to him.

'Jesus, that's all we need,' Brogan continued. 'Why, in the name of God, would she say that? Was the guy wearing a dog collar or something?'

Mulcahy shrugged. 'You'll have to ask her, next time.'

'What do you think she meant? Do priests bless themselves any different to the rest of us?'

'Not that I know of.'

'Well, it can't be because she doesn't understand it, can it? I mean, she's Spanish so she's Catholic, right?'

'I think we can safely assume that,' Mulcahy said. 'Her father's famously right wing. In fact, he's always being attacked for his links with the Church. And, like I told you, she said the cross and chain she was wearing around her neck is missing.'

'It's a strange thing for her to focus on, given all the other stuff this guy did to her, don't you think?'

'You'd know more than me about that, but maybe it's of

27

some . . . Oh, I don't know.' Mulcahy stopped, not wanting to speculate or get any more involved than he was already.

'No, go on,' Brogan prompted. 'What were you going to say?'

'Just that I remember reading a profile of Jesica's father in *El País* or somewhere. I don't remember exactly, but I'm pretty sure her mother died when she was very young and it was himself brought her up alone. Or as alone as you can get with the sort of lifestyle they lead. We're talking real old Spanish aristocracy.'

'All the less reason to worry about a cross and chain, then, you'd think?' Brogan said.

'Unless it had sentimental value. Maybe it was her mother's – or maybe her father gave it to her. It must have had some special significance for her.' He dropped the guttering cigarette beneath his foot and crushed it. 'Anyway, I'm sure it'll all come out in the end. What do you reckon your chances are?'

Brogan brushed a strand of hair off her face. 'Hard to say at this stage. It's not exactly run-of-the-mill, is it? We won't know anything until we get an idea of where she was and who she was with last night. And you never know what the guys from the Technical Bureau might turn up.'

'What sort of sicko could do that, eh? She's hardly more than a child.'

Brogan scowled at him, but not unpleasantly. 'Try working in Sex Crimes for a while, you'll find there's no shortage of sickos in Dublin.'

He shook his head. 'No thanks, I'll stick to what I know.'

Given half a bloody chance. Mulcahy looked at the sky again. The inviting azure of the early afternoon had gone, obliterated by a flat expanse of ashen cloud. And the wind had a hint of rain on it. Perhaps it wasn't a good day for sailing, after all. A dark blue Mondeo rolled up beside them. Inside, Cassidy leaned over from the driver's seat and pushed the passenger door open. In doing so he shot Mulcahy a sullen glare. He hadn't been at all happy when Mulcahy had suggested he make another, more sincere apology to Ibañez. The ignorant fucker should be thanking him for saving him an appearance at a disciplinary hearing.

Brogan glanced back as she climbed into the car. 'Thanks, Mike – and sorry for spoiling your Sunday. I'll let you know how we get on.'

'Do that,' he said, hoping she wouldn't. 'Good luck with it.'

With a squeal of tyres, the car shot away. Mulcahy stared after it a moment. Cassidy was clearly an old-school thug of the first order, a bloody liability. He wondered how Brogan put up with him. Then he shook his head again, took his keys and cigarettes from his pocket, and headed towards the car park.

3

Siobhan Fallon swept up Stephen Street like a March wind, coat flapping open despite the steady drizzle, one arm deep in her shoulder bag, rummaging for her mobile phone. She was fifteen minutes late already. Ordinarily, she'd just blame the weather and flash a winning smile, which usually did the trick. But she liked this guy, and even if that didn't work out there was always the chance of a story in it. She scrolled back through her recent calls and clicked on his number, but all she got was voicemail. There wasn't much point in leaving a message now. She slipped the phone back into her bag and upped her pace. She was nearly there, anyway.

Three minutes later she rounded the corner onto South Great George's Street and saw the Long Hall across the road. The old Victorian pub had enjoyed a bit of a facelift since the last time she'd seen it, when a vast new office block was being built behind. For a while it had looked as if the whole street front would be demolished, and the Long Hall with it. Par for the course during the early days of the boom, when no inconvenient bit of Dublin's heritage lasted longer than it took to stuff a planning officer's pocket with cash. But somehow the Long Hall had made it through, a valiant survivor, doubtless still as decrepit as ever inside. She'd laughed when he suggested meeting her there. Not exactly the place to impress a girl.

She pushed through the door and past the dark mahogany bar, her eyes trailing over the mad mishmash of mirrors and chandeliers, the wood-panelled walls bedecked with mottled old Chinese prints, the crazed fruit plasterwork on the ceiling. She spotted him straight off. He was sitting reading a paper at a table in the back room, long legs stretched out, a pint of stout hardly touched in front of him, jaw jutting towards the story, absorbed. A memory coursed through her of a time years before, when she'd seen him in a posture just like that, but without the paper, exhausted and thoughtful after leading a major drugs bust out in Clondalkin. Herself a rookie reporter and him already in a position that reeked of responsibility and power. The sense that washed from him then, of being in complete control, had gone through her like a charge – his calm, cool determination. And, though her own position had changed a great deal since, she felt shot through by exactly the same feeling now.

Exactly the same.

Mulcahy was about to check his watch when he looked up and there she was, framed by the dark wooden clock arch that divided the front and back bars, smiling at him, looking like the rain hadn't dared touch her.

'I'm *really* sorry I'm late,' Siobhan said, a penitent smile lighting up her face. 'I couldn't find anywhere to park.'

'That's alright. It gave me a chance to catch up on the news.' He folded his paper and started to get up, but she motioned him to stay where he was, shrugging off her coat, delving in her bag for her purse, refusing to let him go up to the bar for her.

He sat back and took a long pull on his pint, watching her as she went, liking the way her black hair kinked and curled as it fell to her shoulders, the way her hips moved under the soft, hugging cotton of her skirt. The way she made the grouchy tosser of a barman beam at her just by asking him for a drink. Mulcahy had liked her from the moment his old pal Mark Hewson – nowadays a minor force in Dublin public-relations circles – had introduced her to him at a birthday bash a fortnight before. Because, despite the changed hair-style and the passing of time, he immediately knew her – the memory rising like a ghost in his mind, something he'd never realised was there but which emerged fully formed and instantly recognisable. Siobhan Fallon, *that* reporter. The one who'd come out on a job with him that time, years ago, after he first got his own team – when he'd flummoxed even himself by bagging one of the biggest caches of smack ever seized in Dublin.

He thought he saw it in her eyes, too, those amazing blue eyes, the surprise and delight at meeting again. For half an hour they'd battled the mad churn of the party, jostled by passing bodies, talking into each others' ears, cheeks brushing casually like old friends, trading laughs. Then they were separated when a bunch of her friends turned up and dragged her away, and he didn't see her again until later, when he caught her eye from across the room as she was leaving with them. She smiled, he waved, and that was it. Or so he thought. It had been on his mind to look her up. But a woman like that, he reckoned, had to be with someone already . . . until she called him a few days later. She'd got his number from Mark. Would he like to go for a drink? Straight out, no messing around – another thing to like about her.

'You'd better put those away or you'll have to arrest yourself,' she said as she sat down, drink in hand, pointing at the pack of cigarettes he'd left on the table.

'I thought I might need an excuse to get out of here quick,' Mulcahy joked.

'Well, be warned, I like a smoke myself now and again, so I'd have an excuse to come after you.'

Her eyes hooked him with a flash of pale sapphire. It was the first thing he'd thought of when she called. That look.

'I heard you on the radio this morning, talking about Gary Maloney,' he said. 'Sounds like you kicked up a storm with that one.'

'Yeah,' she said. 'It's big alright. The nation's favourite footie hero and all that. But it'll be in all the other papers by tomorrow – won't really be mine any more.'

Mulcahy didn't see why that would matter to her. For all that he thought cops and hacks had a lot in common, and could sometimes be pretty useful to one another, he'd never been much taken by the tabloid thing, all that goggling at other people's indiscretions. How she'd go about finding a story like that, on the other hand, did interest him.

'Oh, you know, sources, rumours,' she replied. 'You're a detective, you know how all that stuff works. Half the job is knowing the right people, being in the right place to get the whisper. Other times they come to you. Jimmy X is pissed off with Johnny Y. He wants revenge, or his job. Or just the dosh. That's how you fellas get most of your leads, isn't it? Contacts, informants, general begrudgery.'

She was right. People liked to believe what they saw on television, that for cops it was all about careful weighing and measuring of clues or, even more stupid, high-tech forensics. But the truth was that the majority of cases were cracked thanks to good old-fashioned treachery. More so in his usual area of operation, drugs, than anywhere else, because the stakes were astronomical and grassing up rivals to the police was just another weapon in the aspiring drug baron's armoury. But however right she was, he didn't want to let her off the hook that easily.

'And do they ever expect anything from *you*?' he asked. 'In return, like?'

She looked at him with a faint smile on her lips, like he'd caught her out in something, but said nothing for a moment or two, obviously weighing up something in her mind. Then she let her smile broaden further before replying.

'It kind of depends on how big a favour they've done you.

34

But like I said, I'm usually the one doing them the favour. Getting the story out, you know? That's enough for most of them.'

'So there'd be no question of you paying a source for this kind of story, then?'

This time she was ready for him. 'I'm afraid I couldn't possibly comment on such a commercially sensitive subject,' she said, grinning again. 'Anyway, you know how fanatical us journalists are about protecting our sources.'

He wasn't sure whether she was teasing him or not. She knew full well that he wasn't asking for details.

'Speaking of which,' she continued, taking a drink with one hand and making a small waving motion with the other, 'I wanted to ask you something. You mentioned at the party that you'd been in Madrid with Europol for a while, and I was thinking maybe it might be worth writing a piece about international drug-trafficking, and where Ireland fits into the picture. I read a piece in one of the English papers claiming that more than half the hard drugs over there come in through Ireland. I mean, I knew it was a lot, but is it really that much?'

Mulcahy's spirits took a dive. It wasn't so much the question, as the thought that a story might be *all* she wanted him for. Well, if he was going to be disappointed, he might as well let her know she would be, as well. He was no longer the great mine of stories he used to be.

'Is that what you have me down for then – a potential source?'

It came out harsher than he intended. Again, she held his gaze for a second or two, then laughed, embarrassed.

'Jesus, I've hardly been sitting here five minutes and I'm giving you the third degree already. I'm sorry, Mulcahy. It's the job, you know, honestly. I see somebody, I think, "Aha, a story", and I jump straight in. I'm sorry. It's force of habit. I thought we could . . .'

She trailed off, staring down at her hands.

'No, look,' he stumbled. 'Ah, forget it. I shouldn't be so prickly. Maybe if we just steer clear of work for a bit, we'll do fine.'

She was looking at him again now, that glint of mischievous curiosity back in her eyes. He remembered how persuasive she'd been that time she convinced him to take her out on the raid. How he'd known he'd be up to his hairline in shit if anything went wrong, but he'd let her come anyway. And it turned into one of the most momentous nights of his life. That operation had been a career-maker for him. Her article let everyone know – not only his bosses but every jumped-up smack dealer on his patch – that there was a new not-to-be-fucked-with guy in town. And, when he looked back on it now, it was her that he thought of, there in the back seat of the car, swamped by a Garda stab vest, as high on the excitement of what was about to go down as any of his team. In that instant of memory, he changed his mind about her again.

'Why don't we go out for a smoke?' he suggested, picking up his pack and lighter.

'Good idea,' she said. 'Then we can start over again when we come back in.'

The way he heard it, she might as well have been beside him in a hotel room, somewhere between desire and the cold light of day.

Brogan looked at her watch as she perched on the edge of a cream leather sofa in the living room of one Mrs Edith Mannion. Everything was clinically clean and ordered. Kept perfect for the visitors who, Brogan suspected, rarely came to mess it up. It was getting late and, despite the prospect of making progress, she was beginning to flag now. This would have to be the last visit of the night. Even so, the thought of returning to her own home filled her with the usual form-less dread. Aidan sitting on the sofa, staring at the television, beer in hand and nothing to say, the static hiss of the baby monitor like an accusing whisper in the corner.

It had been a slow, frustrating evening, with little or no progress. By late afternoon they'd got in touch with Frank Harney, principal of the Dublin Summer Language School, where Jesica was enrolled on a four-week course. Given the circumstances, Harney hadn't taken much persuading to curtail his Sunday family outing to the Wicklow mountains. A couple of hours later, looking anxious and uncomfortable in a khaki shirt, shorts and hiking boots, he met them at the school, which was situated on the upper floors of a Victorian building on Westmoreland Street.

From his small office window, you could see the grey

River Liffey cleaving the heart of the city in two at O'Connell Bridge, the iconic statue of the Liberator himself just beyond. Any other day, Brogan might have paused to admire the view, but she was focused on getting Harney to produce a list of the foreign students he thought Jesica might have gone out with the night before, and the details of the families they were lodging with. Then they'd started tracking the kids down, one by one. They'd already drawn a blank with the three they'd contacted so far. None of them had been with Jesica, but all three had mentioned the young girl currently staying with Mrs Mannion as being close to her.

'You'd think we had shit on our shoes, the way she looked at us,' Cassidy muttered from the armchair opposite. Mrs Mannion had indeed been less than welcoming. But Brogan could hardly blame the poor woman for being upset, the Gardai turning up on her doorstep in prim and proper Orpen Close, Stillorgan – at this hour on a Sunday night. Demanding to see a youngster she probably knew little or nothing about, who was only staying with her for the duration of a language course. God knows what awful suspicions were going through the woman's mind.

'Shush, would you,' Brogan said. 'That's them coming now.'

The door opened and in came Mrs Mannion, followed by a pretty, olive-skinned girl of sixteen or so. With long, sleek hair, an expensive-looking pink top, cream hipster jeans and immaculate white Reeboks, she was typical of the middle-class Spanish and Italian kids who flocked to Dublin in their thousands every summer, dispatched by parents desperate for them to improve their English skills. She, too, looked anxious. Brogan guessed their host must have attempted an inquisition of her own while escorting the girl downstairs.

'Now, Inspector, this is Luisa,' the woman said, leaving her standing while going to take a seat herself.

'Uh, there's no need to sit down, Mrs Mannion,' Brogan said. 'We'd like to talk to Luisa on her own, if you don't mind.'

She did mind, but once it was established that Luisa, being sixteen, didn't need to be accompanied, Mrs Mannion didn't have much room for argument. Not even when she suggested she should stay '*in loco parentis*, as it were'.

Brogan thanked her, reminding her how she'd already told them Luisa's English was better than average, then got up and closed the door behind her as the woman left the room. Brogan smiled at Luisa and touched her arm reassuringly, directing her to sit down on the sofa, beside her.

'Don't worry, Luisa, you're not in any trouble.'

Luisa smiled weakly, but wasn't convinced.

'You're a friend of Jesica Salazar, is that right?' Brogan asked.

'*Sí* . . . I mean, yes,' she stumbled.

'Well, I don't want to worry you, but Jesica's had an accident and is in hospital.'

Brogan gave the girl a moment to translate this to herself. A second later, shock and understanding hit home simultaneously, and some of the natural gloss of her complexion faded.

'What happen to her?'

'You don't need to worry about that for the moment,' Cassidy butted in, a little harshly.

The girl looked back to Brogan, anxiously.

'But she is okay, no?'

'Sure, Luisa, she's okay for now,' Brogan equivocated. 'But we need to ask you some questions. Did you see her last night?'

'Yes, of course.'

Brogan glanced at Cassidy, who was hunched forward, all the tiredness gone from his face now.

'You were out with Jesica last night?'

'Yes, we went to, uh, to dancing together, in a club, with some of the other students.'

'Can you tell us where this club was?'

'*Por supuesto* . . . by the crossing in Stillorgan. You know the club, the GaGa? It is not very nice, but is, uh, near to here, you understand?'

'The place near the bowling alley?' Cassidy inquired.

'Yes, this one.'

'And what time did you leave the club?'

Again she looked up guiltily.

'It was late. Mrs Mannion, she wasn't very happy . . .'

'Forget about Mrs Mannion, Luisa. We're only interested in what happened to Jesica. Did she leave the club with you?'

'No.' The girl looked surprised they could even ask the

question. 'No, she go early with . . .' And then the penny, the peseta, the Euro . . . or whatever it was, dropped, and her eyes opened and her face flushed, and all of a sudden she was frightened.

'Jesica . . . she *is* okay, no?'

'Like I said, she's doing alright, Luisa,' Brogan replied. 'But we really need to know who she was with in the club and afterwards. Did she leave with somebody else? With a boy? Is that what you're saying?'

Again the girl looked unsure whether to answer or not. Brogan guessed Jesica must have breached some sacrosanct school rule by leaving the club with someone other than a fellow student.

'Come on, Luisa. We won't tell anybody. This is important. Did she leave with a boy?'

'No, not a boy, exactly.' She hesitated. 'He was more old. Maybe twenty, twenty-two. They were together all of the night, you know. They dance, they, uh, kiss. She said he will take her home to her house. He looked nice . . .' Again she frowned, fear fighting understanding. 'Was he . . .?'

Cassidy pulled the car keys from his pocket and popped the locks before they were halfway down the drive. There was something about the instantaneous clunk and flash of orange lights that he found satisfying. He eased himself in behind the steering wheel while Brogan dumped herself unceremoniously into the passenger seat. Their long day was taking its toll on both of them.

'Right,' Brogan said, 'let's call in at that club on the way back and see if we can get any CCTV. Leave it any longer, they might record over it. Then we'll call it a day. You look done in.'

Cassidy didn't disagree. He wouldn't have disagreed a couple of hours ago.

'And when we get there,' Brogan continued, 'maybe you could give Maura and Donagh a quick call and tell them to get over to the language school first thing in the morning, to take statements from those other kids Luisa just gave us the names of. That should allow the two of them enough time to get back to the office for eleven, so phone the rest of the guys, too, and tell them I want everyone in for an initial briefing at eleven sharp.'

Cassidy groaned inwardly. Done in or not, if he had to track down the entire team at this hour of the night, it'd probably be another couple of hours before his head could hit the pillow. But of course that wouldn't occur to Brogan – no way. They were all the bloody same. And as for that wanker at the hospital, Mulcahy. He had to be called that, didn't he? The name alone was enough to keep the anger fizzing in his veins. Who did he think he was, strutting around like he owned the place? Greasing up to that poncy little Spanish git, him with his fucking apologies. If he ever crossed his path again, he'd make him regret that, one way or another. Cassidy dug the phone from his pocket to start the call-round, when he was pipped by the chirrup of Brogan's mobile. He waited as she answered, grimaced, and mouthed Healy's name.

'Sir?'

Cassidy looked on, curiosity mounting, as Brogan's frown deepened to the point where her eyebrows very nearly met.

'But that's hardly necessary, sir. I mean . . .'

He could just about hear the whine of Healy's voice emanating from Brogan's phone, but not well enough to make out a single word.

'Okay, sir, okay . . . Yes, first thing.'

Brogan said goodbye, through gritted teeth, and hung up.

'For Christ's sake!' she shouted, thumping the dashboard with the flat of her hand. It was as emotional as Cassidy had ever seen her. 'You won't believe what Healy's gone and bloody done.'

Mulcahy slammed his foot on the brake just in time to save himself a respray job. He thought he'd got used to negotiating the ridiculously narrow gateway of his parents' semi-detached house in Milltown during the past few months. But coming back in the dark, his edge blunted by drink, he'd swung the steering wheel too freely into it, and only just stopped short of side-swiping the gatepost. He threw the car into reverse, lined it up, then eased it forward onto the scarf-sized patch of concrete that passed for a drive. He hadn't even had a driving licence last time he lived here.

He sat in the car, damning himself for driving home over the limit. This wasn't Spain, and the days when a flash of your warrant card would get you a nod and a wink and a wave on from the lads in Traffic were long gone. Careers had foundered on less, and his was in a parlous enough state as it was. But that was the bloody problem with everything, wasn't it? It had been a bad night to go out: the interview with that poor Spanish girl still raw in his mind, his annoyance at missing an afternoon's sailing still lingering. But the lure of Siobhan Fallon had been strong. He'd wanted to get something good from this day before it ended. And it seemed like he would, too, after they'd gone outside to have that smoke. From the second they got out there, before he'd even held out his lighter and watched her lips purse round her cigarette and draw in the smoke, they were chatting like old pals. About Mark and the party, who they'd known there, making the connections. Huddled there in the tiny porch of the Long Hall, standing in from the rain, he'd smiled to himself at what a pair they must look. Himself big-boned, crude-carved, towering over her. Siobhan short, shapely, head tilted back to look up at him, laughing. Even in heels, she barely made it to his shoulder.

Back inside, they couldn't steer away from the subject of work for long. It was too big a part of both their lives. Certainly there didn't seem to be much going on in hers apart from work. No man that he could tell, although he'd already adjusted his assumptions in that regard when she called him. Even then, they kept it to generalities. She told him about some of her big stories, how being chief reporter for the *Herald* was alright but no great shakes, how she was still set on bigger things. When she asked him again, he told her more of what his job in Madrid had been, how intelligence work differed from regular policing, the opportunities it offered. He even offered to help her out with some info on EU joint prevention if she did decide to do a story. But by then he was fairly sure that it was him she was interested in, and not just a story.

A flurry of rain drumming on the car roof pulled Mulcahy out of his thoughts. Fat drops burst lazily across the windscreen, snaking away down the long black bonnet. Beyond, behind the garage doors, his dad's Nissan Almera was parked. Untouched for almost a year, like the house and all its contents, it was his now. And, like everything else, he didn't want it. He couldn't bear even to sit behind the wheel and turn the engine over once in a while. It felt wrong. In the end, he'd gone out and bought a car of his own. It wasn't much, a big bruiser of an old Saab. That was all he could afford with the drop in pay and him still forking out for the apartment in Madrid. But at least now, when he woke in the night, he could look out the window and see something that was his.

He gathered his stuff from the passenger seat and hurried to the front door, the bag of takeaway food he'd picked up in Ranelagh interfering with his efforts to get the key in the lock. Probably look drunk to anybody watching, he thought, though he was far from it.

'You liked it over in Madrid then?' Siobhan had asked, leaning in towards him, all interest, the chandeliers above striking sparks off her eyes.

'Absolutely loved it. Best place I've ever worked, by a

mile. There's such a buzz, such a strong sense of life out on the streets there, in the sun, in the heat. It was great, for the most part.'

'So what made you decide to come home?' She sat back a little. 'It sure as hell wasn't the weather.'

'No, it wasn't the weather,' he confessed, trying to laugh his way through the sudden catch in his voice. 'The powers-that-be decided to set up a new operation in Lisbon. MOAC – the Marine Operations Analysis Centre.'

Siobhan nodded. 'Yeah, I think I read something in the *Irish Times* about that. Some kind of global drugs-tracking centre, isn't it?'

'That's it, for monitoring seaborne trafficking across the Atlantic mostly, but also sharing intel with other countries, co-ordinating rapid interventions, that kind of thing.'

'Sounds exciting.'

'It was. Or at least it would have been,' he said ruefully. 'Anyway, to cut a long story short, that put the kibosh on the Madrid operation, everything went west to Lisbon – and my role went with it.'

'So how come you didn't go, too?'

It was the second time in a day that somebody had asked him. God knows how many times he'd been asked it in the six months since his return. And the fact that Siobhan sounded like one of the few who were genuinely interested didn't make him feel any more comfortable with it.

'I could have gone, but I didn't. Like I said, it's a long story.'

He glanced at his watch, anything rather than look her in the eye.

'So go on, tell me. I'm not doing anything else tonight, if you're not.'

His head came up in time to catch the smile rippling across her mouth. Some day, he thought, he might wake up to those lips, those eyes, bathe in their light like the morning sun, and be warm and happy. But not tomorrow – not if it meant first having to wade through all the crap of the past six months, and the twelve that had gone before them.

'I'm sorry,' he said, finally. 'It's too complicated. There was a whole load of other stuff going on, as well. I'd prefer not to go into it right now.'

'That's okay,' she said, though clearly surprised by his reticence. 'It'd be awful if we suddenly got all serious at this hour of the night.' She swirled the remains of her drink around in the glass and knocked it back in one, then nodded towards his empty. 'It's my twist. Same again?'

But the spark was gone from the evening after that, and while they had another couple of drinks, chatting happily enough, they'd called it a night fairly early. He hoped he hadn't killed it completely. As they were leaving the pub he said he'd like to meet up again, and she'd given him that smile and said she'd like that, on the tips of her toes as he bent to kiss her cheek. There was something between them alright. He'd just have to wait till next time to pursue it.

Back in the now, the stale smell of his parents' past enveloped him as he pushed the door shut behind him. The still sharp memory of undertakers bearing their remains out that door, within six months of each other, cut into him as it did every night on his return. He headed for the kitchen in the dark. No need to see the faded green wallpaper, the tired carpet, the half-moon telephone table and the coat-stand in the hallway. He already knew everything was covered in a thin patina of dust. The tiny red bulb in the answering machine blinked at him as he swept past, but he ignored it.

Mulcahy flicked the light on in the kitchen, trying his best to keep the house's deathly atmosphere from settling on him. The kitchen and the spare bedroom were all he ever used now, during the few hours he could bear to be there. Sometimes he turned on the television in the living room for the news, but never sat and watched it, preferring to listen instead from the kitchen. As for the spare bedroom, he had no choice. His own room, with its narrow single bed and wardrobe crammed with relics from his childhood, felt as small and constricted as a tomb now.

He upended the carton of takeaway – a glutinous mass of noodles, water chestnuts and pallid chicken pieces – onto a plate and left it steaming weakly while he grabbed a bottle of Navarra from the counter top, uncorked it and filled a small, short-stemmed glass. One more drink wouldn't make any difference. As he turned, he noticed an odd orange glow above the overgrown hedge at the bottom of the garden. It looked like the shimmer from a fire. Glass in hand, he climbed the stairs and went to the small back room upstairs. Out of the window he could see over the line of high hedges into the small public park beyond. No more than a couple of acres of grass and clumps of stunted shrubbery, but it had been half the world of his boyhood, a place where cowboys roamed and would-be soccer stars scored the best goals of their lives. Looking out across it now, he saw a small bonfire flare up as another log was thrown onto it, flames casting shadows across the faces of the half-dozen kids sitting around it, talking and laughing as they sheltered from the rain under a long sheet of plastic, a makeshift tent. He thought of his meal going cold in the kitchen but felt no impulse to go eat it. The scene outside held him spellbound, recalling how years ago he'd sat round fires there with his gang.

It's not healthy, he said to himself, not healthy living like this in a house that's getting more like a mausoleum by the day.

For a second, like the fire outside, all the faces of his regrets seemed to flare up in front of him, dancing fingers of flame: his parents, his friends and colleagues in Madrid, his ex-wife Gracia, even Brendan-bloody-Healy, his current boss. Then, just as quickly, they faded again and with that came something like peace. In the window now, he saw nothing but the dark and himself reflected in it, realising that for months he'd been doing little more than hiding out here in Dublin, licking his wounds, trying not to feel sorry for himself and failing. That had never been his way.

He turned and looked around the spare room, as if seeing

it for the first time: the knackered old mattress on the bed unused for years, the boxes of hoarded remnants, a limp flap of wallpaper peeling from the corner by the window. He swirled the wine around his glass, then knocked it back. This house meant nothing to him, really. Without his parents it was just empty rooms. With a grim smile, he remembered how he'd spent most of his teenage years dreaming of getting away from it. He'd only moved back in for convenience, for familiarity, because for so long he'd called it home. Getting rid of it had been just one thing too many to deal with.

Well, not any longer. Tomorrow he'd do what he'd been putting off for months: despite the free-falling property prices, despite all the memories wrapped up in it, he'd arrange to have the house put on the market. Then at least he might have some chance of moving on.

4

Mulcahy waited for the gleaming Luas tram to trundle past, then eased the Saab into the queue of traffic at the top of Abbey Street. It was a glorious morning. Clear blue skies erased all evidence of the previous evening's rain, and his inward-looking mood had dissipated with it. The first thing he'd done after he got up was phone a couple of estate agents. They hadn't been confident about his chances of a quick sale, but just making the call lifted some of the weight from his shoulders. Eventually he got to Smithfield and found a parking place in the lee of the high stone wall of the former Jameson distillery. Ahead of him, the sun bore down on what was left of the old market square. Ranks of uniform new-build office and apartment buildings lined the west side, sucking every scrap of age and tradition from their surroundings. Like so many other projects, they'd been a sponge for the flood of Celtic Tiger cash that had swept through Dublin over a decade before, when legions of the newly rich were desperate to stash their cash anywhere the taxman couldn't get his hands on it. Building boomed: in place of crumbling warehouses and inner-city blight came regeneration, young professionals, sleek apartments, smart shops and cafés. Even the old cobbles, worn smooth and black by four centuries of hooves, carts and footfalls had been ripped out and trucked away, replaced by whorls of new, pale-grey granite sets.

To Mulcahy, from the distance of Madrid, the boom had always had the feel of something that couldn't last. The new loaded Dublin bore little resemblance to the one he'd grown up in, and now that the bottom was falling out of it, he could see the old city beginning to reassert itself. Thousands of flats stood empty and tenantless, impossible to sell on. The market square looked as lost and dust-blown as a ghost town. And just a couple of streets back, he knew the smack-heads and crackheads, the burglars and muggers, were all still there, out of sight, waiting their time in the cycle. And it would come. No amount of fancy new apartment blocks could change that.

He double-checked that his car was locked, and headed down towards the river, turning his thoughts to the meeting he was due to attend – a pre-trial briefing at the Four Courts with the state prosecutor. It was one of the few cases he'd worked on during the last six months that was actually making it to trial. Mainly because it was fairly cut and dried. The Colgans were two career low-lifes from Phibsboro who'd got in over their heads, stealing high-performance cars to order for a gang in England, which in turn serviced a substantial part of the illegal car trade in Jordan, Syria and

the Lebanon. Mulcahy had only come on board at the closing stages but he had to admit he'd felt a thrill getting away
from his desk, back on the frontline nabbing bad guys.

Coming round the corner on to Arran Quay, Mulcahy
looked up at the green dome of the Four Courts, standing
out against the sky over the Liffey. A flash of light drew his
attention to a flurry of movement by the main entrance. A
gleaming silver SUV with dark-tinted windows was pulling
up, and a scrum of journalists swarmed around it, cameras
jostling for position, flashes popping, microphones, recorders
and notebooks waving aloft. He couldn't see who was getting
out of the car, but it hardly mattered. Doubtless some gobshite gangster who'd been stoking up the media ahead of
trial – and as usual they lapped it up. For a moment
Siobhan's face drifted into his mind, but he pushed the
image away. It worked both ways, of course. Half the gang-
sters in Dublin would hardly be known to the Gardai if it
wasn't for journalists exposing them. But it still grieved him
to see psychos being treated like celebrities.

He moved around the press pack and up the steps,
between tall granite columns, dragging his focus back to the
case. Entering the round, marble lobby, all echoing footsteps
and murmured conversations, he looked around to see if he
could spot any of the other guys who'd worked on the operation, then stopped in his tracks when he heard a familiar
voice hailing him from behind.

'Mike, wait up there.'

Mulcahy turned and watched as Superintendent Brendan

Healy, all blue-serge uniform and amiability, patted a gowned barrister farewell and strode across the lobby towards him. In his mid-fifties, he was a big man but with a head that seemed too small to match his bulk and, despite the heavily braided cap tucked beneath his arm, a hairstyle of such steely precision it'd put a US news anchor to shame.

'Brendan, what brings you down this way?'

'You do,' Healy replied. There was an edge of castigation in his voice, despite the smile. 'Didn't you get my message last night?'

'What message?'

'You weren't answering your mobile, so I left a message on your phone at home.'

Mulcahy remembered the blinking red light and mentally kicked himself. It was only when he'd pulled on his jacket this morning that he realised he'd left his mobile switched off ever since he was in the hospital. Didn't look good, that. Unprofessional. Trust Healy to use the home number.

'I didn't get it,' he said.

'Ah, no matter. I wanted to come down here and square things with Downey in person, anyway. Never hurts to stay on the right side of those fellas.'

Mulcahy didn't like the sound of that. Downey was the barrister prosecuting the Colgan case. 'I don't follow. What did you need to square?'

'Why you won't be attending today's briefing – on account of more pressing matters having arisen. Look, I hate to spring this on you, especially when you were so obliging yesterday, but I did try to give you notice. You're on the case with Brogan.'

'I'm what?' Mulcahy spluttered.

Healy adopted an expression of sympathetic disbelief. 'The Spanish say they want you as liaison officer.'

'The Spanish? Why in the name of God would they do that?'

'I've no idea,' Healy shrugged. 'Whatever you did yesterday, they took a liking to you and the Ambassador himself asked the Minister for you to be assigned.'

Mulcahy was gobsmacked. Why would the Spanish ambassador have asked for him? Then he remembered the incident with the diplomat, Ibañez, and, with a groan, cursed himself for getting involved. He tried a last forlorn hope.

'But sex crimes is a specialist area of operations. I have no experience—'

'No buts, Mike.' Healy cut in, getting impatient. 'This is right from the top. I told the Minister it's not what you do, but he felt he wasn't in a position to refuse, in the circumstances.'

'And how long am I going to be stuck doing that?'

'As long as it takes. I told Brogan you'll be joining her at Harcourt Square this morning. Go over there now, and you'll make the eleven o'clock briefing. And remember you're just assisting. Brogan is the lead on this, so let her get on with it. Okay?'

But for Mulcahy that caution was so far beside the point

as to be irrelevant. The last thing he wanted was to be tied into some politically sensitive operation while opportunities to get back to where he wanted to be passed him by.

'But that's crazy, Brendan. The whole point of me being with NBCI is so I don't get caught up in—'

'I thought I'd made myself clear, Mike. This is not up for debate.'

A hiss of steely officialdom had entered Healy's voice, and it was probably this more than anything else that pushed Mulcahy too far.

'For fuck's sake, Brendan, that's the last time I'm doing you a favour.'

The anger in his voice was altogether too raw, and he knew he'd overstepped the mark even before he heard the sharp intake of breath, and saw Healy's chest puff up so fast the buttons threatened to pop off his uniform. Healy looked quickly around to make sure no one was within eavesdropping distance, before hissing back at him.

'Now, look here, *Inspector*. I know the last few months have not been easy for you. But we've all been doing our best to sort it out, and we hope you'll be going back to Drugs as soon as something suitable comes up. In the meantime, I would remind you that you're not a one-man band like you were in Madrid, and for as long as you're under my command you're going to have to toe the line like everyone else. Do you understand me?'

Mulcahy glared back at him. 'And what if this "something suitable" comes up while I'm working on this case?'

Healy's eyes narrowed as he pushed his face fractionally closer to Mulcahy's.

'Then you'll just have to wait for the next bloody thing, won't you?'

Brogan checked her watch: quarter past eleven. What the hell was Mulcahy playing at? Helpful as he'd been the day before, he looked like he could be a tricky one. Well, he'd get a shock if he thought he could swan in late and trample all over her team, *her* investigation.

She clapped her hands for a bit of hush. 'Okay, lads, come on, enough hanging around. Listen up.'

Behind her, Cassidy was sticking copies of the medical examiner's photographs of Jesica Salazar's battered face to the whiteboard he'd set up in a corner of the DVSAU's cramped quarters. The Domestic Violence and Sexual Assault Unit, officially, but everybody called it 'Sex Crimes', as if it were one in itself. Ordinarily, on an active op, they'd have been working out of an incident room by now, in whichever station had logged the assault, which in this case was Dundrum Garda Station. They'd have been parachuted in to run the operation with the local lads; to steer, advise, take charge of the investigation but use mostly local manpower and resources. Sometimes, though, when things got overly complex or – as here – required an unusual level of discretion, they had to work out of their own godforsaken offices on the fourth floor at Harcourt Square. Brogan looked around and cursed Healy for his media paranoia again. This was the pokiest, most uncomfortable office accommodation she'd ever had the misfortune to work in. Every chair in the place was knackered, and the muddy-beige walls and threadbare grey carpet tiles looked like they hadn't been cleaned since the building went up in the seventies. Every chance she got, she was gone from the place like a flash. Now she'd almost certainly be stuck here for weeks.

There were only seven of them in the room, including the two uniforms from Dundrum, but already the air was oppressive. It was as big a team as Healy would allow – the more faces, the more tongues might wag, he'd declared. And then, despite all the hand-wringing, he'd snapped at her and said it wasn't as if she was dealing with a murder. Patronising wanker. As for landing her with Mulcahy, she could have punched him. That's all she needed – a spy in the camp checking out her every move.

'Boss?'

She blinked and realised that Cassidy and everyone else in the room was staring at her, waiting for her to begin.

'Okay, guys . . .' She coughed, rallying her thoughts. 'Some of us initiated actions on this yesterday and early this morning, but for those of you coming to it fresh now, Sergeant Cassidy here's going to take us through what we've got so far, just so we're all up to speed. Then we can start thinking strategy. Before that, though, a reminder that we've got blanket silence on this one. No leaks, no exceptions – on pain of the worst transfer you've ever imagined. Okay?'

There was a low murmur of assent from the room, and Brogan turned to Cassidy. 'Andy?'

Standing in front of the whiteboard, using a marker pen as a pointer, Cassidy launched into his what-we-know-so-far spiel. 'Right then, lads, this is Jesica Salazar – at least that's the easy version, so let's go with that from now on, yeah? She's a sixteen-year-old Spanish national, here on a four-week English course. You know the type exactly . . .'

Brogan zoned out and compared her sergeant's face with those of the others looking up at him. His expression, as usual, was glowering to the point of aggressive, his wide-legged stance a parody of the John Wayne gait. As for the suit, if he didn't get it cleaned soon, Health and Safety would be having to prise it off him by force. She ought to say something, take him aside and explain that it wasn't acceptable to go into people's homes scowling and stinking of sweat. But she didn't want to risk alienating him because, for all his faults, he was a good cop. Not the sharpest knife in the drawer but a street fighter to the core, and the others looked up to him.

She surveyed the rest of the team. Three of them were her own: Maura McHugh, Donagh Hanlon and Brian Whelan, all detective Garda rankers and all okay in their own way, but not exactly shit-hot. None of them could hold a candle to Cassidy in terms of getting things done. Maura was about the best of them but she'd be losing her in a few weeks anyway, when she went off on maternity leave. As for the two uniforms in from Dundrum, well, what could you expect? Young, green and thick, cheeks still rosy, hair trimmed down to a stubble that wouldn't normally be visible beneath their caps. They'd hardly be much use for anything but knocking on doors and keeping the coffee hot and sweet. The look of shock seeping into their expressions, as Cassidy summarised some of the more horrific detail from the medical reports, told her all she needed to know about them. Not much of a team, but you got used to that in the DVSAU. And at least Healy allowed her use of the two administratives outside, to help with the paperwork.

'As I said, lads,' Cassidy went on, 'the damage you can see here to the girl's face and chest is nothing compared to what he's done to her down below. But if you're still in any doubt about what kind of a twisted sick fucker we're after, the photos taken by the burns specialist at the hospital are here in a folder for you to look at afterwards.'

He paused as every gaze in the room took in the folders stacked on the table to his left, weighing up whether they really wanted to open them and see the worst – knowing that morbid curiosity would get the better of them all in the end.

'Right, we're not doing too badly on this so far. We tried to interview the victim yesterday, but she was too distressed to give up any detail and our translator wasn't exactly on the ball. Still, we managed to get a couple of things . . . Ah, speak of the devil.'

Cassidy broke off and every head in the room turned to

the back of the room as Mike Mulcahy came in through the door, flushed and short of breath.

'So you managed to join us,' Brogan said, and all eyes returned to her, momentarily, before ping-ponging back to Mulcahy again.

Mulcahy nodded. He'd arrived at Harcourt Square to be told that no one had booked a space in the basement car park for him, and there were none left now anyway. It had taken him the best part of half an hour to find a spot in the crowded side streets nearby and another ten minutes to walk back. Sweating and visibly annoyed, this wasn't the impression he was used to making on entering a room.

Cassidy waded into the gawping silence, drawing the attention back to himself again.

'Okay, lads, this is Inspector Mulcahy. He normally hangs out with the glam boys in Drugs, but he'll be working with us on this. Now, as I was saying . . . Yes, Maura?'

McHugh, the only woman seated in the group, her blonde hair cut in a bob, her short stature emphasised by the swell of a pregnant belly, had put up a hand. She turned to look towards Mulcahy for a moment, before asking Cassidy her question.

'Is there a drugs angle to this you haven't told us about?'

'No, at least not that we know of,' Cassidy laughed grimly. 'But the inspector here is fluent in the old *es-pan-yole* and he was the one who helped us talk to our young victim yesterday.' Cassidy glanced over at Brogan before continuing. 'For which we're very grateful, I'm sure. But not as grateful as the Spanish. They liked him so much they wanted to buy him.'

A few sniggers broke out in the room as Cassidy grinned broadly at his joke.

'Well, at least we prevented *you* from making matters any worse, didn't we, Sergeant?' Mulcahy said, gritting his teeth.

Eyebrows raised, every face in the room now turned from his to Cassidy's in time to see it flush with indignation. At which point Brogan pushed herself away from the table and intervened.

'Alright, lads, settle down. What the sergeant meant is that Inspector Mulcahy here is kindly lending us his expertise in all things Spanish, and in particular liaising with the embassy – for reasons we really don't need to go into just now.'

All heads turned back to Mulcahy again, one or two nodding a bit more respectfully this time as Brogan invited him to take a seat and instructed Cassidy, flatly, to get on with it. The sergeant flicked an angry glance at Mulcahy before resuming.

'As I was saying, we've yet to pin down the actual scene of the assault but given the severity of the girl's injuries she can't have staggered too far from where she was found. What we do know now is where she was beforehand. It's a club called the GaGa, out on the Stillorgan Road, where she was with some of her student pals. We tracked one of them down last night and she says Jesica left the place early to go off with some fella she picked up – an older guy, early to

62

mid-twenties, we reckon. So, for the moment, tracking him down has got to be our number-one priority. Asap, alright?'

Asap, my arse, Mulcahy muttered to himself. Clearly, Cassidy had been watching too many American cop shows and they'd gone to his head. The man was a complete and utter tool. The sullenness, the smart-arse remarks, the fists-first approach: all the redneck, bullshit attitude that gave the Gardai a bad name. Mulcahy looked up and saw the sergeant pointing at a large question mark written on the whiteboard behind him, beneath which were scribbled various notes and key words.

'In terms of ID-ing this guy, so far we've only got the one vague description: tallish, good-looking, brown hair – but that's under club lights – and wearing a stripy shirt. That's all. The good news is that me and the boss popped into the GaGa last night and managed to score some CCTV from around the right time. We went through a couple of hours' worth this morning and managed to locate Jesica's gang of students entering the venue at 9.35 p.m.' – he pointed over his shoulder at a video printout pinned on the board – 'and, also, the rest of them leaving, as they claimed, at about 12.55 a.m. But, so far, no luck on Jesica departing with the mystery fella. That means, Whelan, you and me'll have the delightful job of trawling through the rest of that CCTV footage this morning.'

A skinny, wavy-haired detective in his mid-thirties, a cheap grey suit and what looked like a GAA tie, groaned loudly, and got a poke in the back from Hanlon sitting behind him.

'Before we move on,' Brogan interrupted, 'Donagh and Maura were round at the school earlier, mopping up statements from the other kids – some of who were also at the club. Got anything to add to that, guys? Did any of the kids get a good look at this fella?'

The two detectives shook their heads and launched into a dull summation of why everything they'd got there tallied exactly with what had been reported already. Mulcahy was hardly even listening, still simmering over Healy, over Cassidy, over being stuck on a shitty Sex Crimes case. Christ, he hadn't been forced to deal with this kind of crap for years.

'Okay now, lads.' Cassidy was up at the board again. 'Tasty as this guy may look, one thing we did manage to get from our victim was that her attacker came out of nowhere, and apparently on the street. She only referred to him as, quote, "a man", which implies a stranger. Isn't that right, Inspector Mulcahy?'

Mulcahy looked up, surprised to be consulted.

'Uh, yes . . .' he stumbled, 'you could say that. Although, from the little the victim was able to give us, it's hard to know whether or not she got a proper look at him at all. One thing she did say was "everything went dark", so maybe something was pulled over her head. Anyway, her whole emphasis was on how sudden and brutal the attack was. She gave no sign of knowing who her attacker was.'

'Which would seem to rule out the fella she'd been snogging all night,' Cassidy went on, various heads bobbing in agreement. 'But not necessarily. So, we need to find this guy, pronto.'

'It might be a case of him not getting what he wanted,' one of the others interjected.

'It *might*.' Cassidy cleared his throat and pointed at the medical folders again. 'But something to bear in mind is that one of the first things the medics pointed out to us was that the victim's burns weren't the result of flames, but the application to the skin of a flat, almost certainly red-hot, metal surface, like a branding iron or something.'

There were one or two gasps as this piece of information struck home.

'Technical, obviously, have to come back to us on that, but for the moment it's pretty clear that this fella would've needed some kind of equipment with him to inflict these kinds of injuries – a blowtorch at the very least, and a metal bar, or whatever, to heat. Not the sort of thing everybody carries around with them in the wee hours. Also he'd have needed something to restrain the victim. There's severe bruising on the girl's wrists and ankles consistent with being tied up or otherwise restrained. Probably with cable ties or similar. None of which is easily done out in the open. And what about the screams? The girl's injuries are of a severity nobody could take quietly. Yet we're told there're no obvious signs that she was gagged. So, pinning down the scene of the assault is vital. Who knows, maybe Technical will find something. The point is, this probably wasn't a random spot-and-drag-into-the-bushes job. All the signs are that the attack, if not necessarily the victim, was carefully planned in advance.'

Brogan pushed herself away from the desk and again took centre stage.

'Thanks, Andy. So, guys, apart from the CCTV and the guy she left the club with, a house-to-house on the Kilmacud Road has to be our other big priority for today. An attack as violent as this . . . somebody's got to have seen or heard something. Donagh, you can organise that with the help of our two colleagues here from Dundrum. The station sergeant over there's said we can have some extra uniforms for today and tomorrow as well, so make the most of them. And remember – don't give out any details, especially about the girl's nationality. A "vicious assault on a young woman", that's all we call it. Okay? Any questions?'

She obviously wasn't expecting any, so it was with a look of strained patience that she pointed to one of the young uniformed guards, a skinny, carrot-haired lad of barely twenty years, who'd raised a hand.

'Was the girl raped, then?' the uniform asked, self-conscious in front of all the detectives.

'How long are you out of Templemore?' Brogan asked him, meaning the training college in Tipperary that every candidate Garda attended, on and off, for three years, before graduating.

'Since April twelve months,' he answered, nerves betraying more of his thick Kerry accent.

Brogan's response was as brittle as ice. 'Well, in that case,

Garda, you shouldn't need me to tell you that Section 4 of the Criminal Law Rape Act, 1990, states unequivocally that any penetration of the vagina, however slight, by any object held or manipulated by another person constitutes rape. *Any* object,' she repeated emphatically. 'I think that probably includes a red-hot metal bar, don't you?' She looked at each of them in turn before continuing. 'Which means that when we get the sick fucker who did this, he's going down for life.'

As soon as everyone else had filed out of the room Brogan came over to Mulcahy. She didn't smile or offer a hand in welcome. Then again, he wasn't exactly thrilled about being foisted on her himself, so what could he expect? What she said next, though, surprised him.

'Sorry about Cassidy back there. I'm sure he thought he was being funny.'

'He's not the only one pissed off about me being brought in on this.'

Mistaking his meaning, Brogan put up a hand to stop him. 'You're right, I'm not ecstatic, but let's not get too hung up about it, okay? Anyway, far as I'm concerned, liaison isn't necessarily a bad thing. So long as you keep your Spanish pals off my back, then I'll be happy.'

'They're no more my pals than they are yours.' Mulcahy bridled. 'And if your hair-trigger sergeant hadn't lost his rag, neither of us would be in this mess.'

Again she put her hands up, this time a thin smile playing across her lips.

'Okay, okay, so neither of us wants this. In which case, you stick to your brief, I'll stick to mine, and we'll put on a united front whenever necessary.'

'Fair enough,' Mulcahy said.

She stopped, one arm crooked and resting on her hip, and looked around the room as if she'd rather be anywhere else in the world. Then she came out with it: 'While you're here though, y'know, I thought we might as well make use of you.'

'Did you have something specific in mind?'

'Well, just from what you were saying yesterday, I was wondering if we shouldn't be putting some emphasis on *who* she is, as being a possible motive.'

Mulcahy raised an eyebrow. 'Who her father is, you mean?'

'Yeah, just that as Interior Minister he must have a lot of enemies, right?'

'In Spain, maybe,' Mulcahy frowned. 'But why would they do anything *here*, and to his daughter? Then leave no sign that it had to do with him, not her. A bit unlikely, don't you think?'

'Who knows?' she shrugged. 'I'm ruling nothing out at this stage. I'll go whatever way the evidence takes me, so if we turn up something to point us in that direction, we'll go down that road. In the meantime, you could ask the Spanish police if they have any leads or suspicions along those lines to pass them onto us. I'm sure you can cover all that as part of the liaison brief.'

'Sure,' Mulcahy said. 'Leave no stone unturned.'

She turned to move away, but then stopped and looked back at him.

'Actually there was something else I was hoping you could do for me, as well. It's a bit dull, though.'

'Yeah?'

'Yeah,' she said, smiling now. 'Like I was saying yesterday, it's a racing certainty that this guy's done something, if not exactly like this, then at least similar – less obvious, maybe – before. I've asked one of the lads to do me a PULSE trawl of all reported violent sexual assaults in the greater Dublin area over the last year – everything that's been logged either locally or through us here. I take it you've been back long enough to have familiarised yourself with PULSE?'

'Of course,' Mulcahy nodded. The national crime database had been introduced since his posting to Madrid but he knew enough about it to agree with those who said the acronym – Police Using Leading Systems Efficiently – would have been far more appropriate as THROB, or Totally Hopeless Retarded Old Bollocks.

'What we get back,' Brogan continued, 'is a feed of names, dates, places and offences, but there'll be hundreds of them and I need someone to sift through the lot, and see if anything chimes with this incident – in terms of MO, locality, weapon, or whatever – and, if it does, to pull the file and do a follow-up. It's a bit of a slog, and a one-man job really, but if you fancy it, it'd be a big load off my back and it'll give you a chance to get acquainted with the kind of things we do.'

Mulcahy nodded. It sounded boring as hell but at least it would keep him occupied and out of her way for now.

'So, let's find you somewhere to work.'

Siobhan bent sideways from the waist as she gave the strands of her hair one last vigorous rub with the towel, before shaking them out and straightening herself up again. Twisting the towel into a turban, she paused for a moment in front of the wardrobe mirror, pulling the white bathrobe open and letting her eyes roam over her body, critically, assessing just how much damage these last few days' absence from the gym had done. She pinched her waist and cursed as a couple of centimetres of flesh slipped between her fingers. Not as bad as it might have been, but she was unwilling to let herself off the hook entirely. She'd have to go at it harder tomorrow.

She had just finished a long and reviving session in the gym downstairs: fifteen minutes each on the rowing machine and bike, followed by a quick fifty lengths in the pool. Then she'd had a gorgeous, energising sweat in the steam room, which was always empty mid-morning. Actually, the basement gym was the main reason she put up with paying the astronomical service charge on her flat. Having it there was the only way she could be sure of exercising regularly. Now, after a shower, she felt fully tuned up, tingling for the new day.

As she began tugging on her white Louise Kennedy sweater, the soft cotton slipping over her arms, she felt herself momentarily back in the swimming pool, gliding through the warm water, her back arched, her thighs feeling the burn. Fifty lengths was getting way too easy. The pool was tiny, barely long enough for her to fit five strokes in, so God alone only knew what it would be like for somebody tall. Unbidden, an image of Mike Mulcahy – his big arms making long rhythmic strokes in a slow crawl across open water – drifted into her imagination and found a welcome there.

She pulled the jumper over her turbaned head, flicked the tail end of the towel out, readjusted the delicate little silver cross and chain she always wore and took another close look at herself in the mirror. Surely she couldn't have scared him off with that crack about being free for the rest of the night? He wasn't that much of a prig. A bit reserved, maybe, but she felt something else was at the root of that. She remembered the way his team had all looked up to him that night she'd gone out on the drugs raid with them, how he'd kept them calm, reining in their excitement until just before the go. Real respect was what those guys had for him, and that wasn't won easily. There was something about him, definitely, even if he'd been hiding it well last night.

Siobhan unwound the towel from her head, pushing the thought away while shaking out her hair and reaching for the hairdryer. Mondays were supposed to be still the week-end for hacks who flogged their guts out on Saturdays, working for a Sunday paper. But she hardly ever took the whole day off and, as usual, had a busy afternoon planned. First, lunch with TV presenter Ryan Tubridy, who'd finally succumbed to her request for an interview. Then an afternoon in the *Herald* office beckoned, setting up her diary for the week. She liked it there on Mondays, when usually just herself and Paddy Griffin were on the desk. It was the only time the place was ever quiet enough for her to hear herself think.

And later, drinks in the Pembroke with Vincent Bishop. Again. He'd probably tell her when she got there that he'd booked a table for dinner as well. That he'd like her to join him. Like the last time. Once more Mulcahy's face rose in her imagination, that smile twisting the corners of his mouth. When he'd asked her about whether her sources ever expected anything in return? Christ, he'd hit the nail on the head with that one.

Siobhan had been introduced to Bishop a few months earlier by a friend at a Sport Ireland function, and already she'd come to regard him as a bottomless well of invaluable information. She'd heard of him previously, of course. One of Ireland's new perma-rich, unblunted even by the recession. She knew how he'd sold his father's dance-hall business in the seventies to found the Bishop insurance group – 'Irish security for Irish people' – and made millions, selling that in turn to found a slew of staggeringly successful internet and media-based concerns. In his spare time, wherever he found that, he was well known as one of the main drivers of the Irish art boom in the early 2000s – a dogged collector with a fierce reputation for always acquiring what he wanted, no matter what the price.

In person he was polite but reserved. Guarded. A bit weird to look at. Tall, pale and bone thin, lank black hair – dyed probably – limp handshake, limp everything, probably. Widowed for years, he was a bit awkward, a bit clammy with her at first but seemed to take a shine all the same, and opened up to her when she started getting a bit gossipy. Maybe he sensed she had no interest in his money. His contacts, on the other hand ... Christ, but they were phenomenal, and across the board in business, the arts, sport and politics. How he did it, she had no idea, but he seemed particularly well up on all the dirt. And he knew its value. So they had that much in common, and they'd met up fairly regularly since. Not on dates. As far as she'd been concerned, he just wanted someone to have an in-the-know yak with. But that was then.

She turned off the hairdryer, threw it on the bed and walked through to the living room, straight to the small desk where her telephone was, leaned over and pressed the play button on the answerphone. From the cheap grey plastic speaker came a brief hiss and crackle, like the start of an old 45rpm record, then a single strum of a guitar, and an eerie disembodied voice started warbling.

It was Roy Orbison, singing 'In Dreams', though she hadn't really taken that in when she first played the message. It had seemed a lot funnier when she got home last night, a bit tipsy from the drinks with Mulcahy and a little deflated by the way things had gone with him. Or, more accurately, hadn't. To walk in, press a button and hear that wash of music fill the room. Just the song. Nothing else. No message. Christ, talk about from one extreme to the other. Hilarious. She'd just laughed it off and tottered away to bed – and she went out like a light.

Now it was beginning to creep her out. First thing this morning, it crowded in on her waking thoughts, going round and round in her head – not in a good way. She'd never liked Orbison's music. Her father used to have one of his LPs and as a little girl, something about the cover picture had freaked her out. She could see it now, that image of a puffy-faced old man in dark glasses and weird black hair, trying to look like someone half his age, trying to look cool. She shuddered at it still. As for 'In Dreams'. Jesus. Not in hers. That was for sure.

Similar stuff had happened a couple of times recently. She'd hardly noticed. A call at work, some other Orbison warble. She hadn't even listened to it, had thought it was some cold-calling ad crap and hung up. Then on her mobile, a song on voicemail: 'Pretty Woman'. She'd been intrigued enough to listen to the end. But it had just clicked off. Again, she'd thought nothing of it, really. Some joker taking the piss, maybe, at most. But she'd had second thoughts when Bishop started coming over all courtly during dinner the next time she saw him, saying how nice she'd looked walking down the street and handing her the Gary Maloney story virtually gift-wrapped. Like some old-style suitor offering his lady a token of his esteem. Up till then she'd thought he was getting his kicks just by seeing some of the stuff he'd told her about appear in print. But now?

Maybe she was wrong. Maybe it had nothing at all to do with Bishop. Maybe the other stuff was just coincidence. But that would be even creepier in some ways. Who the hell else could have got her home number? She was ex-directory and only a close circle of friends and family had that number. She hadn't given it to Bishop. But everyone knew money like his could buy such information easily. And somehow the whole clammy, courtly, passive-aggressiveness of those songs seemed to fit him to a T. It *had* to be him. The only question left was what the hell was she going to do about it – without causing a rift? Because in any terms other than romantic, she needed Bishop more than he needed her. Gary Maloney wasn't the only story he'd tipped her the wink on, and she was sure there were lots more there just for the asking. *If* she handled this the right way.

Siobhan shook her head in grim amusement as Orbison came to his vaguely masturbatory climax and the answerphone clicked off. Maybe that was it. Maybe the right way was just to ignore it. What harm could an old song on an answering machine do to her, anyway? All she had to do was press a button, delete it, and it was gone. Compared to that, the chance of getting another cracking story from Bishop had to be worth any little awkwardness that might come up between them. And if he tried to take it any further, well, she could handle that, too, when the time came, she was sure.

'I thought you might like your own space,' Brogan said, opening the door onto a tiny office off the incident room.

Space was hardly the appropriate word for this airless, windowless grey box with a metal desk and chair all but crowbarred into it.

'Thanks . . . I think,' Mulcahy said.

Brogan wrinkled her nose, then stepped back to let him pass. 'It's the best we can do.'

Mulcahy took a breath and reminded himself again that he was the interloper here. It was all a far cry from the sumptuous EU-funded office he'd worked out of in Madrid. Nothing but the best there, from the carpets and computer equipment all the way up to the expensive artwork hanging in the public areas. He'd laughed so often at the jaw-drop reactions of visiting Garda colleagues as they crossed the threshold of the Europol building on Recoletos, but he'd grown used to it in the end. Now he'd have to pinch himself if he ever went back.

'Not to worry,' he said. 'I've worked in worse. I'll leave the door open to keep the oxygen level up and to make sure I don't miss anything going on out there.'

Brogan didn't look any happier with his friendly approach, but he caught her smiling again as he squeezed awkwardly round the desk.

'Is there somewhere I can put these?' he asked, indicating two cardboard boxes that, apart from the computer terminal and phone, were the only things on the desk.

Brogan put a hand to her mouth and coughed. 'Actually, that's some stuff we dug out from our own paper archive, for you to have a look through until the results come in from PULSE. They're all sexual assaults from the last year or so.

That lot on the right are the ones it's been possible to initiate some kind of investigative action on. The positive-outcome cases, where we made an arrest and charged a suspect, are in the small red folder at the bottom. And the big pile on the left comprises reports that have only been investigated locally, or referred to us – for statistical purposes only – as being unactionable, whether due to complete lack of evidence or simply not enough to justify expenditure of scant resources.'

Mulcahy peered into the box on the right. There must've been getting on for a hundred files in that one alone. And there were considerably more in the other box: the unactionable ones.

'Surely these can't all be from the last twelve months?'

'I'm afraid they can – and are,' said Brogan. 'I told you at the hospital how things are with us. Sex crime is one of the few growth areas Ireland's got left these days. And because we compile the stats for the Department of Justice, every logged incident has to be cross-reffed to us. Like I said, it'll give you a taste of what we do.'

Mulcahy shook his head. How the hell could a tiny unit like the DVSAU get through all that work? But the answer, he knew, lay right in front of his eyes. They didn't.

'Yeah, just what I wanted,' he said. 'I suppose I'd better get cracking before the next wave comes rolling in and drowns me completely.'

Brogan bumped into Cassidy in the corridor, coming out of the loo.

'How's he liking his new quarters, boss?'

'I'm beginning to think you're deliberately trying to wind the man up, Andy. Couldn't you have found anything better for him?'

'Not on this floor,' Cassidy grinned. 'But, if he complains, there's loads of space down in the basement.'

'Very funny. You just watch your step with him. He could have you buried before breakfast. He's well in with Healy.'

'I wouldn't be too sure about that, boss,' Cassidy said. 'I've been doing some checking up on him. Turns out I knew his old man years back. He was an arsewipe of the first order, too.'

'For Christ's sake, Andy,' Brogan broke in sharply. 'What's his old man got to do with anything?'

'I'm telling you, he was an inspector with the old "A" Division out in Clondalkin when I was there. A right old stab-in-the-back merchant, he was. Bastard cost me my first chance at stripes . . .'

Brogan shook her head impatiently and suppressed a curse. 'I don't have time for this crap. I don't give a damn who his father was. Or who Mulcahy is either, for that matter, other than the fact that he's here on my patch and will probably be reporting our every move back to Healy. So just watch what you say and do in front of him, alright?'

'Right, boss.' Cassidy chewed his bottom lip for a moment. 'Look, all I'm trying to say is that, for all his airs and graces, there's something not right about him. This pal of mine who just got back to me says he's not even in Drugs any more. And he's only on attachment to NBCI.'

Brogan raised an eyebrow, not sure what to make of that. 'Still Healy's domain though, isn't it?'

'Yeah, but a bit of a comedown from the feckin' European Commissioner for Drugs, or whatever he fancies himself as, don't you think?'

Brogan shook her head. 'I don't know what to think, other than that an unknown quantity's more dangerous than a known one.'

Cassidy screwed his face up, like he always did when she said anything even vaguely abstract to him.

'Anyway,' she continued, 'he's got plenty to keep him out of our way for now.'

'He's going to go through the dregs, is he?' Cassidy wrung his hands together, as if he hadn't left them under the dryer long enough. 'I'm still not sure about giving him that job. What if he misses something useful?'

'And maybe a fresh pair of eyes will spot something we would've overlooked.' Brogan turned and walked back a few paces towards her office. 'Look, Andy, the bottom line is we're under pressure for a result. Whatever else he might be, he's a smart guy and an experienced investigator. If there's something there, he's got as good a chance of finding it as anyone else.'

'He doesn't look very happy about it.'

Brogan followed his glance back up the corridor. Through an open door she saw Mulcahy taking files from boxes, arranging them on his desk, frowning in concentration.

'No, he's okay with it. He knows he'll need a bit of background if he's going to pull his weight over here, for however short a time.'

5

'God, is it yourself again? You're never out of this bloody place.'

'I could say the same to you.' Siobhan Fallon dumped her bag on the desk and switched on her screen, while she waited for news editor Paddy Griffin to respond. The newsroom, as she knew it would be, was empty but for the two of them.

'Yeah well,' Griffin said eventually, 'it's pretty much accepted that I've got no life outside the paper. You, on the other hand, being the young and rather lovely ace reporter that you are . . .'

Griffin's voice was laden with irony, his grey, deeply lined face wreathed in good humour. In his sixties, pushing retirement now, he was leaning back in his swivel chair like a lounge lizard in a hotel lobby, his long, thin limbs like pipe cleaners inside the tubes of his rumpled linen suit. It was a posture born long before computers became the basic tool of journalism. Some said he doted on his chief reporter, but in reality his relationship with her went much deeper than that. It wasn't her body he was after but the same dogged-ness and hunger for a story he recognised from his own glory days. He sucked what he could of it straight off her, like some creature of the night feeding on her energy and need.

'Run out of things to buy, did you?'

'Ran out of spondulicks, more like.'

Siobhan pressed her stomach against the back of Griffin's chair and gave his shoulder a fond squeeze as she stared at the computer screen in front of him. He looked like he hadn't left the office since she'd signed off her copy on Saturday night, as if he'd just stayed there all along, scroll-ing through the wire services, looking for anything that would make a half-decent story for next week's edition.

'Anything doing?'

'Nothing that won't be dead by Thursday,' he groaned. 'Christ, but I miss the dailies sometimes. This place's been deader than a nun's knickers all day. I'm beginning to wonder why I bothered coming in at all.'

Siobhan knew there was more to it than that. Griffin was a minor legend in Dublin newspaper circles. He'd been everywhere, seen it all, done foreign and war for the *Irish Independent*, crime and politics for the *Irish Times*, even a stint as managing editor of the old *Irish Press* before it went splat back in the nineties. Not for him any sense, though, that the *Sunday Herald* was a comedown. No, anywhere there was news flowing in and out, and he was in a position to put it into print, was good enough for Paddy Griffin.

'I heard you on the radio again this morning,' he said. 'You were good, as usual.'

'Thanks. I stayed on for the Pat Kenny show afterwards, but even they were getting bored with it by then. Only gave it the three minutes.'

'Better than nothing, eh?'

'Yeah, I suppose. How's it doing on the wires?'

'Oh, still kicking up a storm with all the Johnny-come-latelys.' Griffin swivelled round and beamed at Siobhan. 'You did well there, my darling, and your instinct was right on the follow-up. They're doing their best to shut it down: the FAI and United are closing ranks. Lenihan's come out with a statement – all the usual bollocks about how him and Suzy are happily married and are certainly not splitting up.'

Siobhan cast her eyes heavenwards. It wasn't like anyone would feel sorry for Suzy Lenihan being caught fooling around with one of her husband's squad members. Especially Maloney who, let's face it, was as fit as they come. Everyone knew she only married Marty Lenihan so she could stay in the spotlight – he had little else going for him – and that together they made up the most toxic couple in Irish sporting circles. Lenihan himself chased every bit of skirt naive enough to get within fifty yards of him. Siobhan, too, had come in for his foul-breathed attention at a book launch in Buswell's one night. A shiver of disgust ran through her, followed by one of satisfaction on recalling the look on his face when she'd told him to fuck right off with himself. But Marty had so far avoided being caught out, and he had lawyers like

Rottweilers. So the headline LENIHAN PLAYS AWAY was still just a tantalising prospect. Her stomach squirmed at the mere thought of it.

'As for Maloney,' Griffin continued, 'he buggered off on the first plane to Marbella this morning, his missus conveniently in tow and definitely not saying a word. So, unless the big own-goaling dope makes an even bigger cock of himself out there, you're right, it won't have the legs to make it through the week.'

'Better get moving on something else then, hadn't I?' Siobhan said. 'If I want to convince Harry that he can't do without me.'

Griffin looked up at her, the lines and furrows on his face rearranged in a crazy-paving of mock pain.

'You got the flowers, did you?'

Siobhan nodded, knowing what was coming.

'I'm thinking that's probably the best you can hope for, just now. He said he'd look at the budget again, but you know yourself what that means.'

Mulcahy was out by the kettle, spooning instant coffee into a mug – they didn't even possess a cafetière, never mind a proper machine – when he heard a commotion break out up the corridor. He turned to see Brogan emerging from her office and making straight for the incident room, her gait a stiff clip-clop of heels, thunder in her face. It took him a moment to realise her fury was focused on him.

'So when were you going to tell me?'

If she hadn't been so tall, he might not have felt her aggression so much; if she'd been a man, he'd have been tempted to deck her.

'Tell you what?'

'That Jesica Salazar has been removed from St Vincent's by some bunch of embassy clowns.'

Mulcahy put the kettle down slowly.

'She's been what?'

'You heard me. She's been spirited away by some gang of bandoleros from the bloody embassy. Came in mob-handed, took the girl away, didn't leave a forwarding address.'

'They've probably just moved her to the Blackrock Clinic, or some other private place. She's a VIP's daughter. You know how it is.'

'No, Mike. I don't know *how* it is. Even more to the point, I've no idea *where* she is now, either.' Brogan ruffled her hair, as if trying to tease something from it. 'You said earlier you'd been talking to your Spanish guy. Are you seriously saying he didn't mention anything about this?'

Mulcahy had been so backfooted by her tone, only now did it register what she was implying. He looked around him to see who else was in the room. One civilian secretary looking at them curiously. And Cassidy, sitting at a desk staring back at him, a malevolent smirk on his face.

'Yes, Claire, that's exactly what I'm saying. And, for the record, what I actually told you was that I tried to contact Ibañez but he wasn't available.'

'Probably because he was the one who marched into the

85

hospital this morning waving an order demanding the girl's release into their care, the little shit.'

'Who'd you get this from? Not Healy?'

'No.' She shook her head. 'I rang the hospital to see how Jesica was and they said she'd been moved out hours ago. I hadn't even thought of Healy. What the hell am I going to tell him?'

'Fuck that,' Mulcahy said, 'it's not your problem. This is the embassy's doing, and they'll have to do the explaining. Don't say anything until I ring Ibañez and tear a strip or two off him.'

'Home?' Mulcahy gasped, unable to believe what he was hearing. 'You're telling me she's been taken home, as in *out of the country?'*

'But of course.' It was Ibañez's turn to sound surprised. 'Where else would we take her?'

Mulcahy couldn't have been more shocked. He'd been all set to give Ibañez a mild upbraiding for moving Jesica Salazar to another hospital without informing them. But the Spanish First Secretary was now telling him that the girl had been put on a plane that was already most of the way back to Madrid. Mulcahy ran a hand through his hair, the phone still clamped to his ear. What a disaster – surely someone must have known?

'Why the hell didn't you tell us?'

'Please, Inspector, there is no need for anger here. It was not my choice to do it this way.' Ibañez's voice was sounding a little strained now. 'Jesica's father, as you know, is a very powerful man. He wanted his daughter back, beside him, safe in her own country without any more hurt, either physical or psychological.' He paused to let the barb hit home. 'You know, Don Alfonso might have been less insistent if it hadn't been for your colleagues' shameful attempt to interrogate his daughter before she was well enough. In these circumstances I understand why he was not so concerned with, uh, niceties, but making certain nothing would delay ensuring his daughter's safety.'

'Don't be ridiculous,' Mulcahy growled into the mouthpiece. 'She was in no further danger and you know it. All this achieves is to leave our investigation high and dry.'

'Which is precisely why her father wanted Jesica repatriated, Inspector. Because, as your reaction shows all too clearly, this was the only way to guarantee she would not be pressured by your officers into talking about this terrible incident until she is ready. Which, I might add, in the opinion of our medical team, will not be for some time yet. So I do not apologise to you, Inspector. We did not do anything wrong. We had all the permissions we needed, including from your own government. If you were not informed, this is not our fault.'

Brogan nearly choked when Mulcahy told her.

'Madrid? For Christ's sake! So now we can wave goodbye to any hope of getting this mess cleared up quickly. How will we get a statement now? Or an ID if we turn up a suspect?'

'I don't suppose they had much confidence in any of us,

after what happened at the hospital.' Mulcahy stared pointedly at Cassidy. 'What I don't get is why you thought I'd have known they were going to swipe the kid? Or why I wouldn't have shared that with you, if I did?'

Brogan had the decency to redden a little at that. 'You're the one supposed to be liaising with them. Who else would have known, if you didn't?'

He felt his annoyance shifting from Brogan back to where it should have been focused all along. He might be pissed off at her paranoia about his presence in her little fiefdom, but what the Spanish had done was unforgivable by any standards of cooperation, and could only make the investigation more difficult.

'We'll find a way around it,' he said, trying to put more reassurance into his voice than he felt. 'All the swabs were done, weren't they? And it's not as if Jesica was likely to give up anything useful, for the moment anyway. We've just got to let it be known upstairs that we knew nothing about her being taken, and that we're very unhappy about the situation. Let the minister deal with the politics. He must have been in on it.'

From the look on Brogan's face, as she walked away, he could tell she hadn't taken a word of that on board.

The incident room was deserted. Mulcahy had already spent most of the afternoon sifting through the files on his desk, alone apart from a civilian secretary in the outer room tapping away at a computer screen oblivious to his presence.

Brogan had done a good job of sidelining him. Shortly after he'd told her the outcome of his conversation with Ibañez, she had buggered off with Cassidy and the rest of them on the house-to-house enquiries and to interview some known sex offenders. Still, their absence had given him a chance to make some phone calls he'd been meaning to make for a while. Not least to his old sidekick, Sergeant Liam Ford, over in the Drugs Squad, who he hadn't seen for ages.

'Jesus,' Ford guffawed, staggered to hear his old boss had been press-ganged into servitude in Sex Crimes. 'Did they whip your bollocks off at the door?'

Mulcahy assured him that they hadn't. They arranged to meet for a pint the following lunchtime, then Mulcahy put the phone down. No wonder Brogan and Cassidy had chips on their shoulders. Whatever his own feelings about the DVSAU, Ford's contempt for the unit was the typical Garda reaction. All the more reason for him to get out of there as quickly as possible. And, the girl being back in Madrid, he now realised, could only work in his favour, since there might no longer be any point to his staying on. The Spanish embassy would probably now loosen its grip on the 'liaising' and he could slip away quietly, maybe in a few days' time. What he'd be going back to might not be much better, but at least he wouldn't be pussyfooting around Brogan and that little shit Cassidy any more.

Just then his mobile rang, but he didn't recognise the number on the screen.

'Mike?'

The voice was Spanish, and instantly recognisable as that of his old colleague Javier Martinez from the Narcotics Intelligence Unit in Madrid. A close friend throughout his seven years in Spain, Mulcahy hadn't spoken to him for months and he felt his spirits lift instantly. It was as if he'd been transported back to his former life.

'Jav? How the hell are you? Christ, but I miss you guys.'

'It's not "us guys" any more,' Martinez chuckled. 'Did you not hear? Like you, like everyone, I was reassigned also.'

'What are you talking about?' Mulcahy said. 'You live and breathe all that stuff.'

'And you don't?'

Mulcahy grunted acknowledgement of the undeniable truth of that statement.

'Like I say,' Martinez continued, 'I was moved, promoted. Now I am in charge of – how do you say it – the Liaison and Protection Division. You know, for VIPs, diplomats, politicians' security and special needs?'

'Jesus, I never had you down as a babysitter.' But even as he said it Mulcahy realised Martinez, the most skilled networker he'd ever met, would be brilliant in the role.

Martinez laughed out loud this time. 'There is a little more to it than that, you know. I don't sit much, because I am pulling strings mostly, arranging favours. Like the one I, uh, arranged for Don Alfonso Mellado Salazar, yesterday.'

Martinez fell silent as he let Mulcahy register, then absorb the impact of what he was saying.

'It was you?' Mulcahy could hardly believe it. 'You organised to have the kid flown out?'

'No, no,' Martinez tutted sharply. 'I did not know about this until Ibañez told me just now. This was most inelegant, but they must have had permission from your government, or they could not do it. No, the reason I'm calling is to tell you it was me who suggested that you be our liaison contact. When I heard Ibañez mention your name during the conference call yesterday, I was naturally very surprised. But, of course, I said there could be no better man to have on our side. I tried to phone you last night but you never answered, and I was diverted to some other thing and forgot. So, I apologise.'

'For Christ's sake, Jav,' Mulcahy groaned. 'I'll probably be stuck on this for weeks now.'

'Yes, but last time we spoke you said how bored you were.'

'That was months ago.'

'And things have improved so much for you since then?'

By the time he hung up again, Mulcahy was feeling marginally more enthusiastic about his new assignment. They'd had a useful conversation about Salazar senior and the chance of a connection with him, although Martinez had been as sceptical as himself regarding that possibility. Mostly, Mulcahy was just pleased to have been able to get his own back on Martinez by forcing him to look into the possibility of a tie-in on his own turf.

'You don't ask much, huh?' Martinez had complained. 'Don Alfonso has every terrorist and lunatic in Spain, from ETA to those bastard Al-Qaeda bombers, hoping to take revenge on him.'

'Precisely, Jav,' Mulcahy said, driving the point home as forcefully as he could. 'Come on, man, don't tell me it didn't cross anybody's mind over there?'

'Sure, it did. But then we think, how paranoid can we get? This is the man's daughter, and nobody claims it has anything to do with him. We think even idiot terrorists and assassins are more, uh, media aware, these days.'

Mulcahy wasn't going to argue with that, but he left the ball in Martinez's court all the same. Then he got stuck into his files again with renewed vigour. He wasn't discovering much, so far, beyond his own disgust and bafflement at the number of sick perverts living in Dublin. In his five years in uniform in the late eighties, he'd only ever come across a dozen or so cases of domestic violence and a few flashers. Of course, a decade later, like everyone else, he'd been riveted by the ongoing scandal of Ireland's paedophile priests. But his deeper reaction to that, back then, had been mostly a heartfelt satisfaction that the clergy's centuries-old grip on the conscience of his countrymen had been shattered at last.

What he was reading here, though, beggared belief – something that hadn't sparked off any general outcry in the media. Hundreds of broken arms and ribs, shattered cheekbones, women and children hospitalised after being beaten by drunk or drugged-up husbands and fathers. Then there were the rapists and paedophiles of every hue – brickies, teachers, solicitors, IT specialists and bankers, as well as clergymen – and the cases he was reading were only the ones where actual bodily harm had been inflicted during the commission of the crimes. What he couldn't get his head round was the fact that this couldn't all have come from nowhere in a sudden rush. It wasn't like the economic boom had sparked a parallel rise in deviancy. The horror was in thinking how much must have been hidden for so long.

In the end, he had no choice but to set his revulsion aside and get on with the job. What was immediately evident was that violence on the scale inflicted by Jesica Salazar's attacker was incredibly rare. As were the rates of stranger assault and rape generally. Irish men clearly preferred to vent their anger on wives and girlfriends, and usually in the privacy of their own homes. Starting with the cases that had actually made it into court, he worked his way steadily through the boxes, sheaf after sheaf of ruined lives, unearthing nothing that bore even scant resemblance or relevance to the attack on Jesica Salazar. Every time he came across a stranger-rape or violent sexual assault, he checked through the details for anything similar, then put it to one side to be reconsidered later.

If the fully investigated cases didn't look very hopeful, there was even less to glean from the huge raft of local reports and 'unactionables'. Again most of these were domestics, often where charges had been laid in the heat of the moment – then hurriedly withdrawn. Here came not only the date-rape allegations that never went anywhere but also alleged assaults so serious that Mulcahy simply couldn't believe they had not been considered worthy of thorough investigation. He'd worked his way through a third or so of the material by the time Brogan and Cassidy clattered back into the incident room, and he realised it was well after seven o'clock. Neither of them so much as glanced in his direction, instead stopping in front of the whiteboard to draw something on the map during a huddled conversation. He got up and went over to them.

'Any progress?'

'Yeah, a little,' Brogan conceded, finally. 'We've identified the scene, we think. Technical are going over it now. We'll know more in the morning. But it looks like she may have been dragged into a van, and the assault occurred there. It would explain a lot.'

'Makes sense,' Cassidy agreed, gruffly. 'A van scenario means he could've had his blowtorch or whatever all fired up and ready to go. We were looking at that as a possibility from the outset – or maybe you didn't get here in time for that part of the discussion, sir.'

Cassidy's eyes darted towards Brogan.

'No, Sergeant, I didn't,' Mulcahy replied, trying to keep the irritation from his voice.

'Well, you'll have a chance to get fully up to speed tomorrow at the nine a.m. briefing,' Brogan interjected quickly.

'I'm assuming you'll join us for that, Mike. In the meantime, you might as well get off. Unless you've come up with anything yourself?'

'No, not at all,' he said. 'Nothing obvious, anyway. Our man is beginning to look like a bit of a one-off judging by that lot. But you know that already.'

'Well, I wasn't expecting you'd turn up anything exactly the same, or I'd have remembered it. But there's a strong chance he'll be in there somewhere.'

'There were one or two that might merit another look, but I'd like to run them by you first.'

'Why don't you see me after the briefing in the morning,' Brogan suggested. 'I'll have a quick look at whatever you've got then. In the meantime, Sergeant Cassidy and myself have a couple of other things to follow up tonight, before we finish. Okay?'

'Fine,' Mulcahy nodded. 'See you in the morning, then.'

The heavy diesel roar of a bus engine starting up outside the window, on Burgh Quay, drew Siobhan out of her reverie. She looked at the clock in the bottom corner of her monitor and realised another hour had passed without her adding significantly to the story up on her screen. It was a work-up of a short piece Griffin had passed her from the Associated Press wire, about a fat kid in Portland, Oregon, who'd held his entire high school to ransom with his father's assault rifle after he heard that hotdogs were being taken off the lunch menu. A couple of phone calls to a nutritionist and a junior minister at the Department of Health, a few choice quotes, and she'd been able to work it up into a nice little piece about the obesity threat hanging over, not just America's children, but Ireland's, too. There was nothing like a bit of waffle to keep till Sunday.

Twenty past eight: time to get going if she wasn't to be late for Vincent Bishop. What little polishing, if any, the piece needed she could do in ten minutes, fresh, in the morning. Griffin had long since given up and headed off for a lonely night in, watching the rolling news channels on TV in his one-bedroom flat in Drumcondra. She closed the file and logged off, then stood up and wandered over to the window, stretching her stiff arms and back as she went.

The daylight looked to be on the wane, but it was always hard to tell through the smoked glass windows of the *Herald* building. She loved looking out at all the faces of the passengers on the top decks of the buses waiting at the terminus outside. Level with her on the first floor, and hardly more than twelve or fifteen feet away, they sat entirely unaware as she watched them through the one-way windows, trying to figure out from faces, hairstyles and clothes what sort of jobs they had, what sort of lives they lived, where they came from, where they might be going to. Once, late on a Friday night, she'd even seen a couple of kids shagging on the back seat of the Number 128. The rest of the deck was empty, the girl hanging off the seat-back, frantically trying to keep a lookout while the boy pumped away furiously, his jeans barely lowered off his arse-cheeks. They had no way of knowing that Siobhan's shriek of surprise had brought the rest of the newsdesk running over for an eyeful, cheering like a bunch of overgrown kids when the boy at last shuddered and collapsed.

Amused by the memory, she walked back to her desk. It was hard to beat the camaraderie of the newsroom sometimes. She was pulling her coat on and reaching to turn off her screen when the phone rang on Jim Clarkin's desk behind her. She hesitated before picking it up. Clarkin, the paper's raddled crime correspondent, rarely if ever made it into the office, preferring to trawl the bars near the Four Courts for his stories, or do the rounds of the circuit courts in his car. He always worked from his mobile. It was bound to be a wrong number. Still, you never knew.

'Hello. Newsdesk.'

To her surprise the caller did ask for Clarkin.

'He's not here. Is it anything I can help you with?'

The caller, on a mobile, was barely audible through the static, but the gist of what he was saying was clear enough. He had information to sell.

'Yeah, well, we're always on the lookout for good stories. I suppose we could sort you out something, if it's right for us. It'd have to stand up, though – we don't hand out money for rubbish. Tell me more.'

As she listened, leaning back against the desk, her face muscles soon slackened into boredom, until the caller revealed the pivotal detail of his story. A Spanish student had been attacked and raped out in the southside suburbs the night before. But it was the injuries he claimed had been inflicted that had Siobhan on her feet again in an instant, reaching for pen and notepad.

'He did what? Ah, jayney, that's revolting.' Disgust tightened her face as she jotted down the details. 'And is the girl alright? . . . Do you have a name? . . . Well, you must know . . . Spanish, and that's all you have? . . . And, what hospital is she in? . . . Okay, what hospital *was* she in, then? . . . Yeah, good . . . What else can you give me?'

But the caller was disappointingly short on further details and, when he began to repeat what he'd said before, she cut him short. 'Okay, look, I suppose it's worth twenty euro. Give me your name and I'll leave the cash at reception for you.'

She fished an envelope from a drawer and scribbled the caller's name down on it.

'No, don't worry, it'll be there – providing the story checks out. And thanks, yeah? Remember my name, Siobhan Fallon, if you ever have any more stuff like that, okay?'

She hung up, grabbed her mobile from her bag and rang Bishop's number. It went through to voicemail.

'Hi, Vincent, something's come up here, so I'm going to be a little late. Give me a call if you have to go.'

Then she turned the mobile off, went back to her own desk and sat down again, eyes flicking from side to side, thinking hard. It was a good two minutes before she shook off her coat, pressed the space bar on her keypad, and watched the screen flicker into life again. Double-clicking with focused efficiency, she called up her contacts file and scrolled down through a maze of names, notes and numbers until she found what she was looking for. She tapped a number into her phone and waited.

'Hiya, is that the Phoenix Park? Look, I know it's late but is Des Consodine still there? Sergeant Consodine, I mean . . .'

The evening was calm and clear, the delicate blue of a soft sky arching down to kiss the flat green sea, as he drove south along the Strand Road. For once, Mulcahy was glad of the sluggish traffic. He wearily took in the wide sweep of Dublin Bay, the tide a quarter of a mile out, the dun reaches of wet sand host now to dog-walkers, arm-in-arm lovers and the distant dots of line fishermen, eternal optimists that they were. Caught in the queuing traffic, looking out at the giant red and white smokestacks of the Pigeon House power station, the boyhood memories came flooding back. Of walking the beach, paddling in cold clear water, dodging the near-flat waves as they rippled in along the shore, his father's trousers turned up to the knee, and the unshakeable certainty of a strong hand holding his, protecting him from whatever might come along. And afterwards, an ice cream from the kiosk in the Martello Tower, or maybe a trip out to Dun Laoghaire for a scoot around the bay in *Seaspray*.

The traffic moved at last, and on a whim he turned the Saab into one of the narrow public car parks that dot the coast road at intervals. Dublin wasn't such a bad place to be after all, he reflected, if only he could rid himself of this awful feeling of drifting without an anchor. He turned off the engine and gazed at the still, calm scene spread out before him. The low evening light seemed to hover above the surface of the water, pressing down on it, as if calming it still further. This tranquillity was totally at odds with the catalogue of assaults he'd been reading all day. But such moments of quiet beauty had always been a part of Dublin for him; the part he missed like crazy when he had moved to Madrid and was instantly overwhelmed by the clamour and rush of daily life over there. He had got used to that soon enough, too, of course, quickly becoming addicted to the exuberance of the *Madrileños*, their love of colour, noise and spectacle. Yet when he'd met Gracia and married her, it was the stillness in her that he'd fallen for. But it hadn't been enough, not nearly enough, in the end.

He raised his hands to his eyes and felt the weight of his mobile phone shift in his jacket pocket. He took it out and stared at it, scrolling back through the call log until he came to Siobhan Fallon's number. Superficially, he couldn't imagine anyone less like Gracia. Apart from her hair, of course. And the eyes. But Siobhan, too, seemed to have that vein of beauty running right down through her. Except in her case it wasn't silent, or in any way interior. It was directed out towards the world. He pressed the call button but was put straight through to her voicemail.

'Hi, Siobhan, it's Mike Mulcahy. Just wanted to say I enjoyed last night, and was wondering if you'd fancy doing it again any time soon?'

She got to the Pembroke half an hour late and, as suspected, found Vincent Bishop had already decamped from the bar into the restaurant and left a message for her to follow. He had a bottle of champagne on the go and he insisted she have a glass with him to toast her success on the Maloney story. Or 'our' success, as he insisted on calling it – a touch too loudly for Siobhan's taste. But they soon moved on to other topics and it wasn't until after they'd finished eating that Bishop brought the subject of Maloney up again.

'I made a cracking deal as a result of that story,' Bishop said, unbuttoning his jacket.

'How do you mean?' she said. A small warning bell jingled in her head but the food and wine had lulled her into relaxation.

'Oh, you know, one of the sports promo companies Marty and Suzy Lenihan head up – I'd been looking at it for a while. I was able to scoop up a sizeable interest when the shares went through the floor first thing Monday morning – you know, after all the rumours that they'd be splitting up. It's a solid little business, so the price'll be back up in a week or two, once people realise it'd take a lot more than infidelity to tear those two apart.'

'Look, Vincent, I really don't want to hear about that.'

'No, wait,' he said, cutting in and putting his hand in his pocket. 'I just wanted to say, thanks. I thought you might like this, as a mark of my appreciation.'

He removed a tired-looking red velvet box from his jacket pocket and handed it to her across the table.

'What is it?' she asked, the full klaxon going off now, as she sat forward and stared at the box, the colour of dried blood against the pale flesh of his spindly fingers.

'Have a look,' he insisted. 'Go on. It won't bite.'

Against almost every instinct, she took the box from him and opened it. Nestling inside was a hoop of dull yellow metal, barely a couple of inches in diameter but intricately wrought in tiny swirls, curls and sinuous protrusions, and studded with what looked like four greyish pearls. In form it reminded her of a Celtic Cross, but when she looked again she noticed a bent metal prong cutting across the back and realised it was some kind of Tara Brooch. Despite the signs of age, it was exquisite.

She lifted her eyes from it and stared back across the table at Bishop, words for once evading her.

'I know a Tara Brooch might seem a bit old-fashioned nowadays,' he said half apologetically. 'But this one's special. Let me show you.'

He took the box from her and removed the brooch, turning it over to reveal the flat, entirely undecorated, reverse side. Weirdly, the plainness of the metal here made it look even more precious.

'There, see,' he said, holding it up to the light. 'It's the mark of George Waterhouse, the Dublin jewellers who revived the Celtic style after the original eighth-century brooch was found in a stream in Meath in the 1840s. They made this piece for the Great Exhibition of 1851 in London. I got it at auction a couple of years ago. Most early ones were silver or pewter but this is a bit more refined, twenty-two carat gold with Irish river pearls.'

'It's . . . it's gorgeous.' She looked around the small dining room, thinking everyone in the place must be staring at them, but no one was.

'So take it,' he said, holding it out to her on the palm of his hand now. 'It'd be lovely to see you wear it, but I'd keep it in the box if I were you. It's a rare piece.'

Siobhan could do nothing but stare across the table at him. The thing had to be worth thousands.

'What's the matter?' He waved it at her like it was a trinket.

'Are you kidding me?' she said, finally, finding her voice again. 'I can't take that from you. Even if I wanted to. I mean, it's incredibly beautiful, don't get me wrong . . .'

He began to say something but she waved his interruption away.

'No, seriously Vincent, it's very generous of you, but it wouldn't be right.'

She paused, watching a shadow creep across his long pale face, trying to find exactly the words she needed. But he got in first.

'To hell with what's right. I want you to have it.' His

voice was a low insistent growl now, his eyes blazing up at her. For an instant she sensed fully what it was that made him so formidable, so indomitable in business and she was sure she didn't like it. She also knew for certain now that she couldn't afford to lose this argument. Not on any level. Leaning in to the table, she dropped her voice to a confiding whisper.

'Look, I'm delighted we're pals, Vincent. And I'm thrilled you liked the splash we made with Maloney. But we're both professionals here. I was only interested in Maloney for his news value. If you made money from it, that's your business. I don't want or need to know. More to the point, there can't be any suspicion that I profited from it. Otherwise, how could I ever write anything again? You see that, don't you?'

She held his gaze, until eventually the fire in his eyes died down. He nodded at her, closed his grip over the brooch, then reached again for the box and carefully pinned the brooch back into its dark red velvet folds. Something about the way his long white fingers worked made her more repelled than ever by the thought of his touch, but she knew a gesture from her would be expected. She reached across the table and quickly patted the back of his hand twice, sitting back again before he could respond, her best smile still in place.

'You *do* understand, don't you?'

'No,' he said, begrudgingly, 'but *dum spiro, spero*, as they say.'

'Do they?' Siobhan laughed. 'I don't think I know that one – or even like the sound of it.'

That seemed to bring a smile back to his face. 'It's just a little Latin motto I have. I only meant, I'll find another way to show my gratitude. You can be sure of that.'

6

He'd only just put his Starbucks down on the desk when they started coming in. First Hanlon, next McHugh, then the rest of them, looking like they'd all come up in the lift together. A minute or so later, Brogan and Cassidy – joined at the hip as usual. He wondered idly whether it went even further than that. He'd rarely seen an inspector and a sergeant so tight. Sure, he'd got on well with Liam Ford, and they'd always gone out for a few pints, but he couldn't imagine meeting up with him before work just to make an entrance together.

'You must've got in early,' Brogan remarked.

'Just as well,' Mulcahy said. 'You look ready to start.'

She looked perplexed. 'Of course we are.'

'You told me nine a.m.'

'But we pulled it forward. I told Andy to . . .' Brogan raised an eyebrow at Cassidy.

'Sorry, boss, I must've forgotten. I was a bit knackered when we finished up last night.' Again the flashing glance, half-suppressed smirk.

Brogan made a vaguely apologetic what-can-you-do-with-them sort of face at Mulcahy.

'You must be driving the old sergeant here too hard,' Mulcahy said, smiling at her. 'Poor fella can't keep up with the game.'

He wasn't looking at Cassidy but could feel the man spitting bullets at him. Mulcahy turned and stared him straight in the eye, daring him to respond. Cassidy, though, did nothing but glare and go a deeper shade of purple, then he swallowed and walked away.

Brogan let out a sigh and stretched her arms behind her back. She was grinning now. 'Okay, lads, we've got a pile of stuff to get through this morning, so we'd better get cracking. Andy, you go see if those video grabs are ready. I'll get the ball rolling.'

There was a shuffling and clattering of chairs as everyone sat down, and Brogan stepped over to the whiteboard.

'Okay, so we now know exactly where the attack occurred and, as a result, a bit more about what happened to Jesica Salazar.' Brogan plucked a pen from the desk beside her, to use as a pointer, and indicated a location on the roughly drawn map – which had expanded and become more detailed overnight. 'Here, just opposite Kilmacud primary school, is where we've got a witness hearing a noise at two-thirty a.m. Out the bedroom window, she sees a van parked on the grass verge outside her house. It's rocking on its axles, so you can imagine what she thought. We showed the woman some pictures; she thinks the van was white but can't be sure, but says it wasn't big. Technical managed to isolate some tracks. Wheel profiles and tyres would indicate a short wheelbase Transit, Sprinter or something about that size.

'They also found blood spatter at the scene, possibly from the punch that broke the kid's nose. We're waiting for forensics to crossmatch and confirm. So what we're looking at here, in all likelihood, is as follows: Jesica's wandering home alone, perv in van spots her, pulls up, jumps out, decks her with a blow to the face, drags her into the van. Instead of taking her off to a lonely spot, though, he's either confident enough, or desperate enough, to continue the assault there and then, in the back of the van. Are you with me so far?'

Everyone nodded and muttered affirmatives as Brogan surveyed her audience.

'Right then, adding to that, the fabric found early on at the scene is definitely Jesica's skirt – we now have three separate confirmations on that from pals and her houseparents. Some interesting red fibres on there too, that Technical are having a look at. One of the lads taking tyre casts found more fabric squashed into the grass. Turns out to be a pair of knickers, almost certainly Jesica's – but obviously to be confirmed whenever we're allowed to have a word with her again. A preliminary exam of both items of clothing shows they were cut off, not torn off – again indicating a high level of preparedness on the attacker's part, despite the possible randomness of his victim selection.'

'A bit careless of him, wasn't it, boss?' The question came

from Hanlon. 'I mean to toss the clothes straight out of the van like that.'

Brogan held her hands up. 'Maybe he threw them out along with Jesica when he was finished with her. Or maybe he dumped them out his window as he was driving away and they went under the back wheels. By the way, Technical also did a fingertip search between there and the point – only a hundred and fifty yards up the road – where she was found afterwards. They're confident this vehicle did not pull up anywhere else along that stretch, meaning the attack was almost certainly initiated and completed all in the one place, and Jesica made her own way to the location at which she was discovered.'

'Do we know what happened to the rest of her clothes?' This question from McHugh.

'Yeah. Well, again, it's impossible to be certain but by comparing what you and Brian got from her fellow students yesterday, and what she still had hanging from her when she got to the hospital, we came up with a checklist and, basically, it looks like that was it. She still had her top and bra on – although both were badly torn and scorched – and her shoes. So it looks like he was only interested in one thing.'

'What about the cross and chain?' Mulcahy asked.

'No sign of it,' Brogan said. 'Both Technical and door-to-door were made aware, but nothing's come back.'

'So that means it could still be in the van?'

'Well, it's got to be somewhere. I suppose it's as likely to be there as anywhere else. For now, we have no way of knowing.'

Brogan paused as Cassidy pushed through the door and into the room, with a sheaf of what looked like A4 photographs in his hand.

'Oh, yeah, and the club's CCTV confirmed the clothing tallies, when we finally pinned down the time at which Jesica left the club. She definitely left with a young guy. Andy will pass the video grabs out to you now. You'll like these.'

A murmur of excitement filled the room as Cassidy handed out the plain-paper photographs scanned from the club's security system. Mulcahy examined them closely. A sequence of monochrome frames, taken from an angle high up and to the left of two open doors, showed a young couple exiting the club, arms around waists, laughing and smiling. Despite the camera's angle, aimed at people entering rather than exiting the club, a number of frames had captured each of them full face, and also in profile, as if they'd been turning to say goodbye, or to see if someone was coming after them. For Mulcahy the most striking thing, apart from how good-looking the pair of them were, was the clarity of the shots.

The girl, unrecognisable from the bruised and broken Jesica he'd seen a couple of days previously, was exceptionally pretty, her dark eyes radiant, glossed lips drawn in a wide smile over bright teeth, her black hair shiny enough to reflect the light over the door. She was wearing a short white top and matching mini-skirt; her long legs and midriff were bare. The young male cut a handsome figure, too. Tall, maybe six-two, narrow athletic frame, early twenties probably, fair hair feathered into a fashionable cut, his smile gleaming almost as much as the expensive leather jacket he wore over a striped high-collared shirt and dark jeans. The final photo was a blow-up of his face.

'Have these been enhanced?' Mulcahy asked, amazed at how good the images were for a club CCTV. He flicked back a couple of sheets and looked more closely. Sure enough, the glimmer of a chain was visible around the girl's neck, the cross glinting bright against her white top.

'No,' Brogan laughed, 'we got very lucky there. Somebody must've invested in some good-quality equipment without knowing it. Or maybe it was knock-off.'

The whole room laughed together, high on the knowledge that identifying the suspect could only be a matter of time. These stills were every copper's dream.

'Okay, so this is a real break for us, as you can see,' Brogan continued. 'Getting an ID remains our number one priority. We circulated copies to all Dublin area stations last night, so hopefully someone local will recognise this guy and contact us this morning. Maura and Donagh, I want you to get out and track down those three bouncers again, and shove this guy's mug in their faces. There's a good chance they'll know him if he's been there before. He's older than the usual crowd at that club, and pretty distinctive anyway. I'd also like you to do some follow-up calls this morning, make sure every sergeant in south Dublin makes all his shifts take a good hard look at that face. We need this badly. Any questions?'

'He's a good-looking lad,' Mulcahy commented. 'No problems picking up girls there, it seems.'

Brogan tutted loudly, like he'd broken some basic rule of detecting.

'And as *we* all know, Inspector, that means nothing. It might even go some way to explain why he did what he did to Jesica. If, indeed, he did it at all.'

'Just an observation,' Mulcahy said, wondering if the reproach was supposed to be some kind of payback for what he'd said to Cassidy.

Whelan put his hand up. 'Is that something dangling from his right hand?' he said, still staring hard at the video grabs. 'Could it be a set of keys? Car keys, I mean, or *van* keys?'

A sound of rustling filled the room, everyone flicking back through their own set of photos, checking they were looking at the same image, squinting hard to see what Whelan was talking about.

'Jaysus, I think he could be on to something there,' Cassidy said, holding up the print in question for Brogan to see.

'Can we get this blown up any bigger?' Brogan asked urgently.

'I'll get straight on to it,' Cassidy said.

'But didn't someone say the girl was walking home?' McHugh asked.

A silence fell on the room, before Brogan turned to Mulcahy, the look in her eyes question enough for him.

He shook his head. 'All she said was that a man hit her. But there was definitely an implication that it was outside. I mean, she said that she fell to the ground. And then, that he dragged her somewhere inside.' He thought back over the exact words Jesica had used, and had no doubt that he was right.

'And her pal said the guy had offered to *walk* home with her,' Brogan said. 'Look, it's just one more thing to throw in the mix. Like I said, the sooner we get on with this the sooner we'll sort it out, so come on, now . . .'

'Hiya, Des,' Siobhan began, cradling the phone on her shoulder with her chin as she finished a sentence on her screen and hit save. She looked over her shoulder automatically, making sure no one was paying any undue attention to her. 'You took your time getting back to me.'

It was Des Consodine, the Garda sergeant she'd primed the night before for information on the attack. Consodine was okay, as sources go, but he could be a lazy old bastard sometimes and she liked to keep him on his toes.

He started making excuses but she brought him up short. 'Okay, but what did you get for me?'

His reply was the one answer she hadn't expected from him. He'd got nothing at all.

'You mean it didn't happen?'

'Not exactly.'

'For God's sake, Des, what're you on about?' She was

about to give up on the whole thing, when her brain kicked in. That wasn't exasperation in his voice: it was unease. 'What do you mean, "not exactly"?'

'I mean, it might have happened. But, if it did, nobody's telling me anything about it.'

'Actively?'

'Very. When I rang Dundrum, they denied knowing anything about it at all. But . . .'

She heard him take a deep breath.

'But?'

'Look, Siobhan, this is as much as I'm going to be able to give you on this one. And, even at that, it didn't come from me, okay?'

'Sure. But at least tell me why, won't you?'

'All I can say is, after I didn't get anything from the lads on the desk, I rang a guy I know in Dundrum – a sergeant. He jumped right down my throat as soon as I mentioned it. Started giving me the third degree over how I'd heard about it.'

'You didn't tell him?'

'No, I fobbed him off. Then he told me to back off and stop asking. And he meant it.'

Siobhan was aware of her chest tightening slightly, as the feeling began to bloom inside her that she'd stepped into somewhere she wasn't supposed to be. She knew the feeling well. Loved it. Craved it, even. 'Bizarre, huh?'

'Too right,' Consodine agreed. 'And it sounded like it came straight from the top.'

She reached for a pencil and scribbled the phrase on to the reporter's pad beside her keyboard, underscoring the word 'top' three times.

'Is there something you're not telling me, Des?'

She thought she heard him swallow during the short pause that followed.

'No, why?'

'Well, so far you've told me nothing I didn't know already, except for some useless little hints. I can't exactly magic up a story from that.'

'Maybe there isn't one.'

'Yeah, well, in that case there's nothing in it for you, either,' she said sharply.

'You've got to be kidding me,' he whined. 'Look, I did what you asked, didn't I? And got a right bloody arse-kicking for my trouble. I need this. I've had a lousy run the last couple of weeks. You've got to give me something.'

It was just as Griffin had told her once: you couldn't beat a betting man when it came to making a good snout.

'And I say the same to you. We're not a charity. No lead, no wedge.'

'But I've told you everything.'

'For Christ's sake, Des, you're just taking the piss now. Let's just leave it.'

'No, wait.'

She didn't say anything, just waited for him to cave.

'Okay,' he sighed at last, 'it definitely came from the top, like I said.'

'From the Commissioner's office?'

'Higher.'

The significance zapped straight from the earpiece into her brain.

'What, from the Minister's office? Why would Harmon stick his oar in?'

She didn't wait for a reply. Her own thoughts were popping like flashbulbs now. It must've been even more serious than the informant on the phone had suggested. Why would the government be interested? Were they worried about the effect on tourism or something? But a cover-up would be a ludicrous over-reaction. She was pulled up by Consodine, speaking again.

'I've no idea, Siobhan. That's all I know. God's honest truth. Even telling you that much, I'm in the shit if it gets out. I'm putting my job on the line here. Are you going to stump up or not?'

'Oh, for God's sake Des, you still haven't told me anything worth having. Can't you give me a name, at least? Who's handling the case? Who's in charge?'

Sounding sick to his stomach now, Consodine mentioned a couple of names who *might* be called in to handle something sensitive like this. Neither of them meant anything to her but it was something to follow up on at least.

'Alright, Des,' she said after she'd scribbled the names on the pad. 'I must be in a generous mood today. I'll put the usual in the post tonight.'

Siobhan put the phone down, her mind racing. Maybe

Consodine hadn't told her everything he knew, but that only meant he was protecting himself from something serious. She was sure in her gut that she was onto something. How big it was, only time, and a few more phone calls, would tell.

'Boss . . . boss?' Cassidy was all gruff urgency as he clamped a hand over the mouthpiece and held the phone away from his face. Brogan, leaning over a desk, talking to McHugh about something, turned awkwardly towards him.

'What is it?'

'It's Sergeant Gerry Leahy from Blackrock, says one of his uniforms down there reckons he knows our boy in the photo.' He paused to look at the name he'd written down. 'Student by the name of Patrick Scully. Even knows where he lives. Wants to know do we need them to go out and pick him up for us?'

'Jesus, no!' Brogan said, the risk of someone their end bungling the break too great. 'No, tell them not to do a thing, and we'll head straight down there.' But as soon as she said it, she had another, alternative vision of the whole thing going pear-shaped and this Scully vanishing without trace before they even got there. 'No, no – wait,' she said, waving a hand at Cassidy. 'Find out the address, then tell Leahy to get someone out there pronto to keep an eye on the place till we arrive. We'll meet them there. C'mon, Maura, Donagh, fingers out, let's get going . . .'

They were all long gone, the incident room empty and hushed except for the occasional hum of the fan from a hard drive, when Mulcahy next raised his head from the files. It was one of the civilian secretaries, rapping politely on the door jamb, a phone held out towards him in her other hand.

'There's a call for Inspector Brogan. When I told the gentleman you were the only one here, he insisted on talking to you.'

Mulcahy took the phone from her.

'Hello?'

The voice that boomed from the other end of the line was a bizarre blend of pomposity and brogue, such a voice as linguists might use to demonstrate the effect of advanced education on vocal chords trained to bellow messages from one godforsaken bog to another in the remotest west of Ireland. Mulcahy recognised it instantly as that of Dr Frank Geraghty, director of the Technical Bureau, the Gardai's in-house forensic science facility. He was a bear of a man with a penchant for baggy tweed three-pieces in bilious shades of green and a gaze so penetrating it could cut you in two.

'It *is* you, Mulcahy, you big sleeveen! When in God's name did you make it back onto these sainted shores? And why didn't you call me? I'd have organised a reception committee, then shipped you straight back whence you came. You were doing a great job for us over there, last I heard!'

'Frank, how are you doing?' Mulcahy said, holding the phone a good bit further away from his ear. 'How's it going over there in Technical?'

As ever, Geraghty ignored the side of the conversation that was not his own.

'Jesus Christ, man, what are *you* doing lurking in Brogan's inner sanctum?'

Mulcahy groaned. He'd spent enough time hanging around courtrooms or attending conferences with the father of Irish forensics to know what was expected of him.

'I've never been anywhere near her sanctum, your honour.'

'Ah, ye dirty brat,' Geraghty guffawed. 'To be honest, I'm not entirely sure she has one, anyway. A mite too imperious for my tastes, the lovely inspector. She's certainly never wanted to indulge my more frolicsome side. But, to get back to my question, if you have been foolish enough to chuck Old Castille for the Old Sod, why aren't you back on crack alley? What on earth are you doing consorting with Brogan?'

Mulcahy spent a couple of minutes explaining the situation, amassing a large number of crude comments along the way. Geraghty was not one to waste words on subtlety.

'Ah well, I don't suppose she'll mind me telling you. I'll be emailing through the results in a minute, but I thought she'd want to know the basics straight from the horse's mouth. Not that she'll be any happier with them. The main thrust is that we found no physical evidence of sexual congress. Or nothing, should I say, to support a charge of rape in the traditional sense, anyway. Clearly, the medics will have to come back with a view on that, from the internal exams, but, on the basis of our analysis of the swabs taken externally there was nothing. No semen traces, no pubic hair, not even foreign skin cells so far as we've been able to establish. She was clean as a whistle – which, I have to say,

119

is most unusual. Normally anything as vigorous as sex, even if it's just masturbation, leaves *some* physical evidence behind. At least, I've certainly never seen a case where it didn't.'

'But you're not saying she *wasn't* raped?'

'No, Mulcahy, what I'm saying is that, from the materials presented to me, and within the limits of my brief, I could find no evidence of anyone engaging in sexual activity with the girl. But it is possible that when this freak tortured her, or whatever he thought he was doing to her, he could have burned off whatever trace evidence there might have been externally. The doctors that treated her must've come to some conclusions about it.'

'Not much good to us, if we've got no forensic back-up.'

'Oh, there's no shortage of forensic evidence, Mulcahy – just none to show the foul wretch had sex with her. That may be unusual, but it's not impossible in the circumstances.' There was a faint wheeze at the other end of the line as Geraghty drew breath. 'One curiosity did emerge, which you *will* probably want to pass on to Brogan post haste. She asked us to venture an opinion on what might have been used to burn the girl and, judging from the photos, we told her it was probably a heated flat metal surface. Sure enough, when we examined the swabs there were metallic flakes amid the residue and so I ran a check on them. Damn me to heaven if they didn't have a high percentage of gold in them. Not your good-quality, eighteen-carat stuff, now, but more the sort you'd find in gold plate. The thing is, it had definitely been subjected to intense heat . . . But all that'll be in the report. I'd have to venture that whatever he burned her with must have had some form of gold-plating on it. Maybe a ceremonial dagger or the like – though obviously it's not my place to speculate. To be honest, it's so unusual we'll have to run more tests. Perhaps he swiped it from Mummy's best cutlery set, but it's not exactly your standard attack weapon, anyway.'

It must've been the twentieth file he'd pulled up and sifted through that morning, but it was proving just as much a dead end as the others. Some young gouger had pulled a Stanley knife on an ex-girlfriend and forced her to give him a blowjob by the communal rubbish bins round the back of a block of flats out in Artane. Then he'd slashed her face and walked away, leaving her screaming, puking and drenched in her own blood. Asked why he'd done it, he said he'd been drinking and, anyway, hadn't she asked for it by getting pregnant with another fella? He was charged, convicted and was doing a three-year stretch in Portlaoise. All of which made a kind of sense to the Garda in Mulcahy. It's how things were in the world: some people were irredeemable shits.

What still didn't make any sense at all to him was what had happened to Jesica Salazar. Less than ever since he'd spoken to Frank Geraghty. A kid gets raped and tortured half to death yet there's no forensic evidence of sex? How the hell could that be? The idea that anyone could get their rocks off by causing that amount of pain was alien enough to Mulcahy. All he knew for certain was that, compared to this, Drugs was a walk in the park. At least there you knew what you were up against most of the time: ruthless greed, abject addiction and heartless exploitation. It was a trade, no matter how evil, and it worked according to its own set of rules.

Mulcahy shook the thought from his head and realised he'd forgotten to call Brogan and pass on Geraghty's message. He dialled the number, got put through to her voicemail and left a message. That was it, then. He grabbed his jacket, squeezing the pockets to check his smokes and lighter were there, and strode out into the empty incident room. Passing the whiteboard, he saw someone had pinned up the two CCTV images of Jesica emerging from the nightclub, one head-and-shoulders, one full-length shot. Such a beautiful girl. Her clothes, though minimal, looked expensive – and why not? Her father was one of the wealthiest men in Spain. What she was doing at a Dublin language school for four weeks, Mulcahy couldn't begin to imagine. He always thought that kind of wealth brought nothing but privilege: private tutors, finishing schools and so on. Then he remembered the photos he'd seen of her father, in newspapers and magazines. A hawkish face, a thin, spare frame: more like a hermit than a politician. More like a grandfather than a father? He thought of what Martinez had told him about Salazar, and wondered what the man must now be feeling. For all his wealth and power, he hadn't been able to prevent this random intrusion of tragedy into his daughter's life.

Mulcahy moved a step nearer to the close-up photo of Jesica: her gleaming hair and teeth, the cross and chain glittering against her white top. Gold on the swabs? That must be it, he thought, recalling how she'd touched the red weal on her neck in the hospital. At some stage the attacker had pulled the chain from her neck. Maybe he tried to choke her with it. Mulcahy imagined a hand gripping the chain, twisting it, breaking it. Had some of the gold flaked off on his hand?

Mulcahy rubbed a hand across his face, massaging his tired eyes with forefinger and thumb. Nothing about this case made any sense. He patted his jacket pocket, feeling for the cigarette pack again, his subconscious reminding him that he'd been on his way out for a smoke. He looked out the window, to where the sunlight picked out the red and black gable end of the Bleeding Horse pub. Make that a pint as well, he thought, looking at his watch. Might as well be lunchtime. He fished his phone out – Liam was probably gasping for one himself by now.

Siobhan was making progress. After only five phone calls to St Vincent's Hospital she'd tracked down someone who had been on duty over the weekend and was able and willing to confirm that, yes, a Spanish student had been treated in Emergency, and subsequently admitted to the hospital, on Sunday morning. No names or clinical details, of course:

123

patient confidentiality and all that, especially where journalists were concerned. Still, on the back of this information she was able to phone Dundrum Garda Station and put the details to them, to see what the reaction would be. The note of panic in the voice of the Garda who answered the phone, and the speed with which she'd been passed on to his unhelpful sergeant, bolstered her belief that Consodine's lead was solid and she was on to something. But what?

Siobhan had a quick word with Paddy Griffin, gave him a rough idea of what she had discovered and got his okay to spread a few euro around, if necessary. Grabbing her keys, she took the lift down to the basement car park and folded down the black cloth roof of her beloved, if ancient, red Alfa Spider. Then she was off, bursting up the ramp towards the bright blue sky, and out on to the quays. She could have just as easily taken a taxi on expenses and that way made use of the bus lanes. But a beautiful cloudless day like this offered too good an opportunity to put the top down, feel the sun on her face, the wind in her hair and any other cliché you might throw at her. She loved them all. The traffic crawled at its usual stop-start pace, but she made good time on a cut-through she knew in Ballsbridge and was soon zipping across the junction at Nutley Lane, and parking in the stunted multi-storey car park that defaced the southern reaches of the hospital grounds. Walking out of it she had a flashback to – what, twenty-five years before? – when her dad had been taken into this hospital. Her, ten or eleven, no more, leading him up the concrete steps, holding his hand, chattering words of comfort, when all the time it was him who was really consoling her, calming her, encouraging her not to be afraid, and to take good care of her mother.

Back then the hospital buildings had been widely spaced, the grounds landscaped with health-promoting shrubbery and lawns. And, even if they were never beautiful, those square-edged sixties buildings had radiated – at least it seemed then – a kind of benign medicinal authority. Nowadays, though, the boom years had allowed for all sorts of add-ons and extensions to eat up the healing green spaces. Inside, the corridors were much as she recalled them, but without the spectral glow of memory. Walls rubbed down to the plaster by too many passing bodies. The floors too footworn now to hold the glossy wax polish that had squeaked beneath the nurses' plimsolls as they took her dad off to his ward. She shivered at the thought: her lovely dad, walking away, waving back to her, the light streaming in from the far end of the corridor eating away at his outline until he was just a stick.

'Jaysus, you're going soft already, and you've only been there a couple of days. They'll have you carrying a handbag next.'

Mulcahy looked up from his *Irish Times* to see Detective Sergeant Liam Ford grinning down at him. He'd been so absorbed in the crossword he hadn't noticed him coming in. Not easy as, at six-foot-four, eighteen stone and always kitted out in the same brown leather bomber jacket, jeans and knackered Nikes, you could normally spot Liam Ford from half a mile off. In his mid-thirties now, some of the muscle was running to fat and the long hair made him look more like an ageing rocker than a Drugs cop. But that was the general idea, and while he was too noticeable ever to excel in the area of discreet surveillance, put him in a small room with a suspect and he came into his own.

'It's only the Simplex crossword,' Mulcahy objected.

'The what?'

'The easy one, you ignorant git. Don't you ever read the paper?'

'Not that one, I don't. The *Sun* or the *Herald*'ll do me. I like to be able to understand what I'm reading.'

Mulcahy smiled at the accent. Over a decade in Dublin and he still sounded like he was straight out of Cork. Ford pointed at Mulcahy's partially consumed pint of Guinness on the bar.

'Another one?'

'Go on, then.'

He called the order to the barman, then dragged up a stool.

'How's it going? Anything I should know about?' asked Mulcahy, laying his paper aside.

'Not a lot. Everybody's a bit on edge with this freeze still on. We're under too much feckin' pressure. Seems like every second desk in the place is empty. Ludicrous, it is.'

Ford broke off to hand the barman a note for the two pints, and took a long gulp while he waited for the change. By the time the glass hit the bar again it was half empty.

'How about yourself? You're being very cagey about what's going on over there. What in Jesus's name would Sex Crimes be needing you for anyway?'

Mulcahy tapped a finger against his nose. 'Nothing that would interest you, Liam. And nothing they couldn't be getting on with all by themselves, either. At the moment, I'm a total waste of space over there.'

Ford looked at him like he had two heads. 'Well, you've got to get yourself the hell out of there then, don't you.'

'Yeah, I guess. But it's not as simple as that.'

Ford leaned an elbow on to the bar and lowered his voice. 'But maybe it is, boss. Look, a fella I know from Southern Region got a whisper yesterday that HR are going to force Tommy Dowling to throw in the towel. You heard about him, yeah?'

Mulcahy nodded. Dowling was head of the Southern Region Drugs Squad. He'd got shot in the liver a few months back, when a raid on a house in Youghal went badly wrong.

'The latest medical didn't go well,' Ford said. 'Looks like he's never going to be match fit again, so they're making him an offer – full pension and appropriate compensation to be agreed. Word is he'll be gone within the month. I reckon you just have to put in for it, and it's yours. Murtagh would be mad not to take you on. I know it might not be exactly what you want, but it would get you back in the groove at least.'

Far from being dismissive of the opportunity, Mulcahy

127

was feeling like a drowning man who'd just been thrown a lifebelt. 'Are you sure about this?'

'As sure as I can be.'

'Who else would be up for it? Who's covering for Dowling now?'

Ford was grinning from ear to ear, getting up some real enthusiasm for the idea.

'That's just the thing. The DI who's been holding the fort, Sean McCarthy, reckons he's a dead cert for it, but word is that Murtagh hasn't been impressed by his performance. He's not popular with the lads, and there've been a couple of bad fuck-ups. But the main thing is, it's a detective superintendent's post. No way does McCarthy have the legs for that, especially not if you put your hat in the ring. I reckon it's got you written all over it.'

Mulcahy tried to damp down the excitement rising inside him. Other opportunities he'd got wind of in the past six months had shrivelled up and died in the face of the recruitment freeze. But they couldn't let a Regional job like that go unfilled – and it *would* suit him down to the ground, even more than Ford realised. Donal Murtagh, the Southern Region chief superintendent, was probably the man he'd collaborated most closely with on intelligence while he was in Madrid. For years they'd battled to combat drug smuggling along Ireland's vulnerable south coast. He had huge respect for him and they'd always got on well.

'Thanks, Liam. Maybe I'll give Murtagh a call.'

'You make sure you do.' Ford grinned again. 'The lads

down there would love it if you came on board. There's lots of 'em remember you from way back.'

'Only one fly in the ointment.'

'What's that?'

'I'd have to live in bloody Cork.'

Ford let out a big guffaw before knocking back the rest of his pint. 'You should be so bloody lucky. They don't call it the Pearl of the South for nothing.'

'They don't call it the pearl of anywhere, as far as I recall.'

Mulcahy signalled the barman to give Ford another pint and tried to stop thinking about just how ideal this job would be. Even the move to Cork would be interesting, as the south coast was the absolute frontline when it came to drug smuggling. Ford, meanwhile, chatted heatedly for a while about his own gig at the National Drugs Unit in Dublin Castle, finishing off with an amusing tale of a well-known small-time dealer who'd been hit by a car while trying to evade arrest.

'Three cracked ribs, a broken collarbone, and his jaw's smashed in so many bits it had to be wired shut. He's not going to be talking to anybody for while. Or going anywhere either, except for the infirmary – we found fifty-three wraps of coke in the lining of his jacket.'

Mulcahy was still laughing when he heard a loud foreign accent behind him. He turned on his stool to see a portly black man in his forties standing at the counter, ordering a coffee and a sandwich. His voice was full of the rounded vowels of Africa, but what was even more striking was that he was a priest. The gleaming white collar encircling his neck stood out in sharp contrast to both his skin colour and his well-tailored charcoal-grey suit.

Craning his neck to see who the priest was with, Mulcahy noticed a whole group of clergymen, a mix of Africans and Europeans from the sound of their conversation, sitting in an alcove to his right. Most had cups, saucers and half-consumed sandwiches already in front of them. He must've been really lost in the crossword not to spot them before. A gang of priests in a pub was a weird thing to see nowadays, even if they were only drinking coffee. Must be some kind of religious conference taking place nearby, and now taking a break for lunch.

'Are you waiting for them to give us dispensation for another one?' Ford asked, holding his empty pint glass in his hand and nodding towards the clerics.

Mulcahy turned and looked at his own barely touched second drink. 'I'm fine for the minute,' he said, taking a swallow. Something was niggling furiously at the back of his mind. 'But you go ahead, Liam. I'm not in any . . .'

As he was saying this, something shunted in his brain and slipped into place. He put his pint down sharply, the smack of the glass on the countertop drawing curious looks from more than just Ford. But Mulcahy was oblivious, his eyes locked onto one of the men sitting facing him from the alcove. Another priest, or a bishop maybe, given his purple shirt. But it was what was hanging in front of the shirt that was the focus of Mulcahy's close attention: a large gold cross dangling from a chain. Big and brash, it was at least five or six inches in length, and flat-surfaced, plain, devoid of a figure of Christ or any other adornment.

'Eh, are you alright, boss?' Ford asked again, a look of amused concern on his face.

'Yeah, no, I'm . . .' He looked at Ford, then quickly at the clergymen, then back again. 'Sorry, Liam. Thanks for all that, but I've just thought of something important. I've really got to go. I'll call you later, okay?'

He didn't wait for an answer. Just automatically checked that his smokes and lighter were in his pocket and half walked, half trotted out of the pub.

Ford stared after him, shaking his head, pouring the remains of Mulcahy's pint into his own.

Mulcahy slammed through the door with such force that the lone secretary nearly leaped from her chair. He stormed over to the table by the whiteboards, and grabbed a picture folder from the stack. Flicking quickly through the first few pictures, he soon saw what he wanted. Although it wasn't completely clear, he knew immediately that he was right.

Eyes glued to the folder, he went straight into his office and turned on the desk lamp, pulling out the hospital photos of the wounds inflicted on Jesica's stomach and groin, spreading them out under the halo of light. He'd looked through the pictures before, but his stomach still heaved on seeing the injuries again – livid bruises, blistered skin, scorched and knitted in ways it shouldn't be, charred

131

black elsewhere. But now the wounds no longer seemed entirely random to him.

There was a pattern to them, not easy to discern at first, but there if you knew what you were looking for. The random scattering of burns all seemed to connect at right angles at some point or another. Broken in places, yes, but if you took the contours of the girl's body into account, especially imagining how a narrow flat surface might be pressed against it, he could see how it was possible to interpret the marks as basic angular shapes. Where the hot metal had been pressed harder or more softly, so the injury was greater or less, and the colours of the burns themselves were more intense or lighter. It was the colours that matched up best. But the width and severity of the wounds did too. He looked at the worst of them, the one that had scorched the flesh around her sex, trying not to visualise the horror of the act, or the pain it must have caused. It took more than one picture to tell the story but it was there, discernible: a wide cross-shape traceable from pubic bone to buttocks.

Un fucking *cura*. Why hadn't he spotted it earlier? What Jesica had said about her attacker being like a priest, making the sign of the cross? But her own missing cross and chain had blinded him to that. What's the most common gold item you're going to find in Ireland, apart from jewellery? Bloody religious regalia. Crosses, for Christ's sake!

He examined each of the pictures again, and saw nothing to make him feel any less convinced. Long vertical burns, intercepted two-thirds of the way along by shorter horizontal

132

ones. The wounds looked exactly like they'd been inflicted with something shaped just like a cross. A big one, too, at least six to nine inches. Bigger than the one the priest in the pub was wearing. Gold plate rather than fine jewellery, that's what Geraghty had said. The sort of thing you'd find in a sacristy or a private chapel, maybe. Plain, cheap, not even a figure on it. Fuck, there must be millions of the bloody things knocking around the country.

He grabbed his phone, hoping that Geraghty might be able to shed some light. But the receptionist at the Technical Bureau told him he'd been called out on a job and wasn't expected back for the day. She also refused to give out his mobile number. Then he tried Brogan, but again went straight through to voicemail. He left a message asking her to call, then hung up, frustrated, and started going through the files again.

He'd been looking for the wrong thing all along.

7

Blackrock Garda Station was a small modern block marooned on an island between the ceaseless four-lane traffic of Frascati Road and the quieter Temple Road on the seaward side. Its position and blank exterior, dark brick relieved only by columns of black glass, suggested the Garda Siochana's desire to keep the folk of Blackrock at bay rather than offer them a place of succour or sanctuary. In other parts of Dublin that would be understandable, but Blackrock was historically one of Dublin's most affluent suburbs, making the station's defensive siting all the more incongruous.

Interview Room 4 was located on the first floor. Cassidy had an eye glued to the spyhole in the door. Brogan was pacing the short patch of corridor outside.

'How long has it been?'

Cassidy pulled back from the peephole. 'Getting on for three quarters of an hour.'

'And he hasn't started sweating yet?' Brogan checked her watch, conscious of time slipping away. Ideally she'd prefer to let this one stew for a bit longer, as everything she'd seen of him so far screamed smart-arse. But it was Aidan's poker game with the lads tonight, the one thing she always tried to get home in time for so she could spend a few sacred hours alone with her boy. Just get on with it.

'Chewing his fingernails a bit,' Cassidy said, 'but apart from that he looks cool enough.'

Sweeping the guy up had been easier than Brogan had expected. As promised, the lads from Blackrock had kept an eye on the house – a well-maintained semi with a large, immaculately kept front garden, in Castlebyrne Park. When they arrived, DS Leahy was able to confirm that Patrick Scully was actually on the premises, having seen him go out to the garage and back about ten minutes after he'd got there. That's the way luck should always work. She let Cassidy and Leahy take care of the talking when they knocked on the door. A woman answered and got into a bit of a flap when she heard who they were and that they wanted to talk to her son. But Scully himself, almost as well groomed and attired as he'd looked in the CCTV footage, was remarkably calm about it, and straight away agreed to come to the station. Didn't even seem surprised, which made her wonder if he had any form. She kept well back and didn't say a word herself, retaining the psychological advantage of presenting him with someone new once it came to the interview.

'Okay, c'mon then, we're wasting time. Let's do it.'

She opened the door and swept in, locking eyes with

135

Scully straight away, but saying nothing. Like all interview rooms everywhere, it was bare of decoration and furnished to the minimum. Its windowless continuum of grey wall was uninterrupted but for two air vents, the door and a bright red plunger-style panic button to the right of it, to summon help in the event of a suspect getting stroppy. Scully sat back in a rangy slouch on one of the four plastic chairs around a metal table that was bolted to the floor. Once again she was struck by how well turned out he was. His long legs were wrapped in cream chinos that looked like they'd come off the designer rails at Brown Thomas. So too with his scuff-free suede loafers, impeccably ironed blue-check shirt and a linen jacket that might have been made to measure. The backs of his hands and his long fingers had the remnants of a tan and his nails shone like they'd been buffed and manicured. Obviously biting them wasn't a habit, so he had to be feeling some anxiety underneath the Mr Cool act. Good.

He held Brogan's gaze as she took her seat, not bothering to alter his slouch. She tucked her own chair under her and pulled it to the table. Only then did he sit up and do the same, positioning his elbows on the table in a mirror image of her own. At this proximity, the first thing she noticed was that he didn't seem in any way disconcerted by her stare. Quite the opposite, in fact. It was his eyes that made her feel slightly uncomfortable. They were so unusual, the irises a deep intense brown that all but merged with his pupils and glinted like jet in the harsh fluorescent light from overhead.

She sat back, to diminish their effect, listening to the scrape of Cassidy's chair as he sat down beside her, waiting as he cued up the digital recorder that was secured to the table top by a steel bracket, then recited the formalities of date, place and people present into the machine.

'Can you confirm, please, that you are Patrick Cormac Scully?'

He nodded, fingers now arched under his chin.

'Answer yes or no for the tape, please,' Cassidy said, a growl of aggression in his voice.

'Yes, I am.'

'Of 43 Castlebyrne Park, Blackrock?'

'Yes,' he said again, to Cassidy, but more confidently this time. He turned his gaze back to Brogan. 'Am I under arrest?'

'No.'

'Then would you mind telling me what this is about?'

'Certainly,' Brogan said. 'It's simple. We want to know where you were and what you were doing three nights ago – that's last Saturday night.'

Brogan thought she saw a flicker of concern cross Scully's face.

'Saturday night?' he asked, struggling to keep the catch from his voice.

The reaction was so faint, Brogan looked involuntarily towards her sergeant for confirmation. Cassidy gave a barely perceptible nod. He'd clocked it, too.

'Yes, Saturday,' Brogan said. 'As in Saturday night/Sunday morning. Can you tell us that?'

'Sure,' he said, adjusting his position in the chair again, sitting up straight, tugging the sleeves of his jacket down over his shirt cuffs, eyes flicked down in concentration, playing for time. At last, with a little jut of his chin, he raised his head and stared back at her. Again, she couldn't help being hit by the intensity of his eyes. It was actually tangible, like a jolt of static.

'I went out,' he said. 'Clubbing, like, you know?'

'Could you be a bit more specific, please? When and where would help – all the details you can remember.'

'Yeah, no problem.' He seemed almost eager to help now, but there was a sense of wariness, of control being exerted behind the words. 'I was at home watching telly with the folks until about eight, then I went upstairs to get ready, and I suppose it was about ten when I went out.'

Brogan smiled. Two hours to get ready? That explained a lot. She hoped for his mother's sake they had more than one bathroom.

'You live with your parents still?' Cassidy put in, hoping to needle him.

'Yes,' Scully replied flatly, not even looking at him.

'And where did you go?' Brogan asked.

'That place up in Stillorgan, the GaGa, you know? I got there about half ten, I suppose. Had a few Buds and a few dances. Left about half one or two, I suppose. Walked back. Got home half two at the latest and went straight to bed. Out like a light, but I'm like that.'

'Is that it?' Brogan asked, thinking it sounded rehearsed.

'What more can I say?' He grinned and turned his palms up. 'Not the best night of my life, I suppose, but I've had worse. Better than staying in and watching Ma and Da getting frisky.'

Brogan gave him a small smile. He was a bit more confident now, thought he could flirt with her. Fine, if that was his comfort zone. She could kick him out of it whenever she liked.

'Getting back to the club,' Cassidy said. 'Did you go there alone?'

'Yeah.'

'Do you always go there on your own?'

'Not always, but often enough.'

'Don't you think that's a bit weird?'

'No more than going to a film or something on my own.'

'Don't you have any friends, Patrick?' Cassidy asked.

'Of course I have friends. Look, what's this about? I go there cos it's just up the road, and it's as good a place to go as any if I need to get out of the house – which I often do. What the hell is wrong with that?'

Cassidy ignored the question. 'Seems a bit *young* for you. The GaGa is aimed at sixteen- to eighteen-year-olds, isn't it? They're just kids compared to you. How old did you say you were?'

'I didn't. But I'm twenty-three. And what can I say? Maybe I like my girls a little bit younger than me. There's no law against that, is there?'

'So long as they're not *too* young,' Cassidy muttered.

Scully bridled at that, alright. 'Hey, what are you trying to say?'

'Nothing,' Cassidy grunted, 'apart from the obvious.'

'Look, I'm getting tired of this. It says on the door that it's for over-eighteens only, so as far as I'm concerned anyone in there is kosher. Now, entertaining as this has been, I'd appreciate it if you'd tell me what you want and let me the hell out of here.'

'Did you meet anyone at the club last Saturday?' Brogan asked.

'Of course I did, I mean, I always . . .' He pulled himself up short.

'Always?' Brogan raised her eyebrows and smiled again. 'That's nice – but then, clearly you know you're a good-looking guy.'

'No law against that either, is there?'

More defensive now, but she could see him absorbing the flattery like a sponge. Couldn't help himself.

'Certainly not. It's to be actively encouraged, I'd say.' Brogan laughed. To her left she felt Cassidy's stare shift towards her, and saw Scully pick up on it, too. Game on.

'So Jesica wasn't anyone special, then, just a casual pick-up?'

'Who the hell is Jessica?' he said, wrong-footed, surprise flaring in those eyes.

'Jesica – you know, the girl you took home on Saturday night.'

'I didn't take anybody home on Saturday night. I told

you, I walked back afterwards and went straight to bed. I've never even heard of any bloody Jessica. Who's been winding you up?'

Brogan glanced at Cassidy and raised an eyebrow.

'So, Patrick, you're actually denying that you left the club with anyone on Saturday night?'

Scully paused, thinking about that one carefully.

'Well, no . . . I mean, I did leave the club with someone, a Spanish girl, but I never even got her name. Is she this Jessica one you're talking about?'

'What if she is?'

'Well, I sure as fuck didn't take her home with me. I mean, we had a bit of a snog on the dance floor, but I could tell she wasn't up for anything else. *She* really was just a kid. I told her I was going, and she said she had to go too, and it turned out we were both going the same way so we walked together as far as the Stillorgan shopping centre.'

'You walked, you say. You didn't give her a lift?'

'No, like I said, we walked.'

'As far as the shopping centre. And then what happened?'

'We split. She went off up Kilmacud way, and I went down Stillorgan Park.'

'Just like that? You didn't stop for another snog?'

'Yeah, well . . .'

'Even though she "really was just a kid", as you put it?' Cassidy remarked, snide and critical.

'Well, you know, a bird in the hand and all . . .'

'In the hand?' Cassidy interrupted, all mock indignation. 'So it went a bit further than a snog, then, did it?'

'No, I just meant . . .' Scully took a breath to calm himself, then seemed to think better of trying to explain what he meant. 'No, it didn't.'

'You must've been pretty tempted, though, right? Not many people up there around the shopping centre at that hour. Pretty easy to push things on a bit, get what you want, yeah?'

'No. No way. I'm telling you, we had a snog and went our separate ways.'

'Are you sure about that, Patrick?' Cassidy pushed.

'Sure of it? Of course I am. I mean . . . Look, hang on a second here. What's this about? Are you saying she's accusing me of something?'

'Why would you say that, Patrick?' Brogan interjected. 'What is it you think she might be accusing you of?'

'Ah, no. Come off it, now.' There was a sense of panic in Scully's voice. 'This has to be some kind of a wind-up. What's she been saying?'

'What is it *you* think she might be saying?' Cassidy jumped in again aggressively, not letting anything go.

'I told you, I haven't got a clue, but whatever it is, it's not true.'

'That's an interesting way of putting it, Patrick.'

'What?'

Brogan was just beginning to think they might be getting somewhere, when the tension inside the room was shattered by a sharp rap on the door.

'What is it?' she shouted, suppressing a curse and sharing a glare with Cassidy.

A young uniformed Garda popped his head tentatively round the door.

'Inspector Brogan?'

'Who the hell else would it be, ya gobshite?' Cassidy muttered, but Brogan was already talking over him.

'Yes, what is it? Quickly.'

'Urgent message for you, outside.'

Cassidy suspended the interview and sat glowering at Scully like a guard dog sizing up an intruder. Outside, the young cop handed Brogan a handset. Who the hell could this be?

'Boss, it's Donagh. Sorry to interrupt, but I thought you'd want to know this.'

'Go on, then. What've you got?'

'You won't believe it, boss. We've got the fucker. There's a small white Transit van in Scully's garage with welding equipment in the back. I did a quick check and, sure enough, it's registered in his name.'

'You beauty.' In her mind, Brogan punched the air. 'What's it look like inside? Anything I can hit him with?'

'Well, it looks clean enough. No blood or anything but then, as soon as I spotted the welding gear, I got the hell out. Thought I'd better leave the rest to Technical, y'know, if it's a crime scene an' all.'

'Good lad,' Brogan said, and told him to tell Technical to impound the vehicle and get it straight over to the lab on a flatbed. 'Top priority, no excuses. Was there anything else?'

'Actually, yes there was, boss. Maura bagged a stack of porno in his bedroom, and a fair old stash of cannabis and what looks like ecstasy tablets. About twenty or thirty of them.'

Brogan felt her chest contracting, feeling certain that she'd got her man. With this lot, the rest should be just a formality. 'Jesus, Donagh, you guys have outdone yourselves. Pints all round on me later, yeah? For now, though, I'm going back in to nail this bastard.'

She hung up and handed the phone back to the uniform who was beaming at her for some reason. She ignored him, grabbed the door handle and took a deep breath, half expecting Cassidy to have wound Scully up into a bate in her absence. But in the interview room everything was exactly as it had been: Cassidy glowering, Scully making a poor job of looking unconcerned. Soon wipe the smirk off that face, she thought as she sat down again, tipping Cassidy the wink as she told him to start up the recorder again.

Siobhan knew better than to trawl the wards. It wasn't her style, and she'd only draw attention to herself. It didn't do to get a reputation for that kind of thing. Of course, there was no point approaching the doctors or the admin staff directly. She'd get nothing from them, not at this stage. Their jobs were far too cushy and well paid to risk losing for the sake of a journalist's curiosity. The nurses, on the other hand, were always a good bet: overworked, underappreciated and, crucially, underpaid. Best of all, though, were the cleaners, porters and ancillary staff, those poor eejits who did the worst jobs for the lowest wages, and were usually guaranteed to lay their hands on any information you wanted, for a small fee.

She reckoned it must have been one of them who phoned her with the story in the first place, recalling the broad Dublin accent cutting through the phone crackle. It might even be easy to track him down, as he'd be one of very few nowadays who was actually Irish. Most of them were Bosnian, Afghan, Vietnamese – asylum seekers and illegal immigrants being the only ones desperate enough to scrape shit, blood and vomit off floors in an economy that, until recently, had enjoyed full employment. Even most of the good citizens now standing in dole queues for the first time in ten years would consider themselves above that sort of thing.

She was standing near the hospital shop, considering the feasibility of tracking her informant down and surprising him, when luck presented her with an easier option. A bell clanged and a pair of wide steel doors opened in the bank of lifts opposite. Out shambled the tall, gaunt figure of Ivo Piric – a man who'd been very useful to her in the past. He was probably no more than forty but, with his deep-set eyes, hollowed-out cheeks and skeletal frame, Piric looked to be in greater need of medical attention than the oldster he was pushing ahead of him in a wheelchair. He'd always looked like that, ever since he turned up in Dublin in the late 1990s as a Bosnian refugee from the war in the Balkans. A man so haunted by the past it was etched on his face, having survived a massacre by hiding under the dead bodies of fellow villagers.

When she originally sold his story to the *Irish Independent* she'd had doubts about a lot of what he claimed. Although there was no doubting he'd witnessed a massacre, something about him made her wonder which side of the atrocity he had actually been on. Even if she had been taken in by him, though, the work Piric was stuck doing here had to be some kind of punishment. As he went past with the wheelchair, he recognised her and smiled. She remembered how unsettling she'd always found that: like an animal baring its teeth, devoid of warmth.

'Hi there, Ivo.'

He put a hand up and parked his charge in the entrance to a television room, where patients and visitors were being deafened by some awful daytime magazine show. Piric loped over, his gaze already fixed on the small brown leather purse Siobhan was pulling from her bag.

'I need some information,' she whispered, putting a hand on his forearm and drawing him towards the far wall. 'And you're the very man to get it for me.'

It took Mulcahy a lot longer to work out how to copy in all the stations in the Dublin Metropolitan Region than it did to write the email itself. He pressed send and his request for information on violent sexual assaults with any religious overtones spun away into the electronic ether, accompanied by a low whoosh from the speakers. He was thinking about trying Brogan again, when the phone rang. It was her.

'Thought you'd want to let your embassy pal know we've got this lad in custody,' she said, her voice humming with excitement.

'Great,' he said. 'Give me some details and I'll start packing my bags.'

'Well, I wouldn't do that just yet. We haven't charged him.'

'But he's the one, right?'

'He hasn't put his hand up for it. But he's admitted leaving the club with Jesica and we found a van in his garage with a load of welding equipment in the back. Technical Bureau are swarming all over it now – should have something for us by morning.'

'I take it he's not a welder, then?'

'Not exactly,' Brogan laughed grimly. 'He says he's a postgraduate research student at UCD. Doing medieval history or something like that.'

'That's interesting.'

'I wouldn't know.'

'No, I meant the academic-welder thing. It's not the most likely hobby for a historian.'

'Absolutely, yeah,' she said, her mind moving on elsewhere. 'Anyway, for the moment I'm holding him on a

147

possession rap. We found a stash of hash and ecstasy in his bedroom.'

'That's useful. Much?'

'Not so much hash, but there must have been twenty or thirty Es.'

Mulcahy knew what that meant. 'That's a lot for a cash-strapped student. You reckon that's what he was doing up at the club – dealing?'

'That's what I was thinking. He's not so cash-strapped, either. His clothes are all designer labels, handmade shoes, that kind of stuff. *So* not cheap student chic. I thought maybe you could check him out with your contacts in Drugs, whether they have any form or intelligence on him.'

'Yeah, of course,' he said, pleased to be able to do something useful at last.

'Quickly, like. It would be good to have it to take into the next interview.'

'No problem. Give me the name and details, I'll make a call and get straight back to you.'

She gave him everything she had on Scully and said she'd be waiting to hear from him.

'Did you get my message about Geraghty?'

'Yeah,' she said. 'How come he went through to you?'

He was glad she couldn't see his eyes rolling heavenwards; he'd almost forgotten her paranoid streak.

'I had a few thoughts about his findings myself,' he said, ignoring her question. 'I'm not certain we've—'

'Look, I'm sure they're very interesting and all,' Brogan

cut in, 'but do you think you could keep them for this evening's briefing? You can share them with everyone then. I really need this drugs gen on Scully. Could you just do that, like right now?'

Stuff it, he thought. His own news could wait. 'Okay, no problem, but before you go, have you said anything to Healy about this guy yet?'

'What's that got to do with anything?'

'I'm just wondering how much to say to the Spanish.'

'It was Healy told me to call you,' she said, her voice prickly. 'I briefed him a few minutes ago. He said to let you – or them rather – know we've got a suspect in custody. They don't need to know any more than that for now.'

Things at the hospital had progressed even more swiftly than Siobhan had hoped. True to form, Ivo Piric was already aware of some fuss having occurred, but he wasn't very strong on facts, rambling on about men in uniform taking a patient away. Intriguing, sure, but it sounded like something he'd dreamed up. For twenty euro, though, he was happy to find her someone who knew exactly what had happened. Siobhan settled into the empty canteen with a plate of sad grey fish and limp yellow chips, expecting a long wait. But barely four chips in, Piric was back. Which was how she'd ended up spending the past ten minutes crammed into a glorified linen cupboard with Nurse Edith Sorenson, flanked by shelf upon shelf of starched white sheets and pillow cases, her shorthand struggling to keep pace with the torrent of indignation spilling from Nurse Sorenson's lips. So far the nurse had confirmed, as obliquely as she could, everything Siobhan's informant had told her about this Spanish girl's appalling injuries. But the stuff she was going on about now – of Gardai interrogating the poor creature though she wasn't fit for it, then a fist-fight breaking out with some official, right at the girl's bedside, and to top it all, what sounded like an invasion party from the Spanish embassy stalking the corridors of St Vincent's Hospital – it was pure dynamite.

'And you're sure this was the same fella who came to get her yesterday, with the troops, as you call them. The original one from the Spanish embassy?'

'I'm absolutely certain. He was only a scrap of a fella but very full of himself, I can tell you. Strutting around like a little Franco, he was.'

Siobhan tutted sympathetically, noting the reference and deciding it put Nurse Sorenson in her mid-forties or so. 'But you didn't get his name?'

'He didn't offer it – on either occasion. I might as well have not been there as far as he was concerned. He was a very rude man.'

'And there wouldn't be any record of his name, in paperwork or anything, up at the nurse's station? It would be a big help, you know, so we could give him his comeuppance in the paper.'

Nurse Sorenson looked tempted by the suggestion but, as she'd already refused to let her have an unofficial peep at the

Spanish girl's records, Siobhan wasn't holding out much hope. Sure enough, the nurse shook her head ruefully.

'No. In any case, it was Sister Philomena who dealt with all the paperwork.'

'And you don't think Sister Philomena . . .' Siobhan said, writing the name down to her informant's evident horror, 'you don't think she'd be willing to cooperate?'

'God no, she'd have my guts for garters if she knew I was talking to you. That'd be the end of me. I'm only telling you this because—'

'Okay, okay,' Siobhan said, trying to calm her down. 'You'll have her in here yourself if you don't pipe down. Look, you needn't worry. I won't let on to anyone about our little chat if you don't want me to. I can't tell you how much I appreciate you telling me all this. It's important that these people shouldn't be allowed to think they can walk all over us, you know.'

Nurse Sorenson relaxed a little, evidently relieved that she'd chosen so trustworthy a member of the fourth estate to share her story with.

'Speaking of which, could you maybe remember the names of the Gardai who came in the day before? The ones who got involved in the fight with this fella. They sound just as bad.'

'They were,' Nurse Sorenson agreed. 'Especially the young woman who was in charge. Nicely dressed she was, but she had a mouth on her. You'd think she could walk on water.'

'And her name was?'

'I don't remember, I'm sorry. I'm sure it began with a B – Brady or Brosnon or something, but I know that's not quite right.'

'Any of the others?' Siobhan looked up hopefully from her notepad. 'The one involved in the fight, maybe?'

'Ah, now, yes, I think she called him Andy. Yes, I'm pretty sure of it. She was calling him that while she was trying to drag him off the other . . .'

'And you're sure it was the Garda who struck first?'

'Oh, yes, certainly. And without any warning, either. Just launched himself at the fella as soon as he came through the door.'

Siobhan was so caught up in getting it all down, she nearly missed the next revelation.

'Inspector Mulcahy was the only one of them who behaved with any sort of decency or respect for poor Jesica.'

Siobhan gawped at her, not quite sure she could believe what she'd just heard. 'Inspector Mulcahy, did you say?'

'Yes, I'm sure that's what he said his name was.' Nurse Sorenson was smiling a little coyly now. 'He was my idea of a proper Garda.'

'As in *Mike* Mulcahy, from the Drugs Squad?' Surely that couldn't be right? There had to be lots of Mulcahys in the guards. But at inspector grade?

'I'm sure I couldn't say.' Nurse Sorenson paused, pursing her lips in concentration. 'I can't see why anyone from the Drugs Squad would have been here. I didn't hear any talk of drugs. But now you mention it, he didn't seem to be *with* the other two, if you know what I mean. To be honest, it was like he was only there because he could speak Spanish, and they were desperate to talk to young Jesica.'

'He spoke Spanish?' Siobhan didn't even wait for a reply: she was already off and racing down the corridors of her mind, opening doors, closing others, putting it all together. If it really was Mulcahy on the scene, maybe there was some major international drugs connection as well? This was turning into one little beauty of a story.

Now all she had to do was get to the bottom of it.

When he phoned Liam Ford, he only had to wait a minute for the search to go through and to hear the ping of a positive hit echoing down the phone line to him. The last time Mulcahy had worked out of the cramped GNDU offices over in Dublin Castle, an outside request to run a check on a suspect would have taken a couple of hours, minimum. Now it was instant.

'Yup, we've got a couple of Patrick Scullys here,' Ford said. 'One from Ballyheige, Kerry, so I'm guessing it's not him. This other fella has an address in Blackrock alright. DOB 25.03.86, so that makes him what, twenty-three? Last-known has him a postgraduate student at UCD. That sound about right?'

'That's him alright. What's he down for?'

'Nothing much. Arrested for minor-possession cannabis – two point two grams – back in May '07 at a university gig.

Got off with a first-strike slap on the wrist that time, and nothing do-able since, except he keeps getting mentioned as a small-time dealer of Es. Nothing heavier, as far as we know. That's all we've got.'

'Typical student dealer, then, making some dosh on the side.'

'Sounds like it, the little shit – making a blip on the radar every now and again.'

'Fine, it'll give us a bit more leverage on him, anyway. With that one on the sheet already, it's enough for us to keep him in custody, for now.'

'String the shitehawk up,' Ford growled. 'Whatever he's supposed to have done.'

'Glad to hear you haven't grown a sensitive side over the years,' Mulcahy laughed.

'Yeah, right. Unlike you. What was all that about, at lunchtime? You ran out of the place like a scalded cat.'

'Nothing you'd be interested in.'

'I suppose you never called Murtagh either.'

'Not yet, but I will.'

'Speaking of calls, some little hottie was looking for you here earlier.'

'For me?' Mulcahy's brow furrowed. 'Over there?'

'On the phone. Feckin' bizarre, man, especially after I'd only just seen you and all. When I told her you hadn't worked here for years, she was a bit surprised, then she said something about Madrid and having your mobile number, so I didn't go on about it.'

'She didn't leave a name then?'

'No, didn't want to talk to me at all after that. And believe me, I tried.'

Mulcahy racked his brains to think of anyone who'd known him when he was at the Castle and in Madrid and would fit Ford's description. He couldn't.

'Oh well, if she's got my number she can get in touch.'

'You'd better hope so. I've never seen you looking more like you could do with having a good time. And she sounded like just the girl to give it to you.'

8

'**O**kay, okay, calm down, you lot.'

Although there were only eight people present, the incident room was buoyed up by enough excitement for twice that many. The babble of voices faded away again as Brogan prepared to wind up the evening briefing. Sitting on a desk behind the semicircle of animated cops, Mulcahy felt more than ever the outsider. Having slogged their arses off all day out on the streets, the team was floating on a cloud of satisfaction that, at close of play, their good work was about to yield a result. It was the best feeling any decent cop could experience and one that he hoped and prayed they were bloody right about. Because, before the briefing began, he'd made that call to Murtagh about the Southern Region job. He'd cut to the chase, making no assumptions about Dowling's departure but letting his own interest be known. And, hallelujah, Murtagh had responded enthusiastically in kind, saying in effect that he really hoped Mulcahy would apply the minute the job became available, because it needed to be filled quickly. The implication being: he was in, but only if he was free to move. That thought had been play-ing on Mulcahy's mind throughout the briefing. That and getting the estate agents to crack on. It would all be so much easier with the house off his hands.

'Like I said,' Brogan was saying, 'it looks like we're on to a winner here but there's no point pushing it until we have the forensics on Scully's van and his clothes back from Technical. As for now, it's not going to do any harm to let Scully stew overnight in Blackrock – and thanks to Inspector Mulcahy's contacts in Drugs we can do just that.'

Mulcahy nodded acknowledgement to Brogan.

'There was something else you wanted to raise, wasn't there, Mike? Something about Geraghty's findings that you thought we should talk about?'

'Yes, there was.' He looked at the faces turned to him expectantly. 'It's to do with Jesica's cross and chain.'

There was a low groan of 'Jaysus, not again' from some-where in the room. Cassidy, he assumed, but he let it go.

'I'm sure if it had turned up in the van you'd have said,' Mulcahy smiled.

'Considering it would have put the case against Scully beyond doubt, I think I would have, yeah,' Brogan retorted.

'It's just that when Geraghty said he'd found traces of gold in the swabs, my first thought was they must've come from Jesica's cross and chain which, we know, was ripped off her during the attack. But he also said the metal traces he found were from cheap gold plate.'

'So?'

'Well, Jesica's jewellery wouldn't have been cheap,' Mulcahy shrugged.

'How can you be so sure?' Cassidy interjected. 'As you're constantly reminding us, we don't have it.'

'It just wouldn't be, not in that family. They're very wealthy.'

'Maybe it was something she picked up herself,' said Maura McHugh. 'You know how girls of that age are. Maybe it was sentimental value, from a boyfriend or something.'

'I got the impression it was of enormous value to her.'

'Look, why does it matter where it came from?' Brogan protested, checking her watch. 'What's your point, Mike?'

Impatience spread like a rash across Brogan's face as Mulcahy related his lunchtime encounter with the priests in the pub and his flash of inspiration regarding the gold crosses and the burn marks on Jesica. As he told them how he'd pored over the photos again to confirm his suspicions, some of the others began shifting about uncomfortably in their seats. For a split second the possibility occurred to him that the couple of drinks he'd had with Ford had gone to his head, and he'd dreamed it all up. But he killed that thought immediately.

'So, really, what I was wondering was whether there isn't some kind of religious dimension to this that we haven't been giving proper consideration to. Or even whether the attacker's primary motivation was sexual at all?'

'Ah, for fuck's sake!' At the far side of the group, Cassidy had clearly heard enough and wasn't going to keep his opinion to himself. He was glowering in Mulcahy's direction now, his jaw thrust forward. Everybody in the room was gawping, waiting to see what he'd say or do next.

But Brogan got in first. 'Like I said before, Inspector, I appreciate that this is a new area of operations for you.' She let her gaze drill straight into Mulcahy, as if to say her vast reserves of tolerance were being stretched here. 'And that you've had a lot of time on your hands for the last couple of days. But what matters here this evening is that we have a suspect in custody and we're trying to build a case against him – not break it down and start all over again. And that case is for aggravated rape, because that's what happened to young Jesica.'

'I'm not trying to break anything down,' Mulcahy replied. 'I never even suggested it wasn't Scully, only that you might be better going into that interview room tomorrow armed with all the facts rather than with just some of them.'

'And what exactly is it that I've overlooked?' Brogan asked.

'Well, motive, for one thing.'

That was it for Cassidy. Pushing his chair back with a loud scrape of its metal legs, he stood up and snorted at Mulcahy. 'What more bloody motive do you want? He didn't get his rocks off, so he came back to take what he wanted and teach the girl a lesson while he was about it.'

'And you think that was enough reason for one of the most violent attacks anybody in this room has ever heard of,

159

do you?' Mulcahy said. 'An attack that, before you landed on Scully, you all agreed had to be premeditated and carefully planned?'

Cassidy didn't have an answer for that, but he didn't need one as Brogan stepped in again.

'Shut up, Andy, and sit down.'

She examined the backs of her hands until Cassidy, cursing beneath his breath, took his seat again.

'Okay, Inspector,' Brogan continued, 'maybe you do have a point there. But remember, just because Scully picked Jesica up in a club doesn't mean he didn't have every detail of the attack planned – other than his victim. Either way, for now I'm not sure we need to concern ourselves with why Scully did it, okay? All I'm hoping for is to get the forensics back and nail him with those, if I can. We can deal with the whys and wherefores later. Now let's move on.'

But Mulcahy wouldn't let it go. 'And all I'm saying is that if you're looking for a motive that fits, and you look at the burn marks on Jesica and tie that in to what she said about her attacker being like a priest, then maybe, just maybe, there's some weird religious element to it.'

At that there was another snort from the far side of the room. Cassidy was on his feet again, this time spreading his arms wide to the audience already turning expectantly towards him. 'Ah, lads,' he scoffed. 'That's got to be it, alright. First we had The General, then The Monk, The Viper, The Psycho, and all that lot. Now it's The Priest. *The Priest*, for fuck's sake – as if we haven't had enough of them in the last few years. Maybe they'll do a film about this fella, too, and make a star of him like they did Martin Cahill. As the inspector's pointed out to us before, Scully's got a bit of the Brad Pitt about him alright.'

Everybody in the room was laughing except Mulcahy. And Brogan, who above the din was telling Cassidy to shut up. But Cassidy wasn't going to do that without getting one last dig in.

'And what about you, Inspector Mulcahy? I'm sure you see your name up there in lights. Who'd you see as yourself? George Clooney?'

Head down, every nerve in his body fizzing with fury at Cassidy, at Brogan and the whole fucking lot of them, the shouted greeting failed to crack the carapace of Mulcahy's angry self-absorption.

'Hey, Mulcahy.'

Louder this time, it got through.

He swung around, startled. She was leaning against a small red convertible in the parking bay outside the gates, looking like an ad for something sunny and aspirational in her big shades, white cotton top, black jeans and heels.

'Siobhan, what the hell are you doing here?'

She folded her arms and scowled at him. 'That's nice. Here I am, after trekking halfway across the city to see you, and all I get is sworn at.'

With the sunglasses on, hiding those big blue eyes of hers, she was more unreadable than ever.

'I'm sorry, I wasn't, eh . . . wasn't expecting . . .'

'And why would you be?'

She smiled broadly at him. She wasn't put out, not really. Door-stepping people was a way of life for her, he reasoned, and she was probably used to far worse reactions. She pushed herself away from the car with her hips and strode over towards him, something feline in her gait.

'So you've been transferred, then?'

His eyes narrowed. 'No, I haven't. But, now you mention it, how'd you know I'd be here?'

She beamed at him even brighter. 'God, you cops, always so bloody suspicious. It's my job, isn't it, to find out stuff?'

'Maybe,' he nodded. 'But it doesn't answer the question. How?'

'Ah, go on, you should know better than try to get me to reveal a source.'

A source? He thought of what Ford had said about a woman calling, wanting to know where he was. The conspiratorial chuckle. Liam must've been a bit more forthcoming than he'd let on.

'Anyone would think you weren't glad to see me.' She didn't pout, but it was implicit. Instead, she raised her sunglasses up and he felt the full blue hit of her eyes.

'No, it's not that . . .'

She was so close now, if he wanted to he could put an arm out and scoop her into him, kiss her hard on the mouth. She laughed and took a small step back, like she could see it or feel it in him. He glanced back at the building behind him to break the spell of her, and drew some air deep into his lungs. By the time he turned to face her again, he was over it.

'It's good to see you,' he said. 'I enjoyed the other night.'

'Me too,' she said. 'I got your message and thought maybe you'd fancy having a bite to eat tonight. It's such a beautiful evening, we could hop in the car and head up the mountains to Johnnie Fox's or the Blue Light, or somewhere. The traffic's not looking too bad – we could be there in half an hour. Watch the sun go down? What do you think?'

'I think that's very spontaneous of you.' He was smiling now.

'I wouldn't be too sure about that. You took a fair bit of tracking down.'

'I hope I'll be worth it,' he laughed, relaxing into the idea, playing her at her own game.

'Seems like a long shot, I admit.' She stood there, blazing him with the smile. 'But, then, you never know. Are you coming or not?'

She didn't wait for an answer, just turned on her heel, opened the car door and slid inside.

Up in the privacy of her fourth-floor office, Brogan leaned into her desk, blessed herself in an only half-ironic fashion, then picked up the phone, cursing Mulcahy and Cassidy. If it hadn't been for their stupid macho squabble, she might have got away on time. As it was, that extra ten minutes put the mockers on everything, because she then got a call from

Dermot Rafferty in Technical saying he hoped to have some initial results back from the tests on Scully's van within the hour, if she wanted to hang on. Well, what was she going to say to that? No, actually, I've got to go home right now or my husband will miss his game of penny poker. Yeah, right. By which time it would have taken a miracle, or a pair of motorcycle outriders at least, for her to get home to Tallaght in time.

She dialled her home number, made the call to Aidan and, by the time she put down the phone again, felt as if her soul had shrunk by yet another small but significant percentage. He hadn't moaned or cursed or shouted. She probably would have felt better if he had. Instead, all she got was the usual surly resentment, a few abrupt words of acceptance, and the certain knowledge that she'd be paying for this with the silent treatment for days. For the millionth time, she cursed herself for ever suggesting that he should give up his job to stay at home and do the house-husband thing. It had seemed like such a good idea at the time.

She was eyeing up the paperwork on her desk, thinking to make good use of her hour's detention, when the faint roar of a car revving wildly outside caught her ear. She leaned back in her chair, looked out the floor-length window and, down below, saw a red convertible reversing, with nothing like due care and attention, out of a parking bay at the front of the building and into the roadway. Some midget-dick from the Drugs Squad, was her first thought. Which seemed to be confirmed immediately when she recognised, with

164

some surprise, that it was Mulcahy sitting in the passenger seat. Then she registered the dark curling hair, the trim figure behind the wheel, and the fact that it was a woman driving. A split second later Brogan was on her feet, pressing her hands against the glass as the car made a tyre-shredding turn, shot across the road and disappeared into Hatch Street opposite.

She didn't turn around again until she heard a knock behind her, and the door opening.

'Everything alright, boss?'

It was Cassidy, a look of concern masking nosiness.

She considered telling him what she'd just seen. Felt a giddy pang of temptation to share the juicy bone she'd just been thrown. But it would only end up being a blunt instrument in Cassidy's hands. This was something to savour and use more judiciously.

She shook her head. 'Yes, fine thanks, Andy. Just some arsehole outside, driving like a maniac.'

'Yeah, I heard.'

Miraculously, the evening traffic melted away ahead of them. Once they got out past Marlay Park and on to the Ticknock Road it disappeared altogether and, more often than not, now, theirs was the only car on the narrow, winding roads that led steeply up into the Dublin mountains. It was years since Mulcahy had been out this way, and it amazed him to remember just how quickly it was possible to escape the city. It wasn't half an hour since they'd got in the car, and already they were hundreds of feet up. Flashing by, behind hedgerows, dry-stone walls and houses, was a view to still the heart: the flat, built-up bowl of the city bathed in a rosy light falling softly from the west, the dark green of the sea to the east broken only by the flecked white wakes of ships and sailboats threading in and out from Dublin port and Dun Laoghaire harbour.

'My dad used to bring me up here all the time when I was a kid,' he shouted over the noise of the engine and the rushing air. 'He was always a country man at heart, had to get out of the city every chance he got.'

She glanced over at him, nodding eagerly.

'Mine too,' she said, turning back in time to ram the engine down a couple of gears and take a hairpin bend with all the confidence of a Schumacher. 'All of us, the whole family, he shoved us into the back of the car every Sunday, and took us up to the Pine Forest, out to Enniskerry or Powerscourt, over the Sally Gap. Or in summer we'd go down to Brittas for the day.'

'Those were our haunts too.' Mulcahy grinned, half a childhood washing over him in one go, pricking his heart with the thought that he'd been away from it all for too long. He'd lost touch with such a large part of his past. 'Very, very occasionally we'd go out to Rush or Skerries. But I think he regarded anywhere north of the Liffey pretty much as for-eign territory. He'd only really go up there for work, or maybe curiosity, but never relaxation. Even if it was just for a couple of hours, he'd be off to Dalkey, Killiney or Bray.

166

But never Howth or Malahide. In fact, I don't think I got out to Howth until I was well into my teens, when I could get there under my own steam.'

'Nort'siders – dey're nuttin' bu' a buncha bleedin' knackers,' she shouted back at him in broadest Dublinese, laughing, her glossy red lips drawn taut against her small, bright-white teeth. He was about to respond in kind when the car crested a rise and they shot out into a vista that took his breath away. The terrain around them was transformed in a blink from grey rock and steep commercial woodland into a spectacular broad, brown plateau of upland bracken and bogland, stretching away for miles towards Wicklow and the mountains proper.

'I just love it up here,' she cried into the wind, slipping the car into fifth and flooring the accelerator. They were totally alone, not another car on the ribbon of road that spun out three, four miles in front of them towards the Sally Gap. Not another soul to be seen in the still, empty landscape they hurtled through, as the sun slipped towards the rim of the world behind them.

They settled, in the end, on the Blue Light pub, high on the slopes of Sandyford at the foot of Barnaculia. An ancient old place that, last time he'd been there, maybe twenty years before, had looked a lot closer to the piggery it once was than a popular spot for late-night revellers. Now, though, it had been rediscovered, done up, and for once was the better for it. Especially when it came to food. Inside, the bar was packed, close and noisy. But outside, in the warm evening air, they found a table that afforded them comparative solitude and a spectacular view out over Dublin, all the more so now that night had begun to draw down, and the million lights of the city below were glimmering like a bowl of diamonds.

She waited until they'd ordered the food and he'd had a few sips of wine before she broached the subject.

'So what were you doing over in Harcourt Square – assuming they haven't just opened up a new outpost for the Drugs Squad over there?'

'It's a temporary assignment. I'll be back to my usual duties in a few days time, I hope.'

'Which are?'

'How do you mean?'

Her mood seemed to have shifted completely from how it had been in the car. Her carefree expression was replaced by a frown of inquisition that was beginning to make him feel uncomfortable. He turned away from her to look out over the sparkling city.

'Look, Siobhan, I thought we agreed we weren't going to do the work thing?'

'We did.' She paused just long enough to make him turn back to her. 'But that was before I went down to St Vincent's today and heard your name mentioned in connection with a story I'm interested in.'

To say he was caught on the hop hardly covered it. He did his best to conceal his reaction, but it was no use. He could see her taking in the surprise in his expression. For all he knew, she was just on a fishing expedition, but it didn't sound like it. Best he could do was try to close it down calmly, maybe find out how much she knew.

'I don't know what you're talking about, Siobhan.'

'Oh, come off it, Mulcahy. Don't give me that. A Spanish kid is raped at the weekend and, from what I've been able to scrape together, it sounds completely horrific. But for some weird reason I can't get a squeak out of any of my Garda contacts about it. If anything, I get the distinct impression they're running scared. Then I hear a whisper that Mike Mulcahy is involved and I think, hang on, rape *and* drugs? And if it's him, it's not just any old drugs but international drugs, big drugs. Jesus, you can hardly blame me for being intrigued.'

That was more than enough for him. 'Change the subject, Siobhan.'

'Why should I?' There was a faint note of outrage in her voice now, as if she wasn't the one who was entirely out of order here.

'Because you don't have a snowball's chance in hell of getting me to talk about this. Look, I meant what I said in that message. I wanted to see you again and I hoped that you might feel the same way. But if I was wrong about that, I'll put my hand up. I'm an idiot, okay? But let's not draw it out any longer than necessary. Let's just finish up here and I'll go order myself a taxi.'

She seemed to think about that a moment, then he saw the tension drain out of her body and she leaned across towards him.

'Oh, come on, you know that's not why I got you up here. I was really pleased when I got your message. I was looking forward to seeing you again. But then your name came up today and, you know, I had to ask the question.'

'Yeah, but you didn't have to ambush me like that, did you?'

This time the air of offence she adopted looked genuine.

'That's so not what I was trying to do. I mean, if that was all I wanted, I could have just clobbered you with it while you were coming out of Harcourt Square. In fact, maybe I should've, because you looked like you were on another planet altogether then, and I'd probably have had a better chance of jumping you into an answer. But I didn't do it.'

He had to laugh at that. 'Okay, fair point, but look, you have to believe me. I'd help you if I could, but I'm absolutely not the person you should be talking to about this.'

'So who is?'

'Have you tried the Garda Press Office?'

'Very funny. You know all that crowd does is read out press releases and spout statistics.'

'Sorry, that's the best I can do. It's the best I'm ever going to be able to do.'

She smiled at that, like she didn't mind him making the assumption.

'Fine, I'll do my best not to bring it up again. Does that mean you'll stay and eat?'

'I'd like that,' he said, beginning to relax again.

'Me too,' she smiled. 'But won't you at least tell me what the hell your job is now? Or is that a bloody state secret, as well?'

'I wasn't trying to hide anything. It's just that it was complicated – a complete fuck-up, if you want the truth of it. And some of it, well, to be honest, it's just not the sort of stuff you want to be getting into on a first, eh . . .'

'Date?' Siobhan prompted, helpfully.

'Yeah,' Mulcahy said. 'I don't know if Mark told you but while I was in Madrid I got married.'

Siobhan didn't look at all surprised, didn't respond in any way other than to nod encouragingly. Protecting her source, probably, even if it was only Mark. Still, it left him feeling freer to tell things his own way.

'Gracia worked at Europol, too, as a policy adviser. Her background was in economics.'

'But was she good-looking, yeah?'

'Yes, really.' Mulcahy smiled, amused again by her directness. 'Incredibly beautiful and elegant, in that dark Spanish way. Totally out of my league, or so I thought. Anyway, to cut a long story short, it was great for a while. Terrific wedding. Lovely honeymoon. We bought a fabulous flat in the heart of Madrid, just behind the Prado. She had her career, I had mine. Life was perfect.'

'So what happened?' Siobhan asked. 'I mean, I assume *something* happened?'

She was making it easy for him.

'Sure. About a year ago, nobody's fault but my own, she asked me to move out.'

'You'd been a naughty boy?'

Mulcahy nodded, but he hardly needed to; the fault was etched on his face like an epitaph.

'And you're not quite over her yet, is that it?'

Mulcahy was surprised to hear an edge of resignation in her question.

'No, not at all. We'd been . . . well, things had fizzled out between us by then. We were well on the way to splitting up already. That just sped things up. I mean, it was upsetting, of course – still is, to be honest – but it would have happened anyway.'

'So what are you saying, that you came back to Dublin to escape her? What about your job? Didn't you want to hang on to that? I thought it was really important to you.'

All he could do was hold his hands up again. 'There's more to it than that. I told you it was complicated.'

'Too right,' she said, shifting in her seat. 'I'm beginning to wonder if I should've brought a cushion. These benches get fierce uncomfortable after a few hours.'

Mulcahy knocked back the last of his wine and felt a wave of relief wash over him. He looked up at the dark mass of the mountain above them, heard the babble of happy chatter coming from inside the pub. He felt happier and more unburdened than he'd felt in months. Whatever you might think about Catholicism generally, he decided, you couldn't beat a good confession.

'Look,' he said, 'why don't I go in and get us a bottle of this stuff, and see what's happened to the food while I'm about it. Then I can tell you the rest when I get back.'

'Okay, but remember I'm driving. You'll have to drink most of it on your own.'

'You got me on the right night for that,' Mulcahy admitted, and headed in towards the bar.

Brogan switched off her computer and bent her head forward, cupping her hands over her ears and massaging the nape of her neck with her thumbs. It was nine-thirty p.m., and she'd waited not one but two hours for Rafferty to come back with a preliminary on the van. And the news was disappointing: so far, they'd found nothing definite to link in Scully. But it wasn't all bad. There were hairs and fibres and skin flakes from the floor to analyse; and, in particular, a length of old matting that had been badly soiled by something recently – but they wouldn't know what exactly until the morning. Then, when they'd put in the UV lamps they'd picked up some blood spatter on one of the side panels. She didn't like to pin her hopes on a slim chance but she had a feeling it would come right. Once again, though, it would take until noon the next day at the earliest before they could get a type comparison with Jesica's blood – and probably days for the DNA to come back. But it might be something to throw at Scully in the interview.

She sat up straight and swept the few items left on her desk – pens, a few loose reports and request forms – into her desk drawer and locked it. She felt almost too tired to drive, especially when she thought of the sulk Aidan would be in when she got home. As she rose from her chair and stretched across to take her jacket from the coat stand, a twinge shot through her shoulder. She gasped from the pain of it. God curse this job and its endless hours.

At the lift she'd just pressed the call button when she saw Cassidy emerge from the Gents' rubbing his hands vigorously, looking unusually animated.

'Jesus, Andy, you nearly put the heart crossways on me. I thought I was the only one left up here.'

'I had a few last-minute things to see to, boss.'

The lift clanged its arrival and the doors lumbered open. Brogan stepped in, but for some reason Cassidy didn't follow her in.

'Aren't you coming?'

'Eh, no,' he hesitated. 'Not just yet. Just got to go downstairs to see someone first.'

'Alright, then. See you in the morning.'

The lift doors shut with a thud and a wide grin ripped across Cassidy's face again. He pushed through the stairwell door beside the lift shaft, skipping down the steps to the floor below, humming to himself, all but tasting the sweetness of vengeance in his mouth as he made his way to a small office at the end of the corridor. Sometimes the ball landed right at your feet, and there was nothing to do but pick it up and run with it.

'How'ya, Mattie – everything going okay, is it?'

Garda Mattie Creasy, sitting with his jacket off and his sleeves rolled up, blinked as he swivelled away from the bank of monitors in front of him, the light behind Cassidy in the doorway being that much brighter than in the security room. Creasy was getting on, by modern-day standards – you hardly ever saw a uniform in his late fifties these days, except in the upper ranks, and his slicked-back, dyed-black hair got him known to everyone in the building as Creasy 2000.

'Ah, I'm alright, Sergeant. Yourself? I heard ye got walloped in the hurling on Sunday.'

'Ah, now, don't get me started, Mattie. That referee should be done for bribery and corruption. But I was actually wondering if you could help me out with something. How would I get hold of one of the tapes from the security cameras covering this place? From outside, like, not the interview room stuff.'

Cassidy's conspiratorial whisper was obviously just what Mattie, bored out of his tree after six hours straight staring at CCTV monitors, needed to hear.

'Outside, is it?' Mattie pondered, as if the question were vital to the security of the entire nation. 'Well, now, I can't see that it'd be a huge problem. We record everything, and keep it for at least a month. But not on tape. It's all saved on a hard-drive system so there's no messing around with tapes and things. No storage problems either. Very fancy it is. A far cry from the old days.'

Cassidy doubted they'd had electricity in Mattie's *old days*, let alone videotape.

'So there'd be no trouble getting hold of some stuff from the Harcourt Street gate earlier this evening – around seven, half-seven?'

'Was there a problem out there?' Mattie's brow furrowed as the possibility dawned that he might have missed the one interesting thing to happen in ages.

'No, no, nothing like that. I just need to check something. On the quiet, like.' Cassidy winked at him, and gave him a roguish grin for good measure. It did the trick.

'Ah, I get the picture, now.' Mattie winked back. 'It's for your eyes only, is it? Well, there's nothing simpler. It'd only take me a couple of minutes to do, but I'll have to wait till Fahy gets back from his break. Is it urgent, like? Do you want me to give him a call?'

'No, no, let the man have his tea. That way we can keep it between ourselves.'

'I'll tell you what I'll do.' Mattie was all enthusiasm for the conspiracy now. 'If you like, I'll download it later and transfer it on to a disk. Then I can leave it on your desk for you.' He tapped his nose as he continued. 'That way you can peruse it in your own time on your own computer. Between seven and half-past, was it?'

'Yeah, that's right.'

'Well, there's two cameras out on that gate, and I can fit over half an hour's worth from each onto the one DVD. Will that be enough for you?'

'More than,' Cassidy grinned. 'Thanks a million, Mattie. You're a star. I owe you.'

176

'Oh, now, don't get carried away, Sergeant. We're here to serve.'

Siobhan knew all about waiting for the lock on a story to click open. And, while she might not have got exactly what she set out to get from him, Mulcahy was more than making up for it with other stuff. In fact, she could hardly remember having a more enjoyable night out of late.

He'd decided on his way back from the bar that, rather than just give it to her straight, they should treat it as a trade-off.

'How do you mean?' she'd asked.

'Like a mutual exchange of information. You know, I tell you something, you have to tell me something back. It'll make it more interesting, what do you say?'

'Okay, so tell me something,' she said.

And he laughed so loud that people all around turned to have a look at them.

'No way,' he said. 'I've just told you about my infidelity and my divorce. It's your turn.'

She started telling him some juicy gossip she'd heard on the grapevine about the personal habits of Johnny Logan, the former Eurovision winner, but he stopped her in her tracks. She wasn't getting off that lightly. It had to be something about her. Something embarrassing. A secret. He was clearly hoping for something intimate. Vincent Bishop and his priceless bloody brooch vaulted into her mind, but that felt too uncomfortable. Or just sleazy. Either way, she wasn't going there. No chance. Not with Mulcahy. Not yet. Probably not ever.

So she racked her brain, and told him how she'd pushed her little brother Paul down the stairs when she was seven and he was five. How he was knocked unconscious and was bleeding so much he had to be rushed to hospital in an ambulance. And nobody ever found out it was her, not to this day. And how she still rubbed the scar on Paul's forehead every time she saw him. For luck.

Mulcahy appeared to be impressed by that. Maybe a little shocked, even. But mostly charmed, she thought. As their meal arrived and they tucked in, she reminded him what he'd said in the Long Hall about coming back to Dublin because of his parents, by way of a prompt.

'Yeah,' he said. 'I couldn't go into all that the last time. I'd had a bit of a rough day. That wasn't a good night for me to be out.'

A line of questioning immediately occurred to her. She couldn't help it. She'd already figured out that if Mulcahy was involved in this Spanish thing, it would have been the same day they'd first met up for a drink. But she forced herself to put the thought aside, not even sure she cared about all that any more, for now. At least, not compared to finding out more about Mulcahy himself. There really was something about him. Something, she was beginning to think, she actually might not want to get confused with work.

'That's okay,' she said. 'It can't be easy talking about it.'

178

'No,' Mulcahy nodded, 'but really that was what started it all. Dad's death, it just knocked me off the rails completely. Coming so soon after my mother died.'

'Oh, my God,' Siobhan said. 'I'm sorry, I didn't know.'

'How would you have.' He shrugged. 'I'm convinced it was love killed him, really. Mam had a stroke the year before and Dad struggled to care for her at home, on his own. He was a proud old fella, and absolutely besotted with her. Wouldn't hear of anyone else looking after her. I tried to do what I could from Spain, came over as often as possible. But Mam never recovered. Then, six months after I stood and held his hand and watched her buried, he went the same way. Peacefully, they said, but it near killed me that I hadn't been there to see either of them go.'

He swallowed hard, disguising his emotion by grabbing for the wine bottle and refilling his glass. She reached across the table, folding a hand over his. 'I really am sorry,' she said. 'I can see they meant a lot to you.'

He nodded again. 'I was mad about them both,' he said. 'My mother was the best you could wish for, and she always spoiled me rotten. But it was my dad's going that really got to me. You can't believe how much I looked up to him: the big hero in his uniform – when things like that seemed to matter to people. It was because of him I joined the Guards. I wanted to be just like him.'

'He was a policeman, too?'

'Yeah, an inspector.'

'Like you.'

'Yes, like me.' He laughed again, but at her this time. 'You better watch it or you'll have me in tears.'

'I'm not so far off it myself,' she said, snuffling melodramatically. She thought of her own father racked by cancer, wasting slowly away, and her alcoholic mother wanting only to be oblivious to it all. Twenty-five years on, the ache of it still hadn't gone away.

'Anyway,' Mulcahy said, sitting up, trying to shake the mood off him with a roll of his big shoulders. 'Dad's death only doubled my domestic troubles in Spain. It was bad enough after Mam died. I don't think I knew how upset I was, cos most of my worry got turned on Dad then. And Gracia, she just wasn't able to meet me halfway. All the things I'd fallen in love with – her calmness, her self-reliance – they all seemed to make her just retreat from me emotionally. In the end it was like *she* was the one who was hiding from my pain. I'm sure it was never her fault. I must have been impossible to live with, but when Dad went I felt so alone all of a sudden, and the last remaining person I had any hope of getting comfort from was backing further away from me . . .'

He stopped and put his hands up. 'Sorry,' he said, 'I'm waffling on now.'

'No,' she said, appalled at the idea he might stop. 'I mean, please, go on.'

He laughed shyly. 'There's not much more to say. Other than that I was out one night and took some comfort elsewhere when it was offered and Gracia found out. By that

180

time, there was all this stuff about MOAC being set up in Lisbon and lots of politicking among the powers-that-be as to what countries would take the key posts of responsibility. Well, I reckoned I could see the writing on the wall for the Europol set-up in Madrid. So, while I was back in Dublin to sort out the will and all that, I met up with an old boss of mine and I asked him what would be the possibility of coming back to Dublin.'

'Why would it have been a problem? I thought you were only on loan to Europol?'

'Yeah, but I'd got kind of caught in the specialism trap – there aren't many top jobs in intelligence-gathering in the Garda Siochana.'

'Intelligence is definitely a rarity in that organisation,' she laughed.

'Watch it, you,' he said, wagging a finger ironically. 'With your damn media cynicism.'

Then he refused to go on until she revealed another secret. So she told him about the time she'd accidentally libelled the Minister for Defence, the one before the current one, in a front page article about an escort agency. The story hadn't been about the minister himself, and it was just an aside, a throwaway comment, but she'd spent weeks convinced he'd sue her and the paper for everything they'd got. But no one ever noticed it or, at any rate, contested it.

'That scar of your brother's really works,' Mulcahy said.

It was then that he told her how this old boss of his had rung up a few days later and offered him a job heading up a new Garda unit coordinating intelligence-gathering on drug smuggling into Europe via Ireland. It was perfect. Made for him. There'd even be a promotion in it: Superintendent Mulcahy. And it was based in Dublin. Even though he'd moved out of their flat by then, he begged Gracia to come with him, to make a new start. But she wouldn't. He gave notice in Madrid, worked out his time, handed over to his replacement and arranged a couple of weeks' vacation with friends in Valencia. Only to hear four days before he was due to take up the new job in Dublin that the whole thing had been killed off overnight in the government's cost-cutting blitz. He'd been credit crunched. Well and truly. Unable to go forward, unable to go back. Stuck. He couldn't even get back into the Drugs Squad because of the recruitment freeze.

'Jesus, you've been through the mill,' Siobhan said. But she knew very well herself how instantaneous and savage the government cuts had been. Mulcahy wasn't the only person she knew who'd been caught out badly by it.

'Couldn't this old boss of yours do anything for you?'

'He tried. But the new unit was supposed to be one last cherry on the cake before he retired. He was gone a couple of months later.'

'So what did you do? What're you doing now?'

He grimaced, picked up the wine bottle and filled his glass again.

'For now I'm stuck in the NBCI pool – the National Bureau of Criminal Investigation – as a hack detective, like

I used to be years ago. Going wherever I'm sent, like a supply teacher.'

'Christ, that's a bit of a come-down, isn't it?'

'They're supposed to be sorting something out for me,' he said, resignedly. 'I'm on a promise that I'll be given the first "suitable" post that comes up. But of course that's where the specialism trap comes in again. And the months are flying by.'

'It's such a waste,' she said.

'Ah, we'll get there in the end.'

And the way he said it, so pragmatic and unyielding, unlocked something inside her. Something that made her lean across the table and kiss him softly on the mouth, and think that maybe she had it in her to give him some of that comfort he'd been missing for so long.

9

'You can let yourself out, can't you? I've got to fly.'

He felt her lips press softly against his cheek but by the time he opened his eyes she was gone. Putting a hand up to shield the light flaring in through thin, unfamiliar curtains he rolled over just in time to see a flash of white shirt and well-tailored, navy-clad thighs disappearing from the room. Then he heard her voice again – 'Call me' – followed by something cheery but too muffled to be intelligible, and seconds later the thump of her front door closing. For a fraction of a second Gracia's face flickered in his mind like a misfiring memory. Then came the happy realisation: Siobhan. It hadn't been a dream.

Rubbing the sleep from his eyes, Mulcahy raised himself on to one elbow. For some reason the tune from some awful Country and Western song was nagging away at his brain. He took a look around to get his bearings. Her place. The double bed, its duvet rumpled and greying, took up most of the small room. Every other surface was covered in newspapers, magazines or crumpled clothes. In a glinting shard of memory he remembered the two of them tumbling into the flat, lips sliding, teeth colliding, hands everywhere, and her – absurdly, breathlessly – apologising for the mess.

He hauled his long legs out of the bed and sat on the edge for a moment, checking his wrist uselessly for the time. Where had his watch gone? Then he saw his shirt and trousers neatly folded on a chair, his jacket hung on the back, shoes paired beneath. Had he . . .? No way. Siobhan must have done it, this morning. He smiled at the gesture but more than anything at the oddness of this tiny oasis of neatness amid the carnage of the rest of the room, then he spotted his watch there too and reached for it. Only seven o'clock still, thank God. Where could she be off to in such a hurry at this hour? He knew the broad, if not specific, answer: work. Which was where he should be heading, too. He took his mobile from his jacket and walked out into the living room, using the speed dial while looking for an envelope, a delivery note, anything with her address on it. He found a pile of bills on her dining table, mostly plastered in red, and the cab company confirmed they could be there in ten minutes.

It was bang on eight-thirty when he got to Harcourt Square, having gone via his own place for a shower, shave and change of clothes. He'd kept the taxi waiting, an expensive option but he was in the mood for self-indulgence, and he'd only have had to call another anyway as he'd left his Saab at work the night before. Feeling fresher, more alive than he'd been for months, he climbed into the taxi again full of drive and focus. It was time to cut through all the crap with Brogan and that arse Cassidy, he decided. Only one thing mattered now: he had to ensure that the case was wrapped up, or at least that his role in it was finished, before Murtagh announced that the Southern Region job was free. Well, he sure as hell wasn't going to bring that about by sitting sifting through files in the background while the others buggered around outside wearing blinkers. He was going to have to push hard, whether they liked it or not. What was the worst that could happen? He'd piss them off so much they'd dump him? That sounded like win-win to him.

He ran into Brogan in the corridor, just about to go into the briefing. She was looking tired, a bit more rumpled than usual – as if the pressure was beginning to get to her.

'Claire, about last night.'

'Last night?' She was looking right at him but also straight through him, her thoughts clearly glued to something else entirely.

'Yes, that farce with Cassidy—'

'Please, Mike, I really don't have time for this.' She went to move around him but he blocked her, smiling.

'Then make some, Claire. Because I wouldn't have brought up the issue of religion unless I felt strongly that it must have a significant bearing on the case. I really feel it deserves to be given more serious consideration than it received yesterday.'

186

Her response was the last one he was expecting. 'Okay, Mike, maybe you're right. I had another look at the exam photos myself again last night, and I can see there's something in what you're saying. It makes sense. Like you said, it's probably best if we take a closer look. Straight after the briefing, yeah? We'll talk it through then. But, for now, I've got a bit of a mess to sort out.'

She pushed through the doors of the incident room and he walked in beside her. Inside, the murmur of conversation faded as they entered. Mulcahy found a seat at the back, wondering at the reasons for her U-turn, and what form this mess she was talking about would take.

'Alright, a bit of hush, please, lads,' Cassidy began. 'The news isn't great this morning, so listen up cos we're going to have another long, hard day in front of us.'

Mulcahy straightened up, as attentive now as the backs and necks ranged in front of him. Up front, Cassidy was dressed the same as always, same grey suit, same greasy hair. Brogan, perched on the desk edge behind him was thumbing her way through a sheaf of papers, clearly dissatisfied with what she was seeing.

'Okay,' Cassidy continued. 'So we pushed Technical to rush through what they could on the van for us overnight. And, miracle of miracles, they did.'

A sarcastic rumble rose from the front but Cassidy shut them up with a wave of his hand.

'Yeah, which is all well and good but that's as far as the encouraging news goes. Not to put too fine a point on it, we got nothing conclusive – as far as preliminaries are concerned, anyway.'

Cassidy's voice had been getting noticeably gruffer as he went on and now he knitted his brow and a thunderous look took up position on his face.

'Now, it's not all bad news. But, while we're on the subject of the van, we do have a bit of a problem,' he said, shooting a glance at Brogan. 'That's because some dense shit-for-brains over in Traffic didn't do his job properly yesterday afternoon and failed to notice that the Patrick Cormac Scully whose vehicle he was running a check on was born in nineteen *fifty*-six and not nineteen *eighty*-six, as advised.'

All the heads in front of him turned towards each other; some puzzled, others quickly getting the picture.

'That's right,' said Cassidy. 'The van belongs to Scully's father, also Patrick C, a plumber of this parish. Which, as you know, could and should have been checked out this end too – by you, Hanlon, ye thick fuckin' eejit.'

Everyone in the room turned towards Donagh Hanlon, who himself didn't seem to know where to look, other than at the floor. Yesterday's golden boy was turning a distinct shade of red. Meanwhile, Brogan pushed herself away from the desk and called for quiet again.

'Guys, look, this is the sort of pointless fuck-up we really don't need. As a result of it, we are on record as citing Scully Junior's ownership of that van as being cause for a full search of the premises. Not only is the fact that he doesn't own it a material error, it's just the sort of technicality that some shitehawk lawyer could exploit in court to make us look like a bunch of incompetent amateurs. That's just not on, not ever, but especially on an investigation like this. So listen, take it as a warning: double check everything and don't rely on anyone else – either inside, or especially outside, this unit – to do it for you. No more stupid slip-ups, okay?'

Mulcahy looked around at the bobbing heads, noting the seriousness on every face, a look which, in Hanlon's case, was still suffused with mortification.

'Okay,' Brogan continued. 'But obviously this doesn't rule Scully out in any way. Just because he doesn't own the van doesn't mean he couldn't have used it. He certainly had access to it, and if his father's a plumber chances are the boy learned how to use the equipment at his daddy's knee. And there are plenty more results to come back still, including the forensics on his clothing. So, Andy and myself are having another go at him in interview this morning. Let's see if a night in the cells has taken the smile off his face. He's still our number-one suspect. No let-up. We're just going to have to dig a bit deeper than we thought. Okay?'

Another murmur of consent. As Brogan and Cassidy started doling out tasks for the day to the others, Mulcahy zoned out, wondering what he'd say to Ibañez when he put in his mid-morning update call. The Spaniard had obviously been taken aback by the speed of the arrest yesterday, especially when Mulcahy stuck in the knife about not being able to get a positive ID from the girl, now that she was gone.

189

What could Mulcahy say to him now? That they still had a man in custody? But were getting nowhere with him? That he was helping them with their enquiries – just not very much? Better go through it with Brogan first. She could always charge Scully with intent to supply the ecstasy and maybe, that way, make it sound like they were making progress after all.

They wound the briefing up after another five minutes and as the others drifted away a small gang formed around Brogan, asking questions, going over the detail. He stepped into his office and switched on his computer, leafing through some of the files he'd left on his desk the day before, keeping an eye out for when Brogan became free.

He was reading a witness statement from a taxi driver, in relation to a violent assault on a woman in Rathgar the year before, when he realised he hadn't yet checked his email. He opened his inbox and saw a long list of replies to his Dublin Regional information request start flowing in. He looked at his watch, then out at Brogan who was still deep in discussion. He had forty minutes or so before the call to the embassy. He clicked the first message in the queue and started to read.

In the *Sunday Herald* newsroom Siobhan, too, was sitting at her computer, fingers flying across the keyboard, words ribboning out across the screen. She was getting occasional fond blossomings of memory from the night before but wasn't going to let that distract her. Hair groomed, face made up, lips a perfect glossy plum, none of her colleagues – not even the more hardened, cynical, long-in-the-tooth hacks – would have guessed that she'd spent the night wrapped in anything but blissful sleep. What they might have spotted was a certain avidity in her eye, a furrow of concentration on her brow, a crinkle of barely contained excitement pulling the corners of her mouth, and recognised them as signs of a reporter who was at last beginning to nail down one blisteringly good story.

On her way into work, in the car, she'd gone over her doubts about whether, up at the Blue Light with Mulcahy, she'd given up too easily on the subject of the Spanish girl. But she'd seen then and knew still that Mulcahy would never have compromised and that they wouldn't have had a hope of getting anywhere if she hadn't backed down. And wasn't it worth it? She could see this thing with him going further, and for once she was completely delighted at the prospect of getting involved. Then, as soon as she got into the office, got a coffee inside her, booted up her computer – what should come along but the confirmation that she'd been right to think of herself for once.

She was listening to the messages left on her landline when it came: 'This is for Fallon, the reporter.' The voice was rough, unfriendly and curiously sexless – mainly due to its being heavily, if amateurishly, disguised. 'A friend in the Force says you're looking for information on a case I'm working. About a Spanish girl. I can help, but it'll cost you.'

The caller knew exactly what he or she was doing, leaving a few choice pieces of information to whet the appetite and show that they were serious, then leaving precise details of when they'd call again – and how much they wanted for the info. She rewound and listened again, guessing it had to be one of the Gardai that Des Consodine had mentioned, hoping to cash in on their role in the investigation but afraid to risk approaching her directly. For a second she thought about Mulcahy and his damned integrity and decided she wouldn't want him any other way. Then it dawned on her: this was actually working in her favour. Whatever small anxiety she'd been feeling about pursuing a story involving a man she'd slept with was now completely laid to rest. He'd given her the perfect excuse, telling her he was the last person she should talk to about the case. Well, now she didn't need to. So long as she stuck to that, she couldn't go wrong.

Most of the email responses to Mulcahy's appeal were useless; quick-hit replies in the negative, to the effect that no information locally matched his request. Those that contained more detail might as well have been negative for all the relevance they had. His phrase 'religious connotations' had exercised the minds of the wags and the witless in quite a few Dublin divisions, and as a result he ended up digging through a pile of reports covering everything from a lengthy investigation into a middle-aged Cabra woman's morbid sexual obsession with the Papal Nuncio (she'd broken into the nunciature one night and nearly given the unfortunate Italian cleric a coronary when he woke up to find her slipping into bed beside him) to a mind-numbing list of break-ins and vandalism to church property in the Santry area over the past five years. Everything else was pretty much the inevitable fallout of the clerical abuse scandals of the preceding decade: rumours and intelligence reports gathered on priests who'd been accused of sexually abusing kids.

Everything else, except one. As he glanced through the brief details in this email, he felt a tingle in the back of his neck that grew as he read through the single-page report attached. It concerned a violent assault on a nineteen-year-old from Irishtown called Grainne Mullins, almost exactly a year before. She'd been attacked on the street outside her home by a man who'd dragged her behind a bush, bound her hands with cable ties, gagged her, exposed himself to her and then carved two crosses into her breasts with a knife. Beyond this one-page report there was nothing other than the status marker *No Further Action* typed into the header.

Mulcahy grabbed the phone and rang the sergeant at Ringsend Station who'd forwarded it to him. The man was on duty but not much help. The file in question had been put on ice after the detective who'd interviewed the girl was seconded on to a major murder investigation. He'd subsequently been promoted and transferred and, it seemed, the case had fallen through the cracks. Until a couple of days ago when the sergeant came across it during a routine case-review process.

'Did the victim not get in touch again at all?' Mulcahy asked, gobsmacked that anything as serious as this could be overlooked.

'Doesn't look like it, does it?' said the sergeant.

'And it was still active when Detective Branigan left?'

'So I understand.'

'Then how come it has a *No Further Action* flag on it?'

'How should I know?' the sergeant replied. Regret was creeping into his voice now, that he'd ever been foolish enough to step out of the usual desk sergeant's mindset and actually try being helpful with a colleague's enquiry. 'Maybe Branigan referred it on, and didn't have the time to file it properly. It's been known to happen, you know.'

'Maybe,' Mulcahy said, unconvinced.

'You boys on the National forget what these local stations are like, y'know. It's a feckin' lunatic asylum down here most of the time. Too much work, too few fellas to do it. You should try coming back to earth sometime and see how ye like it.'

'Yeah, sure,' Mulcahy said, barely aware of what the man was saying now he knew he'd be of no further help. 'Thanks, anyway. I'll see if I can chase it up myself.'

'You do that,' added the sergeant petulantly. 'You'll be the only one has the time for it.'

Mulcahy put the phone down, still staring at the girl's address. What was the likelihood of her still living there if she'd never been back in touch with the local Gardai? But it had to be worth a shot, and it was probably easier than trying to track down this Branigan guy, who'd only get all defensive about the case if it really had fallen into the gully unnoticed. He was jotting down the girl's details on a scrap of paper when a movement in front of him made him look up. Brendan Healy was standing in the doorway. How the hell long had he been there?

'Sir?' Mulcahy said automatically.

'I thought you'd never get off that bloody thing,' Healy said, pointing at the phone.

He looked around the small room critically, slapping the palm of one hand with the leather gloves he was holding in the other, as if searching for somewhere to sit down. Surely he could figure that one out for himself?

'Is there something I can help you with, Brendan?'

Healy frowned. 'The Minister's been on to me.'

Mulcahy glanced at his watch. Five minutes to go before he was due to call the Spanish embassy. Nothing to do with that, then.

'About the investigation?'

Healy nodded. 'The Ambassador called him this morning, asking about progress. Said he'd been informed last night we had somebody in custody. Was that you?'

'Sure, I rang First Secretary Ibañez as soon as Brogan told me about Scully. She said you'd approved it.'

'Did she now?' Healy replied, cryptically. 'Well, the Minister wasn't happy about it. At least, not when I had to tell him how little progress we've made with this character, Scully, so far, if you catch my drift.'

Mulcahy not only caught it, he was already trying to figure out what the hell he'd be expected to do about it.

'You must be pretty sure that this Scully character is involved,' Healy continued.

'I can't take any credit for that. It was Brogan's call. I haven't had much to do with that aspect of the investigation myself.'

'Haven't you?' Healy frowned even deeper. 'Well, you'd better get up to speed on it before we have any slip-ups with the Spanish.'

Mulcahy gritted his teeth. 'That's not what I meant.'

'No? Well there better not be any, Mike. I've told the Minister you'll go over to see the Ambassador in person this morning and use these diplomatic skills of yours to explain why they shouldn't be expecting anything too dramatic to happen any time soon. And while you're there, would you please impress upon them again that *you* are the official liaison officer on the case – at their request, remember – and not the Minister or his private secretary. Do you understand me?'

'Yes, sir.' What's not to understand, Mulcahy thought, feeling his heart sink. He wouldn't be getting out of this place for a few more days yet, then.

'Good man. Now, where's Brogan?'

'Probably questioning the suspect in the interview room downstairs. They had him brought over from Blackrock earlier.'

'Right. I'll call in on them on my way out – see for

myself if this fella Scully is as guilty-looking as everyone says he is.'

She was just grabbing her bag to run out for a coffee, when the ping of an incoming email drew Siobhan back to her screen. She sat down again, shoulders slumping when she saw the message was from Vincent Bishop, not wanting even to think of him on this of all mornings. But she was unable to resist the lure of a potentially good tip, especially one headed: 'I know you'll like this . . .'

She clicked on his name and the email opened, but it was blank. It took a couple of seconds for her to notice there was a pdf file attachment, then she double-clicked on it and was gobsmacked by what unscrolled before her eyes – a scan of a flight ticket from Dublin to the Seychelles, departing the following Monday. In *her* name. Beside it was an itinerary for a week's stay at some hyper-luxurious resort called the Banyan Tree. This, though, was not only in her name but Bishop's as well.

If the sound of her hand slamming down on the keyboard didn't draw much attention in the newsroom, the string of four-letter ordure that exploded from her mouth did. Paddy Griffin raised an eyebrow, rose from his desk and ambled over.

'What is it?' he said, leaning in towards her screen.

'Oh, Jesus, nothing that would interest you, Paddy, trust me.' She closed the attachment before he could read it and hurriedly quit the entire email programme for good measure. 'It's just someone taking the piss.'

'About what?' he said, disappointed, not quite ready to believe her.

'It's nothing, honestly. Go on, get back to work,' she said, batting him away with her hands and standing up. 'I was just going out for a coffee, do you want one? My treat?'

Even more in thrall to the bean than she was, Griffin smiled an affirmative and let her pass. Only when she got outside onto Burgh Quay did Siobhan allow the anger to take hold of her again. Ducking into an alleyway round the corner, the one place that offered enough shelter from the street noise for her to use her mobile, she leaned back against the brick wall and noticed her hands were shaking. She jabbed at Bishop's number, determined to exert some control over the situation.

He answered immediately.

'Hi, Siobhan—'

'Vincent, what in the name of Christ do you think you're doing?'

10

Nodding a comradely farewell to the security guard closing the iron-studded door behind him, Mulcahy stepped into the sunshine and pulled out the cigarette pack he'd been clutching in his jacket pocket for over an hour. He sparked up a cigarette and drew the smoke deep into his lungs, exhaling with a heartfelt sigh of relief, and tried to forget the polite mauling he'd received at the hands of the Spanish Ambassador and Ibañez.

'My government expects the Garda Siochana to treat this case with an urgency appropriate to the status of the individuals involved, Inspector,' Ambassador Escriva had complained. Tall, fair-haired, his manners even more impeccable than his suit, he cut an altogether more impressive figure than his miniature First Secretary.

'I can assure you it is being given every priority, Ambassador,' Mulcahy had responded, and a hundred more variations on the same as the diplomat repeatedly drove home the point.

Mulcahy looked around again as he walked towards

his car, unable to ignore the splendour of his surroundings, the colonial-style house behind him, the lush, carefully tended gardens. Like most of the older diplomatic missions in Ireland, the Spanish embassy occupied a sprawling mansion in the heart of Dublin 4. Whether by coincidence, astute speculation or the glamour that came with diplomacy, this was one of the few areas of the city that hadn't suffered the recent catastrophic drop in property prices. Snobbery always seemed to hold its value, even in recessions.

Suddenly, his mobile shattered the tranquillity around him. He looked at the screen, recognised Javier Martinez's number, and cursed as he answered.

'Jesus, that didn't take long,' Mulcahy said.

A brief, Scooby-style grunt of confusion came from the far end of the line. 'What are you talking about, Mike?'

'I'm at the embassy, Jav, I've just been updating—'

'I don't know anything about that,' Martinez interjected, a hint of defensiveness in his voice. 'I am calling to update you, actually. After we spoke the last time, I asked an investigation team to reassess any recent threats made against Don Alfonso.'

'And?'

'And they think they may have discovered something that has relevance to your case.'

'Seriously?' Mulcahy didn't bother trying to conceal his surprise.

'I really don't know yet,' Martinez said. 'It is little better than anonymous, from an ETA cell who say they will kill Don Alfonso *or his family members* any opportunity they get, when he least expects it, at home or *abroad*.'

Mulcahy let out a deep sigh. 'Christ, that's not exactly specific, Jav. Do you really think—'

'I don't know what to think,' Martinez cut in again. 'My men are thinking that, you know, historically, ETA has links with the Provisional IRA, and so Ireland . . . Like I said, I don't know. But this man you have in custody, he isn't IRA, no?'

'Scully?' Mulcahy gasped. 'No, he's not. I mean, not that we know. And from what I've heard, I can't imagine that he could be. But we'll check it out, now, obviously.'

'Good,' Martinez said. 'Let me know what you find out.'

Mulcahy hung up, shaking his head in disbelief. An ETA/IRA connection? Jesus, this thing was getting crazier by the minute. He had to be able to do something. He was taking his car key from his pocket when his fingers brushed against the scrap of paper on which he'd scrawled Grainne Mullins's details. She was the only lead he'd managed to come up with so far. He looked at the address again. It was only a mile down the road. He turned the car around and set off towards Irishtown.

It might have been less than a mile away but the street Grainne Mullins lived on seemed light years from the sedate, tree-lined avenues of embassy row. A council estate built on landfill on the fringe of the East Link development, in the shadow of the Pigeon House power station, it sat jammed between the wastes of the river's southern docks and three busy arterial routes. A bunch of thin, crop-haired youths in chav caps and knock-off trainers stared sullenly as he drove by, clocking him instinctively as a cop. He parked outside No. 18, the last one in the terrace, locked his car and rang the doorbell, feeling the youths' eyes on his back, hearing the confidence in their cackling jeers. One voice, louder than the others, called out: 'Goan'ta get yer rocks off, are ya, pig?'

He ignored them, noting the feeble, wind-blasted hedge that straggled around the side of the house, behind which the report said the assault had happened. Even if she hadn't been gagged, he doubted whether anyone round here would have responded to a cry for help.

The smell of stale milk and mildew hit him before she'd got the door open wide enough for him to see her. She was small, no more than five foot two, wearing a loose pink scoop-neck top and pale blue jeans, thick hanks of bleached blonde hair flopping around a face that not so long ago must have been pretty, but now looked hollowed out and emptied by life.

'Grainne Mullins?'

'Yeah, what about it?'

She eyed him suspiciously, folded one arm across her chest, and flicked at her fringe self-consciously with the other. Mulcahy froze on the spot. Beneath her hair, slashed across her forehead, was a pale scar. He couldn't take his eyes off it. Nobody could argue *that* wasn't in the shape of a cross. How the hell had it not been mentioned in the report?

'Is there something you want or are you going to just stare at me all day?'

'Sorry,' he said. 'I'm from the Gardai.'

'Yeah, I gathered that, but what d'ya want? I got a baby in there needs feeding.'

As if on cue, the wail of an infant escaped from within the house. He looked in past her, saw wallpaper peeling away from walls, a staircase with dirty pink carpet on the treads, a doorway into a kitchen that looked like a swamp.

'I was wondering if I could have a word with you about the assault,' Mulcahy said.

Her reaction took him completely by surprise.

'You're havin' a fucking laugh, aren't ya?' Her face curled up in a snarl and she grabbed the door to slam it in his face. He only just got his foot into the gap in time.

'No, wait, Grainne, please,' he pleaded.

'Go fuck yourself.' Inside, she leaned her minimal weight against the door. 'Youse lot are fuckin' unbelievable, you are. Why can't you just pay for it like everybody else.'

'I only want to talk to you.'

'Yeah, right, just like that other fucker did, I suppose?'

'Look, I don't know what you're on about, Grainne, but I swear this is important. I think the fella who attacked you has done it again. But worse this time. I need your help – to stop him.'

203

He felt the weight coming off his foot, saw the shadow of her body lifting away from the glass pane. Her face appeared around the door: just her eyes and that scarred forehead.

'Was it another workin' girl?' she asked. 'I'd'a thought I'd'a heard about that.'

'No. Just a kid.' Even as he said it, he was aware of the irony that this woman could be barely four, five years at most, older than Jesica Salazar.

'Well, you better come in, then, I suppose.'

It didn't take him long to work out why her case hadn't been investigated properly. Prostitutes never got a fair deal from anybody, least of all the Garda Siochana. She didn't come right out and say it, but Branigan, the detective who'd been assigned to her case, had obviously decided he could trade some kind of protection for sexual favours, and when she wouldn't play ball any more after the first couple of times, he made sure the case got buried – for his own sake. Grainne Mullins had just assumed that life had given her one more kick in the guts and got on with it, unaware that Branigan had been transferred, and convinced that if she ever pursued the matter he'd only try the same thing again.

Mulcahy told her he'd try to do something about it, but didn't hold out much hope. She wasn't impressed. Cynicism was dyed deep in her by now. The only thing that got through to her at all was the idea that the man who attacked her had done it to somebody else, and might do it again.

'Seems like ages ago,' she said, pointing at the infant in

the rocker beside her. 'Had this little one since. I'd only just been given this place because I already had the other two.'

The baby was asleep, a soother in its mouth, no sign of the other children. She'd brought Mulcahy into the tiny, sparsely furnished living room. A blue foam sofa, an armchair and a small television on an upturned plastic storage box took up what bits of floor weren't strewn with baby gear and toys. Everything was cheap, filthy and falling apart. He looked again at the scar on her forehead, and shuddered to think what her other injuries must look like. How had she even been able to keep on doing business?

She read his mind.

'You'd be surprised what some creeps get turned on by. There's fellas now I can charge extra just to take me top off for them.' She snorted at the stupidity of it. 'The rest of them are usually so blathered by the time they get down to it, they never even notice.'

'What about the man who attacked you?' Mulcahy asked.

'You must be jokin' me,' she hooted, mistaking his meaning. 'That bastard wasn't interested in doin' anything. All he did was fiddle about uselessly, then got on with carving me up.'

'He cut you because he was angry at not being able to do it?'

'How would I know?' she said. 'It might sound kinda obvious, but I was more scared of the knife than anything else. Once he got me down and got me hands tied, he never

205

tried to touch me that way. It was weird. It was only when he cut me bra that he started fiddlin' with himself, but y'could see his heart wasn't in it. But his eyes lit up when he went to cut me. I was so scared I didn't even feel it, just saw the blood comin' out. I lost it completely then. Can't remember much after that, except trying to scream and not bein' able to cos he'd stuffed a cloth in me mouth.'

'What happened to the cloth?' Mulcahy asked.

She looked at him like he had two heads.

'It's evidence. It might give us a clue,' he said. 'I mean, did anyone come and examine the scene afterwards, or collect evidence?'

The look of scorn only intensified on her face. 'Jesus, you're really working in the dark, aren't you? Look, the only fella who came out here was that pig, wassisname?'

'Branigan.'

'Yeah. And, like I said, the only thing he was interested in collecting was his rations. Once he heard I was a workin' girl, that was it. Fair game, that's what he said. Always the bleedin' same.'

'Can you tell me what you were doing before the attack?' Mulcahy asked, deciding it was better to avoid that issue for the moment.

'What's the fuckin' point – you're not going to catch him now, are you? And how d'ya know it's even the same fella?'

'I don't, but I'm kind of hoping there's no more than one freak going around doing this kind of thing.'

'Okay, look, I was just comin' up to the house, lookin' for

me keys. I'd been out doing an at-homer out in Glasthule. The fella's a regular – always pays me a taxi home.'

'Could the taxi driver have seen anything? Didn't he drop you to the door?'

'Yeah, well, that's just my bloody luck, isn't it. The driver said he was runnin' low on petrol and asked could he drop me off at the bottom of the road so he could go over to the garage on Bath Street. I wasn't bothered. Saved me tippin' him. Course it'd have to be the one night a pervert was on the loose.'

'Were you aware of the attacker beforehand? Did he follow you up the street?'

'Haven't a clue. He came at me from the back, as I was putting the key in the lock. It was like he hit me with his chest or something, at a run. My face went smack into the door and I was nearly knocked out. Keys and everything went flyin'. Next thing I knew, I was on the ground, hands tied behind me back, and he was stuffin' this rag into me gob. I thought I was going to puke but when I saw the knife I just froze. I was too terrified to move.'

'So you saw his face?'

'For fuck's sake, what do you think? He'd just knocked me halfway into next week. The only thing I was seein' was stars.'

'But you must've got some impression of him?'

'Not really.'

'What about his age? Was he young or old?'

'Jesus, I don't know. Like I said, I was too groggy and all my attention was on the knife.'

'Well, what would your gut say, your instinct?'

She shrugged. Clearly, this question hadn't been put to her before.

'Well, not a kid, like, but not too old either. He was strong but not huge, y'know.'

'It says in the report that you didn't know the man? What was it made you so sure? Did he say something, is that it – was it his voice you didn't recognise?'

'Are ya kiddin' me? Jesus, ya wouldn't hear that voice twice and not know it. Soft, like, and a bit educated, too, now I think of it. Not from around here, for sure. An' he was mitherin' all the time. Especially after he cut me. He just kept on, low like, not so much excited as fuckin' mad. Cursin' and mumblin' all this crap, like he was sayin' his prayers or some shite.'

'Prayers?'

'Ah, I don't know.' She shook her head again. 'It was double Dutch to me. All I knew was he was a mad shite and he was doin' a bleedin' good job of cutting me up.'

'Did he try to burn you at all?'

'Holy fuck,' she gasped. 'What do you want? Didn't he do enough to me, or what?'

'Sorry, just checking.' Mulcahy smiled apologetically but he didn't get one back. 'I suppose I should be going. Let you get on with things.'

As he got to the door, he stopped and asked: 'He didn't take anything from you, did he?'

'How d'you mean?'

'Something personal, a piece of jewellery, you know, a necklace maybe, or—'

'Y'mean me Versace?' She was staring at him now, something like laughter in her eyes.

'Your what?'

'Ah, go on,' she said. 'The other girls used to always take the piss out of me for it. It was like one of those big Versace crosses you used to see a few years back. You know them?'

Mulcahy said nothing, afraid to interrupt the flow.

'It was a big gold cross all studded with fake jewels and glass and stuff, like the sort them rappers wear, on a chain.'

'And you were wearing this at the time?'

'Yeah, I mean, it wasn't real or anythin', just a piece of crap I got on Henry Street for a laugh. People were always going on about it, y'know, given me line of business.'

'And he took it from you? I didn't see any mention of that in the incident report.'

'Yeah, well, I'm sure I said somethin' about it at the time. But maybe I didn't. It was only a piece of old tat. He'd carved me up, for Jaysus' sake.'

'But he took it? You're sure?'

She shook her head and sighed.

'Yeah, positive. Soon as he got me on my back, he pulled it tight like he was tryin' to choke me with it. Course, it was such cheap shite, the chain snapped as soon as he gave a tug on it. That pissed him off – must've thought it was worth somethin'. That's when he started on with the prayers and rantin' on about Jesus dyin' for our sins.' She paused, then

209

a note of pain mingled with the exasperation in her voice. 'What the fuck would he know about it, eh? Carving me up while spoutin' on about Jesus on the cross.'

'Like a priest,' Mulcahy said, mostly to himself.

'Not like any priest I've ever met,' she said. 'Not that I get many. Most of them lot is only interested in fiddlin' with little boys.'

She waited for the greeting on Mulcahy's answering service to play out, then the beep.

'Hiya, Inspector, it's the chief reporter here. Sorry I couldn't stay for breakfast this morning but I was expecting some calls and needed to be at my desk first thing. I did try to wake you but you were completely sparko. Anyway, just wanted to say, y'know, thanks for last night and hope your head doesn't hurt too much this morning. I'm looking forward to us not helping each other with our enquiries again soon.'

Siobhan put her mobile down and smiled to herself for the first time in a few hours. It had taken most of the day to get back to what she'd been wanting to do most. First, that ludicrous email had taken up half the morning. When she'd called Bishop he'd come over all defensive and apologetic about it. Pathetically so, claiming his name was never supposed to be on the itinerary. That the holiday was just for her – *'if you want it that way'* – the bloody creep. As if she'd even consider it. The thought of his clammy skin coming anywhere near hers was, by now, almost enough to make her retch. But for some reason – the last vestiges of self-interest probably – after he'd promised to cancel the whole thing, she'd calmed down and let him swing the conversation round to some new titbit of gossip he'd uncovered about Marty Lenihan, and they'd eventually hung up on reasonably amiable terms again.

In her gut she knew it couldn't last. Even if Bishop thought his attentions were innocent, to her they were getting creepier by the day. And no amount of stories was worth that sort of hassle. If she didn't put some serious distance between herself and Bishop, she knew it could only get worse. How best to go about that, though, she still wasn't sure. She didn't want to make an enemy of him either. But she had no time to think about that. As soon as she got back with the coffee, she and Paddy had had to go straight in to Harry Heffernan's office for the post-mortem he insisted on holding every Tuesday, where he banged on about every misplaced comma, wrong name, cocked-up photo caption and breached deadline from the previous week's edition – ad-bloody-nauseam.

By the time she got out of there it was lunchtime and of course that was already booked – out in Dun Laoghaire with a Fianna Fail councillor who was helping her with a piece she was researching on the financing of local politics. It was past three by the time she got back from lunch, whereupon she thought of Mulcahy and decided to give him the call. She was glad she only got his message service. Too much else to be getting on with. But just the thought of him was comforting.

She picked up a pencil and pulled a spiral-bound note-book towards her across the desk, then flicked back a couple of pages. She tapped the pencil against her teeth, then used it to circle a name she'd scribbled on the page in front of her. A touch on the mouse brought her computer monitor flickering back to life again. She keyed in her password and double-clicked on a folder entitled *Active* and, within it, one called *JMS*. The number of files inside was growing. A single keystroke brought up the Google search engine and she typed in 'Spanish politicians'. A long list came back, most relating to news stories, but it didn't take long to refine her search and find a roster of the current members of the Cortes. Seconds later, her breath was stilled as her eyes matched the name in her notepad to an entry on the list in front of her.

'Bloody hell,' she said, looking around to see if Paddy Griffin was anywhere in the vicinity.

For once, though, he wasn't.

Over in Harcourt Square, Mulcahy's hopes of making rapid progress had not been realised. Brogan and Cassidy had been in the interview room most of the day, trying to wear Scully down. He'd passed a note through to them about what he'd found out at Grainne Mullins's, and sent an excited-looking Hanlon off to look into the possibility that Scully might have a footprint in the world of Republican subversion – but had heard nothing back on either front. In the meantime he'd done some following up of his own regarding Detective

Branigan and, finally, traced him to an armed-robbery task force working out of Dublin West. But his efforts to get in touch were met with the news that Branigan was away on leave until the following day, and to call back then. After going through the rest of the replies to his round robin, and not turning up anything else interesting, he put in a call to Javier Martinez in Madrid to see if they'd come up with anything on their ETA lead. They hadn't.

When Brogan and Cassidy reappeared for the evening briefing, it proved a pretty dismal affair. While the suspect had been cockily polite and 'helpful' all the way through, they reported back, he had obstinately refused to change his story about leaving Jesica at Stillorgan shopping centre and going straight home. And just to help matters he absolutely denied that the drugs found in his bedroom were his, too. In fact, he'd stated for the tape no fewer than twenty-five times that they must have been planted there by members of the Garda search team. Meanwhile, the forensics on the van hadn't exactly flooded back in, and those that did arrive had yielded nothing. Worst of all, the blood sample taken from the interior definitely did not match Jesica's, although it had been identified as human. It had yet to be checked against either Scully or his father, both of whom had so far refused to give a sample. Overall, then, the case against Scully was beginning to stall. Brogan decided to keep him in custody overnight again and told him she'd be charging him with possession in the morning and to have a legal representative present.

'And guess whose phone number he gave the desk sergeant?' Cassidy scoffed. 'Dermot bloody Kennedy.'

There was a groan of recognition around the room. Every cop in Dublin knew of Kennedy, one of the city's longest-serving, most conniving and disagreeable solicitors. He could be relied on to make life as uncomfortable as possible for Brogan, although there could hardly be any question that she could keep Scully in custody on the possession charge, given his previous form.

'It proves one thing,' Whelan remarked. 'Scully's no full-time student if he can afford Kennedy's fees.'

'Right, but I don't suppose the bench will see it that way,' Brogan said. Whereupon she turned towards Mulcahy and said in rather brighter tones, 'The inspector here seems to be the only one who's actually made any progress today. Would you care to share what you were telling me about this possible earlier victim, Mike?'

There was a rustle of interest and a scrape of chairs as one or two of those present perked up and changed position to get a better view. But the noise didn't quite cover the muttered sigh of 'Jaysus, not the feckin' Priest again' that escaped one pair of lips in the room.

'Sergeant,' Mulcahy said, staring Cassidy down and waiting for the rest to settle, 'if you can't bring any ideas of your own to the table, then my advice is keep your mouth shut.'

Cassidy glowered back at him and muttered something very like, 'I don't take advice from you, tosser' beneath his breath.

'What was that?' Mulcahy stiffened.

'Eh, "If that's your view, sir",' Cassidy said, grinning inanely around the room, eliciting a feeble titter from one or two of the others.

'Okay, now, everybody,' Brogan intervened. 'Inspector Mulcahy is right, we need all the ideas we can get here. So shut up and listen to what he has to say. You might learn something.'

Mulcahy outlined the details of his visit to Grainne Mullins earlier in the day and was gratified to see that everyone in the room, even Cassidy, seemed to take its significance on board.

'Thanks, Mike,' Brogan said, when he'd finished. 'That's really good. I think we all agree this is a very interesting development.'

She walked away from him and addressed the small group from the front again. 'Okay, lads, so it's beginning to look like Scully, or whoever, has done this before. Donagh and Brian, first thing tomorrow I want you to talk to this Branigan character – get his details from Inspector Mulcahy – and find out what happened to the files on his original investigation.'

The two detectives groaned at the idea of having to confront a fellow officer about a botched, or probably deliberately buried case, with Hanlon moaning he might as well be working for Internal Affairs.

'That has nothing to do with it,' she snapped back at them. 'If anything, we're doing him a favour by not passing it straight on to IA. So don't go accusing him of anything. If he kicks off, make sure he knows that if any of what this

Mullins woman says stacks up he's going to get a rocket up his arse from somewhere. And emphasise to him that any assistance he gives us now could make the difference between getting a slap on the wrist or a full investigation and all that brings with it. I have a feeling we'll find that all the original case notes have disappeared, but see what you can get, and then bring Grainne Mullins in to make a formal statement on the original attack, and her allegations about Branigan.'

The two detectives didn't look any happier but murmured their assent.

'And make sure they're separate statements,' Mulcahy added. 'Don't let her mix up what she says about Branigan with the attack itself – for now that's what we're most interested in.'

'It sounds to me like Inspector Mulcahy already did a thorough job,' Brogan continued, 'but you never know what else she might be able to give us to tie it in with Scully, so dig deep. Alright, I think that wraps it up for tonight. Let's hope Technical come up with something useful overnight and we have some hard evidence to pin on Scully in the morning. Anything else?'

There was a low murmur of negatives and chairs started clattering as everybody began to get up and drift out. Brogan dispatched Cassidy on some errand with a whisper, and then turned to Mulcahy as he was leaving the room.

'Thanks again for that, Mike. This'll certainly strengthen our case against Scully if anything comes of it.'

Mulcahy wasn't so certain. 'You don't think it would be worth widening the net a bit at this stage, to look into suspects other than Scully?'

'I wasn't aware that we had any suspects other than Scully.'

'Come on, Claire, you know what I mean. Surely it's worth a go, rather than keeping all our eggs in one basket. I mean, if there is some serial attacker running around out there, wouldn't it be as well to cover our arses, just in case? You know, get the word out, and pull in some of the usual suspects?'

'What do you think we've been doing for the last few days?'

'I know, but don't you think maybe we should look at them all again now, in light of this new information?'

Brogan halted in the corridor and treated Mulcahy to one of her more piercing stares.

'Look, Mike, I meant what I said. I'm grateful you went out and got us that lead. But don't forget that's all it is – a lead. We still have to establish a connection, don't we? So for now, let's not get too ahead of ourselves, yeah? I have a suspect in custody who I still fancy for this. So I can't see the point of continuing to rummage around in bushes when I've got the bird I want right in the palm of my hand. As you can see, I have very limited resources. I want to use them as best I can to get a proper bead on Scully. If I fail to do that, then obviously I'll direct them elsewhere. But not until then, okay?'

Mulcahy had to concede the point. The evidence was there at every briefing.

'I was only suggesting it might be better to get a head start, so you're not left staring at nothing should Scully go tits up.'

'And I just told you. I haven't got the resources for running two lines of enquiry. It's as much as I can do to keep up with this one.'

'So why not get me to do it? I'd handle it on my own.'

Brogan seemed surprised by the suggestion, as if using him productively was still the last thing she'd consider. In the end there was more exasperation than enthusiasm in her response.

'Alright, Mike, why don't you do that? Look around all you like and, if you find anything, come back and let me know. But until then just let me get on with my own enquiry in my own way, okay?'

'Great, I'll be happy to.'

She pushed her hair back behind her ears and swept it round in a loose plait over her right shoulder. In any other circumstance it might have seemed self-conscious or even flirtatious but not, as it was, accompanied by that steely glint in her eyes.

'Just one more thing, yeah?'

'What?'

'I'm pretty amazed that the press haven't got wind of this thing yet – even after all Healy's warnings. I don't suppose you've heard any stirrings?'

Mulcahy looked at her, his thoughts immediately flying to

Siobhan. He'd thought it through and decided there was no merit in telling either Brogan or Healy about Siobhan's approach. It would only complicate matters for him, and while he had no doubts that she'd dig deeper and break into the story soon enough, he was confident she wouldn't bring his name up in connection with it.

'No, nothing,' Mulcahy shrugged.

'It's amazing,' Brogan went on. 'The more I thought about it, the more I was inclined to agree with what you said the other day, about how mad Healy was thinking he could keep something like this under his hat. Especially with the political edge to it. It's incredible nobody's got a sniff. You'd have thought that the Spanish press at least would be making a fuss about it.'

'The silence on the Spanish side is easy to explain,' Mulcahy said. 'The Ambassador went on at length about it to me this morning. He said Salazar is willing to take out as many injunctions as it takes to keep this out of the media over there. For the girl's sake. The privacy laws in Spain are a good bit tougher than they are here, especially when it comes to minors.'

'So it'll be down to us if it leaks, then?'

'Or the hospital, I guess. Like I said, I suppose we'll just have to wait and see. Are you heading home now? You look like you could do with a break.'

Brogan shook her head. 'I'm here for ages yet. I just got a call to say Scully's solicitor is coming to see his client, *tonight*. Says he wants to meet the arresting officer.'

'What's the problem?'

'I'm not aware there is one,' Brogan said. 'But you know what a slippery creep Kennedy is. He's bound to have something up his sleeve. We'll just have to wait and see what bollocks he'll try to push past us.'

'Do you want me to hang around?'

Brogan smiled. 'Thanks, Mike, but I'm pretty sure we'll be able to handle him.'

But the evening only went further downhill for Brogan. She'd just about been able to square Hanlon's cock-up over the van ownership with Superintendent Healy – at least there was someone else to blame for that. But when Dermot Kennedy came marching in downstairs in his Louis Copeland suit, all arrogant gloating and bluster, waving a copy – God knows where he'd got it from – of the search warrant, claiming it was invalid because Cassidy, the authorised officer named on it, hadn't been on the premises when the drugs were seized, she nearly had a stroke.

It was a small point, one for which most judges would not throw out a warrant. Not on its own. But when added to the cock-up over the van, it meant the whole search – and the drugs seizure made on the back of it – might now be fatally undermined. And even though Kennedy didn't seem to have spotted the issue over the van yet, she couldn't afford to take the risk of provoking him into looking any closer at that warrant. So, humiliating as it was, she'd had to agree to Kennedy's request that his client be allowed home for the night on the understanding that he would attend for interview again at ten the following morning to be formally charged for possession under the Misuse of Drugs Act. Healy's reaction to being caught on the hop like this had not been good, not good at all.

Absorbed as she was, the rap on her door startled her. What in the name of Christ could it be now?

'Come on in,' she shouted, a bit sharply.

'Boss?' A cautious head peered around the door. 'Am I interrupting?'

'Maura, what is it? You weren't at the briefing, were you? I thought you were long gone. You must be exhausted.'

McHugh shook her head and waddled up to the desk, standing side on to it rather than facing forward. The curve of her belly was getting more prominent by the day.

'You know you told me to get on to UCD and find out what they think of Scully down there?' she asked.

Brogan listened as Maura related how she'd got nowhere on the phones so she'd driven over to the university herself and been lucky enough to catch the History Department's administrative secretary just as she was leaving and, even better, hit it off with her straight away.

'She'd just found out she's expecting and she took one look at me and, well, you know yourself how it is,' she continued. 'Anyway, turns out she doesn't like our boy Scully much. Thinks he's way too far up his own arse. My guess is they must've had a run-in over something some time. But y'know, it meant she was only too happy to lay the goss out for me.'

'Good girl,' Brogan smiled. Maura could winkle the grit from an oyster, she was so chatty.

'Well, he's definitely doing the PhD, anyway – although this girl did say he's takin' a bit longer at it than most. Getting on for three years, or something. So I asked her what sort of stuff Scully is studying and she says, far as she knows, his specialist area is medieval Christianity.'

'Religion?' Brogan said, her mind jumping immediately to what Mulcahy had been banging on about earlier. When, in interview, she'd asked Scully what he was studying he hadn't been evasive, only said it was medieval history and implied that it was way too complicated to go into. He hadn't mentioned anything about religion. Christ, why hadn't she thought to follow up on that?

'He doesn't look the type, does he?' she said, almost to herself.

Maura wasn't so sure. 'I wouldn't know. I always thought students were supposed to be poor. One or two of the ones walking in and out of the department today looked like they'd come straight off a catwalk.'

Brogan said nothing, still cursing herself for not following up that line of questioning. Scully was such a cool little shit, how had he got that under her radar?

'Anyway,' Maura continued, 'so I push a bit further and she eventually looks up his file and gives me the title of his doctoral thesis. Get a load of this, it's called "Ireland's Inquisition: Echoes of Bernardo Gui in the Annales Hiberniae".'

222

She'd tripped over the Latin a bit but Brogan got the picture. 'The Inquisition?'

'I know, that's what I thought, too,' Maura said, her face lighting up like a beacon. 'That was all about burning people at the stake, wasn't it? I couldn't help thinking of young Jesica.'

'Well, sort of,' Brogan said, trying not to let her own somersaulting thoughts get the better of her, fighting against them, trying to think it through. The Inquisition was definitely all about religion, she knew from the little she could remember learning about it in school. But it was in Spain, wasn't it, not Ireland? Jesus, *Spain*? Surely there couldn't be a connection?

'Did she say anything else about it?'

'Nah, she didn't know any more, but the thing is, she gave me a phone number for Scully's thesis supervisor or whatever they call her.' Maura consulted her notes again. 'Dr Aoife McAuliffe, a lecturer in medieval studies. So I give her a call. In her fifties, I'd say, from the voice, and a right snooty attitude on her. This one was a lot meaner with the info. I got the impression that herself and Scully were dead tight, that she saw him as her star pupil or whatever.'

'She had nothing bad to say?'

'Not a word,' Maura said. 'She was more concerned about getting the whys and wherefores of him being questioned, and whether Scully's human rights were being breached, than giving anything away to me.'

'So did you get anything at all from her?' Brogan just wanted Maura to get to the point. Her breath was getting shorter now, as her chest tightened with anxiety.

'Well, that's just it. Obviously, I didn't tell her what we had him in for. And that's just as well, cos otherwise I think she'd never have said what she did say.'

'Which was?'

'Only that all his work involved looking at the persecution of heretics and witches here in Ireland during medieval times, and its connection to the, eh, wider Inquisition on the continent. Honestly, boss, I didn't understand half of what she was saying. Most of it was about some Dame Alice Kettle or Kittler or something who was burned alive at the stake, or should've been . . . I don't know. The thing is, at one point I stopped her and asked her who this Bernardo whatsit fella in the title of the thesis is.'

'Gui,' Brogan said, wondering why she remembered the name so well. Had she heard it somewhere before? 'Bernardo Gui.'

'Yeah, him,' said Maura. 'Well, you won't believe this. According to McAuliffe, during the Inquisition in Spain, he was the fella who wrote the rulebook on how to torture people into making confessions.'

'Oh, for fuck's sake!' Brogan jumped up and grabbed her jacket from the back of the chair.

'What is it, boss?'

'We've just told them downstairs to let Scully go.'

*

As soon as Siobhan opened the door, she heard it. The low beep of the machine. Responding to its summons unthinkingly, she pulled her key from the lock and went straight to the living room and pressed the play button without even turning the lights on. Instantly, she recoiled when the rich thrum of a guitar blossomed from the answerphone speaker and the high male voice took flight: Roy Orbison again, and creepier than ever.

Recovering herself, she jabbed at the machine to turn it off but in her haste succeeded only in knocking it to the ground. As she knelt down, fumbling between the waste bin and the table, the song continued to poison the darkness around her.

Its tempo was a bit more jaunty by now and a string section had joined the guitar but it still closed in on her, so much she could hardly breathe. She recognised it now: 'My Prayer', more familiar from another version by The Platters that her parents used to play at home all the time. So long ago. So long it felt like a ghost stalking her through the darkness, Orbison's strangled tones turning its message of imagined love into cold psychotic threat.

At last she got hold of the answerphone and found the button. As she felt it click beneath her fingers all the pressure in her head seemed to wash away and the silence that fell around her became still more audible than the song had been. She heard her own breath rasping in and out of her lungs, her trousers brushing against the carpet as she pulled her legs out straight and sat back on the carpet, a feeling of exhaustion swamping her.

'Fuck him,' she said to herself in the enfolding gloom, the lights of the city outside refracting through the window like knives of orange flame. 'Fuck him, if he thinks he can play *me* like some shitty old record.'

11

It was shaping up to be another spectacular summer's day, that rare pairing of clear-blue heaven and bright biting sunlight guaranteed to make any self-respecting Dubliner add a 'Glorious, isn't it!' to their morning salutations. Already, at only eight-fifteen, the heat had built up enough to feel almost oppressive by the city's meagre standards, and Mulcahy was in the Saab, his elbow out the open window, heading into work, thinking hard about what else he might do today to push things a bit further forward.

The Cork job was still very much on his mind again. He'd had a call from Liam Ford the night before to say that Dowling had been approached but was playing for time and more money. Fair enough, that was only to be expected. The man would be a fool to take the first offer he was made, especially for an injury that was cutting short a distinguished career. But it still meant the deal would probably be done within weeks rather than months.

It was beginning to feel like he was running out of time.

Things would have to move soon, or he wouldn't be free to go for the job. He'd spent the rest of the evening checking over and signing off on details and photos left for him by the estate agents. And first thing this morning he'd had a call from one of them to say they had two viewings lined up, with the possibility of one or two drop-ins, too, this being Saturday. The prospect of being unencumbered by either the house or his current job filled him with what felt like a force field of energy. Or maybe that was just Siobhan. He'd spent no small while thinking about her, too. Even the thought of moving to Cork hadn't taken the shine off that. It was only three hours away by train.

His mobile went off.

'Mulcahy?' It was Brogan.

'Yeah. How's it going?'

'Not good.'

Christ, she sounded low.

'Did Kennedy rustle up a get-out-of-jail-free card for Scully?' He wasn't being entirely serious, so her response in the affirmative came as a surprise.

'He did.'

'Bollocks,' Mulcahy cursed. 'I thought we had him covered. How'd he manage that?'

'Look, Mike, I don't really have time to go into it now, but it's actually a good bit worse than us just letting him go.'

'That sounds ominous.'

'It is. There's been another one,' she said, almost as if she herself could hardly believe what she was saying. 'Another assault, I mean. Overnight, out in Marino. I don't have a time yet, as it's only just come in to us from District.'

'Bloody hell, how bad?'

'Even worse than Jesica, by the sound of it. Bad as it gets without the victim being dead.'

His mind swam with the awful possibilities.

'And Scully? He was out?'

'We had no choice. His brief, Kennedy, was on the warpath. The warrant had too many holes. Lucky for me, it was Healy signed off on the release.'

Not so lucky for the poor kid who was attacked, Mulcahy thought, but he kept that to himself.

'And you're sure it's the same attacker?'

'No question. Has to be. Same victim type, seventeen years or thereabouts, found semi-naked and unconscious in Fairview Park. Similar injuries, but even more disgusting, burns not just on the genitals this time but all over her body. I asked if they were shaped anything like crosses. Apparently there are so many it's hard to tell for sure, but they said that's one way of looking at it.'

'Jesus, that's awful. He's getting worse.'

'Looks like it,' she said.

'Was the victim a student?'

'Hard to say, but they don't think so. Not a foreign one at least. But same age, same dress style – her clothes were dumped nearby – all that. No ID yet.'

'A working girl?'

'Not that we know of.'

'Is she still under? I mean, can she talk?'

'She's barely alive, as I understand it. She's in Intensive Care in the Mater Hospital, under heavy sedation. It's not looking good. The medics don't give her more than a one-in-two chance.'

God, but that was bad. He wondered briefly if Jesica might be well enough yet to be re-interviewed, then cast the thought from his mind. She'd be so well wrapped up back in Spain now, it could be weeks before anyone would be allowed near her again.

Brogan went on, 'Can you do something for me?'

'Sure, name it.'

'I've got to go brief Healy on this, and then head in to the Mater to look in on the girl and see if I can get anything from the guys who treated her. The local lads already called in Technical to do the CSI stuff out in Fairview, and apparently they're still out there. What I really need is for someone with a bit of sense to get over there right now to do some nosing around. I'd send Cassidy but he's on his way over to Scully's, to bring him in early and check his whereabouts last night. He undertook to remain in the family home.'

'Did we have anybody out there keeping an eye?'

'What do you think?'

'Doesn't look like Scully kept his promise, does it?'

'Don't, Mike, I can't bear to think . . . Christ, this is turning into a total fuck-up.'

He heard her sigh deeply into the phone, and felt for her.

This really wasn't looking good. In fact, the worst possibilities hardly bore thinking about. She'd have to pull herself together or it would drag her under.

'Don't let it get to you, Claire. None of this was your doing. Look, I was on my way in anyway, so I'll just head over to Fairview now, okay?'

'Yeah, good,' she said. 'You know, let them get on with it but bring back a few initial ideas for us to run with, and make sure they don't overlook anything that only we might see the significance of. See you back at Harcourt Square once you're done.'

She gave him the location details and, as soon as the cars ahead of him moved, he swung the car round in a tight tyre-squealing U-turn, heading down Haddington Road towards the East Link Bridge. The streets were fairly free now he was no longer heading into the centre so he put his foot to the floor and, as he did, the blood began to accelerate around his system too. Out of frustration that another young kid had been so abominably assaulted, and that somehow the team's failure to find an answer in time could have contributed to it. Suddenly all his earlier doubts about Scully's guilt were thrown into relief, like so many minor misgivings.

As he sped on towards the river, Mulcahy passed the entrance to the estate where he'd interviewed Grainne Mullins the day before. Whatever she might think, it was clear to him that she'd had a lucky escape. He tried to picture Scully coming down to Irishtown from Blackrock, and taking out his anger on a working girl. Had it been an experiment? A trial? There seemed such a gulf in the levels of violence. He hardly noticed himself paying the bridge toll, such was the rush of thoughts crowding his brain. He made a mental note to double-check that someone else on the team had sounded out the Vice lads down in Store Street regarding other assaults on prostitutes. Despite Grainne Mullins's experience, it was hard to believe anything similar could have occurred to another working girl and gone unreported. They might moan about the way the Gardai treated them, but they were usually quick enough to kick up if they felt any real threat out on the streets.

His mind raced as he weaved through the heavier traffic on the East Wall Road, getting a broadside of angry horns as he ran a red light turning on to the North Strand. A couple of minutes later he spotted the team from Technical on the far side of the inbound carriageway, opposite the row of shops on Marino Parade. Their cars and vans were jumbled on the pavement, with still more of them inside the grounds of Fairview Park. He looked for somewhere to turn.

They were packing up already. Mulcahy enquired after the crime scene manager and was directed towards a skinny, hawk-faced man called Eddie Keane. He was dressed in the standard white coveralls staring intently at the screen of a small digital camcorder he was holding at arm's length, videoing a series of small red flags set on thin metal rods inside a patch of ground cordoned off by blue-and-white scene tape. The area was about five metres square and lay

232

immediately behind the park railings which, together with a line of thin hedging, partially screened the spot from the sight of any traffic surging past on the Fairview Road.

A bizarre spot to dump a victim, Mulcahy thought, as he headed towards Keane. Sure, it would have been much quieter in the early hours of the morning, but even so, this was a major thoroughfare, with cars and people passing day and night. He looked behind him, past the traffic, at the parade of shops across the wide road. A chemist's, a mini-market, an estate agent and a café were topped by what looked like a floor of residential accommodation, all with net-curtained windows overlooking the park. A couple of security cameras, too, bolted high on the brick frontage, though probably not at an angle to take in this patch of ground across the road. Even so, the chances of being spotted by someone were pretty high.

'Either he needed to get rid of her in a massive hurry or he didn't give a shit who saw him,' Mulcahy said after introducing himself.

'Or maybe both,' Keane replied, pushing back a strand of floppy black hair off his forehead.

Mulcahy guessed he was in his early thirties, wiry with an intelligent demeanour that was probably attributable to the thin rimless glasses perched halfway up his hooked nose.

'He didn't take much time over it, anyway. As far as I can tell, he must've pulled up, jumped out, hoiked the girl over the railings – followed by everything else – and then skedaddled. Didn't leave much trace of himself behind, anyway.'

Mulcahy took another look around. Fairview Park was a broad expanse of grass, pathways and small clumps of weatherbeaten hawthorn and poplar. The land, reclaimed from the sea and the muddy estuary of the Tolka river, was bisected by a curving embankment across which now clattered a lime-green Dart train heading towards the city centre. Beyond, a grey-blue expanse of sun-brushed seawater lit up the horizon, and to his right, far in the distance, he could just make out the twin humps that marked the southern exit of the Dublin Port Tunnel. Why dump a body here, Mulcahy wondered. Why had he chosen this busy spot? Could he really have been so desperate to get rid of her? Or was he trying to make some point? Did he want her found quickly? So she wouldn't die?

'Can we be absolutely certain he didn't attack her here?' he asked.

Keane frowned and pushed his glasses a little further up the ridge of his nose.

'No way did anything happen here in the open. Nothing corresponding to the injuries she received has been found on the ground. It would've been impossible to inflict that much, and especially that type of, physical damage without leaving some traces behind.'

'And she couldn't have crawled here from somewhere else, trying to get help?'

'There's nothing to indicate it.' Keane shrugged. 'I mean, this whole area's been badly compromised, from our point of view. First by the fella who spotted her – he was staggering

234

home from a party half scuttered, having a piss through the railings when he saw her. Then by the ambulance crew and the lads from Fairview station. Because she was still alive, their priority was seeing to her medical needs rather than preserving the scene. The one bit of luck we had was the weather, which was fairly clear. But even at that, things got pretty churned up all round.'

'So there's no way of telling?' Mulcahy said.

'Ah, I wouldn't say that now.' Keane repositioned his glasses on his nose and grinned.

'Well, are you going to tell me, or do I have to guess?'

The CSM's tooth display grew wider. These techie guys were always such smart-arses. Spent their whole lives imagining themselves wise-cracking on some TV show.

'Well now, for instance, if you look closely at this excuse for a hedge over here?' He pointed to the straggly, exhaust-choked line of spiny hedging that grew against the railing. 'There's damage along the outside edge, our side that is, consistent with the sort of crushing and tearing you get from something heavy and – from the surface area affected – roughly horizontal, being tipped over it. We also got quite a few samples of skin that'd been scraped off by the spines.'

'So she was, what, unconscious when she was pushed over?'

'Or semi-conscious at best. It's a reasonable deduction given the proximity of the hedge, and the fact that there's no other evidence of her moving around much before she was found.'

'And you've got something else, right?' Mulcahy said. 'You mentioned something about him throwing "everything else" over after her. What was that?'

'What we're assuming at this stage to be the girl's clothes.'

'He dumped them with her?'

'Flung them after her, more like. With the result that all the stuff immediately around her got squashed into the ground by the crew that took her away. But one or two items, like some more bits that got snagged on the hedge, might provide us with something useful. Not that there's many of them. A thin cotton skirt, cut. A strappy silk sort of top, torn. We got both shoes for once – white stiletto heels, of course – and, even more surprising, we got the knickers. Not too ragged, so they may not have been ripped off her, but they're not in great nick, so we'll have to take a closer look. There might be something latent on them, you never know.'

'Can I see them? Everything, I mean.'

'Sure, it's all bagged up, ready and waiting for a process request.'

Keane walked over to a Garda Technical Bureau van that still had its back doors open. He mumbled something to a technician in the back, who handed out a sealed clear evidence bag containing a small bundle of clothing that couldn't have weighed more than six ounces.

'See what I mean?' Keane said. 'She must've been flashing the flesh for a bit of action last night and got more than she bargained for.'

'They look like party clothes, or the sort of things she'd wear to a club. Do we have any idea where she was before-hand?'

Keane pushed his glasses up his snout again, and rolled his eyes a little. 'You're the detective. All we can do is tell you where we found the stuff, what's on it and what we might surmise from that – if anything. But not yet, obviously.'

'Well, can you at least tell me what *these* might be?'

Keane bent to look at the bag. Mulcahy was crushing the plastic against the fabric inside, rubbing it gently between finger and thumb to try and get a better look at something. He held it up for Keane's perusal. Three thin red fibres, each a couple of inches long at most, were snagged on the glittery material that gave the top its sparkly sheen.

'Oh, yeah,' Keane said. 'I spotted some of those on the skirt earlier and took a couple off and bagged them up sep-arately. I can't say for sure but they look man-made to me. Some kind of plastic, maybe? My guess would be it's some type of netting, like what they use for thick plastic sacks, you know, for coal, logs, hundredweights of onions, that kind of thing. So they're unlikely to have come from any kind of clothing, unless our man has very unusual taste in clothes.'

'Something you might find in the back of a van, though?'

'I guess so, but obviously, like I said, we'll have to run tests before we can confirm it.'

'Run them,' Mulcahy said. 'Top priority. I'll get the authorisation sent through to you later.'

*

237

Although Brogan had asked him to get back to Harcourt Square as soon as he was finished, something in Mulcahy made him spin the wheel and turn the Saab back towards Dorset Street and the Mater Hospital. His route took him up the Clonliffe Road and past some of the citadels of Holy Catholic Ireland. On his left loomed the hulking concrete stands of Croke Park, high altar of the Gaelic Athletic Association, where his father took him to worship regularly at both hurling and football matches. To his right, almost facing it, was the great institutional edifice of Clonliffe College, once second only to Maynooth as a maker of the nation's priests, now all but defunct as a seminary such was the fall-off in vocations. Behind that lay the Gothic sprawl of the Archbishop's Palace, for decades the centre of clerical power and political sway in Ireland. More Victorian sprawl awaited him at the Mater. Brogan, he learnt, had been and gone. He made his way through the labyrinthine corridors and disinfectant fug to Intensive Care but wasn't allowed any further than the door. Not that he would have wanted to go in, anyway. One look beyond was enough, into the cubicle where the bruised and battered girl lay quiet and unmoving, breathing through tubes and with seemingly every electronic gadget known to medical science attached to her. Enough to let him close the circle and take into his heart what he'd known in his head and gut already; that the man who'd attacked this girl was unquestionably the same evil bastard who'd beaten and tortured Jesica Salazar. The same guy who'd cut up Grainne Mullins, too.

He left the Mater Hospital feeling sick, a hollow gnawing in his stomach that at first he didn't recognise but, as he wound his way south, began to realise was something he hadn't felt in years. Anger. Real, burning anger. Righteous anger. What he used to feel all the time when he was a fresh young cop with something to prove. Like when he first made detective and joined the Drugs Squad and he knew he'd found his vocation. A bit like falling in love – the world became a different place. But this feeling had eventually congealed into a cold, hard, angry focus day after day, year after year watching addicts wasting away in misery, squalor and criminality. Dull-eyed kids prostituting themselves to death for a few quid for the next fix. Girls barely old enough to conceive leaving their infant children wailing and starving while they went out shoplifting or whoring for a score. And all the while the bastards who fed their habits lived high on the hog in gated mansions in Kinsealy or on stud farms down in Kildare.

That was when the anger used to flow like lava through his veins. It gave him clarity and focus, drove him on, up through the ranks from detective Garda to detective sergeant to detective inspector – all in the space of ten years. It was an emotional state he'd have bet his life on never relinquishing. And yet here he was, back in Dublin, realising it had grown unfamiliar to him – how he hadn't really felt it since he'd gone to Madrid and become absorbed in statistics, policy, intelligence and initiatives, and the prestige of working for Europol. What had happened? Had he got lazy?

Bored? Maybe he had just matured. But some tectonic shift had occurred in his way of seeing things and he hadn't even noticed it happening. Maybe that's what he'd been missing over there. Not love or home or any of the soft, good things he'd assumed. But something harder, darker and fiercer, the lack of which hadn't even registered. But it was back now. And it felt good, natural and necessary to have it there, burning in his blood, stoking up his heart.

Phone cradled between her chin and shoulder, Siobhan looked up from her notepad as Paddy Griffin arrived back in the newsroom. She tried to catch his attention as he passed by on the far side of the room but, with just the one hand to wave with while she continued writing notes with the other, she couldn't attract his attention.

'I see, uh-huh,' she said, turning her attention back to the phone call again, flipping over a page of her notebook and scribbling. 'And I can quote you on that, can I?' She smiled as she got the response she wanted. 'That's terrific. You've been a great help. That's exactly what I needed.'

She put the phone down with a clatter and rushed over to Griffin, grabbed him by the arm and pulled him into Harry Heffernan's empty office.

'You won't believe this, Paddy.'

She shut the glass door behind her as Griffin parked his skinny behind on the edge of the desk, his arms folded, a man convinced he'd seen it all and who would take a lot of convincing that there was anything new in the world. Still his eyes glittered as he ran them over her, as always ready to indulge his star a little, not so much the professional that he couldn't enjoy a sly glance at her chest heaving in excitement.

'So what've you got now, Scoop?'

'This Spanish kid . . . the reason we can't track her down?'

'Go on.'

Siobhan's eyebrows pitched her story as effectively as her words. 'What that nurse told me about the girl being taken away by a crowd in uniform turns out to be even righter than we thought. I've just spoken to someone at air-traffic control who says they received statutory notice in the early hours of Monday morning that a Gulfstream jet would be inbound for Baldonnel Aerodrome with an ETA of nine a.m. This guy's a bit of a hothead about CIA renditions, so he decides to check it out and—'

'Hang on, for Christ's sake,' Griffin interrupted impatiently. 'What the hell's the CIA got to do with anything?'

Siobhan shook a hand at him to hush him up. 'Nothing. And if you'd be quiet a second, Paddy, you'd see that's what I'm trying to tell you.'

Like all news editors, he was incapable of waiting for a story to flow out, had to have it all in the first paragraph. She stared at him until he put both hands up, then pretended to zip his mouth shut before indicating that the floor was hers. She pushed her hair back and began again.

'Look, I'll make it easy for you. By law, the Air Corps has

241

to notify the Airport Authority of all military air traffic that crosses Irish commercial flight paths. So on Monday, this guy at Aer Rianta spots that, among the usual stuff – fisheries protection flights, air-sea rescues and the rest – there's something out of the ordinary. It's this Gulfstream flying into Baldonnel. Like I said, he's a member of one of those internet groups that monitor unusual flight patterns to track illegal CIA rendition flights. A concerned citizen, no less. With me so far?'

Griffin nodded, maintaining his silence, but rolled his eyes in exasperation.

'Okay, I'm getting to it. The flight is logged as coming in from an airbase in northern Spain, so he thinks something funny's going on. A good few rendition flights have gone through Spain, supposedly. And the CIA just love Gulfstreams. But when he checks this one, it turns out it's leased by the Spanish Air Force – so there's no obvious CIA connection.'

'And no story, either,' Griffin snapped, his frustration getting the better of him.

'No, not for him, maybe – but for us, yes. Because the guy keeps an eye out and the jet comes through bang on time, sits on the ground for three hours and then takes off pronto, on exactly the same flight path back to Spain.'

'So?'

'So those three hours correspond exactly with the time it would have taken for a Spanish military unit to get from Baldonnel airfield to St Vincent's Hospital and pick up a severely injured Spanish government minister's daughter from under Nurse Sorenson's nose at around ten o'clock on Monday morning. Do you get it now?'

Griffin's posture had stiffened, his back a fraction straighter, his eyes now much more alert.

'You're saying Mellado Salazar sent a military unit over here to get his daughter?' Paddy Griffin grinned, teeth bared like a wolf's, his arms unfolded now, fingers clutching the edge of the desk. 'Bloody hell!'

'I can't see how it'll read any other way.' Siobhan nodded excitedly.

'Christ that's a good one, alright. But what's at the bottom of it? There's got to be more.'

'More? The Spanish interior minister's daughter gets raped, and he sends the cavalry in to save his little girl, presumably not trusting our boys to do the job. How much more do you want?'

'Look, Siobhan, it's good but I can feel it in my gut – there's more to it.'

'Oh, for God's sake, Paddy!' Siobhan looked at her watch, then for extra impact shoved her wrist in Griffin's face pointing at the time. 'It's twelve o'clock already and I've still got tons of stuff to follow up on the actual attack on the girl. This bloody source of mine kept me waiting till late last night to unload all the really good stuff. I'm going to have enough on my hands just writing that lot up and checking it, let alone go off and find something else.'

He waved away her objections. 'No, shut up a minute and

listen to me. I'm not telling you to stop or to do anything other than what you've been doing all along. This is just an interesting sidebar as it is, but that doesn't mean we couldn't work it up into something better. Like, them coming over here could be seen as a kind of trespassing on our sovereign soil, couldn't it? I mean, they must've had permission from the Air Corps to land. But what if it was all a bit sneaky and under the radar? A favour from one minister to his Spanish counterpart, maybe? We could work up a hell of a big stink. "Spanish army – or even armada – invades Dublin", something like that. What do you think?'

Siobhan laughed, not sure whether to believe her ears. 'I think that would be completely outrageous and deeply provocative. Are you serious? Do you think we could make it stand up?'

Griffin grinned at her, his face wreathed in an expression of malevolent mischievousness. 'Damn it, we haven't given the government a decent hammering for weeks. As my old mentor Arthur Hayes used to say: "If the eejits are thick enough to hand us a stick, then we'd be bigger ones not to beat them with it." Harry'll be mad for it, I bet. I'll tell you what, I'll sort it myself. You concentrate on following up on the girl and the assault and what the Gardai are doing about it. But discreetly – we want to keep a lid on it until we see how it's all panning out. I'm still seeing that as the splash. Make sure it's absolutely airtight because we'll really want to stick it to them if they've cocked up on it. In the meantime, I'll get a couple of lads to start stirring things up on the political side. Who should we be talking to, do you reckon, about the flight, and nailing down all that stuff?'

'My Aer Rianta guy says he's happy to be quoted,' Siobhan said. 'But for the real confirmation you'll have to talk to the Air Corps Command, I suppose.'

Griffin batted the suggestion away. 'They'll just deny everything, give us the usual national security bollocks. I reckon we should go straight for the jugular. Why don't I try the Department of Defence? Whack 'em right between the eyeballs and ask for a statement from the Minister on why a Spanish military unit was here operating on Irish soil. If they deny it, we have them by the knackers. If they don't, then they'll just have to tell us where the authorisation came from, and then somebody else'll have one heck of a lot of explaining to do on the subject of cover-ups. Good girl yourself, let's get—'

A knock made him snap his head round as one of the subs poked his head around the door.

'What is it?' Griffin asked irritably.

'It's for Siobhan,' the sub said, all huff and attitude. 'A phone call. Says it's urgent.'

'Put it through to her here, on extension 538.'

The sub sloped off to transfer the call and Paddy Griffin headed for the door.

'I'll go ring Defence and then see if I can track down Harry. He'll want a heads-up on this straight away. And if that call's anything to do with the Spanish girl, I want to know about it.'

He slipped out the door and Siobhan snatched up the phone as soon as it rang.

'Siobhan Fallon,' she answered, wondering who could be ringing her now and how to palm them off as quickly as possible. But her eyes lit up as soon as she heard the voice at the other end. 'Have you got something else for me?'

She listened to the distorted voice coming down the line.

'Another one? Holy Jesus! Yeah, too right, I do. Go on . . .' was all she said before kicking the door shut with a thud, grabbing a pencil and a sheet of Harry Heffernan's headed notepaper and settling down at his desk, writing furiously.

Mulcahy arrived back to find the offices of the DVSAU had changed beyond recognition, packed with a sea of unfamiliar faces, buoyant with chatter. There must have been twenty, maybe thirty new arrivals, standing around, drinking tea or Starbucks, and the tiny incident room felt as crammed as a sardine tin in a glut. A few words of enquiry established that this influx of manpower was all Brendan Healy's doing, and that the man himself was due down any moment to conduct a briefing. Mulcahy moved through the throng, heading towards Brogan's office but was barely halfway there when he was waylaid by Maura McHugh.

'Hey, Inspector, do you have any idea what we're all supposed to be doing next?' she asked above the hubbub, perching herself on a desk edge while removing a sandwich from a paper bag and tucking into it.

'Not yet,' he said. 'Have you seen Brogan? How's it all going?'

She shrugged, then swallowed. 'It's a mess,' she said, echoing the words Brogan had used in describing the situation to him earlier. She then went on to tell him how things had begun to unravel as soon as the news of the assault on the girl in Fairview came filtering in. But things had really kicked off after Cassidy arrived out at the Scully family home in Blackrock.

The story that followed unfolded like a farce. Scully's parents had refused the sergeant entry to their house on the grounds that he was an hour early. Cassidy said he'd wait but wanted some proof that their son Patrick was actually on the premises. But while the parents repeatedly assured him that Patrick would soon be out of the bathroom, the minutes kept ticking away. Until Cassidy lost his rag and threatened to do them for wasting police time. At which point a fracas broke out, a forced entry was effected and the discovery was made that not only was Patrick Cormac Scully not in the bathroom, he hadn't been anywhere in the house for many hours and certainly hadn't slept the night there.

'I could hear the Sarge bellowing down the phone at the boss from over here, y'know, while it was all going off,' Maura continued, swivelling her eyes. 'After that she went straight up to Healy and I think he must've given her a terrible rollicking cos I've never seen her come back from anywhere so pale-faced. Jesus Christ, it was tense . . . Anyway, it's been mad here ever since. I've been on the phones, calling in anyone who's available. Most of these guys are giving up their free Saturday to help.'

Just as she was finishing, a fresh murmur of anticipation ran through the room and Mulcahy stood up to see a grim-faced Healy, flanked by Brogan and Cassidy, entering the incident room from the corridor. As they came in Healy surveyed the room, spied out Mulcahy and, with a jerk of his head, signalled him to join them up front by the whiteboards. Mulcahy pushed through the mass of bodies and positioned himself beside Brogan, trying to catch her eye to see how she was doing, but she avoided his gaze. Even Cassidy seemed unable to drag his eyes from the floor for once.

'Okay now, c'mon, a bit of whisht now, I'm going to have to keep this brief,' Healy began, nodding appreciatively as silence fell upon the room. He gestured vaguely behind him at the boards. 'I'm sure you've all gathered some idea by now of why you've been asked in today. In a few minutes, Sergeant Cassidy here and a couple of his colleagues will give you newcomers a crash course on the two hideous sexual assaults that have occurred on our city's streets this week. One last Sunday, another this morning – both of them off the scale in terms of violence but last night's stopped so short of murder, I'm telling you, it's a miracle we're not talking in those terms yet. In fact, there's a strong possibility that this second victim – a young woman, whose name we don't even know for now – will yet succumb to her injuries.

'I'm telling you, lads,' Healy continued, his brow furrowing even deeper, 'it's no exaggeration to call this the work of the devil. But don't forget it's a man who's attacking these young girls, a very dangerous, sick and evil man, who's out there committing these offences and leaving a trail of agony and grief behind him. But that's not the only trail he's leaving. And that's what we have to focus on. Every move this fella makes, he leaves a trace. And together we're going to find those traces, put them all together and track him down. Every single one of us, lads, we're going to work our bollocks off so that we can string him up by his. Are ye with me?'

There was a muted roar of encouragement from the crowded room but Healy put a hand up to quell it. 'Good men,' he continued. 'I'll be leading this investigation from now on, with Inspector Claire Brogan here on point and Inspector Mike Mulcahy assisting. Any questions you have, address them to Sergeant Cassidy or another of his team for now. I need to sit down with these guys right away and talk tactics.'

The murmuring rose loud again as Healy swept out, followed by Brogan and Mulcahy. The sound of Cassidy calling for quiet was the last thing they heard as they slipped into Brogan's office and closed the door. Healy made straight for Brogan's chair behind her desk.

'Any news on Scully?' Mulcahy asked her, as they dragged the two spare chairs away from the wall.

'No,' she shook her head vigorously. 'Not yet.'

'Good to see you here, Mike,' Healy interrupted sharply, obviously in no mood to waste time. 'Tell us what you got from the scene. Anything we can run with for now?'

'Not much that you don't already know from the prelims, Brendan. It looked to me identical in every significant respect, apart from location. I've absolutely no doubt this is the same offender.'

'I heard you were in the Mater Hospital afterwards. What took you down there?'

'Just wanted to see her for myself. Get the feel, you know?'

Healy nodded, tolerating the gesture as a good one. 'Anything else from the scene?'

'Three things struck me. None crucial, maybe, but worth mentioning. One was the location – major route, phenomenally busy. You must go past there yourself all the time. Opposite that row of shops on Marino Parade, near where the Clontarf and Malahide roads meet. Even in the early hours there's traffic constantly going by. This guy parks up and heaves a semi-conscious girl over four-foot railings and the hedge behind it. Vehicles passing, loads of first-floor viewpoints from across the road. Somebody *must* have seen something. And there were more sheltered spots available to him either side of where he did it, even within a few hundred yards. Which makes me think he must've wanted to be seen this time.'

'Interesting,' Healy remarked, looking at Brogan.

'Yeah,' was all she said in reply.

'Or maybe he wanted the girl found quickly,' Mulcahy added.

'So why not leave her on the pavement? Why throw her over the railings?' said Brogan.

'I don't know,' Mulcahy said. 'It was just a thought.'

'You have any more, Mike?' Healy asked.

'Yeah, some short red plastic fibres found on the girl's clothes. I've rushed them over for priority analysis. I thought I remembered seeing something similar in the Technical reports from the Jesica Salazar assault.'

'You're right, there was,' Brogan said. 'We thought she might have acquired them from the floor of the attacker's van.'

'That's what I thought. Good for a possible match, then. It would tie the attacker to both offences. Which brings me to point number three, regarding the van. Or rather *a* van, any van.'

'What about it?' asked Healy.

'Well, the CSM said he couldn't tell what kind of vehicle had been parked up on the pavement. I suggested he look for short wheelbase Transit type tyre marks and he said he'd have another look but didn't hold out much hope. The point is, if we do get an eye witness in Marino and they confirm a van was used, then maybe we should think again about Scully. I mean, what's the likelihood of him having access to another van – that's assuming Technical still have his father's van impounded.'

Brogan nodded that they did.

'Even with him on the run, you don't fancy him for it?' Healy said. 'Some coincidence, don't you think?'

'I honestly don't know. My concern would be the drugs. Could be he's more worried about the ecstasy possession charge. With his form, he'd be facing three to five years. I've known plenty of dealers who'd keep a stash of cash and a passport handy to do a runner from a stretch like that.'

'Well, obviously it's something we've already given a lot of thought to this morning,' Healy said, again glancing over at Brogan. 'Claire's come up with some pretty compelling new information about his academic interests that points it back towards him, which I'm sure she'll fill you in on in a moment. But for now, I agree, it's best we keep an open mind and widen the scope of the investigation. For now, we've got alerts out at all ports and stations and Scully's description has been circulated as priority one. What we've now got to consider is: what if it *wasn't* him?'

Healy paused to draw a breath. 'One thing I'm thinking we can say for certain, though, is there's almost no chance now of any Spanish political angle to this.' A tiny upward twitch of his lips betrayed a flash of relief before the stern mask of formality returned. 'It's not about who Jesica Salazar's father is. Are we agreed?'

Mulcahy and Brogan shared a glance.

'The guys in the ambulance said our new victim mumbled a few things before she was sedated,' Brogan said. 'Nothing useful for us, but they're pretty sure she's local.'

Mulcahy nodded. 'That was always a long shot anyway.'

'Good,' Healy said. 'Let them know at the embassy, Mike. Now, going forward . . .'

The next few hours went by in a tumult of briefings, job allocations and technical meetings. The strategy agreed on was to put a small specialist team in place to lead the manhunt for Scully using the Garda Network – a battery of electronic tools for monitoring the use of mobile and landline phones, cash cards, email, internet service providers and any other electronic signatures and imprints a suspect might leave – plus four detectives following up on Scully's known associates, relatives, ex-girlfriends and so on. In the meantime, the majority of the new bodies on board were to be thrown at the second incident, in a co-ordinated drive to collate as much information on victim, perpetrator and crime as was achievable in a condensed space of time.

As a result, by early afternoon the information on the second assault began to trickle through. The most important piece of the jigsaw provided an ID for the girl and, as a result, a location of sorts for the actual attack. A door-to-door inquiry in Pearse Avenue, Fairview, turned up a Mrs Fidelma Plunkett who was beginning to wonder why her daughter hadn't yet returned from a night out at a club up the road with friends. Alarm bells rang, a description of clothing matched the victim's, and a car was sent round. By mid-afternoon a team of detectives had gleaned enough information from shell-shocked relatives and friends, about the victim's background and movements, to give the key facts: nineteen-year-old Catriona Plunkett was a pretty dental secretary who'd gone out for a Friday night bop at the Kay Club up in Killester with her pals, drank a bit too much, felt a little tired and decided to leave early. The bouncer, pulled out of his bed, confirmed that he'd seen her leaving the club alone at around 12.45 a.m. Both these facts were subsequently confirmed by the club's exterior CCTV. At which point the trail went ice cold, until Catriona turned up half dead a couple of miles away in Fairview Park at 5.25 a.m.

Another team of four Gardai, led by Maura McHugh, had already been dispatched to seize and view the footage from all CCTV and traffic cameras covering the many roads and approaches that converged on Marino Parade and Fairview Park. But that was a mammoth task which could take days. One small fact that did bloom into significance out of the many flooding back was that yes, Catriona did have a cross and chain, a lovely gold one bought for her from Fields on Henry Street for her eighteenth birthday. Catriona loved it so much, her mother claimed, that she never took it off, not even to have a bath. Mulcahy knew it hadn't been on her when she was found and a double check with the hospital and Technical confirmed that it wasn't among the items dumped with her in Fairview Park either. He led a brainstorming session for case officers on the significance of crosses, chains, burning, branding and the rising level of violence – with some useful ideas emerging. Further out in the circle of operation, arrangements were put in train for Catriona Plunkett's item of jewellery to be identified with the help of staff at Fields, should an example be required for comparison purposes. It wasn't until after five that Mulcahy got out again, only to be called straight into Brogan's office where she and Healy appeared to be engaged in a private conference.

'Sit down, Mike. Claire said you should sit in on this,' Healy said to him.

'What's up?'

'Bit of an emergency. Last thing we need is another bloody distraction, but the press are on to us.'

Mulcahy shrugged. 'Hardly surprising, given the number of people we've brought in on this today.'

'Yeah, but this is a bit different, Mike. I've just had a call put through to me – from a tabloid journalist called Siobhan Fallon from the *Sunday Herald*. Wouldn't talk to anybody else but me. Wants me to tell her all about "The Priest".'

'The *Priest*?'

'Claire here says it's the nickname you came up with for our attacker.' Healy raised his eyebrows at him in a what-do-you-have-to-say-about-that expression. 'I'd've thought that with sensitivities towards clerical abuse being what they are, you could've been a bit smarter about—'

'Hold on a second, Brendan,' Mulcahy interrupted, doubly defensive at Healy's accusing tone and the mention of Siobhan. 'I didn't come up with any nickname. In fact, I'm pretty sure it was—'

'Forget that,' Healy snapped back. 'The point is, how did this Fallon woman get hold of it?'

255

'I've no idea. How would I know?'

'Do you know her, Mike?'

The question came from nowhere but he knew he couldn't afford to fluff it.

'Yes I do, as it happens. But I sure as hell didn't give her any information.'

'You're certain about that?'

'Didn't I just say so?'

Healy looked sideways at Brogan and gave her a nod.

'Glad to hear it, Mike. So how do you suggest we respond?'

'Well, do we know how much she's got?' Mulcahy asked. 'I mean, has she said yet what she wants, specifically?'

'She's being very cagey about her information and where she got it from. At first I thought she was just fishing but then she gave me some detail. She seems to have quite a lot of detail. More than she could have got since lunchtime from some newbie on the case. Most of it had to do with young Jesica Salazar.'

'So she did tell you what she wanted?'

Again Healy and Brogan exchanged glances.

'Yes, she did, Mike,' Healy said, licking his lips as if they'd suddenly gone as dry as dust. 'She was very specific about it. She wants a statement from me as to why myself and the Minister for Justice shouldn't be held personally responsible for the torture and near death of Catriona Plunkett, since we've both known for a week that there's a madman called The Priest loose on the streets of Dublin attacking teenage girls and we did nothing to warn the general public about it.'

'Shit.'

'My sentiments exactly, Mike. And, you can be sure as fuck, somebody around here is going to be neck-deep in it as soon as I find out where she got that from . . .'

12

He was skimming across calm, flat water, a strong breeze filling out the sail, pulling away towards a pale blue horizon, when the trill of his ringtone shattered the dream. He opened a bleary eye on the clock-radio beside the bed. What were they doing ringing him at a quarter to eight? He wasn't due on duty until eleven.

'Ungho,' he said into the mouthpiece, rubbing his face with the back of his hand.

'Have you seen the papers?' It was a woman's voice and for a second he thought it must be Siobhan. But of course it wasn't.

'What papers? No, no, of course not. Christ, I haven't even got out of bed yet.'

'Well you'd better have a good look at them before you come in, especially the *Sunday Herald*.'

With that Brogan clicked off, leaving him sitting fog-eyed on the edge of the bed, staring into the swirling spiral galaxies of the bedroom carpet, cupping his head in his hands like he was afraid it would roll off his shoulders. Why the hell had she done that? The evening before, they'd spent a good couple of hours hammering out a media plan with Healy, discussing the pros, the cons, what to give and how much to hold back. They'd eventually decided the only chance they had of dealing with the *Herald* would be to hold a press conference in which they did precisely what Siobhan Fallon had been accusing them of stalling on: warning the public. Or at least that's how Mulcahy had argued it.

It wasn't a political decision so much as a pragmatic one. As soon as the second attack happened, it had been inevitable that some press leakage would occur. The girl was local, her discovery was public, her family were upset and getting increasingly vocal about it. Siobhan Fallon, it transpired, hadn't been the first reporter to ring the Garda press office about it that day, but she *was* the first who refused to be fobbed off with the low-key information Healy had provided them with. Once she'd pulled the pin out of the grenade and lobbed it at them, the only way to go was full disclosure. Or at least as full as they could without handing out an open invitation to every freak, weirdo and pervert in the city to have a go for themselves.

On that issue, Brogan had been particularly forthright. 'Maybe Mike's forgotten what an irresponsible bunch of gougers the press in this country can be with a story like this, sir,' she'd argued to Healy. 'Especially the tabloid element who, you can guarantee, will seize on the more lurid elements and pump them up out of all proportion. The only outcome that is likely to generate for us is complete panic on the part of the public, and the possibility of copycat attacks. Our resources are limited enough without having to deal with that.'

It was a good point. They agreed which details would be definitely held back and Healy and Brogan went downstairs to conduct the hastily convened press conference at eight-thirty p.m. By then, of course, all but the late editions had gone to press, but that was half the point of doing it. Nobody could say they hadn't responded. It would be interesting to see who'd pick it up. Mulcahy, who'd gone home directly, flicked on the main RTE news bulletin and saw that they hadn't. A good sign, he'd thought. After which he'd tumbled straight into bed.

Now he pulled on a grey cotton sweater, jeans and a pair of trainers, thinking that if Brogan had gone to the trouble of warning him, he'd better go discover the worst. The streets were empty and he knew the shop where he usually bought his *Irish Times* and *Sunday Tribune* wouldn't be open yet. Long gone were the days when they used to sell the papers outside the local church after mass but he headed down that way anyway, past the imposing single-spired, grey stone building from which the mumble of a responsorial psalm was already reverberating through the chill morning air. Sure enough, across the road from the church and beside a shuttered-up pub was a newsagents he'd never noticed before and, miraculously, it appeared to be open for business, despite the early hour. Inside, he was greeted cheerily by a kid in a T-shirt and baggy surf shorts, who was dragging stacks of bundled newspapers out in front of the magazine racks that stretched the full length of one wall.

'Howya, grand morning,' the boy said without looking up.

Mulcahy barely grunted, his breath catching in his lungs as his eye roamed the newspapers arrayed in front of him. Almost every front page carried the same story, but most looked hurriedly cobbled together in a late-edition rush compared to the massive headline splashed below the *Sunday Herald* logo. THE PRIEST! it screamed across the full width of the page, dwarfing the heading FRENZIED RELIGIOUS RAPIST ATTACKS TEENAGE GIRLS that ran underneath. To the right and lower down, a smaller headline SPANISH TROOPS IN DUBLIN topped a sidebar running down the outside edge, a border of words framing two grainy, blown-up photographs of Jesica and Alfonso Mellado Salazar.

Fucking hell.

Siobhan's byline was all over the page, twinned with that of someone called Paddy Griffin, news editor. Hers alone headed up the 'exclusive' main story which focused heavily on the assault on Jesica Salazar but led, vividly, with the second attack, on Catriona Plunkett. As he pulled the paper open he saw there were five or six more pages of coverage inside, complete with pictures of Catriona Plunkett, her family, more of the Salazars and even maps and graphics illustrating the locations of the attacks. Where the hell had Siobhan got her information from? And so quickly? This wasn't so much a leak as a cracked main.

As he read on, Mulcahy was astounded by what a credible blend of accurate reporting and wildfire conjecture Siobhan's writing was – gruesome detail of the two attacks garnished with blood-curdling speculation about the terrors of having 'a maniac in our midst'. It was exactly as Brogan had predicted. There were even quotes from some of the medics who'd treated the two girls. Worse, though, was the fury with which, on the inside pages, both the Garda Commissioner and the Minister for Justice came under fire for incompetence and procrastination. The poor sods in the Garda press office had been caught on the hop – the only statement reproduced being the first one Healy had left them with. There it was, word for word, pathetically inadequate. The criticism tilted into the red zone as the time lag between the two assaults was highlighted; a years-old file photo of Brendan Healy in uniform, looking grim, was captioned: 'Could he have done more?'

As if that weren't enough, the leader page launched yet another vicious attack on the Minister for Foreign Affairs for shaming the entire country by allowing military representatives of a foreign power, albeit a friendly one, to barge into an Irish hospital and remove a patient. Were our medical and justice systems held in such low esteem by other EU nations that we couldn't be trusted with the care of their citizens? Surely the Minister should tender his resignation forthwith?

Mulcahy knew all the political stuff was piss and wind, but that didn't mean there wouldn't be hell to pay. He could picture all too well the repercussions: two ministers and a Garda Commissioner on the warpath, hundreds beneath them desperate to avoid the flak, frantic to find answers to the inevitable storm of questions that would be asked in the Dáil, and even more so to find scapegoats to throw to the slavering press.

And the woman whose bed he'd slept in on Wednesday was behind it all. How in the name of God had that happened?

He was still turning it over when he got into Harcourt Square at eleven. On the fourth floor, Brogan's office door was shut but a light was visible through the opaque glass so he stuck his head round it. She was sitting at her desk looking frazzled. He'd never seen her so much as glance at a newspaper before, but there was a collapsed heap of them strewn across the floor beside a jumble of box files.

'How goes it?'

'I'm sitting in the middle of the biggest shitstorm I've ever been involved in, so how do you *think* it's going?' she said, looking up from the file she was studying. 'Action this, review that, double check the bastarding other. By the way,' she paused, indicating the box files. 'I had to take those back from your office.'

He shrugged. 'The fallout's bad?'

'Nuclear.'

'Anything I can help with?'

'No,' she said, lowering her head again. Then, almost in

passing: 'Healy says he wants to see you, upstairs, soon as you get in.'

'Upstairs?' Healy rarely saw anyone in his office on the sixth floor, preferring to emerge occasionally to poke his nose into everyone else's business instead. 'Any idea why?'

Brogan shook her head. 'I've got enough crap on my plate without worrying about yours.'

He headed back to the lift, pressed the button for the top floor. There the accommodation was more salubrious. Even the difference in carpet grade was immediately obvious. His shoes sank into thick Garda-blue tufts the second he stepped out. Here on the sixth there was no open-plan space, just corridors and discrete offices, some with small secretarial areas outside with desks and monitors. These were mostly empty now, it being a Sunday. Except for Healy's, whose secretary was sitting there with her coiled hair and her two-piece suit, typing something on a screen.

'Go straight in, Inspector,' she said.

Apart from the standard-issue lamp on his desk, Healy's office couldn't have been less like Brogan's. It was four times the size, with a big oak desk, executive chair and three monitors. There was also a two-seater sofa and armchairs over to one side, plus an assortment of filing cabinets and bookcases. But above anything else it was spotlessly tidy.

'Come in, Mike, come in,' Healy said, getting up. He was looking tired, Mulcahy thought, noticing the dark semicircles forming beneath his eyes. When he put a hand out it was not to shake but to point at the straight-backed chair in front of his desk. 'Sit yourself down there. Can I ask Noreen to get you a coffee?'

Mulcahy refused the offer.

'Right,' Healy said, sitting into his chair again. 'You've seen the press, I suppose. Christ, we took some pasting there. The bloody Minister and Commissioner have been taking turns hauling me over the coals since six this morning. I'm telling you, if I could've got my hands on that reporter, Fallon, I know what *I'd* be doing with the rest of my days. Serving them out in Mountjoy prison for bloody strangling her.'

Mulcahy smiled as politely as he could.

'The thing is, Mike, we can't afford to be having leaks like that. I said to Claire last night that, after this settles down, I should get you to have a look into it to see if we could root out the rotten apple. You impressed me a lot yesterday, I don't mind telling you, so I was all the more surprised when Claire said she thought you knew Fallon. Then you seemed so offhand when I asked you about it, I thought, fair enough, we all know journos. And then, fuck me, what should drop into my inbox this morning but this. I'd like you to tell me what you make of it, Mike.'

Healy swivelled his computer screen round so that Mulcahy could see him double-clicking on his email queue, then on an attachment within the email he'd opened. He just had time to read the two-word message 'hacked off' before the media player launched a black subscreen which stalled a moment, then ran some good quality CCTV footage of two people, a man and a woman, approaching each other on the street, stopping to chat, then climbing into an open-top sports car.

Oh shit.

'I recognised *you* straight away, Mike.' There was a strain of incredulity in Healy's voice now. 'But, would you believe it, I had to ask a colleague who the woman was. She said she thought it might be Siobhan Fallon from the *Sunday Herald*. Tell me it isn't true, Mike?'

Mulcahy swallowed, completely wrong-footed. The video clearly came from one of the gate cameras outside Harcourt Square, and the imprinted timecode identified it as being from the previous Wednesday. No getting away from that. But how the hell could anybody have got their hands on it? More to the point, who had sent it? He immediately thought of Healy's exchange of glances with Brogan during the media meeting the night before.

He straightened up in his seat and looked Healy in the eye.

'I told you last night that I knew her, Brendan. And I also told you I hadn't given her any information about this investigation.'

Healy snorted. 'Sure, you said you *knew* her. But didn't you think it worth mentioning, especially last night, that you'd been off for a jaunt in her car with her only three days earlier? I'd call that one hell of an omission, Mike. I mean, you must see how that looks?'

It was Mulcahy's turn to become irritated.

'Of course I see how it looks. It looks like someone's trying to stitch me up.'

'So, what're you saying? You're trying to tell me this meeting didn't take place?' By now Healy was jabbing his finger at the screen.

'No, obviously it did. But what I'd like to know is who sent you this material. It's clearly malicious. Haven't you considered why someone would want you to see this?'

'Sure I have. So I'll tell you who sent it to me. "A friend" it says here. Untraceable, of course, but do you know what? Right now, I'm thinking, maybe they have been a friend to me. Or at least a hell of a better one than you've been.'

Mulcahy decided it was best to roll with that one. 'Brendan, as I keep telling you, I was not the source of this leak.'

'So you just happened to meet Fallon straight after you'd left a briefing regarding this very case, and at no stage did she bring up the subject of either Jesica Salazar or The Priest?'

'No, not as such.'

It would have been easier to lie, but he couldn't. That might only backfire worse in the long run if it ever emerged. And of course Healy pounced on it like a starving cat.

'What the hell does that mean, "Not as such"?'

There was only one answer left to him. 'It means she asked me if I knew about a Spanish girl who'd been attacked, and I refused to discuss the matter with her in any way, shape or form.'

'Jesus Christ!' Healy hissed at him. 'She asked you this on

Wednesday evening, and you didn't think it was worth mentioning to either Claire or myself?'

'No. How could I have known what Fallon was planning? Like you, yesterday, I just thought she was on a fishing expedition. I didn't think it was relevant.'

Healy stood up. He was seething now, his voice shrill, barely able to control himself.

'Relevant? I'll tell you what's bloody relevant. Someone's been leaking like a drain to this bitch all week, as a result of which I've had my arse chewed off and my prospects blown to buggery for Christ knows how long. And you couldn't even be bothered to give us a heads-up? I can't believe it, Mike, that you, of *all* people, who I've been carrying for months, giving you an easy time, waiting to pop you back into your bloody beloved Drugs Squad, could come in here and see me drowning last night, and you couldn't even be arsed to throw me a lifeline.'

That was it. He couldn't just sit there and take that. 'With respect, Brendan, that's bullshit. I spent most of last night busting my balls to come up with an intelligent media response that would leave us looking as good as we could in the circumstances. And now I come in here and find you're happier to believe some anonymous shit-stirrer—'

'Bollocks,' Healy cut in again, his finger jabbing the air. 'This is about loyalty, trust and fair play. And I'll tell you, this isn't my idea of any of them. Nor is it a decent return on favours done. So I'm telling you now, Mike, you can go fuck yourself as far as I'm concerned. Don't you come in here looking for favours from me in future, because I damn well won't be doing you any.'

In the event, Healy didn't have enough manpower to freeze Mulcahy out of the investigation completely. Later that day, he called to say he would be handing responsibility for liaising with the Spanish back to the Minister's office but, beyond that – and a distinctly chillier note to their day-to-day encounters – there was little practical difference to Mulcahy's role over the next few days as the investigation was ramped up beyond all previous measure. The long hours went by in a blur of frenetic activity, peppered by briefings, meetings and general slog. Healy might have considered himself to be leading the investigation but, as his chief representative on earth, Brogan was still in everyday charge. Much to everyone's relief, rumours that she was to be replaced by a big-hitter came to nothing as Healy's rearguard action, essentially a fight for self-preservation, was more effective than most would have anticipated.

So, for all that everyone felt the pressure increase a hundredfold, the most palpable effect was a welcome further injection of manpower and resources. For those on the ground the storm itself seemed to move off now, up to another level, the one above them where a war of words between press and politicians raged. Down below, a kind of bunker mentality set in, one where teeth were gritted, shoulders were squared and every member of the crew focused on one thing only – getting a result.

As for the world outside, it seemed to the Garda team as if madness had taken hold. Not just the city of Dublin but the whole of Ireland was in a full-blown panic over The Priest. From that Sunday lunchtime, the entire media apparatus had gone into absolute tunnel-vision hyperdrive. Every front page, every TV news bulletin led on the story. Every radio talk-show fell on the subject with pornographic glee, inviting every under-informed pundit, over-opinionated academic and the verbally diarrhoeic public at large to hash and rehash, corrupt and over-inflate the threat, oozing raw sentiment and fantasy, and above all whingeing about the incompetence of the Gardai, the government and anyone else they could think of blaming.

Mulcahy got through it all by adopting much the same attitude as everyone else. There was talk of an internal investigation to trace the source of the leak, but it was just talk. Mulcahy had his own suspicions – how could he not have? – but in the absence of any evidence, or the time to go find it, he was happy for things to stay as they were for now; not so bothered about clearing his own name as avoiding the risk of being stitched up by some ambitious Internal Affairs weasel keen for a quick and easy result. Tasked by Healy to review the case against Scully, he spent untold hours with his face glued to a computer screen reading and rereading all the initial interviews, poring over negative forensics reports, and going through the material on Scully's seized PC with a detective Garda from the IT Dept. There was nothing of interest there, no buried files, no hidden sado-porn, no password-protected portals to websites advocating the torturing and mutilation of young Spanish or Irish women.

He even ploughed through Scully's thesis work on the so-called Irish Inquisition, the title of which had understandably come close to giving Brogan a stroke. But it was nothing more than a dull historical account of the persecution of a young Irish noblewoman from Kilkenny who'd been tried for sorcery in the early fourteenth century. Scully had clearly been trying to work it up into a shocker but the material was doing its best to resist. Like everything else, it was a dead end that led Mulcahy back to the conclusion he'd reached earlier about Scully. He was an unsavoury character, there was no doubting that, and it was easy to see why Brogan had become convinced there was more to him than met the eye. Because indeed there was: he was a drug dealer worried he was being nobbled for something he hadn't done. And so he ran. But for now, at least, Mulcahy could turn up nothing further to link Scully to the attack on Jesica Salazar.

Having delivered his conclusions to Healy, the superintendent handed Mulcahy another poisoned chalice straight away, putting him in charge of the tips and leads team. As Brogan had predicted, the result of the press and public hysteria about The Priest, in information-gathering terms at least, was pandemonium. So much so that a rota of six guards had been assigned to field and respond to the deluge of phone calls, letters and emails coming in from the general public.

They all had to be followed up, wherever feasible: every

suspicious neighbour, every idiot with an axe to grind or just ringing in to share their fears, preoccupations and morbid fantasies. The prospect of further public humiliation as a result of missing a vital piece of information, especially one handed to them on a plate by a right-thinking citizen, simply didn't bear thinking about. Mulcahy became the filter. It was up to him to assess and prioritise, task initial responses, hand on to the appropriate quarter what wasn't pertinent to the team's own investigation, and pass up anything that was relevant, to Brogan, whose people would then do the onward enquiries. It was hard, intense work. It kept him busy, and so tired when he got home of an evening that he was unable to dwell on anything much else in his life. Not even Siobhan, the thought of whom still generated a maelstrom of contradictory feelings in him.

Coming out of Harry Heffernan's office that Wednesday morning, Siobhan Fallon was beaming so bright even the word-blunted subs perked up and took a look at her. Everyone had been taking a lot more notice of her. These last few days she'd never been so busy, never been anywhere near so big. Doing radio shows over the phone, TV news interviews in front of the brass *Sunday Herald* sign by the main door downstairs. Once, even, up here in the newsroom, much to the annoyance of every begrudger in the place. All that tutting when the camera crew set up their lights. She couldn't help wondering if it was because she was leaving the rest of them in the shade.

And now Heffernan had finally gone and bestowed on her the only acknowledgement of success that meant anything to him, or to any of the rest of them when it came down to it. He'd called her into his office and announced that he was going to talk to the chief exec about getting her that raise she wanted. Twenty per cent minimum, he'd said. It had better be. She'd already had a sniff that morning from Alan Hanley, the news editor over at the *Irish Times*. And a pal at the *Sunday Tribune* said her name had been mentioned as a possible poach over there, as well. If the ball kept rolling her way, she might be able to name her own price by the end of the week.

The very thought of it made her go weak at the knees but she kept up the face, scanning the room for Paddy Griffin. She spotted him perched on sports editor Brian Meany's desk, arms folded, half listening to what Meany was saying but one eye all the while watching her emerge from the lion's den. She shot two thumbs out at him and widened her smile still further. He grinned and batted her away with a flap of his hand. He'd already given her all the praise he could manage for one week. He had even offered to take her out for a slap-up dinner the night before, his treat. Or rather, his expenses. But she couldn't, as she'd been asked to go on *Questions and Answers*, RTE's political discussion show. She'd never had high-end TV exposure like that before. And she brought the house down. Every word she said, the studio audience clapped. And then they booed the junior minister who'd been dragged on from the Department of Justice. Even John Bowman, the presenter, was impressed and he'd congratulated her warmly after they wrapped up the show. 'We'd have had you on again,' he'd said. It was a shame they were retiring the show just as she got her foot in the door.

Still, the big time really did feel as good as she'd always suspected it would.

Even Siobhan was staggered by the strength of the public reaction. If it wasn't interviews and phone-ins on every talk show on RTE – and Lord knows they could keep you busy for two lifetimes in themselves – now the story was trickling out into the wider world. Sky News had picked it up, and the BBC as well. She'd even been interviewed by some Spanish radio station she'd never heard of. From experience she knew well how some stories can sprout wings and take on a life of their own. It happened all the time, whenever a little kid went missing or some politician was caught with his hand down a rent boy's trousers. But there was never any telling for sure which would be the stories that would really catch fire, take over the front pages and the news reports for days, even weeks at a time.

She'd had a gut feeling about The Priest but still she hadn't expected anything remotely like this. Every woman in Dublin, young and old, seemed to be in a panic, looking over their shoulders for fear of God or the devil or whatever else lurked in their sublimated terrors and desires. And all the other hacks in the city, from lowliest reporter to loftiest cultural commentator, seemed to be doing their level best to whip it up still further, and at every opportunity. Front doors were being reinforced, there had been a run on locks in the DIY shops, radio phone-ins were full of young wans saying how they could hardly sleep in their beds at night for fear. For her own part, she'd actually tried to calm things down a bit. Whenever she got the chance, she pointed out that this guy had only struck twice and he had never attacked anyone in their own home – so far as anyone knew. But it didn't make any difference. Hysteria had taken hold and showed no sign of releasing its grip any time soon. What could she do but ride the wave?

Success had its downside as well, though. Exciting and flattering as all the attention was, the fact that the world and his wife now turned to Siobhan Fallon whenever they wanted to know anything about The Priest was becoming a pressure in itself. She'd run out of anything fresh to say. And repeating the same things over again by rote was just plain boring. Fortunately, she had plenty of ammunition to fire off about the awful rates of unreported sex crime in Ireland, the government's shameful under-funding of this most sensitive area of law enforcement, and so on.

She meant every word of it. The facts spoke for themselves, providing you could unearth them. And she was spending every spare second digging up more, searching through statistics and government reports, gathering information from every rape crisis centre in the country, fielding calls from experts and academics who were bending over backwards to get their names into one of her pieces. Some were downright nasty, too, accusing her of all sorts of ignominy and infamy. Well, you got that reaction on lots of stories. And it wasn't like she wanted to be a voicebox for every woman in the country. Leave that to the social scientists and lecturers out in Belfield. No, this had been thrust upon her. She'd tapped into something deeper than just a story. And she'd keep right on digging away at it until she'd got every last inch of decent copy from it.

It was bloody knackering, though, and in the last two days she'd barely stopped to think. Now, by the time she got from Heffernan's office to her desk, her brain had filled to the brim again with things she had to do. But first a private satisfaction: an email to Vincent Bishop telling him where to stick his stupid bloody record needle. He'd been leaving messages, texting and emailing since Sunday. First congratulations, then peevish little jabs about why she hadn't been in touch – as if it wasn't obvious. Not least because she was too damn busy for anything other than work. And then last night, when she'd just got in from RTE on top of the world after her *Questions and Answers* triumph, her phone rang and she picked it up – naive fool that she was – thinking it would be someone calling to congratulate her, and there it was again, the scratch and hiss of the record player followed by Roy buggering Orbison, this time squeaking 'Love Hurts' at her.

'It fucking will do if you don't fucking stop this,' she'd roared down the phone at him – the few drinks she'd had in the green room at RTE helping that one along the way. But Roy just kept on singing and she'd slammed down the phone. That was the weird thing. It hadn't seemed to matter whether she was there to pick up the phone or not. The record played anyway. Was there anyone at the other end of the line, even? She'd dialled call return, but of course the number was blocked. Feeling dirty and tired then, she'd gone and run a bath and, settling in, listened to the late news on the radio, eventually drowning out all thought of it.

Now, though, a pay rise in the bag and her confidence at an all-time high, it was time to knock this on the head for good, she thought. All the exposure she'd been getting, she wouldn't need to be beholden to the likes of Bishop for decent stories any more. They'd come by themselves. She tapped the space bar ready to compose the email. Then she thought, stuff that, and got her phone out. This was a message she'd rather deliver in person.

'Somebody wanting to talk to the ranking officer,' one of the tips team called across the room to Mulcahy, holding up an imaginary phone as substitute for the headset he was wearing.

'Why?' Mulcahy asked, annoyed at having his attention taken away from the prioritisation list he was trying to put together on his computer.

'Some old copper, won't talk to a mere mortal like me,' said the uniform with a sneer.

'Okay, put him through.'

The voice was thin but amiable, the accent from somewhere in Munster. 'Are you looking after that Priest case?'

'Yes, I'm Inspector Mulcahy. How can I help you, sir?'

'Oh, now, don't you be sirring me. I only ever made it to sergeant before I retired.'

Mulcahy's barriers dropped a notch or two. 'You were in the force?'

'I was indeed, yes,' the man answered, sounding like he'd still like to be. 'Sergeant Pat Brennan, retired. It's been a few years now, mind – and I didn't go till I was pushed.'

'Good for you. My old man served the full term, too. Broke his heart to leave, truth be told. Maybe you knew him, Inspector John Mulcahy?'

There was a thoughtful silence at the other end of the line, a brain flicking through the Rolodex of possible acquaintance, and then: 'Ah no, not *Johnny* Mulcahy from Dun Laoghaire! You're his boy?'

Mulcahy was happy to indulge the wave of nostalgia that washed out from the phone. He loved hearing stories of his father and his colleagues, and of their times. He'd grown up on them. Invariably they sounded like they came from a golden age of innocence before drugs, organised crime and serial sex attackers had taken the bloom off the holy island of Ireland. This guy was from a slightly younger generation, but he'd still spent virtually the whole of his career in the one place, Rathgar Garda Station. That almost never happened nowadays, when uniformed guards were regularly moved around.

'The thing is, being in a place for so long, you get to see and hear things that wouldn't come your way otherwise. You get a feel for people, you know?'

'I do,' Mulcahy said. 'So what've you got for us?'

'Well, we're going back a few years now, but do you know Palmerston Park?'

'Sure I do, I grew up in Milltown.' Mulcahy had often wandered past the semicircle of elegant Victorian villas on his way home from school.

'Like I said, this is going back a few years, but there was a young fellow lived there. Sean Rinn was his name, from a very good family.'

The name sounded vaguely familiar to Mulcahy.

'His grandfather was a High Court judge,' the sergeant continued. 'But the boy was a nasty piece of work. Got into a few scrapes with me in my time, but of course Chief Justice Rinn was always there with a word in someone high up's ear to get him off.'

A note of whingeing resentment entered the old man's voice, the same note that featured in so many of the calls they received; Mulcahy was instantly inclined to put his barriers back up.

'And this has what, exactly, to do with the case you're calling in about?'

He must have said it a bit harshly, because the old guy started apologising. 'Ah, the wife told me not to go bothering you with my old stories. Sure, what good's a name to you? I never managed to pin anything on him myself. It's just that when I saw the stuff in the paper about The Priest, I thought of Rinn, and figured maybe I should give you a call, on the off-chance, like.'

279

Mulcahy felt a twinge of guilt. The man was only doing his duty, after all. 'Well, give me what you've got and we'll look into it.'

But all the sergeant had was a few vague, meandering stories about a number of violent 'sex pest' attacks, as he put it, that occurred in and around Palmerston Park in the mid- to late eighties, which he'd been convinced this guy Rinn was responsible for but could never pin on him.

'CID just refused to have a look at him, because of who his grandfather was,' Brennan said. Which was entirely plausible at the time, Mulcahy knew, although the absence of any shred of evidence was likely to have swayed them even more.

'Or maybe it wasn't him?' Mulcahy suggested.

'Oh, it was him alright. One girl got a good look and gave us a description that convinced me. But I didn't have anything to back it up. Not with the judge riding our backs over it.'

'So what happened?'

'Well, there's not that much more to it, except that a few months later the attacks just stopped – suddenly, just like that. And guess who'd been sent away at exactly the same time?'

'Sent away as in sent down?'

'No such luck,' the sergeant tutted bitterly. 'No, sent away as in packed off by the grandparents. They sent him off to All Hallows to train for the priesthood.'

'The priesthood?' Mulcahy's ears pricked up again.

'You heard me right.'

'How long ago are we talking about, Sergeant?'

'Well, eighty-eight or eighty-nine, I suppose. No later than that.'

'And what about after that? Any more attacks?'

The line went silent for a second or two. 'No, they stopped.' The old sergeant was sounding more defensive than ever. 'But that's just my point.'

'And that's it? That's the connection you made with The Priest?' Mulcahy threw his eyes heavenwards.

'Yes but . . .'

Mulcahy's mobile rang. He snatched it off the desk and saw the caller ID was Brogan's.

'I'm sorry, Sergeant, I have another call. Give me your number and we'll get back to you.'

He asked Brogan to hold while he scribbled the number down and promised the old man somebody would call him back for the details.

'Claire, how can I help you?'

'Any sign of things slowing up over there?'

A swish of noise in the background gave him the impression she was calling from a car.

'You're kidding, right?'

'I wish. The press office guys are going ballistic. Apparently it's absolute lunacy over there. They want an extra body to field press enquiries. I thought maybe you could spare one of your guys?'

'Not a chance. The phones are ringing off the hook.'

'Christ, what a mess. I told you this would happen.'

'Yeah, you did,' he said.

'What in the name of God are you talking about, Siobhan?'

Either Vincent Bishop was the best actor she'd ever had the bad fortune to encounter, or he really, genuinely, categorically didn't have a clue what she was on about.

'Look, calm down. Or at least sit down, would you? You're embarrassing everyone. What's the matter? And what the hell has Roy Orbison got to do with anything?'

He was holding the CD case up at her, its clear plastic wrapping flaring under the restaurant lights. Shaking his long, narrow, lank-haired head like she'd slapped him in the face or something. Which she had, sort of. It'd seemed such a great idea on the way over: the spike of anticipation as she strutted into HMV and bought the copy of *Roy Orbison's Greatest Hits*, the rush of satisfaction when she thrust it at him as soon as she'd reached the table and hissed: 'Get yourself a fucking CD player, Vincent. You can afford it.'

Didn't seem such a great idea now. She'd seen more than her fair share of gawps of shock and surprise in her years of door-stepping people for the job. The full gamut. Real and put on. But she'd never before witnessed anything like the look of naked incomprehension that currently held Vincent Bishop's wan features in a gape of slack-jawed confusion. He couldn't be faking that, no way.

She had intended to walk straight out again. Now she was stuck, as if her shoes were glued to the floor right there in the middle of a packed-out Marco Pierre White's, of all places. Half the faces in there, staring at her now from every other table whispering, nudging, sniggering over their lunches – were fellow hacks, for Christ's sake. What in the name of God had possessed her to do this here?

'Come on, Siobhan. This is really not acceptable. The whole place is staring at us like we're a pair of spares. Or worse. I think you owe me an explanation, now.'

Oh, sweet Jesus . . .

It wasn't until a couple of hours later that it came to Mulcahy. He'd gone out to get some lunch and was coming back, a latte in one hand and a beef and coleslaw sandwich in the other, obsessing over how, the night before, exhausted and with too much wine in him after yet another takeaway meal at home, he'd called Siobhan to tell her what he thought of her. But greeted by her messaging service he'd found himself suddenly tongue-tied and rung off. *I don't think we should see each other again*, he'd texted instead. An act that mortified him now every time he thought about it. Not only cowardly, but bloody presumptuous as well.

That's what was going round and round in Mulcahy's head when, out of the blue, it struck him. From nowhere. What that old sergeant, Brennan, had said to him on the phone earlier. About some young kid called Rinn. He *had* seen the name Rinn somewhere before, he was sure. Written somewhere. He racked his memory but it still wouldn't come.

The first thing he did when he got back to Harcourt Square was slip into Brogan's office. She was out somewhere but the boxes of files were still where he'd last seen them. Except that a messenger was there, too, preparing to load them onto a trolley. He was a small, frail-looking man in his mid-fifties, his balding head a gleaming network of oiled-down comb-over strands.

'These are the boxes that are going back to the archive, right?' the messenger asked Mulcahy, his accent so thick with old Dublin it should have had a preservation order on it.

'If that's what you've been told,' Mulcahy said. 'But hang on just a sec, I need to grab something from one of them.'

The messenger tutted loudly and screwed up his face. By now Mulcahy had a third of the files out of the main box, strewn across the floor. 'Look it, are they ready to go or not?'

'I'll only be a minute,' Mulcahy insisted. 'I'll know what I want when I see it. Why don't you have a smoke or something while you're waiting?'

'Ah now, I don't know about that.'

Mulcahy put his hand in his pocket and quickly dug out his pack and lighter.

'Here, go on over to the window. No one will ever know.'

The man nodded, looked around to be on the safe side, then took the cigarette and strolled over to the open window. Mulcahy heaved out the last armful of files and, bingo, there it was in his hand. He knew it straight off: a buff folder with a scrawl of previous recipients on the front, and a few loose-leaf typed reports inside. Case No 6B420703SSA: Coyle/Temple Road, D6, 03/08/09. In the status box the handwritten word 'Active' had been obliterated by a red stamp – NFA.

He quickly opened the covers and recalled the details as soon as he started reading. He scanned the first page quickly. Mrs C. Coyle, walking home from the Luas stop in Milltown . . . attacked . . . dragged into a garden . . . screams alerted the householder and a passer-by . . . assailant ran off . . . victim suffered bruising . . . clothing ripped. He shuffled through the paperwork to the back, saw what he wanted. Two sheets of paper with *Witness Statement* printed across the top.

The first statement was from the householder, Quigley, who'd scared off the attacker. Nothing out of place there. But the second, that was it. A taxi driver who said he'd heard screams as he was passing, and had gone to help, whereupon he'd found the householder tending to the victim. No sign of the assailant. Mulcahy flipped over the page to the end of the document and there it was, the driver's name, typed and signed at the bottom, alongside the home address he gave. He knew he'd seen it before. The name the sergeant had given him, Sean Rinn. And still living in Palmerston Park, just around the corner from where the woman was attacked.

Mulcahy heard a cough and looked up. The messenger was standing by the window, stubbing out the cigarette end on the metal sill outside.

'They always say they'll be ready for me,' he moaned to the unlistening city outside. 'But they never bleedin' are.'

The house on Palmerston Park was about as grand a semi-detached villa as it was possible to possess in Dublin. Late Victorian, solidly brick built, it rose through three floors of diminishingly elaborate casement windows, the uppermost arched attractively and poking out from a fine mansard roof. Like all the houses overlooking the quaint semicircular park opposite, it was set back from the road by a low granite wall topped by black spearhead iron railings. Only the choice of hedging behind them differed. For some it was laurel. For others privet. For this one, the choice had been an impenetrable, close-clipped Irish yew.

One hell of a place for a taxi driver to be living, Mulcahy thought, as he walked through the open gates, noting the satisfying crunch of gravel as he stepped onto the drive. But immediately he stopped in his tracks. A small arc of grass was all that remained of the front lawn. Most of the garden had been carved away to make more space for parking, although there was plenty of that already in front of the huge detached garage, converted from a coach house, over to the left hand side. What caused him to halt was a van – a filthy, but still discernibly white, Transit – that was parked in front of the garage. It was just the type described by the eyewitness in the Jesica Salazar case, and caught on the edge of a CCTV frame pulling in where Catriona Plunkett had been dumped in Fairview Park. Sure, there were thousands of similar ones in the city, and they still hadn't even pin-pointed the precise make or model they were after, but its presence on this driveway immediately put Mulcahy on the alert, the hackles on his neck tingling.

He mounted the double step to the stout, six-panel door and gave the large brass bellpush a shove. He was rewarded with an old-fashioned jangle from somewhere deep within the house – but nothing else. He waited a minute, then tried again. No response. He was thinking about the van again, wondering why nobody was answering the door when he thought he heard something, a clatter of tools, maybe, coming from round the back? Of course, it was a fine day – they might not have heard the bell if they were out in the garden. Mulcahy walked over to a narrow passage between the house and garage, where a wooden gate was open. He went through and at the far end came out into a magnificent garden, at least fifty metres in length, with mature beech and apple trees, a profusion of colourful flower beds, and a design sense straight out of a homes magazine. Only when he stepped on to the patio did Mulcahy spot a man on his knees, surrounded by planks, a pile of soil and other build-ing materials, working on the far side of the garden. He was wearing camouflage-style combats and a thin, heavily soiled white T-shirt, and the muscles rippled on his arms and back as he worked.

'Mr Rinn?'

The man straightened his back as suddenly as if he'd been lashed with a whip but otherwise stayed in the same position, his arm outstretched with a lump hammer in it, not even turning.

'Mr Sean Rinn?' Mulcahy tried again. The man slowly swivelled round now, his eyes shielded by the tatty peak of an army-style baseball cap.

'Get out! Get out or I'll have the Guards on you,' he shouted suddenly, his face contorted in anger. Or was it fear? He stood up and began to advance, holding the hammer out threateningly, until Mulcahy put a hand up and pulled out his warrant card.

'I *am* the Guards,' Mulcahy said. 'Now put that bloody hammer down and stop acting the goat. I need to talk to you.'

That seemed to do the job pretty quickly. The man dropped the hammer on the patio with a clatter and immediately started wringing his hands. Something here wasn't right.

'Are you Sean Rinn?' Mulcahy asked, approaching him carefully.

The man shook his head, the peak of his baseball hat swishing the air in front of him.

'No, sir, he's out. I'm just doing some work for him, laying the path, like.' His accent was flat and uneducated, with the pinched nasal quality of the Irish midlands. The way he spoke, Mulcahy figured he wasn't the sharpest knife in the box. Probably been in trouble with the Gardai before, too, given the anxiety he was currently displaying.

'Any idea when he'll be back?'

'Didn't say, sir.'

Mulcahy took a look around. Everything seemed normal enough now. He'd just startled the guy. 'Do you work here regularly?'

'Once a week, sir, on the garden. I just gets on with what he tells me.'

Mulcahy nodded. 'And that's your van outside, not Mr Rinn's?'

'N-no, sir,' the gardener stammered, anxiety seeming to get the better of him again. 'It's mine, sir.'

'Right, then, I'd better let you get back to work,' Mulcahy said, deciding there was nothing further to be gained from the conversation.

He scribbled a note on the back of a business card, asking Rinn to get in touch, and popped it through the letter box, then went and sat in his car. He shook his head. What in the name of God was a taxi driver doing living in a house like that? Not to mention employing a gardener? He looked at the case file lying on the passenger seat beside him. What to do? He was enjoying his time out of the office, away from the ceaseless ringing of the phones and his computer screen. But, as likely as not, old Sergeant Brennan was just a grumpy old fucker with a grudge, just as Rinn witnessing an assault was probably a complete coincidence.

Mulcahy looked at his watch. Plenty of time, and besides, he was out here now. He snatched up the file and opened it again, turning to the victim's statement and scanning down through it. The woman stated clearly that none of her belongings had been taken. No missing cross and chain, nor any mention of one. He flipped back to her details: Caroline Coyle, 22 Cowper Road, Dublin 6. Only a minute up the road. DOB 17.6.78. That made her, what, thirty-one now – thirty at the time of the assault? She was way outside the victim profile; all the others were teenagers. Even Grainne Mullins was a teenager at the time of her attack. He thought of what his visit to Grainne had turned up and decided that wasn't likely to be repeated here. The victim was clearly a respectable, articulate woman. The investigation had been thorough, as far as he could see. But they'd had nothing to go on. She was attacked. Her assailant got spooked and fled, leaving no trace of himself. It happens. A woman that age would probably be out at work at this hour of the day. But where was the harm in trying? He got his mobile from his pocket and tapped in the phone number listed in the file.

The first thing that struck Mulcahy about Caroline Coyle was how wealthy she looked. He'd half expected it, given the shimmering Jaguar coupé parked on the driveway of 22 Cowper Road, a classic Rathgar townhouse with a fan of white granite steps leading up to a double-pillared entrance. But when she opened the shiny red front door, Mulcahy was almost knocked over by the air of money and refinement that wafted out. And from her own carefully groomed person, as well.

She invited him to 'come through' and his eyes could

hardly decide what to land on. Everything in sight was stunning, from the hand-woven carpet on the floor to the polished and gilded antiques that glittered from every nook. He thought he spotted a painting by Paul Henry in the hall, and he was sure the enormous oil painting above the fireplace in the sitting room she led him into was by William Orpen: a glorious scene of a young woman in a white dress reading in a sun-dappled green garden. He'd seen one similar on the *Antiques Roadshow* a month or so before, valued at some astronomical figure.

It was only when Mrs Coyle smoothed her dress beneath her hips and sat down on a sofa opposite him that he noticed how young she looked. On the phone she'd expressed surprise that he was following up, a year on, but he'd said it was routine. He'd more or less dismissed her as a possibility for The Priest's sick attentions the instant she'd opened the door. Now, again, he wasn't so sure. Beneath the poise, the make-up and the perfectly styled hair was a face that could probably quite easily pass for an eighteen-year-old's. When she told him she'd been on her way home early from a fancy dress party, his ears pricked up.

'I'd gone as a tart,' she said. 'As in vicars and tarts. With Daithi, my husband, who was supposed to be the vicar.'

'Vicars and tarts?' Mulcahy asked, bemused.

'An English thing we used to do when we were at Trinity together, and one of our pals decided to revive it. The boys dress up as priests, the girls as, well, slappers, I suppose. But Daithi got delayed in surgery – some emergency procedure he had to perform – and I was forced to go along to the party on my own and wait for him.'

She'd already told Mulcahy that her husband was a surgeon, which went some way to explaining their wealth, but he still couldn't imagine how the man could have accumulated so much just by scalping patients.

'Anyway, I'd been there a while when one of Daithi's juniors phoned to say there'd been a complication and he wouldn't be coming at all, and I couldn't bear to stay on without him.' She paused, biting her lower lip a touch shamefacedly. 'I think I must have had a little too much champagne. In fact, I'm sure I did, because normally I'd have jumped straight into a taxi. Especially wearing that outfit – although I did have a coat on, too. But for some reason I caught the Luas. The tram was a novelty for me and I knew there's a stop just down the road from here and I wanted to try it out and . . . what a stupid, stupid fool I was.'

Mulcahy was about to assure Mrs Coyle that people using public transport were as entitled to a safe journey home as anyone, but she rushed on, explaining how she'd felt 'a little drowsy' and missed her stop but woke in time to get off at the next one, and so began walking home.

'By then I was glad of the chance to get some air. So much so, I even passed up the chance of a taxi home, can you believe it? God, how I beat myself up later for not taking it,' she sighed.

'A taxi?' Mulcahy asked. 'I didn't see any mention of a taxi in your statement.'

'Well, no, you wouldn't have. Like I said, I didn't take it. I told him I was enjoying the fresh air too much, and it was only a few hundred yards.'

'What do you mean, you "told him"? Are you saying a taxi driver offered you a lift?'

It was a small point but one that, in the circumstances, rang alarm bells. It was illegal for taxi drivers to canvass fares and any driver caught doing so risked losing their licence.

'Well, maybe it was a little unusual, now you mention it,' she replied, and he saw a little flicker of alarm fire up in her eyes. 'But his light was on when he pulled up and I didn't think anything of it. I just said thanks but no thanks and walked on. You don't think it was him, do you?'

'I don't know what to think,' Mulcahy said quickly, wanting to get his next question in. 'Did you happen to get a look at the driver?'

On her face, he could see the scared thoughts taking hold, tautening her pale, pampered skin, making her look still more like a child in grown-ups' clothes.

'Um, I . . . I don't know. I mean, it was dark by then. I remember him pulling in beside me, and his window was down. But he was on the far side, in the driver's seat. I don't think I even looked in. Why would I? I just remember him calling me, offering me a lift, and I said, "No thank you, it's much too nice an evening", and . . .'

Her voice trailed away, her brow furrowed in concentration. Mulcahy could see that the assault had hit her deeper than she'd given away at first. But he had to take her through it again.

'Did he drive off straight away? Do you remember what kind of vehicle it was?'

'No, I don't, really. Only that he offered. All I was thinking about was how much I was loving the evening air on my face and on my legs . . . Oh, I must have been so drunk, and I didn't even realise it. And in that silly outfit, too. I might as well have gone begging to be attacked.'

She plunged her face into her hands and Mulcahy thought she might be crying. But when she drew them away and looked at him again, there was no trace of tears, just embarrassment.

'Maybe you could tell me what happened after that?'

Mulcahy knew it all already from reading her statement but he wanted to hear her tell it again. She'd walked on, she said, past the big houses on Temple Road with their huge front gardens, without a care in the world, or so she thought. Then it happened so suddenly: her attacker came from behind, clamped an arm around her neck and dragged her into one of the gardens where it was pitch dark. It was her screams that had brought the householder out. In response to Mulcahy's prompts, Mrs Coyle confessed she couldn't remember anything about the second man who came to her aid other than that she'd been told he was local, and no, she wouldn't have remembered the first one, Mr Quigley, either, except that she had called in on him a month or so later to thank him for rescuing her. It had all been such a shock.

Mulcahy smiled sympathetically, interested to note that she clearly hadn't been told that one of her rescuers was a taxi driver. He had no intention of telling her now, either, he thought, wondering what were the chances it was the same one who'd offered her the lift. In which case it would have been Rinn. Was it possible that he'd been following her?

Mulcahy decided to wrap up the interview. Mrs Coyle was seeing him to the door when he asked her if she was sure the attacker hadn't taken anything from her, or whether she'd noticed anything missing afterwards. She smiled and shook her head, but then ran a hand across her chest in an unconscious grasping motion and seemed oddly preoccupied as she opened the door.

'Why did you ask me that?'

'What?'

'About me missing something.' There was a tremor in her voice and a look of real fear in her eyes. 'You think it might have been this fellow, The Priest, the one on the news, don't you?'

Mulcahy was surprised but wary of acknowledging that it was the only reason he was looking at her case again. 'It was one of a number of possibilities.'

She nodded, then hacked a sharp cough into her hand.

'Jesus Christ, he might have done *that* to me,' she whispered. And suddenly her legs seemed to buckle but Mulcahy caught her before she went down. He helped her back inside and sat her on a chair in the hall. She was shaking like a leaf.

'He would have, wouldn't he?' she said, her face as white as a sheet beneath the sheen of make-up.

'You had a lucky escape either way, Mrs Coyle, but these other attacks have only started recently and the likelihood has to be that it wasn't the same man.'

Anything to reassure her.

'No,' she insisted, 'you don't understand. It must have been him.'

He stepped back, there was such certainty in her voice. 'Why do you say that?'

'When I took the costumes back to the shop a couple of days later, they made an awful fuss because the crucifix from Daithi's vicar's costume was missing. The *cross*. They wanted something outrageous like fifty euros for a replacement. I thought they'd lost it themselves as Daithi hadn't so much as tried his costume on. But then I remembered that we'd looked at them together and laughed about them the night we got them home. And I knew I'd seen it – a big, cheap old brassy thing. So I paid up, thinking it would turn up somewhere eventually. But it never did. Now I can't help thinking maybe I wore it myself that night, as a bit of a joke, on impulse. You know, to go with the tart's outfit. And I forgot about it afterwards. From the shock, maybe? I never made the connection before. I mean, I can't be certain. It never even occurred to me until now.'

Back in his car, Mulcahy sat and waited for his heart to stop thumping and wondered what the hell he should do next.

He'd done his best to calm Caroline Coyle, then left her to her own thoughts. But what she'd said had unsettled him: it wasn't what he'd been expecting. And hadn't it all come out just a little too easily? He decided he'd better put the brakes on and think things through clearly. Even Mrs Coyle herself hadn't been a hundred per cent sure about the cross. She admitted it was the first time it had struck her. Stranger things had happened. People saw stuff on the television and read about it in the papers and assumed the same had happened to them. It was something they had to deal with over and over again while handling the tips lines at Harcourt Square. Nobody realised better than himself now how some people were capable of absorbing external events and weaving them into their own personal narrative. But it was a shock to see it happen right in front of his eyes – if that, indeed, was what had happened here. To his mind, it still merited further investigation. Careful, dispassionate investigation. He'd have to get Brogan to set someone onto it as soon as he got back. But he also knew he'd have to be careful how he put it to Brogan. She'd been acting twitchy around him ever since he'd done the Scully review for Healy and the last thing she'd appreciate would be him bounding up to tell her he'd pulled another rabbit out of a hat.

Stepping back from it, he could see now that letting Sergeant Brennan's witterings get so far into his head had been a mistake. Even if Mrs Coyle had been solicited by a taxi driver that night, even if it had been this guy, Rinn, who was to say he'd been the attacker as well? And as for The

Priest, the one thing they knew for sure about him was that his targets had all been teenage girls. And anyway, he used a van, not a bloody taxi. His memory snagged on Grainne Mullins again. Hadn't she said she'd only just been dropped off by a taxi when she was attacked? But the taxi driver was gone by then. He'd dropped her off early so he could get petrol. Could it have been a ruse? Had the driver maybe parked somewhere and come back for her? Christ, it was all coulds, mights and ifs. The best thing he could do was lay it out for Brogan when he got back. That way he could stay on his side of the line and she could follow it up if she wanted to. If it came to anything, she was welcome to the credit.

13

Any fears Siobhan might have had that a bigger story could come along and knock The Priest off the front pages never materialised. She was busier than ever. Even her mortifying showdown with Vincent Bishop in Marco Pierre White's had produced some upsides. Prime among them, of course, being that Bishop had cooled off faster than a streaker in an ice storm. Crazed outbursts in public places were never going to be okay in his book. He had made that quite clear, despite her garbled, on-the-spot apology – in which she attributed her inappropriate eruption to crossed wires, stress, overwork and just about anything else she could think of as she anxiously glugged most of the bottle of St Emilion Grand Cru he'd ordered to go with the medium-rare rib-eye lying uneaten on his plate. She hadn't heard from him since, which suited her just fine.

But there were other benefits, too. As expected, given the number of her fellow hacks who'd witnessed it, a few snibby comments regarding her outburst appeared in the *Irish Independent*, *Mail* and *Sun* – PRIEST-BREAKER UNLOADS ON

BISHOP, that kind of thing. But as they had nothing to pin the incident on and as, like herself, Bishop had refused to comment to enquiring hacks, the tongue-wagging died down as quickly as it had flared up. An appearance in the gossip columns, though, was a first for her and could be regarded as yet another indication of her leap into the media stratosphere. It certainly hadn't dented Heffernan's determination to get her that pay rise. Quite the opposite, if anything. Next morning he'd strolled up to her desk, winked at her and said: 'I see you're working on keeping your profile up. Nice one.'

He'd even had a word with Griffin and instructed him to assign a couple of editorial assistants to help research her follow-ups. They were just kids, and utterly clueless, but at least they were able to help with the donkey work – in particular on a piece she'd pitched about the authorities' shameful clear-up and conviction rates for domestic violence and sexual assaults generally. There'd be plenty of room for headlines in that, she knew, but it wasn't anything the other papers couldn't cook up for themselves. What she really needed was something new and exclusive on The Priest.

That was her biggest headache. What she hadn't told Griffin or Heffernan was that her source in the Garda sex crimes unit had gone to ground on her. Dried up. The spotlight was suddenly too bright to allow any leakage at all. And there was nothing she could do about it. Normally she'd have had some hold over such an informant by now, if only the mere fact that they had taken her money. But this one, having handed it to her on a plate, had vanished. He hadn't even come in to pick up the cash, yet. Damn it.

But she could hardly blame the guy for staying away. It seemed like the whole of the Garda Siochana had gone into paranoia overdrive following publication of her Priest scoop. Even that creep Des Consodine was refusing to talk to her. And as for Mike Mulcahy, he was blaming her just like all the rest of them. Why he had to take it personally, she had no idea. What had she done that was so wrong? She'd been careful. She'd made absolutely sure his name hadn't come into it. If he didn't want to believe that, so be it. But it still hurt. Especially as he'd dumped her by stupid text, as well. Didn't even give her a chance to explain. Maybe, if she kept her distance until the next big thing broke and things moved on, he'd get it into perspective after a while.

The other fly in her ointment was that Roy Orbison hadn't stopped phoning either. She'd had two more calls since. Both on the machine when she got in after working late. The first, ironically, just hours after she'd wrongly upbraided Bishop – as if she'd needed any further proof. She listened so hard to it, trying to get some clue as to who else could be behind it, that it took her a minute or two to hear what the song itself was telling her, to realise that every verse ended with the same line – the song title: 'You Don't Know Me'.

'You could've told me that before now and saved me the trouble,' she'd whispered grimly into the phone, before deleting it. But something about that particular moment chimed with her own dark sense of humour, and she'd laughed at it, too. And while the calls were still freaky, and no more bearable for knowing now that it wasn't Bishop making them, they also seemed a lot less serious after that. So much so, she hardly even registered the next one: caught the first five seconds, pressed delete, then forgot about it straight away.

Maybe if she'd been less busy it would all have played on her mind much more. But now, as things were, she barely had time to go to the loo. She looked around the *Herald*'s still busy newsroom, then checked her watch. She wanted to be sure she had time to pop to the Ladies' before her live link-up with Gerry Finucane's *Crime Week* radio show on 2FM. She was reaching for her bag when the phone on her desk rang. Damn. They preferred to make the connection over a landline. They'd probably keep her hanging on for ages now until they were ready. But she picked up anyway.

'Siobhan Fallon?' The voice was cultured, by Dublin standards – bound to be someone from media central in Montrose House.

'Yeah, it's me,' she said. 'But listen, love, do you think you could give me a couple of minutes and ring me back. I'm desperate for—'

'*Deus non irridetur.*'

Siobhan shook her head as if something in her ear had come loose. 'Excuse me?'

'*Deus non irridetur,*' the voice intoned. 'In the words of Saint Paul: "God will not be mocked."'

302

Ah, for Christ's sake, Siobhan thought. Not another one. Ever since she'd appeared on *Questions and Answers* the cranks and creeps had been coming out of the woodwork. The price, she was beginning to accept, of even her small modicum of fame was being a loon magnet. And even though she'd asked the operators to stop putting anonymous calls through to her extension, to let the newsdesk filter them, still some got through – this was the fourth or fifth nut job she'd had that day. All of them men, naturally, all of them saying the dirty young trollops deserved everything they got from The Priest, or some rancid rubbish to that effect.

'Look, pal, whatever it is you're after, I'm not interested.'

A low growling laugh came back down the line. 'You should be interested. You make a living out of peddling filth, don't you?'

'Is that what you're after, some filth?'

Again the horrible laugh, but this time the voice came back sharper.

'I have no filth in my life except what you and your kind bring into it. I saw you on the television the other night, talking all that filth about this so-called Priest. And there you were, parading yourself, with your low-cut top and your whore's lipstick, defiling the symbol of Christ's sacrifice that you wear around your neck. Does it mean nothing to you?'

Siobhan self-consciously put a hand up to her neck, touched the little silver cross at its base, an automatic act of security, though her mind was elsewhere, gathering rage.

'I'll tell you what means nothing to me, pal,' she spat back

303

at him. 'Bullshit artists like you ringing me up and mouthing off because you're too pathetic to get your thrills any other way.'

Normally that would have been enough. But not for this one.

'You spout torrents of corruption, your every word drips with it. And you remain blind to the message. You have the gall to condemn a righteous man.'

His voice was becoming laboured now, his breathing heavier. She could imagine all too clearly what was going on at the other end of the line.

'Righteous, did you say? That's a laugh. Do you think I don't know what's going on? Do you think I can't hear you at it, you sad fucker? Let me give you some advice – piss off and play with yourself on somebody else's time. Or I'll have this call traced and it won't be yourself you'll be pleasuring but some seven-foot stinking crackhead in a prison cell in the arse end of nowhere!'

She slammed the phone down. Behind her she felt the re-assuring presence of Paddy Griffin drifting up, putting a hand on her shoulder, his nose for trouble as unfailingly sharp as ever.

'Are you alright, love? What was that all about?'

'I'll give you one guess.' She looked up at him, a smile automatically snapping back on to her face. Never let anyone see you're fazed – his advice, she recalled.

'A crank, eh?' Griffin replied. 'Well, sounds like you sent him away with a flea in his ear.'

304

'It's what he had in his hand that I was worried about.'
She balled her right hand into a fist and jerked it up and
down obscenely.

'Oh God,' Griffin grimaced, his laugh diluted by nine
parts sympathy. 'That's Holy Christian Ireland for you – full
of tossers.'

'Yeah,' she said absently. Her mind was already turning
back to the radio interview, wondering about the time again.
She looked at her watch and saw she still had a minute to
spare. Only then did she notice that her hand was still trembling.

'Paddy, love,' she said, grabbing her bag. 'Could you
listen out for the phone for me. It'll be RTE for that *Crime
Week* thing, but I'm dying for a pee.'

The door to Brogan's office was open, so Mulcahy just
knocked and went in. She was staring intently at her computer screen and when she looked up she gave him that
tired, wary smile he'd been getting from her for the past few
days whenever he turned up to go through the best of the
leads coming in over the phones.

'Got something for me?' she asked.

'Yeah, maybe,' he said. 'How's it going? Making any
progress today?'

They still had a couple of hours before the main evening
briefing and she could have asked him to wait till then, but
instead she smiled and invited him to sit down while she
scrolled back through her email and called something up.

'Looks like you were right about Scully, by the way,' she said. 'We got a call from police in the UK earlier today – Scully's cash card was flagged being used to withdraw £250 sterling cash at Harwich ferry terminal, in Essex, on the east coast. By the time they realised what they were looking at, he was gone. I'm assuming across to the continent, but not under his own name. At least, not according to the passenger manifests.'

'There's a service to the Hook of Holland from there, so Amsterdam would be my guess. It's his kind of town. We can always get the Dutch to check out the hotels there.'

'Not much point,' she replied. 'Healy's saying we should hand the lot over to the Drugs Squad now that it's chiefly of interest to them.'

In response to Mulcahy's quizzical expression she pointed at another document she'd called up on screen. 'We got back the last of the forensics on the van today. Clean as a whistle. The hair's definitely not Jesica's – so that's pretty much the end of that. Because even though the blood spatter *was* blood spatter, it was matched to Scully's father who finally relented and gave us a sample yesterday. Seems he must've cut his hand on a bit of pipe.'

Mulcahy gave her a sympathetic smile but said nothing. He hadn't really been expecting any other result.

'And they drew a blank on those fibres, too,' Brogan continued. 'No sign of anything remotely like them in the van.'

'Do they even know what they are yet?'

Brogan shook her head. 'They say they're not sure – i.e.

they haven't got a clue. All Technical will say for definite is that the ones found on Jesica's clothes are an *exact* match for the ones found on Catriona Plunkett's top, too.'

'That's something, I suppose: find the fibres, find the man. How is she, by the way – Catriona? Any improvement?'

Brogan shook her head again. 'Still under heavy sedation and they say they're going to have to keep her that way for days. At least until some of the burns begin to heal over and she can't make herself worse just by moving. She's in a terrible state, poor kid.' Brogan sighed heavily and nodded towards her screen. 'I was just going over the CCTV of her outside the Kay Club again.'

She clicked on the black subscreen on her monitor and Mulcahy saw a grainy image jerk into life, revealing a young woman in teetering heels standing outside an open doorway. A length of thick rope hanging between two waist-height stainless-steel poles indicated the area where club-goers queued for entry. She was looking away, her face turning first to peer up, then down, the street, and she was alone except for a large shaven-headed man in black standing by the door behind her.

'The bouncer?' Mulcahy asked.

'Yeah,' Brogan nodded. 'But look at this.'

They watched together in silence as the girl turned and engaged the doorman in what seemed to be a bit of friendly banter and he responded, gesticulating with his hand. Brogan froze the image. 'Okay, so according to the bouncer, here she's asking him why there aren't any taxis waiting outside like there usually are, and he's telling her there won't be any taxis because the local firms decided to boycott the pubs and clubs in the Killester area.'

'Boycott?'

Brogan nodded. 'Apparently, two or three taxi drivers got robbed at knifepoint around Killester in the space of a week and they were all up in arms about it. I checked it out and it's true, although the boycott only lasted a couple of nights because it hit the local drivers too hard in the pocket. But this particular Friday was the first night of it, and the one night the ban held firm.'

'So there were no taxis at all out in Killester that night?'

'None of the local ones that do the clubs. To be honest, I'd kind of discounted that as a factor until now because Catriona lived only a few hundred yards up the road. And look, here she turns and walks in the direction of home, as you'd expect.'

Sure enough, the CCTV caught Catriona turning and walking away, saying goodnight to the bouncer with a flirtatious twist of her fingers. 'God love her,' Brogan said. 'We thought that was the last we had of her on camera. But look at this. One of Maura's lads spotted something else this morning. It's from a traffic camera a hundred yards further up the same road. It only lasts a few seconds, which is how it was missed first time round. Just watch . . .'

She clicked on another subscreen and a rougher, greyer, wide-angled image emerged of a girl – the same girl, if you looked hard enough – walking up the road towards the camera, swinging her handbag by its long straps. There didn't seem to be any traffic on the road. Then, just before she passed the camera, she lifted her head, turned suddenly and raised her right arm. At which point she disappeared from the frame.

'Show it to me again,' Mulcahy said, intrigued.

Brogan played the footage once more, this time at half the previous pace. 'Do you see what I'm talking about?'

'Yeah,' he said, still puzzling as she played it for him a third time, slower still.

'So what do you reckon she's doing?' Brogan asked.

'Well, if I didn't know better, I'd say she was hailing a taxi. Either that or she recognised someone who happened to be driving past.'

'That's what I figured, too,' Brogan said.

'My bet would be on the taxi,' Mulcahy said. 'Maybe someone who didn't actually know that there was supposed to be a boycott that night?'

'How do you mean?' she said, slightly spiky. 'We *did* check it thoroughly. None of the ranks was operating that night.'

'No, that's just my point. It's to do with something I unearthed today. Just a feeling for now, but if you have a few minutes . . .'

14

The call came in at around 2.15 a.m. Her mobile, trilling on the bedside table, cut through a waxy dream of something slipping from her grasp.

'Get yourself over to the Furry Glen asap,' the voice instructed, 'if you want to see something interesting.'

The voice was distorted, as it had been before, but instantly recognisable as that of her elusive source. A ten-second instruction that penetrated her sleep like a knife slicing through flesh, before the click and vast nothingness of disconnection. Siobhan was instantly awake, rummaging in the darkness for the jeans she'd peeled off only four hours before, razor-keen to know what was going on, not content to wait until she got there to find out. Didn't even stop for a coffee. She had a can of Red Bull in the car if she needed a hit later. For now, the adrenalin pumping through her like a piston was more than enough.

She jumped in behind the wheel and roared up the ramp out of the garage, regardless of anyone sleeping in the flats overhead. Her mind raced ahead all the way there, weighing up the possibilities, the permutations. Why the Furry Glen? By day it was an overrated beauty spot in the Phoenix Park. By night its quiet, bosky pathways made it a favourite hangout for gay men. Had The Priest switched sides? Had he maybe targeted a guy this time?

She slowed the car as she reached the lights at the bottom of Grand Canal Street, then gunned the engine and sped through on red across the bridge. The tip-off wouldn't have come if they weren't already thinking it had something to do with The Priest. And if it was a crime scene she was going to, they had probably been there for a while already. Which meant there was a good chance that whatever it was they were interested in would be there still, too. Not in a hospital. Was it a dead body? Was that it?

She drove on through the still, quiet streets of the city, her progress marked by the split-second intervals between the sodium orange streetlights, her foot easing off the accelerator only on the rare occasions she encountered another vehicle. Within seconds of crossing the river and entering the Phoenix Park, she could see that something major was afoot. The mouth of Wellington Road, which ran the couple of kilometres down and around the southern rim of the Park as far as the Furry Glen, was blocked by a Garda car, its blue emergency lamps flashing in the night. She drove on up Chesterfield Avenue, the main route that splits the Park in two, but found a similar blockade at the next turn-off, and then at the next again – patrol cars parked across the side roads, denying access, every time with a uniformed

Garda leaning against the bonnet or sitting inside with the windows down. By then she knew there was no point trying to get any further in the car, so she pulled over onto the grass verge, into the shadow of a copse, and killed the engine.

From there it was a twenty-minute hike, across flat grassy parkland and around dense patches of woodland, to reach the Glen. How she made it she wasn't quite sure, thanking Christ for the light of the full moon, and herself for having the good sense to have slipped her trainers on and not the mules she'd been wearing earlier. On the downside, it did feel a bit mad to have a handbag swinging from her arm. But by then it was too late to go back and she was already closing in on her target, guided from some distance out by the unmistakeable flare of spotlights, a canopy of light domed in the night ahead of her. When at last she reached the Upper Glen Road she spotted two more cop cars, but they were at least two hundred yards apart at either end of the access roads leading down into the Glen itself. No one had thought to guard against anyone arriving from across the park on foot.

She crossed unnoticed between them and slipped into the shadow of the trees beyond, making it all the way to the rim of a wide and steeply sloping bowl in the ground that looked to be almost as deep as the thirty or forty feet it was across. Hiding behind a rough-barked tree, leaning into its trunk for support, she took in the scene below, lit harshly by a battery of arc lamps set up on the opposite edge of the hollow.

There were eight, maybe ten men down there, all dressed head-to-toe in ghostly white overalls, some standing, some taking photographs, some on their knees, searching. A white forensics tent had been awkwardly erected over the centre of a thick concrete pipe that spanned the base of the hollow. Siobhan's heart skipped a beat at the thought of what might be beneath it, and how she might manoeuvre herself into a position to get a look. It was probably the furious churning of her imagination that closed off all her senses to the movement behind her. The looming form. The long arm reaching out to grab her.

They gave her pretty short shrift despite her well-practised protestations. The young cop who'd rumbled her was nice enough. If anything he was more shocked to stumble upon her in the dark than she had been at getting caught. But the sergeant he marched her down to meet was another matter altogether – all crew cut, red neck and stripes, the sort who liked to ask questions he already knew the answers to.

'What the hell do you think you're doing here?' His Sligo accent was as thick as his neck. He was staring at her press card and *Sunday Herald* ID like they were smears of something nasty on his hand.

'I'm doing my job, Sergeant. To the best of my knowledge they haven't passed any law against that, yet.'

It was while waiting for him to think up some devastating riposte that she spotted them: three figures – two men and a woman – emerging from the gloom about fifty yards

313

in front of her, walking towards the hollow. One of them, in the same white overalls she'd seen the men down below wearing, was talking and gesticulating at the others as if engaged in some elaborate explanation. The other two were in plain clothes, detectives without a doubt. As they neared the edge of the hollow and peered over the rim, the light from below carved out their facial features in sharp relief. Siobhan was sure she recognised one of them – but not sure enough.

'We'll be here all night waiting for you to make up your mind, Sergeant,' she said. 'Eh, isn't that Inspector Brogan I see over there? She knows me well.' She beamed the special smile at him, anything to cover the lie.

The sergeant followed the direction of her pointing finger. He peered, looked back, then back again at Brogan, scepticism evident in the arching of an eyebrow.

'She knows you, how?'

'Ah, sure, we're great pals. We go way back. I'm sure she'd be happy to talk to me. Do you think you might go over and ask her for me?'

'She's busy,' said the sergeant, handing back her ID cards.

He was right. Just then the white-domed heads of two men in coveralls appeared over the rim of the hollow, and the others stepped back to let them clamber out. They turned and pulled up behind them what appeared to be a lightweight metal stretcher, which in turn was being pushed carefully from below by another two men, arms upstretched

314

to keep their load as level as possible. The four of them struggled to balance their long and narrow burden, and it wasn't until they were all out and upright again that Siobhan was able to see for certain what it was they had strapped on the stretcher. A body bag, no doubt about it.

'Holy mother of God,' said the sergeant beside her in hushed tones, blessing himself and touching an imaginary crucifix to his lips. Like Siobhan, and the rest of the uniformed cops standing back on the perimeter, he was totally transfixed as the stretcher bearers halted by the waiting detectives. The one who'd been doing the talking unzipped the bag at the top end and made several rapid hand gestures towards what could only be, in Siobhan's mind, the head and chest of a dead body. Remembering the stranger in their midst, the sergeant turned to her with a baleful look.

'Like I was saying, I don't think the inspector will be wanting to be disturbed right now.'

'Yeah, maybe you're right,' Siobhan conceded, opening the flap of her bag and shoving her notebook, pen and cards back into it. She'd been tempted to shout out, do anything to get a quote from Brogan but couldn't help feeling all she'd get for her trouble would be a night in some stone-cold cell somewhere. Now was not the time to make a fuss. She'd seen more than enough already. Her priority was to get away as soon as possible and get the story out.

'I'll just have to hang around for a bit, then,' she said to the sergeant. 'Take in the sights. Unless you could get one of your fellas to give me a lift back to my car?'

The sergeant looked over at the five or six patrol cars parked up on the roadside behind them, their drivers standing or leaning against them, still absorbed by the activities of the stretcher bearers who by now were loading their burden into the back of an ambulance. The detectives had already disappeared.

'For a friend of Inspector Brogan's?' the sergeant said, a considerate tone entering his voice now. 'Where did you say you left it?'

'Way over on the main road,' she said with a sigh, and a small pout for added effect. 'It took me half an hour to walk here, thanks to you fellas blocking all the roads.'

'Ah, sure, like you said yourself, we're only doing our jobs. And do you know what?'

His smile was now on the verge of saintliness and had completely transformed his features.

'No, what?' she gleamed back.

'That doesn't include chauffeur services for scum like you.'

She was so taken aback by the snarl with which he said it that she was stunned into silence. By the time she'd composed herself enough again to respond, the sergeant had put up the palm of his huge bogman's hand in front of her face and turned to summon the same Garda who'd found her in the woods.

'Crilly,' he said, 'walk this bloody parasite up to the road where you found her and shove her off in the direction she came from. Then stay there and make sure she doesn't come back again. Cos if she does, I'll have your bollocks for breakfast.'

She may have cursed him to the very highest heaven all the way back to the car, but bless his heart, it was the redneck sergeant who gave Siobhan her second most precious gift that morning. Because if he hadn't forced her to trudge back the route she came, across the trackless, sodden parkland, she'd never have seen it. Even though she was dog-tired and her legs felt like lead pipes welded to her hips, she'd been making good progress. For some time, dawn had been diluting the darkness and the pink shimmer of daylight in the sky was growing paler by the minute. Skirting a dense clump of tangled vegetation, Siobhan came to a sudden standstill. Ahead of her a small herd of fallow deer was emerging slowly from the trees, grazing as they came, snouts gently nuzzling the thin layer of white mist that tickled the top of the grass. But beyond them, out across the flat expanse of open ground stretching away to the east, was what took her breath away, so completely she could only stop and gaze in wonder.

Towering in the distance, half a mile away or more, vast against the empty skyline and the rising sun beyond, was the enormous steel cross erected for Pope John Paul II's visit to Ireland in 1979. Her father and mother had taken her to the Phoenix Park that extraordinary day when almost half of the population, one and a half million people, flocked from all corners of the country to see and hear the charismatic father of the Catholic Church celebrate mass in the open air. Six years old, wearing her white communion dress, the same colour as the Pope's vestments, the same colour as the cross, she remembered the press of the vast crowd, the flapping of the banners and flags in the breeze, the excited cries rising and falling as the Popemobile drove round and round to get him within viewing distance of all the throng. Mostly, though, she remembered when the Holy Father finally made it to the altar, her own father cheering madly as he held her aloft in his long, strong arms, high above his head, as the roar of the crowd carried her higher and higher and she felt like an angel ascending to heaven.

'Young people of Ireland, I love you,' the Pope said, and an entire nation fell at his feet.

Where had all that feeling, that spirit, gone, she wondered? It was like nothing she'd ever experienced again. She couldn't imagine it occurring today. Ireland was so totally different back then. It was like any other country now. People would barely remember that day if it wasn't for the Papal Cross. She looked at it again, its white steel burned deepest black against the fiery red orb of the sun rising, huge, behind it. The cross had been a symbol of hope, of faith, back then. This morning, though, it was more like some awful sign from a wrathful Old Testament God, throwing its long flat shadow across the park like an accusing finger towards her, and all the death and Garda activity going on in the Furry Glen behind her.

A lurid image to fit lurid circumstances, Siobhan thought, recognising it instantly for all its tabloid worth.

'Okay, guys, gather round. This is important. Come on, now, wakey-wakey.'

There must have been fifty people crammed into the tiny incident room but, as soon as Brogan clapped her hands, the murmuring came to a swift halt. Suit creased, hair a mess, she looked like she'd been up all night, her eyes puffy but on high alert. Buzzing on something, for sure, Mulcahy reckoned, hoping it was legal. Cassidy, too, exuded a bristling energy. He was holding something rolled up in his hand, a peculiar expression of expectancy crinkling his face.

'Some of you will have heard this on the news already, but for those of you who haven't, a body was found in the Phoenix Park last night. A couple walking their dog – I won't spell it out, you know the score – found the remains of a young girl, a teenager, wrapped in plastic sheeting, stuffed under a drainage pipe in the Furry Glen. We suspected it from the outset, but once we got her back to the mortuary there was no more room for doubt. It was our man did her, alright.'

As Cassidy unfurled the large print-off he was holding there were muted gasps in the room. The image had all the stillness of death. A girl cocooned in clear plastic turned opalescent by a camera flashing on the layers that had been peeled back from her bare head, shoulders and torso. Her hair was a dark auburn, thick and wavy, framing a face that

319

was alabaster-white – angelic almost, with eyes closed as if in sleep – except for one smudge of dirt on the forehead. The look of peace on her face was in stark, barely credible contrast to the appalling injuries that had been inflicted on what could be seen of her chest and upper arms. Everyone present had seen those marks before, on Jesica Salazar and Catriona Plunkett – the horror that results when white-hot metal is applied to flesh – but these appeared to have been applied with still more fury. There was hardly a square inch of skin that hadn't been burned, hideously blackened and blistered. Mulcahy guessed he wasn't the only one offering up a silent prayer that death had come swiftly and protected the girl from the worst of it.

'So, as you can see, this case is now a murder inquiry.' Brogan paused for effect. 'I got called in at three a.m. to confirm the Murder Squad's suspicions that this was our man's doing – although with all the press coverage we've been having they were never really under any illusion that it could be anyone else. Whether that press coverage actually contributed to an escalation in The Priest's campaign is something that remains to be seen.'

A rush of whispered anger rippled through the room.

'Alright, alright, settle down,' Brogan said. 'What's done is done, and there's no going back. Let's get on with it now. The time of death has yet to be established, but as rigor was still pretty much full on when she was found the medical examiner was willing to give an unofficial initial estimate of twenty-four to forty-eight hours since she was killed. That puts it roughly between midnight Tuesday and midnight Wednesday, although it looks as if the poor kid's ordeal started long before that. The points being this – and there are two of them – that, since his appearance in the press, our man has decided to up the stakes and cross the border nobody can come back from. He has killed. The second point is that, as a result of this now becoming a murder investigation, the case is being reassigned.'

'Ah, for fuck's sake!' Hanlon shouted in disbelief, unable to control his feelings and pretty much summing up the sentiments of everyone in the room. 'Do they not know that we've been working our arses off on this thing?'

'Shush, now.' Brogan patted the air to quell the swell of disgruntled voices. 'I understand your disappointment, but you all know the score. Murder is murder.' While she was waiting for that to sink in she turned to Cassidy, who for some was reason was trying to stop himself grinning. Mulcahy was beginning to wonder if he was hallucinating, or dreaming, when Brogan turned back to the room and she, too, was smiling.

'One last thing,' she said. 'I want you to listen more carefully to me from now on. I said the case was being reassigned. I didn't say we weren't going with it. In fact, I made a very compelling case for them to take us on as a job lot. We're on the murder team, you dozy bunch of prats. They're throwing everything we've got at it.'

There was a roar of triumph as smiles and applause broke out all around the room. It was ever thus, Mulcahy knew: the bigger and bloodier the case, the more any decent cop wanted to be involved in it, all the way to the finish. Especially when they'd invested as much time and emotion as this team had. For most detectives, working a murder was the best, most exciting job they could ever hope for. The fact that a girl was dead had not been forgotten. They just knew they had a bigger, even more important job to do now.

Cassidy was waving for a bit of hush, holding up Brogan's arm as if she'd just won a challenge cup.

'She even got herself made deputy senior investigating officer, lads – so we won't be pushed to the sidelines.'

There was another flurry of approval and applause.

'Right, so gather up all your paperwork and discs,' Brogan continued. 'Anyone with laptops bring them with you. The main incident room's now over in Kilmainham Garda Station. Be ready to reconvene there for a full briefing from Detective Superintendent Lonergan at eleven hundred hours. Make sure you call ahead to get your cars cleared through for parking. Sergeant Cassidy here has the number.'

As the noise of scraping chairs filled the room and bodies began milling about excitedly, Mulcahy noticed Brogan's gaze searching him out and, with a jerk of her head, calling him aside.

'Congratulations,' he said. 'Smoothly done.'

'Yeah, thanks.'

'A bit bizarre, don't you think? Him hiding the body like

that. Especially after all the trouble he'd gone to mark her and all.'

'Weird,' she agreed. 'The same thought occurred to me. Stuffing her under that pipe, she could have been down there for months before anybody stumbled on her.'

'You couldn't get more opposite to what he did out in Fairview.'

'I know, it doesn't make any sense. Why would he want to hide her?'

'Why does anyone want to hide anything?'

She eyed him directly, trying to figure out exactly what he meant by that. 'Are you thinking all this press coverage was maybe too much for him? That he couldn't take the heat?'

Mulcahy shrugged. 'I doubt it. Everything else, he's done in such a way that you'd have to think he wanted it to be known about as quickly as possible.'

'So you're thinking maybe he's ashamed of it suddenly? How likely is that, given what he'd already done to the others? He might not have killed them, but he as good as left them for dead.'

'Maybe that's not how he sees it. Maybe for some reason it was important for him not to actually kill the girls, who knows? And now he's overstepped the mark, got carried away or something – I don't know. Maybe it wasn't part of his plan.'

'Whatever that may be,' Brogan nodded, still thinking about it, filing the conversation away for future consideration.

Then she took a half step back and looked closely at him. 'You know this is the end of Healy's involvement? Lonergan will take over control of the entire investigation.'

Mulcahy nodded, wondering what she was getting at. 'You know him?'

'No,' she said, 'but I'm sure I will by the end of the day.' She smiled a little hesitantly before continuing. 'The thing is, Mike, I asked this morning, you not being part of my team and all, and Healy says you're to hang back. That you're not being reassigned with the rest of us. I don't know why that is. All I know is, he says he'll be in meetings all morning for the handover but he asked me to tell you to hang around – to "await further orders" is how he put it. Sorry.'

She said it like she was expecting Mulcahy to be devastated about this but his reaction to the news was precisely the opposite. All he felt – in light of Murtagh and the upcoming Southern Region job – was relief. Jesus, if he'd been sent over to the Murder Squad on some mass temporary transfer ticket, it could have taken him months to extricate himself.

'That's fine, Claire. I'm sure I'll find something useful to do.'

'Yeah?' she said, looking at him like she couldn't quite believe how well he was taking this.

'Yeah,' he said. 'I'll be fine.'

'Well, I know we had our moments, Mike, but . . .'

If she was on the brink of saying something nice she was

saved by Cassidy's intervention, a shout from across the room.

'Boss?'

She looked over, then back at Mulcahy. He decided to put her out of her misery. 'You go on, Claire. I'll see you around.'

She was just turning away when it came to him. 'Oh, one last thing. I don't suppose you got a chance to look over that case I was telling you about last night – Caroline Coyle?'

She blinked, seeming unsure of what he was talking about. Clearly the events of later that evening had wiped her memory of it temporarily.

'Oh, shit. No, Mike, I'm sorry. That sounded really promising but, you know, I've been up all night on this. It completely slipped my mind. Could you put it in an email for me? I'll get somebody on to it right away, okay?'

'Sure,' he said, watching her back as she walked away, spotting Andy Cassidy smirking triumphantly at him from the far side of the room. The twat. He wasn't going to be sorry to see the back of him. What to do about Sergeant Brennan, though, Mulcahy was not so sure.

'That's it, Siobhan, you're clear now,' the disembodied voice of producer Seosamh Gaffney floated into her ears. At least she could see and make eye-contact with the news presenters in the glassed-in studio in front of her small interview booth. But Gaffney, who had brought her in and sat, with widening eyes, discussing what she had for him while she was being miked up, was nowhere to be seen. He'd been off pressing buttons in a control room nearby during the whole show. 'And thanks a million, again. We haven't had such an exciting story break on air for ages.'

She took the cans off her head and gave her tingling ears a rub. She hated having to wear headphones, didn't like the way they made her voice echo back up her ear canal. But that was the way they did it on *Morning Ireland* and Gaffney had insisted. Especially as they wanted her free to come in on any discussion with the others they'd managed to raise for interview over the phone. It had been a hell of a good session, with everyone in the small RTE news studio buzzing in the knowledge that they had a solid-gold scoop on their hands, something no other broadcaster or news agency had even had a sniff of before them. The two pre-senters, Lawlor and MacCoille, had been falling over themselves with the questions, eager to get the most out of it knowing just how many people would be waking up startled in bed or letting their cornflakes go soggy for fear of missing a detail with a mistimed crunch. This was, after all, the most listened-to radio show in the country. The one that set the entire day's news agenda. And on RTE that meant the entire day's radio, because whatever went out on *Morning Ireland* got endlessly rolled over and recycled into every talk show that followed during the course of the day.

She had phoned Gaffney, an old pal from journalism school, as soon as she got back to her car in the Phoenix

Park. He'd all but gone down on his knees, begging her to come in, even offering to send a limo out there to fetch her into the studio. But what was the point of that when she had her own car and, anyway, the drive in would give her a chance to get her head together and her story straight? And time to phone Paddy Griffin and get the nod first, of course, laughing as he howled invective down the line at the curse of being a Sunday news editor. Barely ninety minutes after being given the boot by that bogtrotter sergeant, she was sipping coffee in the RTE studios in Donnybrook, yakking to Gaffney while some other guy did sound checks on her mike. And, after an introduction in which she was described as 'the *Sunday Herald*'s brilliant chief reporter Siobhan Fallon', she began recounting in graphic detail everything she'd witnessed in the Furry Glen earlier that morning. Of course she mentioned the *Herald*'s name as much as possible – she wasn't going to risk upsetting Harry Heffernan until she had that pay rise carved in stone – but she also made sure to take the lion's share of the credit for herself. It wasn't like she didn't deserve it. She'd only had to embroider the odd patch here and there. There was no shortage of colour to fill in the vague outlines of what she'd seen: the spectral glare of the arc lights in the night, the ghostly toing and froing of the investigators in the hollow, the sad spectacle of the stretchered body being borne away. But, most of all, it was the giant Papal Cross that she used to illustrate her story. The image of it burned black against the rising sun. And it went down a storm.

So much so, that when they asked her to stay on to do the Pat Kenny show, later, the old stager led with the image of the burning cross himself. And so it was for the rest of the morning, traipsing from studio to studio, from radio to TV and back again, milking it for all it was worth, until she literally didn't have the strength to say another word about it. That was when she rang Gaffney and told him to send round that limo he'd promised her. She wanted to go home. Even as she was wafted back to her flat in the soft, enfolding, new-leather comfort of a luxurious Mercedes, barely able to keep her eyes open, she heard on the radio the story being taken up by others, rolling it on, building it ever bigger, that image of the Papal Cross taking on a life of its own. She knew then that by end of day, even as she slept on in her own bed, it would have been adopted by every hack and rent-a-comment on the airwaves as a kind of catch-all shorthand, a symbol of whatever malaise they might suddenly decide had taken hold of Ireland.

And she knew, too, that however big a story it had been to begin with, the murder and that image of a burning cross would make The Priest into the biggest source of outrage that Ireland had seen for a hell of a long time. There was nothing like a society that thought it was over something for diving straight back in again at every opportunity and having another worry at it. And Catholicism was still that something in Ireland, capable of tweaking every button, clanging every bell, pulling every knob it ever had, with the added fury of those who now presumed themselves to be above all that – but weren't. As she finally succumbed to sleep in the back of the limo, she was sure she saw her name, Siobhan Fallon, as if by angels held aloft, transported upwards seeking out its rightful place among the stars.

15

'Ah, sure, when we bought this place, it was like our holiday house in the country. Now, with all the development there's been, it's barely better than living in the suburbs.'

'It looks a lot nicer than that to me,' said Mulcahy.

Sergeant Pat Brennan, retired, hadn't done half bad for himself, Mulcahy thought, as he stood outside the man's home high on the wooded slopes outside the village of Kilpedder, twenty miles or so south of Dublin. The house itself was nothing much to look at, one of those ubiquitous white bungalows that scarred the lower faces of the Wicklow mountains like a pox. But its location – at the end of a winding drive on what had to be at least three acres with fine views out over Bray Head, Greystones and the sweeping bay beyond – was spectacular.

'Got it for a good price, too, back in the early eighties. The owners were desperate to get away to England to look for work. Heaven knows what it's worth now,' said Brennan with a tilt of his eyebrow.

Like hell, Mulcahy thought. The shrewd old goat probably knows its value down to the nearest tenner. Even with the collapse of property prices, it had to be worth a couple of million easily. For a second Mulcahy was gripped by the thought that he hadn't heard a peep from his own estate agents since they said they'd lined up those viewings . . . how many days ago? He couldn't remember. Then the thought was gone as he followed the sergeant in through the front door.

Meeting Sergeant Brennan face to face had made Mulcahy revise the impression he'd got of him over the phone. For one thing, there was a vivaciousness about him that just didn't come across in his voice. In person, Brennan was fit, tanned, smart of dress and straight of back. He still sported the No. 1 buzz cut he'd probably worn to maximise the grip on his Garda cap for the best part of four decades on the force, and he looked at least ten years younger than the seventy-plus he had to be if he'd held out to retire at sixty like he'd said. Nothing at all like the bitter old buffer Mulcahy had imagined. And he didn't seem to mind at all the interval that had passed since he'd spoken to Mulcahy. In fact, he seemed strangely chuffed, as if the wait had somehow made the return even more important.

'I knew you'd come back to me eventually. That's why I wanted to speak to someone like yourself, who knows the value of good intelligence. That young galoot I spoke to first had me written off the minute I opened my mouth. You have to go to the top if you want anything done, nowadays.'

'Yeah, well, a lot's been happening over the last few days,' Mulcahy replied. 'Maybe you could tell me a little more about this fella Rinn now? Didn't you say he trained to be a priest?'

That, more than anything else, was what was nagging at Mulcahy. On the file, it had said Rinn was a taxi driver. How the hell did that fit? But he couldn't afford to tell Brennan about the file or anything else to do with Caroline Coyle. He didn't want to prejudice the man's already coloured judgement any further.

'Well, I was just about to get to that when you had to go. The grandparents packed him off to All Hallows, but he never made it. I mean, he did a few years in the seminary there but he was never ordained into the priesthood.'

Okay, that cleared that up. Mulcahy looked around the kitchen, wondering where to go next. 'You said he had a well-connected grandfather, but where were his parents?'

Brennan drew in a big breath and let it out again slowly. 'Well, that's just it. It was a tragic case, really. The parents died in a car crash, both of them, when the boy Sean was only six or seven. While they were on holiday down in Killarney. Terrible thing. The boy was with them in the car and was severely injured himself when it caught fire. But he survived.'

'And so the grandparents brought him up?'

'That's it. He was an only child like his father before him, so he went to them. And ordinarily, like, you'd have nothing but sympathy. But, whether it was the accident did it, or it was just in him all along, there was something twisted in that young man – twisted to the core.'

Mulcahy said nothing, unsure whether he wanted to encourage Brennan any further, thinking the young Rinn sounded an odd candidate for the priesthood in that case. As if reading his mind, the old sergeant took up his theme again.

'They must have thought he needed divine intervention, to hand him over to the priests so young. He was only fourteen or so. But I sure as heck didn't mind. Everything went quiet for three or four years and then he turned up in Rathgar again – in civvies. I made some enquiries and the whisper came back that he'd been kicked out of All Hallows. Some awful scandal, they said, but it'd all been hushed up by the priests and everyone else involved. Doubtless Mr Justice Rinn called in a few favours to ensure the family name stayed unsullied. Anyway, I got a pal of mine over in Drumcondra to make some enquiries with contacts he had in the college. What he heard – only rumours, mind – was that young Rinn had been involved in some incident at the judge's holiday place up in Gweedore over the summer, and that the priests had got wind of it and asked him to leave the seminary. That was all he could find out. So I tried to make a few enquiries myself, but I didn't have any contacts in those parts and, well, I got nowhere with it. It was clear enough that *something* had happened up there, but for the life of me I couldn't get anybody to open their gob. I tell you, though, I made sure I kept a closer eye than ever on him after that.'

'And?'

'And nothing. A few months later he was packed off again, to teacher-training college, down in Maynooth this time, and I never heard of him again. I've been living down here in Kilpedder since I retired in ninety-five – before he would have qualified. But I presume he did, and went off to become a teacher. Some role model he would've been for children, don't you think?'

'Maybe. I don't know,' Mulcahy said. 'But to be honest – and I hope you won't mind me saying this, Sergeant – you never had any evidence he did anything wrong at all, did you?'

'Only the evidence of my own eyes. And, if you could've seen the state of some of the young women brought into my station, you'd believe it too. In bits they were, and the coldness in his eyes when I questioned him. You'd think the same, too. The little bastard, Lord bless my soul, never even denied it to my face. Just waited for his grandfather to come and get him, while CID refused to lift a finger. I'm telling you, there were times I would've happily strung him up myself.'

Mulcahy flicked back through what the sergeant had told him on the phone: the scrapes he said he'd had with Rinn back in the late eighties. They hadn't sounded too serious, mostly involving incidents in Palmerston Park, the secluded couple of acres of well-tended lawns and rose beds in front of Rinn's grandfather's house. Brennan now told him again how, during the few months Rinn had been home between colleges, a number of 'courting couples' had been attacked in the park after dark, as a result of which one young guy had been hospitalised after being beaten round the head with a brick.

'This girl you said got a decent look at him,' Mulcahy said. 'How come she got so close?'

'She was the one whose boyfriend was hurt. Susan Roche.' All the anger was gone from Brennan's voice now. 'I remember her like it was yesterday. Crying over her young fella in the dark, while we waited for an ambulance. She was drenched in blood, got a thump herself but was lucky it was only a glancing blow. The boyfriend was on top when he was struck first and he'd managed to shield her from the worst of it. I went with her to the hospital and she told me, in the ambulance, how she'd seen their attacker's face as he stood over them. From her description it was Rinn alright, I had no doubt. But the case got handed over to CID straight away, and those guys . . . oh, they interviewed him, but you could tell they'd been got at. Chief-bloody-Justice Padraig Rinn again. Never was justice so ill served by anyone in the judiciary.'

'It can't have been easy for you,' Mulcahy sympathised, genuinely. He'd felt similar frustration himself on one or two occasions, when the system he was desperately trying to uphold seemed wilfully directed away from the side of good.

'You're right there,' said Brennan. 'I almost packed it in. Went through a bit of a rough patch, so I did. But I didn't give up, in the end. Because the girl, young Susan, came

335

back to me a couple of months later and thanked me for what I'd done. She said even though she felt let down by the investigation she knew I'd done my best. A lovely kind girl, she was, didn't deserve that. She even said some day she'd find it in her heart to forgive him. "I might even get around to saying an *Our Father* for him, Sergeant" – that's what she said. An *Our Father*. That really impressed me.'

'Why so?' Mulcahy said, wondering at the sudden emotion in the old man's voice.

'Because that's what Rinn was bawling at her all the while he was beating her fella with the brick.'

Although she'd only had a couple of hours sleep back at her flat, Siobhan looked immaculate when, just after three o'clock, she emerged from the lift at the *Sunday Herald* in a scoop-necked Betty Jackson top, tailored black trousers and a pair of pointy black Christian Louboutins she'd blown the budget on a good few months back but which still looked as good as new. She strode across the open-plan floor of the newsroom, thanking heaven for the reviving miracles worked by make-up and curling tongs. Almost before she put her bag on her desk, Paddy Griffin was there beside her, dangling a long arm around her shoulder and giving her a squeeze.

'Good work this morning, girl – especially all that malarkey about the Papal Cross. Nice touch. Shame we had to waste it all on RTE, though.'

Siobhan extricated herself as politely as she could and leaned across the desk to turn on her computer monitor. 'It wasn't a waste, as well you know. And anyway, there's loads left in the tank for Sunday, don't you worry.'

Griffin's eyes lit up immediately. 'What you got?'

Siobhan looked at him and laughed. 'You don't want much, do you? Another scoop? No chance. I only meant I can work up what I've got into something special. "Eye-witness exclusive: fear and loathing in the Furry Glen", etc,' she laughed. 'You know the kind of thing. All the gory details. They'll be lapping it up come Sunday. Anything yourself?'

Griffin sighed and swatted at the air in front of him.

'Not really. Foreign Affairs has been on the ropes in the Dáil over whether there should be an official enquiry into the "Spanish invasion" or not. Word is they might agree to one, if only to kill the media coverage by putting it all on a *sub-judice* footing for now. I've a couple of the lads looking into it. Actually, I was wondering if you'd be free to help them with it, later.'

'Ah, come off it, Paddy, does it look like I'm not busy or something? Or is getting up at two o'clock in the morning not enough for you? I only brought you the biggest story of the week.'

'So far,' said Griffin glumly.

'So far,' Siobhan parroted, and leaned over to touch her desk for luck – though the closest thing to wood in it was the chipboard under the laminate. 'And what'll be my chance of improving on it, if I'm stuck weighing up the likelihood of a dull-as-ditch public enquiry?'

'Okay, okay!' Griffin held his arms up in surrender. 'Christ, I forgot for a moment that you were a fucking celebrity now, and that you don't have to play by the same rules as the rest of us mortals. Forget it.'

Siobhan's triumphant smile was broken by the trill of her mobile. She put a hand up to block out Griffin's whingeing.

'Yeah, that's me,' she spoke into the phone, then her eyes widened. 'Are you serious? When? . . . Yeah, of course . . . What time? . . . Great, yeah, thanks.'

Siobhan snapped her phone shut, looked at her watch, then turned to Griffin again. 'Maybe we're not going to need that public-enquiry piece after all.' She grabbed her bag from the desk and shut down her monitor again. 'You're not going to believe this.'

As soon as he got back on the N11 northbound, Mulcahy put his foot down and worked the car in and out through the heavy traffic heading into Dublin, trying to make up time. It really hadn't helped when Mrs Brennan, a spritely little woman who looked as fit as her husband, had appeared carrying a mountainous plate of smoked-salmon sandwiches and a pot of tea and insisted that he stay for lunch with them. Nice as it was, the conversation had ground to a halt at that point. Brennan was not one to discuss 'work' in front of his wife and Mulcahy found himself sitting there politely, talking about the great weather they'd been having and wondering what the hell he'd got himself into. Sure, everything Brennan had told him about Rinn had set alarm

338

bells ringing. But he still couldn't see how, if Rinn was as out of control as Brennan said he'd been, he hadn't been caught – regardless of who his high-powered grandfather was. It was the eighties when all this had supposedly gone on, not the bloody Middle Ages. Why the hell hadn't Rinn been active in the meantime? Surely somebody would have to have picked up on that?

The one thing that did continue to niggle away at him was the Caroline Coyle connection, since there was something just not right there. Everyone, from his dad to the fat-necked martinets who'd trained him years ago at Templemore, had bludgeoned the same thing into him: never trust a coincidence. His own hard-won experience had taught him to temper that maxim with a healthy dose of common sense, convincing him that sometimes life just throws up entirely random conjunctions. But, even so, his gut told him the Coyle thing wasn't right.

He was trying to manoeuvre past an overtaking lorry when he heard the pips for the news on the radio.

'Reports are coming in of an arrest in the so-called Priest case.'

Mulcahy pressed the tab on his steering wheel to raise the volume, willing the newsreader to get the words out of his mouth faster.

'A Garda spokesman announced a few moments ago that a man was detained by Gardai at his home in Chapelizod, Dublin, earlier today and is now helping Garda investigators with their enquiries relating to the so-called Priest case. The spokesman said that, following the discovery of the body of a young woman in the Phoenix Park in the early hours of this morning, the case had progressed rapidly, resulting in an arrest. No other details are available at present but a further announcement will be made at a press conference later today. In related news, the row over a Spanish military unit allowed to operate on Irish soil continues. In the Dáil today, the Minister for Foreign Affairs resisted calls . . .'

Mulcahy made a long, low whistle and turned down the volume. Christ almighty, that was fast. What the hell had happened to bring about an arrest so quickly? He spotted a lay-by ahead and pulled into it. He had to find out immediately what was going on. He scrolled down to Brogan's number and tapped the call button, but got put straight through to voicemail. Of course he did. Everybody and his wife would be ringing her now. He left a message asking her to call him back. He'd barely hung up when the phone rang.

'Is that Inspector Mulcahy?'

It was a man's voice, light and refined, the accent full of the rounded vowels of Dublin 4. Mulcahy had a quick glimpse of the number before responding. He didn't recognise it.

'Yes, it is.'

'My name is Sean Rinn. You left a card at my home yesterday, asking me to call you.'

It wasn't so much a statement as a question: *why?* Mulcahy sat back in his seat, wondering what to say. News of the arrest had knocked all thoughts of Rinn from his head, replacing them, it seemed, with a vacuum.

340

'Um, yes, Mr Rinn. Thanks for getting back to me. It was in relation to an incident you were a witness to last year. I was reviewing the case and wanted to have a word with you, if that would be possible?'

'Is it really necessary?' Rinn complained. 'I told the Gardai everything I knew at the time. It's all in my statement. Nothing's changed since then, has it?'

Something about the way he said it irked Mulcahy. A fleeting memory of Caroline Coyle's face as she nearly collapsed in her own front door flashed through his mind. Followed by one of Brennan describing a boy beating another with a brick.

'It's routine but necessary, yes, Mr Rinn.' He looked at his watch. Everybody back at Harcourt Square would be fixated on the arrest for hours now. This might be the last chance he'd get to do anything about it. Fuck it, why not?

'Look, I'm going to be in your area in half an hour, Mr Rinn. Will you be at home?'

When the door bell jangled this time, he was rewarded by the sound of footsteps approaching across a tiled hall. The door swung open and the man who answered it was not at all what Mulcahy had been expecting: not exactly a small man, five ten or so, in his mid- to late thirties, slim built with sandy hair and a narrow kind of face distinguished only by the sort of absence of features that sinks into the background in photographs. Somehow, from Brennan's description, he'd imagined he would be entirely different – younger, certainly. The only notable thing about this guy was that he dressed a little bit older than his years, a red polo-neck sweater hanging from his thin frame, a pair of well-worn tan cords sagging above battered brown leather brogues.

'Mr Rinn?'

'That's right.'

'I'm Inspector Mulcahy. We spoke earlier . . .'

'Yes,' he said, looking at the warrant card Mulcahy was holding up.

'Can I come in?'

'Oh,' Rinn said, as if the thought had never crossed his mind. 'Well, of course, yes. Come in.' He stepped back to allow Mulcahy through the front door into a huge hallway. The floor was a worn mosaic of brown and white tiles, leading to a fine mahogany staircase that was let down by a threadbare pale green carpet. The hall furniture looked dated – dark, bulky antiques – and the paintings and pictures on the walls looked relentlessly gloomy.

'Excuse me, Inspector,' Rinn said. 'I don't get many visitors. Why don't we go into the sitting room? The doors there are open on to the garden.'

Mulcahy followed him into a marginally brighter room. There the furniture seemed somehow less heavy; the carved marble mantelpiece had a lightness to it, as did the faded silk shades on the table lamps, dripping with tassels and frills. It was a room that felt like it had the hand of a woman about it.

'You certainly have a fine big house and garden here, Mr

Rinn,' Mulcahy said, moving towards the open French windows and looking out across the wide flight of lichen-stained stone steps leading down to the garden below. From this elevated position it looked even more strikingly beautiful than on his previous visit. Only the half-laid path in front of the left-hand borders marred its elegance.

'Yes, my grandparents left it to me. I'm lucky, I suppose. I spent a long time teaching abroad, never living the high life exactly. And then I came back to this. I do rattle around in it a bit, and both the house and garden take quite a bit of upkeep. But it's worth it. Will you sit down?'

Mulcahy chose the armchair closest to the window.

'You lived abroad, you said?'

'Yes, until a couple of years ago.'

'And you live here now,' Mulcahy continued. 'On your own?'

'Yes, I do,' Rinn said. 'Why?'

Mulcahy shrugged. 'As you said, it's a lot for one person.'

Rinn didn't respond to that, so Mulcahy went on. 'Like I said, I'm here about the assault over on Temple Road last year.'

'Yes,' Rinn said, 'nasty incident. I was hoping you'd caught someone for it, at last, when I saw your card.'

'I'm afraid not. But we are reviewing the case. I was wondering if we might go back over a couple of details in your statement.'

'I suppose so. Although I'm not sure how well I remember what I said in it now.'

'That's okay. I have a copy right here.' Mulcahy flapped the thin folder in front of him. 'But maybe first you could tell it to me as you recall it now – to see if anything new comes up.'

'Alright, if that's what you need.' Rinn scratched his head and took a deep breath. 'As I recall I was driving up Temple Road at the time. It must have been a warm night as I had the window down. I heard screams coming from one of the gardens and, well, it sounded like a woman in trouble, so I stopped the car and ran back until I came upon a man standing over a young lady who was sitting on the grass. She was crying and shaking, and the man was trying to calm her.' He paused, as if replaying the scene in his mind before continuing. 'It was so dark it was hard to tell exactly what was going on, so I challenged them, and the man said the woman had been attacked and that the Gardai were on their way. I didn't know the man, but the front door was open and the light was on so I assumed it was his house. I asked him if he'd seen the attacker and he said no, that he must have panicked and run off. So I waited with them until the patrol car and an ambulance came and next day, as requested, I made a statement at Rathmines Garda Station. And that, Inspector, was it, I'm afraid. I didn't see or hear anything else.'

'Thank you, Mr Rinn. Nobody passed you as you ran up after parking?'

'Not that I was aware of. Perhaps he went in the opposite direction—'

'That'd be the direction you were coming from in your car. You didn't see anything then, either?'

'No,' Rinn said flatly.

'Very public spirited of you to stop.'

'Well, like I said, the young lady sounded like she was in trouble.'

'And nothing else has occurred to you about the incident since you made your statement? Sometimes things come back, small things that—'

'Recollections in tranquillity?' Rinn interrupted, and moved away from the mantelpiece to look out over the garden through the open doors.

'If you like.'

'No. I did think long and hard about it at the time. I was quite disturbed by the incident, in fact. As you can imagine, things like that don't happen very often around here.'

Mulcahy stared at him, wondering just how deeply Rinn might have thought about it afterwards, and how often.

'I was hoping you might tell me in more detail how you came upon the incident, Mr Rinn. I wasn't very clear on that from your statement.'

Rinn turned to him quickly, surprise on his face. 'No? I thought I'd made it quite explicit.'

Mulcahy said nothing.

'Well, as I said, I was just driving up the road.'

'Going to? Coming from?' Mulcahy prompted.

'I'm afraid I don't remember, Inspector. I must have been coming home from somewhere, I suppose.'

'You weren't working then?'

'Working?' Rinn sounded genuinely surprised. 'All this occurred at ten o'clock at night.'

'Nine forty-five,' Mulcahy supplied, helpfully.

'Whatever,' Rinn said, slightly tetchy now. 'The thing is, Inspector, the time is irrelevant because I wouldn't have been working anyway. What I mean is, I don't work. As I said, I'm very lucky. My grandparents left me well provided for. I don't need to work, so I don't.'

Now it was Mulcahy's turn to be gobsmacked. 'But in your statement it says that you're a taxi driver by profession.'

He'd rarely seen a jaw drop quite as precipitately as Rinn's did, followed by a great boom of laughter. 'A taxi driver? Me? You must be confusing me with someone else, Inspector. Or maybe a colleague has been pulling your leg? Where does it say that? Show me.'

Mulcahy flicked the file open and checked the statement. Sure enough, in the box marked occupation, the words 'taxi driver' were typed. He showed it to Rinn, and pointed to his signature at the bottom of the page.

'I'm sorry, Inspector, but whoever typed this statement made a mistake. Obviously, I wouldn't have signed it if I'd noticed that at the time. But I'm sure you'll see there's no such reference in my statement. There couldn't be. I'm sure I checked it thoroughly at the time.'

Mulcahy scanned through the body of the statement and, as Rinn said, there was nothing about him driving a taxi, only a car. How the hell could he have missed that?

Somehow the Garda who'd taken the statement must have inserted the wrong details. And now Mulcahy had gone down completely the wrong track after him. Not only that, he was being made to feel a complete prat in front of Rinn, just to cap it all.

Mulcahy stood up, apologised to Rinn for disturbing him, and was heading for the door when his eye was caught by a small, bright painting on the wall: a lush coastal landscape, with a sailboat cleaving through blue-green water in the foreground. It reminded him so powerfully of sailing with his dad on childhood summer holidays in Cork, he just had to stop and look. Somehow, the artist had captured all the pleasure of sailing in a single scene.

'What a beautiful painting.' Mulcahy leaned in closer to examine the small brass lozenge embedded in the frame. *Gweedore Summer by Padraig Rinn*, it read.

'Yes, my grandfather was a gifted amateur artist,' Rinn said.

'Looks like it.' Mulcahy's eyes were still entranced by the swirl of blue and green on the canvas, but not so much that the rest of him couldn't sense a crackle of anxiety coming from Rinn beside him. The man's mood seemed to have turned in an instant.

'It's so summery,' Mulcahy said. 'You can practically feel the light bouncing off the water.'

'Indeed.' Rinn seemed unbearably uncomfortable now, fiddling with the neck of his sweater as if feeling the heat of the day for the first time. For just a second, Mulcahy caught

347

a glimpse of what appeared to be a spectacular scar of purple puckered skin wrapped around his throat, and he thought of what Brennan had said about Rinn being badly injured in the crash that killed his parents. That explained the polo-neck sweater, at least. Then it hit him – Brennan had mentioned something about Gweedore. Some incident or another.

'Gweedore?' Mulcahy said, looking Rinn full in the eyes. 'That's up in Donegal, right?'

'That's right,' Rinn replied, a slightly strained tone in his voice now.

'You have family connections up that way?'

'My grandfather was raised there. He dragged us up there for a month every summer when the courts were not in session. Beaches, safe swimming, rowing boats to take us out fishing. And, of course, the sailing, which he was passionate about.'

'It shows,' Mulcahy said, thinking Rinn's tone didn't exactly exude enthusiasm. 'You don't get back there very often yourself, I take it?'

'No,' Rinn replied. 'I haven't been in years. Why do you ask?'

Again Mulcahy could feel the tension radiating from Rinn.

'No reason,' Mulcahy said. What a weird reaction. What the hell was he being so defensive about? The grandfather, maybe?

'Is this the man himself?' Mulcahy pointed at a faded old photograph in a glass frame on the mantelpiece. It was a head-and-shoulders portrait of a glum-looking man with slicked-back hair, a large fleshy nose and thick tortoiseshell glasses, his expression as stiff and unyielding as the starched shirt collar that dug into his neck. Beside it was another photo, retouched by hand in muted colours, of a group of young men standing formally to attention, all wearing some kind of green uniform. Mulcahy recognised the man at the centre as the one in the portrait, younger but with the same heavy glasses and what looked like a gold chain of office around his neck. In the background, a long white banner read: *International Eucharistic Congress, 1932.*

Rinn hadn't replied to his question, so Mulcahy turned and asked again. 'Is this your grandfather, sir?'

'Oh, for God's sake . . .' Rinn spluttered, his agitation getting the better of him. 'Yes, it is. Now please, Inspector, if you have nothing else pertinent to your enquiries, I really must get on.'

Mulcahy stared Rinn down for a couple of seconds, then took one last look at the painting of the boat on the water and made his way out through the gloomy hallway to the front door.

'Okay, Mr Rinn. If you do think of anything, you have my details.'

He was sitting in the Saab outside, still trying to get his head round how he'd tell Brogan that his great tip-off about a taxi driver had turned out to be nothing but some fucker in uniform's typing error, when his phone went off. Another voice he didn't recognise, a woman's this time.

'Noreen from Superintendent Healy's office here, Inspector. He wants to see you.'

Mulcahy looked at his watch. Two thirty-five. God alone only knew what the traffic would be like.

'I'm just on my way back in, Noreen, I'll probably be half an hour.'

'Shall we say three, then?'

'Yeah, fine.'

The line went dead. He started the car and pulled out. This was one meeting he really didn't want to be late for.

His mobile rang again just as he was about to get into the lift in Harcourt Square. It was Brogan, finally getting back to him. He let the lift go and walked over to a quiet corner, congratulating her on the arrest and begging her for details. From the rush in her voice, he could tell she was still high on it.

'To be honest,' she said, 'it was more to do with Lonergan than us. That guy has some luck: I couldn't believe how fast it happened. Apparently, when the Techs were preparing the girl's body for the post-mortem exam, one of them noticed a piece of paper stuck to a corner of the plastic wrapping. It was all torn but there was some half-legible typing on it and also some kind of a code. I'm telling you, Mike, these guys can work like lightning when they want to. In under an hour they matched it to a gardening wholesaler – Hartigans, in Chapelizod. You know how close that is to the Phoenix Park. So we all go screeching round to the place and this

350

weedy little guy in Hartigans says, "Oh yeah, that's the back end of one of our delivery numbers", like it's no big deal.'

He heard her break off on the other end of the line and say something muffled to someone else. Then she was back. 'Are you still there?'

'Yeah, go on.'

'Okay, look, I have to go in a minute, so I can't go into details, but here it is in a nutshell. The guy in Hartigans looks up their records and says, yeah, here it is: a delivery of half a ton of coconut-husk chips to a gardener called Emmet Byrne. And one of the local guys, who knows him, says Byrne's got form for indecent assault. So we all go tearing over to his place and, when we get there, first thing we see is a white Transit van, the side door open and what's all over the floor of the van except a load of sacks from this coconut stuff. And what are the sacks made of? Exactly those same red plastic fibres we got on the other victims. I mean, they're so distinctive, they literally couldn't be anything else. So we had him, bang to fucking rights. It was amazing.'

Mulcahy laughed as she broke off again, her excitement infectious even down the phone line. Then she had to go. 'Lonergan's calling me. We're going in to do the press conference now. I've got to go.'

'Yeah, good luck with—'

But she was gone before he could finish the sentence.

Healy kept him waiting for a few minutes before Noreen's phone buzzed and he was ushered in. This time the office was in semi-darkness; only the glare from a huge flat-screen TV on the wall supplemented the meagre light penetrating the curtains drawn shut across the huge window. Healy was standing by his desk, remote control in his hand, raising the volume on what revealed itself to be a press conference. The cameras showed a long table on a dais, where four people – one in heavily braided uniform, three in suits – were seated in front of microphones, answering questions. One of them, he saw, was Brogan.

'Brendan, I just heard—'

Healy put a finger to his lips and swept a hand towards the chair in front of his desk. 'Sit down there for a minute, Mike, this is just coming to the end. RTE's putting this news conference out live.'

In close-up appeared the man they all worked for. The heavy-set, furrow-browed Garda Commissioner Thurloch Garvey, his smoke-grey uniform trimmed with enough gold to underpin a third-world economy, was looking eager to wind up the session, as he asked for any other questions. The camera switched back to the room and a flurry of raised arms, picking out one in particular from the pack of jostling reporters. Mulcahy instantly recognised Siobhan Fallon's mop of curly black hair and curvy frame. Just what he bloody needed with Healy hovering beside him.

'Don't you think it's all a little bit convenient, Commissioner Garvey?' Siobhan inquired, flashing her familiar smile. 'I mean, a murder last night and you pick up a suspect by lunchtime. This despite the fact that another team of detectives has been looking for The Priest for weeks already?'

Garvey bridled. 'That's a ridiculous assertion. Of course it's not a question of convenience. Next question, please.'

The camera panned back to the throng of reporters, from which came an indignant shout. Siobhan was trying to ask a follow-up but Commissioner Garvey flatly ignored her. 'Okay,' he said into the microphone. 'If there's nothing more, we'll wrap this up now. Any further enquiries will be dealt with by Superintendent Lonergan via the Garda Press Office. Thank you.'

As they gathered their papers and left the room the camera cut back to the RTE news presenter and Healy pointed the remote at the TV and lowered the volume.

'She has a way of getting up people's noses, that girl,' he said as he walked back around the desk and settled into his swivel chair.

Mulcahy thought it best not to respond to that.

'Anyway, it's a great result for us all,' Healy went on.

'Sounds like it – and solid too.'

'You spoke to Claire?'

Mulcahy nodded.

'As soon as those forensics come through,' Healy said, 'it'll be in the bag. Lonergan told me so personally.'

'It's just a shame his crew has to get all the credit.'

There was a creak of leather from the chair as Healy leaned forward and put his elbows on the desk, pressing his fingers to his nose, staring at Mulcahy.

'You know, if I'm honest, I'm not so sorry about that. It'll still be a long road preparing the case for the DPP, and this whole thing has been a bad lot from the start. It's never good when politicians get too closely involved.' As he said it, Healy made a cleansing motion with his hands, as if throwing something imaginary into his waste bin. Mulcahy wondered whether Healy really thought a girl's life was a price worth paying to pass the buck to Lonergan and the Murder Squad.

'Anyway, things have moved on now,' Healy continued. 'All the investigations are being linked and dealt with under the one umbrella by Lonergan and his team. But there's still a loose end, and it's one the Minister wants tied up quickly. That's the Spanish involvement – which, as you know, is still causing the government a bit of stick. Thanks chiefly to your friend Fallon and her colleagues.'

Something must have cracked in the poker face Mulcahy thought he'd adopted because Healy smiled and sat back in his seat.

'Don't worry, Mike. All we want you to do is go to Madrid and take a statement from young Jesica Salazar. I got a call through this morning saying that she's well enough now to be formally interviewed.'

'I thought you were handling all that yourself now, sir?'

Healy shifted in his seat a little uncomfortably. 'Yes, well, according to this fella Martinez who called us, it seems Señor Salazar is insisting that the interview should be conducted by someone the girl is familiar with, namely you. There's also a

354

continuity-of-evidence benefit, and the Minister is particularly concerned that there shouldn't be any holes in the judicial process due to Miss Salazar's, eh, unorthodox removal from our jurisdiction. Especially with the possibility of a public enquiry looming. So, given that you've interviewed her before and know the sensitivities of everyone involved, we thought you'd be the right man for the job.'

Mulcahy had to stop himself from smiling. He knew damn well that this could only be Javier Martinez's doing. How many strings must he have pulled to get that one to fly?

'Well? Don't you have anything to say?'

'Yes. I mean, no, sir,' Mulcahy stumbled. 'Will anyone else be going?'

'No, you're only going over to take a statement from her. Someone there can witness it. I'll ask Lonergan if he wants you to take some mugs of this fella they've arrested and try for a positive ID. But that may not be necessary at this stage. Word is the girl still doesn't recollect much of the incident at all. So it's mostly a formality, but we have to be seen to respond quickly to their offer. Lonergan can always send one of his own team further down the line if she comes up with anything else subsequently. I just want it wrapped up at our end for now, okay?'

'Of course.'

'Good. See Noreen outside about your travel arrangements. You'll be going tomorrow. Short notice, I know, but we want to get this done as soon as possible.'

355

'Not a problem.' Mulcahy glanced over at Healy, who was now apparently preoccupied by the muted television screen on the wall again. 'Will that be all, Brendan?'

'No, Mike, there was one more thing.' Healy sat forward in his chair. 'I had a call from Chief Superintendent Murtagh from Southern this morning. He said a job had come up in Cork that you were interested in applying for.'

Mulcahy's spirits lifted. At last, Dowling must have agreed to take the compensation package – and his timing couldn't have been better. 'Yes, head of the Southern Region drugs task force. He thinks I'd be good for it.'

'I've no doubt you would, Mike,' Healy smiled at him. 'I've no doubt of that at all. But as I told Chief Superintendent Murtagh, I'm afraid you won't be available to take up his offer.'

Mulcahy's innards instantly felt hollowed out, his head as if it'd been pumped full of air.

'Excuse me?'

'I said I told Murtagh you wouldn't be free to take it up.'

'Why the hell not?'

'Well, I should've thought it would be obvious. With Brogan out of commission for the foreseeable future over on Lonergan's murder team, we're an inspector down here, so obviously I can't afford to lose you as well. Especially not in the current climate. You're going have to stay on in Sex Crimes until we get Brogan back.'

It hit home like a punch in the gut, a real sucker punch, and now Mulcahy felt the breath go out of his body from it.

'But for God's sake, Brendan, that could take ages. What about the job? I've been waiting months for an opening like this to come up.'

'I know, it's a tough break, Mike, but I really can't afford to let you go just now. Even if I'd wanted to do you the favour' – he paused, filling the momentary silence with a vengeful little smile – 'I wouldn't be in a position to. Not unless I wanted to make a rod for my own back. And anyway, Murtagh was very understanding about it – as I'm sure he'll tell you himself. So, when you get back from Madrid, you can take Brogan's office and I'll be in touch regarding her caseload. We'll have to sort you out with some staff as well, of course, seeing as she's taken all hers with her.'

Mulcahy didn't even hear the rest of it. A horrible pounding in his head was blocking everything out.

He needed somewhere to go, somewhere to sit and calm down and stop the damn torment that seemed to have taken up residence in his skull. Jesus, what an idiot he'd been. How could he not have seen this one coming? He should have phoned Murtagh himself as soon as he heard Brogan was being transferred and asked when he might be needed. At least that way he could have gone in to see Healy prepared, had ready some kind of fait accompli. But now? Now, he was just plain buggered. He looked at the itinerary sheet in his hands. Noreen had pounced as soon as he came out the door. 'It's the nine-fifteen Aer Lingus flight to

Madrid, check in eight-fifteen, arrive . . .' Again he hardly took in a word of it. Without even thinking about it he made his way back down to the fourth floor. He saw the door to the incident room was open and knew it was one place guaranteed to be empty now. But he was wrong again. So bloody wrong.

'How'ya, Inspector.'

Christ almighty, what the hell was Cassidy doing back here?

'Sergeant? I thought we'd seen the last of you.'

'No such luck,' Cassidy grunted, unpinning an A3 blow-up of Catriona Plunkett from the board and rolling it up.

For a second the awful thought flashed through Mulcahy's mind that Cassidy, too, might be being held back from the Murder Squad, that he would be expected to work with the man for the foreseeable future . . . but it seemed he was to be spared that indignity at least.

'I was just on my way back from the post-mortem on the girl,' Cassidy said. 'I thought I'd stop off to pick up these bits and pieces. She was only fourteen, you know.'

There was real anger in Cassidy's voice, a sense that he, too, had been seeking the sanctuary of an empty incident room to find some calm. Mulcahy thought of the dead girl himself and felt the weight of a tragedy considerably greater than his own career problems settle on him.

'Christ, that's young,' he said. 'The ID came in fairly quickly, then?'

Cassidy nodded, pulling some photocopied forensics

358

sheets from the wall and adding them to the pile in front of him. 'Paula Halpin, from Dartry. Missing persons had her, reported gone by her parents Tuesday night. Went out to the shop to get fags for her mother, didn't come back.'

'God, how would you live with that?' Mulcahy said, thinking how guilty the mother must be feeling. 'From Dartry, did you say?'

Somehow it struck an odd note. Then again, there was no particular geographical cluster relating to The Priest's victims. Cassidy looked at him as if to say: *what of it?*

Mulcahy let it go. 'So, how did the PM go? Do we have a cause of death?'

Cassidy continued staring at him, as if considering whether or not to share. In the end, he turned away again and nodded. 'The preliminary results indicate that she died of a major myocardial infarction.'

'A heart attack?'

'Yeah, brought on by shock from the severity of her injuries, the doc said. Seems she'd suffered from a heart murmur since birth. Did for her, apparently – but they're still looking into that.'

'The poor kid.' Mulcahy shook his head.

'You can say that again,' Cassidy said, as he loped off.

The Long Hall was deserted, the lunchtime rush long over and still too early yet for the after-work crowd. Mulcahy, grateful for a sense of isolation at last, mounted a stool at the long mahogany bar and ordered a pint, thinking of the last time he'd been in here, with Siobhan Fallon, and of that other night – the night they'd spent together before the whole thing blew up about The Priest. Christ, what an unmitigated cock-up the last few weeks had been.

The barman gave him a peculiar look as he set the pint down and Mulcahy realised he'd been leaning into the counter, rubbing his temples, staring like a madman into the huge Victorian mirror behind the bar. He sat up, straightened himself out, breathed deeply in, then out again. He reached for the pint and took a long gulp. Immediately, the wash of cold stout through his system exerted a kind of calm. Then the thought of losing the Southern Region job sent his stomach into spasm again. He took another pull on the pint, trying to think his situation through rationally. It could take months for Brogan and the others to prepare the case for the DPP, assuming they had the right man. And, now they had this Byrne guy in custody, you could be sure they'd take their time getting it right. Meanwhile, because of Healy's intransigence, every opportunity that came up in Drugs would be closed to him. In other words, he was totally fucked – stuck spending all his time chasing wife beaters, rapists and child abusers.

Mulcahy started flicking through his mental address book of acquaintance and influence. Who could he phone to give him a hand, get him out of this fix? But he knew it was pointless. He'd called in his entire stock of favours when he'd first returned from Madrid and all that had got him was a place in the NBCI, beholden to Brendan Healy.

He took another long gulp. The thought of his career going down the pan – with Healy gleefully pulling the chain – was almost too much to bear. Maybe it was time to face the inevitable, he thought, swirling the remains of his pint in the glass. Maybe it was time to throw in the towel.

He was about to order again when he caught another glimpse of himself in the mirror and something clicked in his head. What was it that had bothered him when Cassidy spoke earlier about the murdered girl? Paula Halpin. From Dartry. That was it. Dartry wasn't that far from his parents' house. More to the point, it was miles away from Chapelizod where Byrne lived and worked, but only a couple of hundred metres down the road from Palmerston Park and Rinn's house.

He tried to shake the thought away. It made no sense to focus on it. An arrest had already been made. And Rinn, apart from acting a bit weird about his past, had seemed a perfectly, maybe even more than averagely, respectable guy. It wasn't even much of a coincidence. Still, the fact of it pulsed like a live electric cable in his head: Dartry. In his mind's eye he saw a young girl, fourteen years old, all milky-white skin and curly auburn hair, sauntering up the Dartry Road from Milltown Bridge, past the old Laundry Mills and Trinity Hall. In her hand she held a little red plastic purse that seemed to beat and throb, and around her neck hung a glittering cross. But instead of walking on up the hill towards light and life, she turned to take a shortcut through—

'Are you havin' another one, boss?'

Startled, Mulcahy was wrenched from his thoughts by the barman, who was holding up an empty pint glass. He shook his head, put his hand in his pocket, and pulled out his phone.

16

Father Touhy, the parish priest of St Imelda's in Chapelizod, looked like he'd long been on the wrong side of seventy. A frail, slightly hunched man, he had a pale, gentle face and, above his black clergyman's suit, a shock of white hair like the head on a pint of Guinness. He made only one enquiry – 'Are you the young woman who asked that question on the television?' – before agreeing to speak to her when she answered in the affirmative. Siobhan had phoned his number on the off-chance. His church was locked up and already swamped by reporters and camera crews, spilling off the pavement outside. A whole mob of them had gone racing down there as soon as the Garda press officer, in response to a leading question, announced that yes, Emmet Byrne, the suspect in the Priest case, *did* indeed have an association with the Catholic Church – he worked as a part-time gardener for the parish church of St Imelda's, Chapelizod.

Seeing them all there already, Siobhan told the taxi driver to keep going. Mainly because she spotted Anne-

Marie Cowen from RTE News doing a piece to camera outside and didn't feel like talking to her. Just as well. A simple phone call later, and the parish priest was letting her slip in the back door of the tiny semi-detached presbytery around the corner, and sitting her down with a cup of tea. He was glad she'd called, he said, as he felt sure he'd need more direct intervention than God's to convince the Gardai that they were wrong about 'poor Emmet' – who was, Fr Touhy insisted, a man more sinned against than sinning.

Siobhan looked at her watch, eager to get on with it, figuring she had half an hour, maximum, before the rest of the pack realised where the presbytery was and started beating a path to its door. The poor old priest looked like he might be close to tears from the stress of it all already. He even confessed, straight out, his fear that a Catholic clergyman might not be considered the best defender that a man accused of a sex crime, let alone rape and murder, could have these days in Ireland. So maybe he wasn't so naive after all.

'I'm sure people will respect the opinion of a parish priest of long standing, like yourself,' Siobhan said. 'They'll want to hear what you have to say about Byrne anyway. Whether they believe it or not is up to them, I suppose.'

He smiled at her, understanding what she was saying. 'Do you think I'd have him working here if I wasn't a hundred per cent confident in him? He's a good man, gentle. On the slow side, yes, if I'm honest. And that's the problem – his friendliness can sometimes be misinterpreted.'

'Misinterpreted?' Siobhan said, her antenna zinging. 'How exactly do you mean, Father?'

'Well, you know, like that last time he was arrested.'

She nearly gagged on her ginger nut, but just about managed to cover it up with a cough.

'Sorry, I think a bit of biscuit went down the wrong way there, Father. You were saying, about the arrest?'

'That's right,' Fr Touhy said. 'For interfering with that child. A terrible thing, it was.'

'A child.' She put the cup and saucer on the table, trying not to let them rattle. Thanking every saint in heaven that she'd remembered to switch on her voice recorder, she reached for her notepad anyway, just in case. For the second time that week she wondered if she hadn't been accidentally promoted into the ranks of the blessed. Could fate be any kinder to her?

'You didn't know about that?' Fr Touhy asked her, a little coyly she thought.

'No, the guards didn't release that information. It does kind of change the picture, though, doesn't it?'

'Yes and no,' the priest said, rubbing his clean-shaven cheeks in frustration, and looking a lot less innocent now. 'I'm telling you this not only because it's bound to come out anyway but because it needs to be known that he didn't do it. It was a horrible, vindictive accusation by a young girl who wanted to make trouble for Emmet and knew exactly how to go about it. Luckily, her mother learned the truth before it went too far. Emmet was never charged with any offence.'

'You know what they'll say, Father,' Siobhan said, composing the piece in her head even as she spoke. 'No smoke without fire.'

'That's why I need your help,' he said, 'because it'll be all too easy for them to make out he confessed again.' He broke off, rubbing his chin with a pale hand, his small eyes assessing her.

'Confessed again?' By now Siobhan wasn't entirely certain who was using who here, but she wasn't sure she cared, either. This story got better by the second.

'Yes,' Fr Touhy said. 'They didn't want to drop it last time, even after the accusation was withdrawn, because the Garda who arrested him said that Emmet had confessed. In the end they couldn't do anything about it, apparently because he'd made this supposed confession before he was cautioned. It was a close thing, but they had to let him go.'

'And you think that's why . . .?' Siobhan trailed off, wanting him to say it for the tape.

'Yes,' Fr Touhy obliged, 'I'm convinced that's the only reason they came knocking again this time – because they hoped they'd get a quick confession. Emmet has a thing – Lord help me, I should know – about confessing to things he didn't do, thinking that it'll make him sound more important. Some of the stuff he comes out with can sound a bit off if you don't know him. But he doesn't mean any harm. If you met him, you'd know he was incapable of doing such things.'

Siobhan wasn't so sure about the sound of that, at all. 'I

hate to break it to you, Father,' she said as gently as she could. 'But from the whispers I've been hearing, Emmet is in a lot more trouble than that. To be honest, I haven't heard anything about him confessing. Only that the Guards are claiming they've got forensic evidence that's as solid as you can get in a case like this. I think maybe you should prepare yourself for that.'

She did a quick calculation in her head. It was Friday afternoon, so she only had another thirty-six hours to get through. If she could keep the information about Emmet's previous arrest exclusive for her own front page, it would be a spectacular coup. And she couldn't help feeling a little bit sorry for the old priest, anyway.

'Look, Father, if you want my advice, I wouldn't mention this to anyone else. As you say, it'll probably all come out, anyway. But there's no point handing people another stick to beat Emmet with, either. You must know how bad this information could look for him if it got into the wrong hands.'

What he said next took her by surprise.

'And your hands are the right ones, Siobhan, are they?'

If she hadn't taken so much care over her make-up earlier, he'd have seen her blushing to her roots.

'I'd have thought you'd be forgetting about Rinn now that you've arrested this other fella,' Brennan said when he picked up the phone.

'Yeah, well,' Mulcahy replied, not wanting to say too

much on that score. 'You know how it is. That's the major focus of the investigation now. But not the only one.'

Brennan didn't sound entirely convinced but his deep-rooted wish for someone, anyone, to put the screws on Rinn must have overcome the ex-sergeant's fixation on procedural correctness.

'Right, well, I rang my old pal like you asked me to,' Brennan said at last, exhaling heavily like a man deciding that, sometimes, you just had to bend the rules to get results. 'I thought maybe the fact that he's retired for years now might loosen his tongue a bit, but I reckon it's his brain that's got something loose in it. He could barely remember who I was, let alone Sean Rinn.'

Mulcahy waited for the rest, praying this wasn't going to be a waste of time. But Brennan sounded upbeat. Maybe he was just teasing – enjoying being back on the job, if only by default.

'But his wife gave me the number of another fella he was working with at that time, by the name of Tommy Casey,' the sergeant chuckled. 'I gave him a call, and it turned out we knew each other from way back, and he was a bit more helpful after that. He remembered Rinn alright, and all that fuss up in Drumcondra. Seems it was worse than I thought. According to Tommy, Rinn was kicked out of All Hallows after an incident with one of the staff there.'

'An incident? An assault, you mean?'

'Yes, but not sexual. It was a fight – with a fella, we think. Tommy couldn't give me exact details but as far as he knew a complaint was made at Drumcondra Garda Station then quickly withdrawn, and there were rumours that a pile of money had changed hands, and the whole thing got swept under the carpet.'

'Sounds much the same as what you said before,' Mulcahy said.

'No,' Brennan said. 'I always thought he was thrown out of the seminary because of something that happened up in Donegal. But this "incident" actually happened in Dublin, at All Hallows college itself. What Tommy said was that this other fella, the one Rinn had the fight with, was from that part of the world himself, from Gweedore, in fact. Which is where Rinn's grandfather, the High Court judge came from. Do you get me?'

'So?' Mulcahy said, his brain pinging back to the oil painting he'd seen on the wall in Rinn's house.

'Tommy said the rumour at the time was that a huge amount of cash changed hands. I mean, for a fist fight? Unlikely, huh? And Rinn getting thrown out? An overreaction, wouldn't you say, when most of them seminarians were a bit mad, anyway? I mean, all that celibacy, they had nothing else to vent their unholy hormonal urges on, so those boys were always taking lumps out of each other with hurleys and the like, out on the playing fields.'

'Okay,' Mulcahy said. Maybe it *was* a bit strange now he thought of it, although he still wasn't sure where the sergeant was going with this.

'Well, that's just it,' Brennan said. 'Don't you see?

Whatever it was caused the clerical bigwigs in All Hallows to kick Chief Justice Rinn's grandson out of their sacred ranks must've been pretty damn serious. The old man was a big noise in the Knights, for heaven's sake.'

Mulcahy's mind spun back to the photo he'd seen on Rinn's mantelpiece of his grandfather in all his regalia. So the old judge had been a leading light in the Knights of St Columbanus, the principal powerbrokers in Irish society for decades after the republic won independence. But so what? It would be more of a surprise if a poor boy from Donegal had grown up to be a High Court judge *without* being heavily involved with the Knights. As with the Masons in other countries, the Gardai and the judiciary, in particular, were riddled with the Knights back in the old days. All the same, Brennan did have a point. It was weird that someone with such strong connections to them would be kicked out of a seminary, of all places, especially back at a time when the Knights still had considerable power and influence. Bizarre, Mulcahy would have said.

'So what I'm thinking,' Brennan continued, 'is that whatever it was happened in Donegal a couple of years earlier, must've been at the root of it all. And it must've been pretty big. Maybe this guy from Gweedore knew all about it, and threatened to blow the whistle, or blew it, until he was nobbled by Rinn senior and the priests. Maybe by then there was no going back for Rinn as regards All Hallows. Whatever it was he did, it was too much for the clergy to look the other way.'

'And as we now know, there wasn't much they wouldn't cover up for one of their own,' Mulcahy agreed.

'Right,' said Brennan. 'They wanted him out of there for some very good reason – and straight away.'

'So whatever happened in Gweedore holds the key to Rinn.'

'That's exactly it,' Brennan said, triumphantly.

Mulcahy sat back. It made a kind of sense. And that it probably had no relevance whatsoever to The Priest was almost beside the point now. If Rinn really did have some secret to hide, it might be something that would justify reopening the case on Caroline Coyle. With Rinn as prime suspect. That way, Brennan might get his closure, too.

'Jesus, Sergeant,' Mulcahy laughed. 'You were a loss to CID and no mistake.'

Siobhan spent a couple more hours out in Chapelizod, pounding the pavements, calling into local shops and businesses, reporter's pad in hand, asking if they knew Emmet Byrne. In the process, she began to get two very different impressions of the man. On the one hand there were those who saw him as a local character, a few cent short of the full euro but likeable enough all the same, and fairly harmless with it, by all accounts. 'Ah, sure, poor Emmet, there's no bad in him at all,' said the woman who ran the newsagents. So, too, with the barber down the road and the women in the greasy spoon on the corner, where Emmet often had breakfast or lunch. It was a different matter, though, whenever she spoke to anyone from the Garda side of the fence, or anyone who was sharing information they'd got from them. Rumours were flying about what a search of Byrne's flat had thrown up. A reporter pal from the *Irish Independent* had phoned to say that all sorts of weird shit had been found in Byrne's room: crosses, candles, chains, and a big pile of porn. She said she'd got it gospel from one of the Guards who'd been in on the search, and that the place was full of newspaper cuttings about The Priest. 'Like a bloody shrine,' she'd said.

So Siobhan phoned Fr Touhy and asked him if he knew anything about that.

'Take it from me, I've been to his place many a time, and there was nothing like that,' the old priest insisted. 'I mean, certainly, he has crosses and candles and a little shrine, but it's a shrine to the Blessed Virgin. He's a man of faith. Why wouldn't he have such things?'

'And what about these cuttings about The Priest they say he kept?'

'Ah no,' the old man demurred, 'I never saw anything like that. But I know he had a couple of pictures of the Pope and Padre Pio on the walls.'

Siobhan's source on the investigation team had stayed completely dry until about four p.m. when he called to say the dead girl's parents had been informed and to give her their address in Dartry. She was a little taken aback by that, but hightailed it over there anyway. Sometimes the first one in was the only one in with things like that. The parents would only make the mistake of opening the door once – to a reporter, that is.

But there was already a press mob outside the house when she arrived. So she decided to make her way back in to the office. By then she'd had enough, and knew – not having heard about it from anyone else – that Fr Touhy must have kept quiet about Byrne's previous arrest as she'd advised him to do. There was always the risk, of course, that it would leak from somewhere else, namely the investigation team. But given that it wasn't already out there, she was thinking maybe the cops had decided to play the long game with that piece of info. They'd wait a few days to see what might come out of the woodwork on Byrne before they started on the dirty tricks proper. In which case, her front page still had a good chance of holding firm. If it did, it would blow every other paper, every other reporter, out of the water. Come Sunday, hers was the story everyone would want to read.

It was late by the time Mulcahy got back to Harcourt Square but he was in the grip of an obsession now and he knew he wouldn't relax until he'd checked out a few more details about Rinn. At the back of his mind he suspected this, in reality, was only a substitute for going upstairs and beating the living Jesus out of Brendan Healy. But as that was never going to be an option, he worked with what he had: Rinn. The first thing he did was try and call the uniform who'd taken the statement the night Caroline Coyle had been attacked. But he was told by the desk sergeant at Rathmines that the Garda in question had finished his rotation earlier in the week and was off for a few days. 'Give us your number and I'll have him call you when he gets back,' was the best the sergeant could suggest. For the next two hours, Mulcahy sat at the computer terminal in Brogan's office and searched through the Sex Offenders' Register, PULSE, the Drugs archive and every other arrest and intelligence database available on the Garda Siochana Network. He drew a complete blank from all of them, apart from one minor traffic offence: an on-the-spot fine for a blown headlamp on Sean Rinn's car eighteen months previously.

Mulcahy knew his search hadn't been all-inclusive. It couldn't be. Whatever the system's accuracy in regard to Dublin and the other major centres, few of the more outlying rural Garda stations would have computerised their records dating back more than five or six years. Up in Donegal, he doubted they had the manpower or motivation for that kind of work. In some cases they probably didn't even have the hardware for it. Gweedore was a case in point. A quick call to the local Garda station in Bunbeg revealed, by recorded message, that it was only manned three hours a day, in the mornings, and not at all at weekends. If he was going to find out anything from them, he'd have to wait till Monday. And yet a creeping sense that he couldn't afford to wait till then was getting the better of him. No matter how he tried, he couldn't shake off that waking dream of Paula Halpin strolling innocently up the hill in Dartry to her death. It was as if some supernatural creature had opened up his head, climbed in and taken up residence, not calling or taunting him but just sitting there, claws embedded in his brain, eyes blazing like a demon.

That's when he thought again of the blown headlamp. He pulled the Traffic Offence file up on the monitor again and scrutinised the page more closely. And there it was. 'The driver Mr Sean Rinn, of Palmerston Park, Dublin, was issued with an eighty-euro on-the-spot fine for driving on a public carriageway in a vehicle not properly equipped with lights, viz driver's-side headlamp on cab was defective.' Fuck! Mulcahy did a double take and checked it again. Cab, not car. His eye must have skipped over it first time round. He scanned the document for further evidence that he wasn't going completely mad and, seconds later, saw it. There, at the bottom of the document, underneath the vehicle registration number for a grey 2003 Toyota Corolla 03-D-35982, the vehicle's taxi plate number was also inscribed: 19374. Now that *couldn't* be a coincidence.

Seconds later, he was calling up the register of taxi-licence holders but Rinn's name was not listed on it. He cross-reffed for the taxi plate but found it was registered to someone else entirely, a Mr Eric Dawson of Clondalkin, and that the licence was currently inactive. Which could mean only one of two things: that Rinn was the victim of yet another bizarre Garda typing error, or he was driving around with a fake sign attached to the roof of his car, pretending to be a taxi driver.

By now Mulcahy's head was hurting from the screentime and his lungs were bursting for a smoke. He grabbed his jacket and headed for the lift. Maybe a cigarette would help him think it through more clearly. He'd only just sparked up outside when his mobile rang.

'*Buenas tardes, Mike. Cómo estas?*'

It was Javier Martinez. Christ, how did he always manage to sound so bloody happy?

'I've been better, Jav. How about you?'

'Yes, good. Sorry to call so late but you have heard about Jesica Salazar? You are coming tomorrow, no?'

'Yeah, for sure. On the first flight out. It'll be good to see you. It's really good, too, to hear the girl's recovered enough already.'

It was hard to believe; it didn't feel so long since he'd seen the poor kid lying there in a hospital bed, her face all bruised and broken, the pain and terror working through her like she was possessed. The young were so resilient. Suddenly, he felt something stir in his head, a sensation that was almost physical, shifting, sinking sharp talons into his memory. An image mushroomed in his mind, of Jesica touching the red welt on her neck where the chain had been ripped from it, and reaching out to him.

'*Hizo la señal del Cristo,*' she whispered. '*Hizo la señal del Cristo.*'

By the time Siobhan finished writing up her notes she was feeling pretty tired, but still running hard on the excitement of it all. After three hours' work she now had two more stories, in outline at least, to add to her stock for Sunday. Not a bad haul, and still a day in hand. Time to think about getting home and catching up on the ironing. Or the telly. Or maybe both. That was enough to make her change her mind and instead – probably from some odd sense of obligation to Fr Touhy – open up another new file, to begin an altogether more speculative piece on whether Byrne was actually the right man. Round and round her thoughts went, fingers lapping the keyboard like waves, trying to tease out and reconnect every strand, every loose morsel – getting it all down. Not for this Sunday, but for the following week's paper, maybe. News was news, and in this case that amounted to Byrne's arrest and his dodgy past. Any doubts she might have over the arrest, she could afford to hold in reserve. After all, they hadn't even charged him yet. It would only make an even better splash further down the road – in the unlikely event that the boys in blue really were trying to stitch Byrne up.

Her email pinged and she clicked on a reply from a psychologist contact of hers who she'd emailed earlier. She was so engrossed in reading its contents that she only grunted when – it must have been about eight p.m. – someone came and placed something on her desk. Not until ten minutes later, after she'd bashed out another string of questions in reply and sent them on their way, did she drag her eyes from the screen and notice the padded envelope now sitting by her elbow, with nothing but her name scrawled on the front. Picking it up and tearing it open, she went to grasp whatever was inside. But the second she touched it, she knew there was something wrong, and then the smell hit her and she yelped like a kicked dog, and dropped the lot onto her desk. Trembling now, she looked down and saw, half drawn out from the envelope, what looked like a sheet of folded paper. But it didn't feel like any paper she'd ever touched before. It was cold and hard yet slightly greasy to the touch – and as for the smell, it was absolutely horrible. Like burned skin or something, like . . . oh, for God's sake.

She picked up a pencil and poked at the envelope, looking inside to see if there was anything else, anything dangerous inside. But all she could see was the folded sheet. Taking a deep breath, she coaxed it out further and what flopped open onto the desk, she now saw, was a thick parchment folio, hide-like in its yellow opacity and grainy texture and flex. What sent a rivulet of cold anxiety coursing down her spine, though, was that it was scorched all over with cross marks of different sizes, some deep black gouges, others burned all the way through, leaving only ragged x-shaped holes, charred black around their edges.

She grabbed the phone and dialled the front desk, demanding to know where the package had come from. The girl below said she thought it had been handed in at reception about an hour earlier, but nobody had seen who delivered it. It had just appeared there, left, presumably, by someone who'd come in off the street. Siobhan rang security, only to be told the CCTV over reception had been down for a week, waiting for the contractor to come and repair it. She cursed, but then nothing about how cruddy the equipment levels were at the *Sunday Herald* ever really surprised her. She sat down and poked at the sheet of parchment with her pencil again, looking it over more closely now, trying to figure out who it might have come from. Was it somebody's idea of a sick joke? She wouldn't put it past some of the ghouls who worked at the *Herald*.

Then, between all the scorch marks and gouges, she saw something different: a few words of text that seemed to have been tattooed on to the fabric, or else burned with a much finer . . . a much finer what? But her mind had gone beyond that now, as she realised what the message burned into it said. Suddenly she was cold around her shoulders, and noticed that her hands were shaking. She looked around, across the banks of monitors, to see if Griffin, Heffernan or any of the others were still there. But she already knew they weren't. It was too late in the day. Even the guys from the sports desk had given up. There was nobody around but herself, and she was instantly aware of how looming, dark and empty the newsroom – the whole deserted floor – was. At just that moment, her phone rang and she lunged for it, glad of the chance to hear another human voice.

'Hello,' she said. And then she said it again. But she got no reply, just a faint hiss from the other end of the line. 'Is there anybody there?'

'God will not be mocked,' the man's voice said, angry,

loud – the breathing heavy as it had been before. 'You'll see. You will be the witness to it.'

The line went dead and Siobhan put the phone down, cursing. It was the same wanker who'd been on to her the other night, but ten times scarier now. It must've been him who left the packet. What the fuck was he talking about, she'd be 'the witness to it'? What the hell had he meant by that? The witness to what?

She gathered her jacket tighter round her shoulders and looked behind her again, shaking from head to toe now. What if he hadn't just left the envelope? Nobody had seen him. What if he'd passed the security barriers as well? He could be lurking out there in the dark, behind any one of the desks, right now. Would she have noticed him come in? No way – she hadn't even seen the messenger deliver the envelope. If it was the messenger? Oh, Jesus, fuck.

No, she thought, forcing herself to calm down. Be sensible. A freak or a nut job wouldn't have just left it there; he'd have tried to deliver his message in person. She slipped her jacket on awkwardly, without standing up, and started saving and closing the files on her screen one by one, as quickly as possible, then logged off. 'I've got to get out of here before I go mad,' she said to herself, sweeping the envelope and its contents into her bag, and hurrying for the door. She was jabbing at the lift button impatiently when her mobile rang. She looked around suspiciously, half believing still that there was someone hiding there, staring at her, stalking her, following her every move.

Her mobile trilled again, and she answered it but again heard nothing at first, just the crackle and hiss of the line. Totally spooked now, she was about to hang up when she heard the voice coming through, all jagged and remote: 'God will not be mocked.'

Then the lift doors clanged open in front of her, and she nearly collapsed in terror.

17

'Mulcahy? Is that you?'

He knew her voice instantly, even though it sounded so shaky.

'Yeah, of course,' he said, trying to push past the spark of wariness in his own voice. For a moment, the only sound at the other end of the line was of a long breath being released. 'Are you okay, Siobhan? Is something the matter?'

'No, it's okay. I'm fine now.' She laughed, but it didn't sound very heartfelt. 'I just got a fright, that's all. I don't even know why I called you. I suppose I panicked. I was waiting for the lift, and when the doors opened all I saw was this yawning blackness. Put the heart crossways on me, it did. I thought someone was going to jump out and kill me but it was just that the light was broken inside. Anyway, I wasn't going to chance it. I legged it. I'm taking the stairs now.'

As if in confirmation, he heard a clacking of heels on a hard surface echo down the line.

'You're still at work?'

'Just leaving. Where are you?'

'Just coming around College Green.' He looked up at the brightly lit façade of Trinity College behind the railings, its elegant curve mirrored across the road by the sweeping blank colonnades of the old Bank of Ireland.

'That's only around the corner from me.'

'You sound like you could do with a drink.' He heard his voice falter even as he said it. What sort of idiot would she take him for? She'd as good as admitted she hadn't intended to call him.

'Are you kidding me?' she said. 'I'll need about six just to stop shaking.'

It had to be either the Palace or Mulligans so they opted for the latter, mostly because it was on Poolbeg Street and more or less beside the *Herald* offices. Siobhan didn't want to be out on the street. She must have got in there a minute or two before him at most, but as he went in the door, into the crowded dark interior, he couldn't see her amid the throng yakking noisily around the bar. Then, as his eyes adjusted to the gloom, he spotted her, sitting by herself in a dark corner cranny, well away from the main bar, with a couple of drinks sitting untouched on a small table in front of her.

'I ordered for you,' she said matter-of-factly as he sat down opposite her, even though there was plenty of room in the corner beside her. The dark wood, the mottled mirrors on the walls around, and the buzz of conversation all around cocooned them in privacy immediately.

'Thanks,' he said, taking a pull on his pint. Now she was there in front of him, he wasn't sure what to say to her. 'You sounded kind of scared on the phone.'

'I was, a bit,' she said, still not looking him in the eye. 'I mean, I got a bit spooked, all by myself in the office, you know? Somebody sent me . . . I mean, I wanted to show you something. See what you think, maybe?'

'Sure,' he said. 'What is it?'

Siobhan leaned over to open the shoulder bag lying on the floor at her feet, then changed her mind. She sat up again and glared at him.

'You needn't think I've forgiven you, y'know,' she said.

'You, forgive *me*?' he laughed, shocked. 'Shouldn't that be the other way around?'

'Why?' She wasn't smiling, wasn't pouting, wasn't playing any games at all, that he could see. She was being serious. 'All I was doing was my job. I even warned you in advance. You didn't have to cut me off like that. I mean, a bloody text, Mulcahy. Couldn't you even say it to my face?'

'Christ, Siobhan, you can't even begin to understand how much trouble you've caused me. Everyone from the Commissioner down assumes it was me who gave you the story. We were seen out together. I as good as got kicked off the investigation, and now I'm going to be stuck in bloody Sex Crimes for Christ knows how long as a result.'

This time she at least had the good grace to look upset.

'Why would they think you had anything to do with it? I mean, you made it clear enough to me you wouldn't help.

And I made sure to keep you out of it. And that wasn't easy, trust me. Your name came up a lot, and it wasn't all complimentary either.'

That came so far out of the blue, he almost had to repeat it to himself.

'What the hell are you talking about? When did my name come up? Where did you come by all this information of yours, anyway?'

'Look, Mulcahy, you know I can't talk about sources, so just don't start, okay?'

'No, that's not good enough, Siobhan,' he said, real anger in his voice now. 'You've as good as said someone was bad-mouthing me. Who the hell was it?'

'Shush, now,' Siobhan reached across the table and put a finger to his lips. Her touch jolted through him like a lightning strike to ground. 'On my life, Mulcahy, I can't tell you who it is. I'm not even sure who it is myself. But look, anyway, that's not the point. What I wanted was to—'

'Not the point?' Mulcahy pulled away from her, fuming. 'I'm up to my neck in shit because of you and you say it's not the point? Jesus Christ!'

That seemed to take her by surprise. She sat back, away from the table, then rubbed her eyes with both hands; anything, it seemed, rather than look at him. When she spoke again it was as if a soft, cold wind was blowing beside her words.

'You know as well as I do, I couldn't tell you even if I did have a name. But for what it's worth, I got a call, the morning, you know, after we were up in the Blue Light. This guy said he was working the Salazar case and could deliver the goods. Gave me the whole thing on a plate and again when Catriona Plunkett was attacked. Then I heard nothing for days, I swear. I was actually relieved to get the call from him when Paula Halpin's body was found. "Get yourself over to the Furry Glen, asap." That's all he said. And I've only heard from him the once since. So shut up now or I'll have a jinx on me and I'll never get another decent tip-off again.'

Mulcahy threw his head back and let out a long, low groan. 'That's how he said it, is it? "Ay-sap"? Just like that?' He thumped the table with his fist. 'I knew it. That treacherous shitebag. I knew it had to be him all along.'

Siobhan stared at him, panic in her eyes, knowing she'd said too much – knowing she'd said more than even she knew she'd said.

'Look, Mulcahy, whoever it is you're thinking of, you didn't hear about him from me, okay? On my life, nobody'd ever tell me anything again. I'd be ruined.'

But he wasn't even listening to her, seeing it now from Cassidy's point of view – the perfect set-up, shafting the uppity inspector while pocketing a bit of easy cash on the side. He must've thought all his Christmases had come at once.

'Look, Mulcahy,' Siobhan broke in on his thoughts. 'For what it's worth, I'd never have done anything to get you into trouble. I liked you, y'know. I still do. Christ, I mean, I can't even help myself, can I? Who's the first bloody person I think of when I need a big strong man to come and rescue me?'

She looked away from him then, leaned down and picked her bag up from the floor. He thought how tired she looked suddenly, hurt even. It was there in her voice, too. He put a hand out and stopped her as she was getting up to go.

'Wait. What was it you were going to show me?'

She shook her head, her black hair flowing like a dark sea in winter. 'It doesn't matter. It was all in my stupid head. I'd better be going.'

'No, don't,' he said. 'Have another drink, come on. You said you were going to have six.'

But she got up from the table anyway. 'What's the point? If it's not this time, it'll be the next. We're never going to be able to get on.'

It was only when her bag fell open slightly, as she hitched it up on her shoulder, that he saw it poking out from between the handles, like a dried-up chamois leather, black marks scorched on it, all over it, like a piece of burned . . .

'What in the name of Christ is that?' he said, pointing.

He carefully examined the stiff fold of parchment in his hands. He'd slid it into a clear plastic evidence bag the minute she told him what it was but he could still catch the strong back-of-the-throat stench of charring from it. The frenzied jumble of crosses burnt on to it looked just the same as the ones he'd seen on all The Priest's victims, only smaller.

'Just look at that, will you?' she said, her voice a tense

whisper. He looked closer, at what she was pointing to, and only then made out the thin line of text scorched into the skin.

Deus non irridetur

'Any idea what it means?' It gave him the creeps just looking at it.

'God will not be mocked,' she said. 'Latin. St Paul, one of his letters to somewhere, warning his flock not to go to the dark side.'

Mulcahy must have raised an eyebrow at that because she laughed, nervously. 'No, nor me either. While I was waiting for you I rang a contact of mine who knows a bit of Latin.'

'And you have no idea who sent it to you?'

'No,' she shook her head. 'For a second back there, I thought it might be this guy I know. He likes to throw the odd Latin motto into the conversation, and for a while I thought he was leaving me weird messages at home. But then I realised that this was exactly the same as what some freak said to me on the phone the other day.'

Mulcahy raised an eyebrow.

'Yeah, before they arrested anyone,' she said, leaning across and turning over the evidence bag in his hands. 'But, look, there's another one in English on the other side.'

He looked at where she pointed. Again it was seared on to the parchment in tiny script: *The body is not meant for lust but for the Lord.*

Mulcahy stole a glance at Siobhan again, impressed by how well she was taking it.

'Were any of your colleagues, or anyone on the other papers sent anything like this, do you know?' Mulcahy asked.

'Not that I'm aware of.' Siobhan shook her head.

'And there's no reason for you to be targeted, especially?'

'Gosh no,' she said. 'Other than the fact that I broke the bloody story and I've been mouthing off about The Priest all over the radio and telly ten hours a day for the last fortnight. No, I don't suppose he'd know me from Adam.'

Mulcahy had to concede the point, but it still didn't make much sense to him.

'I don't buy it, it doesn't feel right,' he said. 'But it's still evidence. You've got to show it to Brogan or Lonergan as soon as possible.'

'Can't *you* get it to them?'

'No, they need to see this first thing, and I'm away tomorrow.'

'Away? Away where?' she snapped, like she had any right to know.

'Don't ask.'

'God almighty,' she said in exasperation. 'I forgot, every bloody thing you do is top secret. Still, I suppose it'll give me time to get it photographed and everything for the story.'

'What are you saying?' He was horrified. 'This could be important evidence. You can't go splashing it all over the front page.'

'Why not? It'll look bloody good on the front page.'

Mulcahy stared at her, incredulous. 'Look, we have no way of knowing yet if this is a hoax or a sick joke, but it could derail the entire investigation if you give it undue prominence in your paper, and everyone has to go hightailing off on a wild-goose chase.'

'Yeah, well, that's easy for you to say. I deal with jerks and cranks every day of my life, and I'm telling you, Mulcahy, this one gave me the creeps – big time. Y'know, they took Emmet Byrne into custody this morning. This was delivered to me *by hand* between half seven and eight tonight. What if they've got the wrong guy? What if he's after me now?'

'Look, I honestly don't think you need to worry. I don't think you're his type,' Mulcahy replied, but even as he said it, his eye was drawn to the small silver cross glittering between the buttons of her shirt. 'We've still got to get this examined as soon as possible. Call Brogan. Let her follow it up.'

Siobhan sat back straight and stared at him like she'd seen inside him.

'You don't think it's Byrne, do you?'

He didn't know the answer to that question himself. 'From what I've heard, we have a very strong case against him.'

'Sure,' she snorted. 'I thought so, too, until some loony started sending smouldering skin samples to me.' She looked over her shoulder before continuing in a whisper. 'You know, I interviewed an old man this afternoon who's known Byrne for years and swears he's a saint.'

'Everybody has friends, Siobhan. Even rapists and murderers get good character references in court.'

'Yeah, well I got an email from a psychologist contact of mine earlier tonight. And do you know what, she said every one of these attacks had hallmarks of something called an "anger-retaliatory" personality type. She said the levels of brutality indicated displaced aggression, someone harbouring feelings of "cumulative, uncontrollable rage". Not necessarily related to the act itself, since the root of it, she said, could be anything. Maybe a severe trauma in childhood, or whatever. But the trigger and focus of the aggression would nearly always be the same. And the thing is, most people I spoke to who actually know Emmet Byrne seemed to think he was sound. A bit on the slow side but always nice, always cheerful. Definitely not your stewing-away-till-he-bursts type, anyway.'

Mulcahy hardly heard most of it. He was still stuck on 'anger-retaliatory'. He realised suddenly what had been nagging at him since he'd been out in Palmerston Park. Jesica Salazar's whispered '*Como un cura*'. Rinn's erect posture, the superior manner, the dressing like an old man. Like a sexless man. Rinn was exactly like one or two priests he'd known as a boy. So held back, so constrained, so packed with repression and anger they all but stank of it. That's what had been crackling off him when Mulcahy was looking at the pictures on the wall. Anger, not anxiety.

He looked up and saw Siobhan was staring at him, just like the barman had in the Long Hall. Like he was off his nut.

'Are you alright, Mulcahy?'

'Sure, yeah . . . sorry,' he said, trying to regroup his thoughts. 'I was just thinking, y'know, the guys on the murder team probably know all that stuff, too. I mean, Brogan's done all the courses, she knows all the psychology.'

'But she's not in charge any more, is she? And they're always up for a quick result. It wouldn't be the first time you guys let enthusiasm get the better of you.'

He didn't even feel the dig. He was too busy with what was evolving inside his own head. Rinn was occupying most of the space in there now, and behind him, barely visible in the gloom, those photos of his grandfather and that glorious sunlit painting, the one he had been so defensive about: *Gweedore Summer*.

'What're you so distracted about, anyway, all of a sudden?' The darkness dissolved as he felt the prickle of Siobhan's piercing blue gaze search his face.

'Nothing,' he said, shutting it down.

'Yeah, sure. You're a hopeless liar, Mulcahy. Come on, I was right just then, wasn't I? You *are* thinking about another suspect, aren't you? You must've had others. Is it someone who fits the bill better? Are you thinking of someone in particular?'

'Don't be ridiculous, I—'

'Jesus, you are, aren't you?' she interrupted excitedly. 'I can tell. Look, c'mon, I can help. We have resources at the paper. You don't even have to give me the whole story now. Just let me in first when you've got it.'

And there it was, and he hadn't even had to ask for it, his chance to look into the past.

'Okay, then,' he said, 'maybe there is something you can help me with.'

Brogan pulled the door of the observation room shut behind her, leaned back against the corridor wall and breathed in a lungful of heartfelt satisfaction. Despite being deep in the bowels of Kilmainham Garda Station, the air tasted remarkably cool and fresh. That, though, could have been because she'd just spent the last hour and a half in close, hot, sweaty proximity to five other detectives, all big men, in that tiny room, watching something she'd never seen before. At least, not to that degree of intensity.

She rubbed the back of her neck, hardly knowing whether it was excitement or exhaustion she was feeling more keenly. Although her back was creaking and her arms and legs felt like sacks, the blood was still rushing through her veins like an express train. She actually felt more alive than she had at any time since her boy was born. Eighteen hours on the trot already, with almost no sleep the night before. But what a day it had been.

Only an hour or so after she and the others had arrived and settled in at Kilmainham with Lonergan's murder mob, rumours had started trickling in of a breakthrough in the case. Then, just before noon, Lonergan had come in, absolutely buzzing. She'd liked him when she'd first met him, earlier, at the scene in the Phoenix Park – a big, easy guy, six-foot-three at least, early forties but fit with it and smart green eyes that somehow never seemed to land in the wrong place. She'd liked him even more, then, when the first thing he did was invite her into his office for a one-on-one briefing in which he outlined the rapid progress the investigation had made over the course of the morning. So unlike Healy. So unlike any other superintendent she'd met. There was real respect in everything he said to her and, weirdly, she'd felt this mad kind of warmth bubbling up in her towards him, like instant loyalty.

It had all been a bit of a blur since then: the massive break about the order code on the plastic sheeting, the raid on Emmet Byrne's place and the discovery of the fibre bark-bags in the van, the briefing Lonergan had asked her to 'co-host' for the sixty-strong murder team, and the press call with Commissioner Garvey announcing Byrne's arrest. Jesus, as if the day hadn't had enough in it already.

Then, to cap it all, she'd just watched Lonergan interview Emmet Byrne and reel him in like an absolute master. The man had been beyond brilliant. Lonergan and a grim-looking detective sergeant doing a classic double-hander, but with himself very much taking the lead. Never aggressive but always keeping the pressure up on Byrne to the max, the line of questioning relentlessly clear and focused, yet stepping back whenever the suspect got in any way confused or befuddled, which was often. Lonergan, she'd noticed, always gave Byrne the space and time to get his story exactly the way he wanted it, and only then came back in hard to smash it to pieces.

It had been such a thrill to watch. All of them in the room

next door glued to the interview through the mirrored glass, breathless at times as Lonergan coaxed yet another small but crucial admission out of Byrne, never really going at him direct but constantly chipping away, helping the man drag himself deeper and deeper into a maze of self-incrimination. In the end, ninety minutes was all it had taken him to reduce Byrne to blubbering remorse – and a confession to all three attacks. 'Yes, yes, okay, I done it. I burned them. I made them bleed. All of them, may the Lord forgive me. I'm sorry, I'm sorry,' Byrne had wept at the climax.

It would be a long time before she forgot that moment, how all of them in that room had let out a whoop of delight and punched the air when Lonergan looked over into the mirror and winked at them through the glass. He'd nailed the big admission. Over the next few days they could work on Byrne for the detail, but for now they had enough to charge him with, whenever they wanted to.

Christ, but that man was an inspiration.

Brogan looked at her watch: ten-fifteen p.m. already. She felt in her pocket for her mobile. Even the thought of calling home and listening to her husband, Aidan, griping about her long absence couldn't bring her down. Aidan could go fuck himself, she thought. How dare he say she didn't spend enough time with the boy. Aidan was the one who'd said he was happy to stay at home. Well, it was up to him, not her, to make that work. And as for the boy, she'd always found the time, and always would find it, no matter how hard she worked.

She stepped away from the wall as the door beside her opened and two of the lads she'd shared the room with for the last couple of hours – Lonergan's lads – came out, laughing together, and bade her a friendly goodnight. She looked at their broad backs as they walked down the corridor, the clatter of their footsteps echoing against the old tile walls, and she knew something for certain. It'd been a long time since she'd found somewhere she wanted to be this much. Now she had, she was going to doing everything in her power to keep things that way. Somehow, she was going to get herself transferred onto Lonergan's team permanently.

He'd been at it for well over an hour, sitting at the *Herald*'s long newsdesk, a couple of fluorescent ceiling lights illuminating their small patch of floor space, everywhere else in darkness or bathed in the orange glow drifting in through the windows from the streetlights outside. For a man who'd never been inside a newspaper office before, Mulcahy found it all a bit of a let-down. Ranks of desks and computer screens sectioned off into individual fiefdoms, like any office anywhere. The only difference he could see was that there were a hell of a lot of TVs around, on shelves, on walls, on stands; you wouldn't be able to hear yourself think if they were all on at the same time. And Siobhan, of course, clacking away at her keyboard behind him.

All he'd asked her was if he could look up the *Herald*'s news archive sometime. And she'd been all over it right away, saying, 'Yeah, come on, come over and we'll look it up now.' He could see why she was good at her job – she wouldn't take no for an answer. She'd dragged him back to the *Herald*, sat him down and showed him how to look material up on the system. She had explained to him about the various online cuttings services they used for other publications. And he had tried . . . but there was no magic bullet. The in-house archive had only been computerised as far back as the mid-nineties. Even then, all he got was floods of random stuff that meant nothing to him. He did his best to winkle out some information about Rinn, his grandfather or the big mystery in Gweedore. And once or twice he thought he'd found something, but they were just wisps – hints that something bad had happened – that dissolved as soon as he tried to pin them down.

In the end he was just plain knackered, his eyes watering more and more with every new search he called up. Until he suddenly caught the flicker of a TV screen blooming into life beside him. He looked round. Siobhan was standing behind his chair, a remote in her hand.

'I just wanted to catch the late news,' she said.

'Sure.' Mulcahy turned to watch as the headlines ran out and Siobhan raised the volume. No surprise, the lead item was the Priest arrest, and he leaned forward as he saw Brogan onscreen, briefly, at the centre of a swirling crowd, with a tall guy he recognised from the press conference, Lonergan presumably, leading this other guy out, with a coat over his head, through the car park at Kilmainham

Garda Station. It was a real scrum, with cameras flashing and all the press monkeys pushing in and jostling to get near. Then someone caught hold of the coat this guy had covering him and pulled it away, and the suspect's face was exposed for a few seconds and he looked absolutely shit-scared. But it wasn't the expression of fear that made Mulcahy sit up and gawp, but the face it was on. He was sure he'd seen the man before, very recently, but it wouldn't come.

Then Siobhan pushed the volume up another notch and he heard the newsreader saying: 'The suspect who's reported to run a gardening business in Chapelizod was arrested just after noon today when Gardai from the Murder Squad raided his flat in St Imelda's Road . . .' Mulcahy felt the breath go out of him from the shock. The gardener! He saw the face again now, but in his mind's eye, with a baseball cap on, anger in his eyes and a hammer in his hand. It was him, the fucking gardener from Rinn's place, the one who'd been working there that day he'd gone round. He'd seen him, met him, even been bloody threatened by him. And the van, for Christ's sake. The fucking van sitting there outside the house and he'd walked straight past it.

Mulcahy felt sick to his stomach, had to put a hand to his chest to stop himself being wiped out by the thought of it. He desperately needed to think straight. That wasn't while Paula Halpin was missing, was it? No, he reassured himself, he'd only gone over to Palmerston Park after her body had been found, and he felt a tiny trickle of relief at that. But then the anger came again. Any money, he'd bet any bloody money that, if they checked the dates back, they'd find that Byrne was working at Rinn's the day Caroline Coyle was attacked, too. And, as for poor Paula Halpin, walking up from Dartry, it wasn't Rinn's clutches she'd fallen into, it was his bloody gardener's. Christ, how could he have come so close yet got it so totally, hopelessly wrong?

For a moment or two he felt totally emptied out by the thought, as good as paralysed from head to toe by the shock of it. He glanced over at Siobhan but thankfully she didn't seem to have noticed his reaction, absorbed as she was in the news report. He sat back in the chair, thinking about Byrne, thinking about Rinn, feeling it all go round and round again. He rubbed his forehead, his head began to pound again – and his lungs jumped on the bandwagon, screaming for a cigarette. He stood up slowly, stretching his arms, pretending a calmness he was utterly devoid of, as Siobhan turned to him.

'I've had enough of this for one night, Siobhan. I'm knackered and getting nowhere. Sorry to waste your time, but I've got to get out of here now, before my head explodes.'

He'd been really very sweet down at the main door, insisting that she contact Brogan first thing about the package, fretting over the fact that she was going back into the office on her own. He'd even come over a little shy when she asked: 'So are we friends again, now?' But he hadn't held back when they kissed goodnight, with his big arms folding her into the hard warmth of his chest. It felt like he wanted her to stay there for ever, and she'd be lying if she claimed she wasn't tempted just to forget about it all and hop into the taxi beside him, there and then. But maybe he would have drawn the line at that. Something was all too obviously still eating away at him. And it was probably better to take things slowly this time, anyway. There was no way he didn't want to get involved with her, she could sense that. They'd just have to be careful, in future, and avoid the work thing altogether.

In future, maybe, but not just yet. Back upstairs she went straight to the terminal he'd been working on, which she'd pretended to turn off when he left, but had actually only put to sleep, making sure the hard drive stayed up and running. She touched the space bar and the screen flickered back into life. A few keystrokes later and she was able to call up the log, and then a list of the files he'd gone through in the archive. It didn't take long to find the one she wanted. He'd stared at it for a good five minutes, not realising that from where she was sitting she'd been able to read the catchlines on just about everything he had looked at.

She called up the story. It must have been one of the earliest on the database, from 1995, and it looked like something from a gossipy political diary. The sort of thing they published back in the day when the *Herald* took itself more seriously, and fancied itself a player in the power market rather than primarily a purveyor of scandal. It was a brief, snibby insert written under the name Oisin MacCumhaill, which she vaguely recalled was the pen-name of a once-renowned political columnist from years back. By the look of it, he'd been an insider writing for other insiders, trading in the sort of weasely winks, nudges and innuendo that were incomprehensible to anyone who wasn't already in on the joke, or who wasn't in the know.

GONE BUT NOT FORGOTTEN?

We're all saddened, I'm sure, to note the departure, from the ranks of the exalted, of the last of the Great Ones. But, while it might seem churlish to mention it now, there are those who will not mourn his passing. A heroic role in the formation of our great nation is all well and good. As is a lifetime devoted to the cause of justice, equality and fair hearing. But, occasionally, even heroes get it terribly, terribly wrong. So much so that great deeds in the past and even a lifetime's devotion to Church and State cannot redress the balance. Most good folk who were in Gweedore in the August of 1988 will remember it as a place and a time of sunshine, beauty and joy. For a few, though, it will always remain a time of darkness, a high-water mark of hypocrisy, of the blackest of stains on a character regarded by many as the next best thing to sanctified. He, of all men, should have known that covering up evil for the sake of vanity, or family, in order to excise it from the public record, was nothing but a perversion of the justice he affected to hold so high.

Siobhan stared at it, bemused. She read it and reread it, and tried to get her head round it. What the hell could Mulcahy have seen here that was so important? It yielded nothing at face value. Clearly it was written as a kind of riddle, to begin with – something the writer could only half say and hint at, for fear of being sued, presumably, or of some greater retribution. Damn Mulcahy, anyway: he was on to something, she could feel it so strongly. Still, if *he* could be, so could she.

She scrolled back up to the top of the story. She knew for sure this was the one he'd stared at like he'd witnessed a revelation. The one he'd sneaked back to when she'd gone out to the loo, and been so absorbed in, he didn't hear her coming back at first, then closed it hurriedly when he finally heard her behind him, making out it was nothing. 'I was just trying to see if I could get to grips with some of those cuttings services you mentioned,' he'd claimed.

Yeah, right.

So what was it? From the log, she could tell that for Mulcahy the keyword had to be Gweedore. That's what he'd put in most of the searches. That and maybe a dozen other criteria: most frequently the word *justice* and the surname *Rinn*. All that had yielded him was a pile of references to some old judge who'd died years back, which he'd seemed vaguely interested in at first, but then he'd whipped though the files with barely enough time to read them. Towards the end, it looked like all he'd been doing was putting random-looking searches about crucifixes and torture and sexual assault into the mix – and getting nowhere with them, by the look of it.

She scrolled back to the original story. The headline: GONE BUT NOT FORGOTTEN. It was obviously some sort of riddle, but a riddle meant for who? The writer had a grievance against somebody, but why and about what? And what was this 'evil' he was talking about?

Keywords.

She grabbed a pen and started writing down the words that seemed to stand out. *Great Ones*: a quick Google search led her precisely nowhere, the term being so vague it brought up references to everything from spiritualist nut-cases to Brazilian footballers. She tried again with *Gweedore* and *1988* but, again, came back with nothing other than a pile of tourism junk and meaningless timelines. She was on the point of giving up when it occurred to her that, actually, it hadn't been her who'd opened the web browser on Mulcahy's terminal. She'd only booted up the Archive-search system on the monitor for him. She'd just assumed he would know how to launch the browser himself. And obviously he had, but when? That time she was out in the loo?

She moved the mouse again and clicked on the History button in the tool bar. Thank God she hadn't closed the terminal down. There it was, just before her own more recent searches. A list of hits each titled *Donegal Courier . . . archive.* The sneaky bugger. Mulcahy had been checking out the local press in Donegal behind her back. How the hell had she not noticed him doing that? She clicked on a link at random which took her to the *Donegal Courier* search page. And there they were: the keywords *Gweedore* and *assault,* the date, *1988.* She could see straight away that the *Courier*'s archive, too, only went back to the mid-nineties, so she clicked out and scrolled straight to the last page Mulcahy had browsed. What she saw there made her sit up straight and lean in towards the screen. It was a story from the *Courier*'s news pages from 1997. And, like the story from the *Herald* archive, it referred back, in part, to a mysterious, and apparently shameful, incident that happened in Gweedore in 1988.

Bingo.

She read through the story again, this time for the detail. It was a fairly typical court report about the successful prosecution for assault of a visitor to Bunbeg, a Dublin businessman called Anthony Michael Blaney, who'd rented a house outside the town for his family for the summer of 1997. Blaney had assaulted a local youth, Aidan Lowry, who'd apparently dared to lean against Blaney's brand new BMW outside McClusky's bar one evening, and the Dubliner had compounded the offence by trying to bribe the Garda who was called to the scene. But as far as Siobhan was concerned, and Mulcahy too, she assumed, the real significance only came in the final paragraph. It was a throwaway remark to all intents and purposes, but a bitter one.

Outside the court the victim's mother, Theresa Lowry, said Blaney's conviction for **assault** *was a triumph for local justice. 'There are those of us in* **Gweedore** *who remember how, less than a decade ago, in* **1988**, *rich and powerful men could make even the worst crimes go away, sweep them under the carpet with a pile of cash. We all remember Helen Martin. Well, this one tried it too and, thank the Good Lord, he didn't succeed. Now at last we can say that justice is alive and well again in Donegal.'*

Siobhan exhaled slowly. There could be little doubt that this referred to the same incident as Mulcahy had found in the *Herald* archive search. Gweedore. 1988. Rich and powerful people covering things up in a remote part of Donegal. She felt her stomach squirm, sensing she was on to something here, even if she didn't yet know what. But she reckoned she might be able to get to the bottom of it. She took a note of the reporter's name, Eamon Doherty, called up a fresh search on the *Donegal Courier* site, and typed it in to see if he still worked there. A blizzard of hits came back at her.

Not only was Doherty still working there. He was the editor of the *Donegal Courier* now.

18

'Excuse me, sir, any drinks or snacks?'

Mulcahy flicked his eyes open as he felt the brush of fingers across his shoulder. No, just let me sleep, he thought, then shook his head as he realised what the flight attendant had been asking him. He pulled himself upright in his seat, trying not to get in the way as she handed a dribble of clear liquid in a plastic cup and a can of chilled Schweppes, to the middle-aged woman in the seat beside him. He looked at his watch blearily. Ten twenty-five in the morning, and they were doling out gin and tonic, Christ. And over an hour still to get through before they landed.

He rubbed his eyes, realising he must have dozed off almost as soon as the aircraft had got into the air. He felt rotten – and looked worse, to judge by the wary glance the lady alcoholic had given him when he first sat down. Better have a tidy-up at the other end, before heading into town. He'd slept badly, and what sleep he'd had was fitful and filled with nightmares. Dreams of Byrne, driving out of Rinn's gateway in the van, spotting Paula Halpin, grabbing her, pulling her into his van, murder in his face and a burning cross in his hand. Over and over again.

Dragging his bones out of bed at seven, slinging himself into the shower, racing to the airport to catch his flight, hadn't done anything to make him feel better. But at least he was doing something useful, and it would be good to get back to Madrid for however short a time. The last thing he'd done before going to bed the night before had been to ring Gracia to let her know he'd be in town. There was still so much to sort out between them, not least the question of the apartment. But although it was past midnight, there was no answer, so he'd left a message saying he would call again when he landed. He couldn't help being infected by a jab of jealousy, or possessiveness, at the fact that she hadn't been at home. Knowing this was ludicrous didn't make him feel it any less.

He stretched awkwardly in his seat now, the stiffness in his arms prompting another memory, of folding them around Siobhan outside the *Sunday Herald* and kissing her good-night. The way she'd pressed her body into his. Why the hell did it have to feel so right, when it was so obviously never going to work with her? Suddenly, he felt a tightness in his chest, as if his lungs were contracting inside him. He felt the woman beside him shift an inch or two further away, and wondered if this was what it was like to suffer an anxiety attack. But it only lasted a moment and once it passed he felt nothing but a great wave of relief wash through him. He thought of the envelope, now in his case in the baggage

407

locker above his head, which he'd found on the mat by the door when he got home. Healy had come through on his promise to ask Lonergan if he wanted to try getting an ID from Jesica. Two 5 × 4 blow-ups of Emmet Byrne's mugshots were in the envelope, a note attached with 'Go for it' scrawled in a clumsy hand.

Maybe, he thought, he would be able to play some small part in calling The Priest to account after all.

Siobhan, too, rose at seven, having slept the sleep of the driven, so she was up, showered, ironed and out, all in the space of twenty-five minutes. A coffee she could pick up on the way. Even so, she wasn't in the office before Griffin. Not on a Saturday. He was already hard at it, so absorbed he didn't notice her come in, didn't drag his eyes away from the Reuters or PA feed or whatever it was he was scrolling through on his screen. Fishing for a big one, or else racking up the more mundane stuff for the shift guys and subs to work up into nibs and fillers during the day. She shouted a hello, expecting him to jump up and congratulate her for delivering yet another cracking lead. But all he did was raise a rangy arm in greeting, didn't even bother to turn her way.

'Didn't you get my message?' she asked.

'I did,' was all he said, flatly, still not turning around.

'And . . .?' Christ, the man could be infuriating sometimes.

'And nothing.' He swivelled round in his chair then, his

face hard as stone, and put his hands up in front of her. 'We're not running it.'

'We're not *what*? What are you talking about? You haven't even seen it.'

'Not my decision,' he said. 'I phoned Harry at home, as soon as I got in. To prime him for the "*Herald* reporter gets Priest death threat" splash. And, for some reason, he took it upon himself to ring Lonergan – you know, the superintendent in charge of the murder team – to insist you must be given round-the-clock protection.'

'Oh, for fuck's sake!' Siobhan groaned. 'Where is he? I'm going to bloody murder him.'

'I actually thought it was a good idea,' Griffin said. 'It would have spiced up the whole focus on you and the *Herald*, and you can't buy publicity like that.'

'So what happened?' Siobhan asked, beginning to see his point now.

Griffin moved his hands to his face, rubbing his eyes as if he couldn't bear to look at her while telling the rest. 'Lonergan killed it dead. Apparently they charged Emmet Byrne with the murder this morning, and now they're saying this letter of yours is evidence material to the case.'

'But that's bollocks!' she shouted. 'It has nothing to do with Byrne.'

'With the best will in the world, Siobhan, I don't think you could argue—'

'Did Harry,' she interrupted, 'point out that it came *after* Byrne was taken into custody?'

'No, he didn't . . .'

'Well, that's it!' she said, clutching at straws.

'But *I* did, Siobhan, and to no less a man than the Director of Public Prosecutions himself – who then spent half an hour, probably in his pyjamas, shouting chapter and verse at me down the phone and describing the ton of bricks he'll bring down on us if we even think about printing it.'

'And that's it?' She was actually shaking with frustration now. 'That's *it*?'

'Yup.' Griffin nodded. 'Harry says it's not worth us going to court over.'

'Easy for him to say,' she said. 'I bet I'm not getting any protection, either.'

Griffin laughed. 'Funnily enough, no.'

'So what happens now?'

'They're sending someone over at eleven o'clock to take a statement from you. And to formally take that *thing* into evidence and, of course, initiate investigative action, or some such bollocks.' He smiled sympathetically as she shook her head in disbelief, then leaned forward and squeezed her arm gently. 'Can I see it, at least? You only left me a photocopy.'

She went over to her desk, unlocked the drawer where she'd left the parchment overnight and handed it to Griffin. He whistled as he examined it through the plastic.

'Jesus, you weren't wrong, were you?' His eyebrows went up when he realised it was in a Garda evidence bag. 'What's this?'

She shook her head again. 'Long story.'

'Oh, well, you can't win 'em all, Scoop,' he said, smiling broadly again. 'And anyway, the way your career is going, I've no doubt there'll be plenty more death threats to come.'

'Mike! . . . Mike! . . . Mulcahy!!'

It was midday in Madrid, and Terminal One at Barajas Airport was swamped with humanity. It was only the appalling abuse done to his surname that made Mulcahy stop and stare into the crowds jostling at the barriers to greet the passengers disgorging into the arrivals hall. Then he heard the voice again.

'Mike! Over here!'

Mulcahy scanned the phalanx of meeters and greeters to his left. There, leaning against a pillar and waving a rolled-up newspaper, he recognised the tall, thin figure of Javier Martinez.

'Jav!' he called out. He wasn't expecting to be met, and had intended taking the Metro into Principe de Vergara before contacting Martinez for details of where and when the interview would take place. 'What are you doing here?'

Grinning broadly, Martinez pointed towards the end of the line of barriers and started walking in that direction. Mulcahy followed and gave his old friend a warm embrace when they eventually converged. For a split second, all the heaviness and worry was gone from his shoulders and he was transported back a year, two years before, to the Narcotics Intelligence Unit, fighting the good fight, working for the cause. Martinez had been the one colleague he'd worked alongside for the full seven years of his Europol tenure, a man who'd combined the skills of guide, language coach, cultural consultant, drinking buddy and bloody good friend. He'd even met Gracia through Martinez, although that wasn't necessarily a plus point any more.

Mulcahy laughed, slapping Martinez on the back for good measure. His mood had skyrocketed. 'Christ, but it's good to be back.'

The Spaniard smiled, waving his car keys and heading towards the exit. For Mulcahy, the mere fact of being back in Madrid and seeing his old pal had loosed a flood of endorphins into his bloodstream. Even the wall-hard shock of heat that hit him as they left the air-conditioned terminal building felt good; even the sweat prickling out under his shirt. He was so heady with it, Martinez had to grab him as, looking the wrong way, he stepped into the road and almost directly under the wheels of a large taxi that was just pulling away. It was a huge thing, an MPV or van, and the driver had to swerve sharply to avoid him, sticking his head out the open window and shouting a selection of choice *Madrileño* obscenities.

But Mulcahy only laughed. 'Christ, Jav, I really have been a long time away.'

They reached the car, a silver Mercedes two-seater convertible that looked to be brand new. No surprise there. Martinez had always had money: a huge apartment in the Salamanca district; a wardrobe full of finely tailored English suits, shirts and handmade brogues, like the ones he was wearing now. It was an affectation he'd picked up from his 'filthy-rich Anglophile family', as he told Mulcahy years back. He was incredibly well connected, which presumably was how he'd got his current job. The one question he'd never answered to Mulcahy's satisfaction was what a Spanish playboy was doing slumming it in the *Policía Nacional*.

Martinez reversed out of the parking space with a screech of tyres that was deafening in the enclosed space of the multi-storey car park. Some things never change, Mulcahy thought. He'd never got used to the crazed machismo of Spanish driving. It wasn't until they'd negotiated the route out of the airport and roared onto the motorway that Martinez opened his mouth again.

'Don Alfonso knows the requirements of the investigation process, so he is aware you need to talk to Jesica sooner, not later. He demands, though, that you can only do it if Jesica's doctor is also always present in the room. That's okay, yes?'

Mulcahy didn't reply, thinking it through, although he couldn't see it being a problem.

Misinterpreting his silence, Martinez glanced over at him a little shamefacedly. 'I know it's not ideal for you but he was very, eh . . . insistent.'

'No, no, what's to be sorry about?' Mulcahy shouted back at him. 'It's not a problem. And thanks again for sorting it out so quickly. Honestly, we appreciate it. If we'd had to go through official channels, it might have taken weeks, knowing what you bloody Spanish are like.'

He grinned across at Martinez, who responded with a broad grin of his own and a push on the accelerator that took the engine from a purr to a growl, and shot them forward at an even more ridiculous speed. By now the ear-buffeting airflow was too much to allow for easy conversation. Mulcahy tucked himself further into the body-hugging leather of the car seat, letting the speed and exhilaration of being back in Madrid rush over him. By the time they reached the outskirts of the city proper, and the traffic had slowed to a more metropolitan crawl, he found himself more relaxed than he'd felt in weeks. The two of them chatted away during the journey, Martinez pressing for details of the wider story of The Priest, Mulcahy seeking to fill out his sketchy knowledge of the powerful politician he would be meeting that afternoon: Don Alfonso Mellado Salazar.

'You know, most politicians we have now, they were babies when Franco was around,' Martinez said, 'but Don Alfonso, he was in politics even then. He was one of the new ones who oversaw the transition to democracy, and one of not many whose career survived it. Because he can change, I think, but without being hypocritical like most. *El Juez* – you know they call him this, the Judge. He is tough but respected. And a big Catholic, too. Many older people like this.'

Mulcahy nodded. 'He must be getting on a bit. From what I remember of seeing him on the news, he looks more like a grandfather than a father.'

'Sure. He must have been sixty when little Jesica was

born. His first wife died in an ETA car bomb in the 1980s. He married again later to a very beautiful, very aristocratic lady with many names and titles. Jesica was their child. But this wife also died, very tragic. I think he only works to forget it. Maybe that was why he wanted his daughter back so quickly from Dublin. I know it caused trouble for you, Mike, but she is everything to him.'

Mulcahy shrugged, not wanting to commit one way or the other on that point. His concentration wandered as he glanced around him. Everything foreign, yet familiar – not so long ago, this had been his life. Normality had been heat and light beating down from above, not the dull hug of a scarf or overcoat. Even the brown pall of pollution that hung permanently above the city seemed normal back then. As Martinez drove down the great spine of the Avenida de las Americas, and on into Castellana, it hit Mulcahy full on just like the heat had: the car horns, the waspish buzz of scooters, the hurtling, bustling sense of humanity always on the move. For so long they had been the things that had made him feel alive. He was actually finding it hard to believe that going back to Dublin could ever have seemed like a good option to him. Indeed, he was so absorbed by sensations, so swamped by the familiar sights and sounds around him, that he realised too late that Martinez had taken the wrong turn off Plaza Cibeles and was heading up Gran Via.

'Hey, where are you going, Jav?' he protested. 'I thought we were going to your office first. I badly need to freshen up a bit before we go see Salazar.'

Martinez didn't make any effort to stop, simply grinned at Mulcahy and pointed at his Rolex, tapping the face.

'That is for later. You have been travelling, so you need to eat. Fortunately, I plan ahead and booked for lunch at La Bola. You look like you could do with some *cocido á la madrileña* to get the colour back in your cheeks.'

It couldn't have been a more disastrous morning, as far as Siobhan was concerned. In the wake of Griffin's early-morning skirmish with the DPP, and the confirmation that Byrne had been charged with murder, orders had gone out from the editor's office that they were to go easy on the Priest stories today. Straight-down-the-line reporting was all they could use: no messing about with speculation, however justified it might be. Harry Heffernan had no intention of wasting money being dragged through the courts for contempt, and the Saturday papers were swamped in reports on the arrest already, anyway. For the moment the plan was still to lead with Siobhan's piece about Byrne's previous arrest, simply because that at least looked like it might keep fresh until the morning. But, even at that, it had been so filleted by Heffernan and blue-pencilled by the lawyer, it didn't look so very exciting any more. As for her 'I Saw the Body in the Park' piece, which they were still intending to run as the centre spread, it was beginning to look like the old news it was, especially since the general opinion was that The Priest was safely behind bars.

Now that Byrne had been charged, as far as Griffin and

the rest of them were concerned, the story was as good as dead in the water until it came up again in court. Not only that, but every other hack on the paper knew that if anything more exciting came up during the day, Griffin would clear the decks for it, and her Priest stuff could end up buried on page seven. Nobody, least of all the two Murder Squad guards who came to take her statement and collect the parchment, seemed to give any credence to the idea that there was a madman still on the loose. As for the prospect of Griffin allowing his chief reporter to go tearing off on a wild hunch that maybe Byrne was the wrong man? Forget it. On a slow day, maybe, but not on press day, and especially not today.

That Griffin was probably right hardly mattered. The suspicion had a grip on her gut tighter than a stomach staple, and it wouldn't let go. All she needed was a little time to herself, to get back into it again. Mulcahy was on to something, she was convinced, and she was determined to find out what. But, for the moment, all she could do was get on with the job she was paid for, making as few waves as possible. That way, she might be able to use the hour Griffin spent in conference with Heffernan and the other section editors to get in a few calls of her own, and so set the ball rolling.

As soon as Griffin disappeared, she was straight on the phone.

'Hello, *Donegal Courier*,' she heard, when she got through, the accent thick enough to make cheese from. She got an immediate image in her mind of a fat woman in a fleece with a scowl on her face and a chocolate eclair poised halfway into her gob.

'Can I speak to Eamon Doherty, please?'

'He's not here – only me on the small ads and notices.'

It took a second for Siobhan to twig that the editor of a regional weekly wouldn't need to come in on a Saturday. That it would be the weekend for him, like any normal person.

'Do you know where I can get hold of him? It's urgent.'

A big sigh came from the other end of the line. 'I suppose he'll be out on the golf course by now. That's where he usually goes on a Saturday morning. You can get him on his mobile.'

'And his mobile number is?'

'We don't give out that information over the phone.'

No matter how she pleaded, the woman refused to give Siobhan the number. But after a bit of cajoling she did agree to get in touch with Doherty and pass on to him a message to call.

'Tell him it's Siobhan Fallon from the *Sunday Herald* in Dublin. Be sure to say it's urgent.'

Siobhan grumbled away to herself as she put down the phone, convinced the woman wouldn't do as she'd asked. In the meantime she scrolled down through her contacts book, searching for someone else who might have a connection with Doherty and know his number. She'd just identified a couple of likely candidates when the phone rang.

'Eamon Doherty from the *Courier* here.'

'Wow, that was fast.'

'Is that *the* Siobhan Fallon I'm talking to?'

A shiver of pleasure went through her when he said that. It was kind of how she'd always imagined life should be. She heard him cupping a hand over the phone and telling someone to go on without him, as he had an important call. He'd catch them up.

'I hope I'm not interrupting your round of golf,' she said, when he came back on.

'I'm not playing golf,' he said. 'If I was, I wouldn't be available even for *the* Siobhan Fallon. I'm actually down your neck of the woods today, for the big match in Croke Park. We're just up the road from you, packing away some pre-match hospitality in the Shelbourne Hotel, you know, on St Stephen's Green.'

There was a flirtatious lilt and a vein of wickedness in his voice. Used to being a big fish in a small pond, she thought, and he sure had that confidence. She looked at the closed door of Harry Heffernan's office and made a snap decision.

'Do you think you could drag yourself away from the bar, Eamon, for a quick chat, if I was able to join you there in the next few minutes?'

The clock hadn't yet struck noon but even so the Shelbourne Hotel's elegant Georgian tea room was packed with clumps of men in jeans and football shirts, knocking back pints of Guinness. The spill-over from the Horseshoe Bar, Siobhan knew – and incongruous as they looked, she also knew it was ever thus on match days. Siobhan found Doherty by the reception desk and, as soon as she'd introduced herself, grabbed him by the elbow and drew him over to a couple of empty chairs in a quiet corner of the lobby. He wasn't what she'd been expecting: shorter, hairier and a good deal older-looking than she'd imagined. But she saw straight away that *she* wasn't disappointing him. He'd obviously already downed a fair bit of that hospitality he'd mentioned. She only prayed to Christ it wouldn't affect his memory.

'So what's so urgent that you had to interrupt my drinking for it?' he twinkled at her, not quite as irresistibly as he thought.

She told him about the report of his she'd seen from 1997 and asked him if he remembered anything about it, especially its connection with the earlier story about Helen Martin. After his initial grunt of surprise, she all but heard the cogs creaking into place in his brain. Sure enough, before he gave an answer, he came back with a question himself.

'Do you mind if I ask why you want to know this?'

She gave him the smile. 'It's just some background I'm doing for a story, Eamon. Look, I know I should never have said it was urgent. It's just that your receptionist didn't sound very keen on letting me crash your weekend. But, if it comes to anything I'll give you and the *Courier* a credit. I'll even try for a few quid for you, if you like.'

She hadn't really answered his question, but it seemed to satisfy him for the moment.

'Well, I'm not sure what I can tell you. I mean, that thing with Helen Martin must be more than twenty years ago – before my time, anyway. I didn't join the *Courier* until 1994, so I'd have been still in college in 1988. And I'm from the other end of the county, anyway, down Killybegs way. But you hear things going around, alright.'

Siobhan heard a raucous burst of laughter from the bar and looked up at the clock. Griffin and the others wouldn't be coming out of conference for a while yet.

'Like what?' she asked.

'Well, Helen Martin was a young one from Gweedore. Lovely girl by all accounts, but the family moved away shortly afterwards, so Lord knows where they are now. Anyway the story, as I heard it, was that she was attacked – she was fifteen or sixteen at the time – by this other kid, a young lad from Dublin who was up there for the summer. And then there was a big cover-up, caused a lot of bad feeling locally.'

'Any details?' she asked.

'Not really, only that this young lad is supposed to have battered Helen to within an inch of her life with a . . . with an iron—'

He broke off suddenly and sat up from the slump he'd settled into while talking. For now he said nothing but, from the flickering of his eyes, she could see his head was working hard.

'Hey, Eamon, are you still with me?' she said, prodding his arm gently.

Boy, was he still with her – he was right on top of her, turning towards her intently now. What he said next nearly made her hair stand on end.

'This has to do with that Priest fella, doesn't it?'

If she'd been eating or drinking anything, she'd have choked on it. As it was, it still took a huge effort of will not to betray herself. She took a deep breath before replying. 'What are you talking about, Eamon?'

'The cross,' he said.

'What cross?'

'The cross he battered her with,' Doherty whispered, looking around to see if anybody had heard him. 'A big old iron thing. The story goes they went into the churchyard in Gweedore together, for a lie-down in the long grass. But instead of giving her, y'know, a cuddle, he started clattering the bejaysus out of her with this big iron cross that he picked up off one of the graves. I thought that was a bit of a local legend, you know, a kind of fairytale to give the girls a scare. But that's why you wanted to know, right? Because of the cross. It was him, wasn't it – The Priest?'

She saw a bead of sweat break out on his forehead, and could see he was almost shaking with the excitement as he searched her face for an answer. Now her own mind was in the grip of the tremors, too. Mulcahy *had* been bloody on to something. But she hadn't expected it to jump out at her anything like as quick as this. And, fool that she was, she'd let the cat out of the bag to Doherty. She had to close it down. Think quick. Quicker than him, at any rate, and find a way to keep him calm and not leap to all the same conclusions she was leaping to. If he did, the story would be splashed across every other newspaper as well as her own.

'Hey, hey, Eamon, steady on there, will you?' She laughed out loud at him, thanking Christ that he was half cut already – she could work with that. 'I think the drink might be making you jump the gun a bit. All I'm doing is a bit of background. I mean, the boys in blue are convinced they've caught The Priest. I'm just doing a sidebar on, you know, other weird religious crimes that've happened down the years. You'd be amazed how thin on the ground they are. In Ireland, of all places. A pal of mine mentioned that he'd heard about this thing in Gweedore – so I thought I'd do a bit of digging and called you.'

She tried to make her tone as patronising as possible, playing on the fact that, for all his swagger, he still probably thought he was a provincial yokel compared to her working on a big Sunday paper. It seemed to work.

'Really?' All of a sudden, he didn't sound so sure of himself.

''Fraid so,' she laughed again. 'Sorry to disappoint you, like, but as far as I know, there's no connection. I mean, I don't even know this kid's name. Do you? The one who attacked Helen Martin? But I'll bet a thousand euro it wasn't Emmet Byrne, the guy they have in custody here.'

That one seemed to stump him. Siobhan spotted a waitress walking past and nabbed her. 'Could you bring a nice cold pint of Guinness over for my friend here?' she asked.

Doherty looked a little flustered now – even he was beginning to think he must be pissed.

'Yeah, yeah, okay. Maybe you have a point, Siobhan. And maybe we don't get enough excitement up our way, either.' He laughed, but it was tinged with embarrassment. 'You're right about the name as well.'

'Yeah?'

'Well, to be honest, I'm not sure what the kid's name was. As you know, it never went to court and—'

'Why didn't it go to court?'

'Oh, the boy was connected to a local bigwig. Or used to be local. His grandfather was a senior member of the judiciary, an old IRA boy who'd risen high.'

'IRA?'

'Yeah, but as in 1922 and all that. A friend of De Valera's, y'know – a founding father of the Republic. They called them "The Great Ones", a gang of Donegal lads who were hugely influential at the start. I think this guy was President of the High Court at some stage.'

'A judge?' The hairs rose up on the back of Siobhan's neck, as all the keywords from Mulcahy's searches started pinging in her brain. She remembered the obituaries he had been reading. They were all about some old judge. She dug in her pocket for a ten-euro note as the waitress returned with the pint for Doherty, waving her away quickly and telling her to keep the change.

'Yeah, a judge,' Doherty said, taking a glug before continuing. 'A local boy made good, Gweedore born and bred.

Had a big old house by the sea that he used when the Dublin courts weren't in session. And a right old bastard, too, by all accounts. He had the power to silence people and used it – with the guards especially. As I heard it, after the attack the boy was whisked away and never seen again. Helen Martin was sent to a private hospital and the whole thing was hushed up. The judge even pushed through an injunction on the *Courier*. Not a word could get out. I'm told he paid the girl's family off but I don't imagine they had much choice but to shut up about it. Young Helen must've recovered alright in the end, anyway, cos they all moved away soon after. To England, I think.'

Poor girl, Siobhan thought with a shudder, wondering what sort of hillbilly backwoods place Gweedore would have to be to let that happen as recently as 1988.

Doherty must have seen in her expression what she was thinking. 'If she'd died it would've been different, y'know. Even in the eighties, the old ways of kowtowing to priests and politicians still had a hold up there – especially with the Troubles at their height across the border. But their power was on the wane. And, after something like that, well, people were just sickened by it.'

'This judge, though, he got away with it?'

'Yeah, but like I say, times were changing. There was a huge amount of bad feeling about it round the place. He never came back after that, and the big house stayed empty until it was sold after he died. That must've been before 1997, or else we'd never have published even the small reference that you read online. The editor back then wasn't exactly the campaigning type, if you know what I mean.'

'Oh, I know, alright,' Siobhan said, just to keep him happy. 'I'm beginning to think it might be a bit too dodgy for my editor to wear even now. I mean, whatever about a court case, there probably wasn't even an arrest, or a police record of the incident, was there?'

Doherty sat back in his seat and shrugged. 'If there was, it'll have disappeared years ago. But, now that you come to mention it, it might be worth looking into. I think everyone's forgotten about the whole thing, to be honest.'

'Well, don't go doing anything on my account,' Siobhan said hurriedly. 'I'm pretty sure I won't be using it now. But if you do dig up something, will you promise to let us have first dibs?'

Doherty laughed. 'Right you are then, Siobhan. It's a deal. Although I've a feeling it won't be knocking anything off our front page next week. This match today and the cutbacks at Letterkenny General Hospital are what people are interested in, up my way.'

Siobhan apologised again to Doherty for wasting his time and said she had to get back to the grindstone, leaving him to saunter back towards the bar with his half-drunk pint. It had been risky, that final double-bluff, but she was as confident as she could be that Doherty wouldn't pursue the story now. Unless he was an even cuter operator than she gave him credit for. But she didn't think so. By saying she wouldn't pursue it herself, she'd effectively pulled the plug.

For him it was nothing more than old news again. And even if he did do some digging, she was sure he'd be enough of an old hack to want to sell it on through her to the *Sunday Herald* first; get a bit of the big time out of it.

She ignored the doorman's offer to get her a taxi, and ran down the steps outside, snagging one for herself straight away, right from under the eyes of a startled tourist. In under five minutes, she was back in the newsroom again, checking out Harry Heffernan's office. She was in luck, the conference had overrun – the rumble of conversation was still coming from behind the closed door. Heated it sounded, maybe even heated enough to give her time to do a quick follow-up on this old judge. And his grandson, who'd be, what, in his mid- to late thirties by now? If God really was being kind to her, the grandson would be a scion of the male line. Lovely word that, scion. And there couldn't be many people in Dublin with that surname, now could there?

For the first time that day, Siobhan felt a genuine smile playing on her lips.

19

The Salazar residence took up the entire top floor of a majestic period block situated between the Palacio Real and the Opera, a huge wedding cake of a building, the swirls and swags of its stucco-work like white icing baked in the glare of the midday sun.

'This is only their pied-a-terre, you understand,' Martinez whispered as they were ushered into a finely appointed sitting room by a middle-aged man in a charcoal-grey business suit – the uniform, Mulcahy assumed, of the modern-day butler. 'The family of Don Alfonso has a nice house, too, over near the Retiro,' he continued. Not a sound intruded from the busy city outside. 'But I hear that it is currently leased to a Russian billionaire.' He laughed. 'The family's historical residence is even more impressive, Palacio Salazar, out in the country near El Escorial. Which shows you for how long they have been close to the centre of power, here in Spain.'

Mulcahy understood alright. The old power systems, those of family, wealth and privilege, were still very much alive in Spain, even if hidden from view by the youthful thrusting face that was the nation's preferred image to the outside world. He looked around him. The room was sparsely but elegantly decorated in a style that was antique in itself. Everything from the carved furniture to the pale silk wall hangings had an air of faded elegance, as if the very notion of home improvement were beneath contempt. Just then came a sound of footfalls from the corridor outside, and the door swung open. Martinez was on his feet instantly, smoothing down his suit with one hand and striding across the room towards the tall, lean man who entered with a loping, authoritative stride.

Mulcahy recognised him immediately from television and the newspapers. Don Alfonso Mellado Salazar. Dressed in a dark grey pinstripe suit, the silver of the stripe a perfect match for his hair, he had to be in his early seventies at least. But while not exactly burdened by age, he looked a little weakened by it. His thin, hollowed-out face still had a hawk-like imperiousness to it, the silver hair swept back from a broad forehead that topped a high-bridged nose, intense brown eyes, and pale fleshy lips. But his posture was more stooped, less fearsome, than Mulcahy had anticipated.

'Don Alfonso, thank you so much for admitting us to your home.' Martinez was formal to the point of obsequiousness, approaching Salazar with his head bowed and a hand outstretched. Salazar nodded as he took the proffered hand and shook it warmly.

'Good afternoon, Javier. Thank you for taking the time to handle this personally.'

By now, after just a few hours back in the city, Mulcahy could feel the language returning to him. During lunch he'd suggested to Martinez that they switch to speaking Spanish, and after half an hour or so of stumbling it had started flowing for him again. Enough to pick up now on the subtleties of the exchange taking place before him, and to be surprised that his friend was on what amounted to first-name terms with Salazar, the older man using the intimate '*tu*' when addressing him. Quite clearly, they had met many times before. Mulcahy wasn't the only one who'd been done a favour by Javier's trip to the airport, it seemed.

'This is the police officer from Dublin, sir,' Martinez announced, as he steered Salazar across the room. 'A good man, and a friend of mine, Detective Inspector Mike Mulcahy.'

'Yes, yes, I know of him,' the old man said. 'They thought highly of him at the embassy there. He speaks the language, yes?'

The question was directed at Martinez, but Salazar had his gaze fixed firmly on Mulcahy.

'Good afternoon, sir,' Mulcahy said. 'It is an honour to meet you. My Spanish is far from perfect, but I hope it will be sufficient for the task ahead. I will do my best to make the process as painless as possible for your daughter.'

This formal approach was what Martinez had suggested but Salazar wasn't interested in niceties.

'So this man you arrested, is he the same one who attacked my daughter?' The old man's tone was accusing.

'They tell me he has murdered a girl since – another child. Is that correct?'

'The investigation is ongoing but, yes, our suspect may have committed both crimes, and at least one other. But it is not possible to say more than that, at this stage.'

He paused as Salazar harrumphed and shot a sceptical glance at Martinez, who did a magnificent job of pretending not to notice it. Before the old man could say anything else, Mulcahy went on. 'We're hoping that any information your daughter can give us will greatly help our efforts to take this man off the streets permanently.'

For a second or two Salazar looked like he was about to say something combative in reply, but then a shadow crossed his face and his entire posture seemed to slump fractionally. A faint air of sadness seeped out of him now. He extended a hand to Mulcahy.

'I believe I owe you a debt of gratitude for halting the interrogation my child was subjected to, so disgracefully, on the day she was attacked. That should never have occurred. It was an outrage. But, for your intervention, I want you to know I am most grateful.'

Mulcahy wasn't sure how to respond to that, since it wasn't entirely true. As he couldn't really see how contradicting the man would help progress matters, he shook the hand offered and remained silent.

'I thought it would be good for her, you see,' Salazar continued, the gaze with which he fixed Mulcahy now sadder, more resigned than the gruff public persona of the politician. 'To get away from me for a few weeks, from the bustle of politics that surrounds us, to see how ordinary people live. So I gave in to her pleading to be allowed to go to Dublin with her schoolfriends. I thought it is Ireland, and a Catholic country, so it will be safe for her. I should have known better.'

Retrospect, the politician's greatest friend, Mulcahy thought. But again he resisted the impulse to respond. It was better to move on, stay on neutral ground.

'May I ask how your daughter is now, sir?'

'Thank you, she is as well as can be expected. In fact, we should proceed. The sooner it is done, the sooner she can begin to put it all behind her. I will take you to her now.'

Salazar asked the butler to show his visitors the way, and they walked through a series of tastefully decorated but dismal corridors, Salazar lagging behind a little, engaging Martinez in a whispered conversation of which Mulcahy could make out nothing other than that it was about some mutual acquaintance. When the butler eventually opened a door and ushered them through, Mulcahy was surprised to find himself in a kind of sparsely furnished anteroom, where three other people were already waiting. From the way they turned and looked at him appraisingly – the man with a decidedly lawyerly sneer – he could tell they already knew why he was there.

Salazar made the introductions. 'Inspector Mulcahy, this is Doctor Mendizabal, my daughter's psychiatrist, and Señor Don Ruiz Ordonez, my lawyer. And, eh . . .?'

'The police stenographer, Don Alfonso,' Martinez inter-jected hurriedly. 'To record the interview for the purposes of the witness statement.'

'Ah, good. Well, please, let us go in.'

Mulcahy shot a questioning glance at Martinez. He'd only agreed that the psychiatrist could sit in, and obviously the stenographer, too. But where the hell did the rest of them think they were going? Martinez shrugged, at a loss himself, leaving Mulcahy, in the end, to stop them at the door and suggest that the fewer people were present, the better. At which point the psychiatrist stepped in to agree, tactfully suggesting to Don Alfonso that while his daugh-ter would doubtless be comforted by his presence, she might be inhibited by it too. As for the lawyer, he could read the stenographer's transcript afterwards. Neither Salazar nor Ordonez were happy about this but, like Mulcahy, Dr Mendizabal stood her ground. He smiled gratefully at her as they went through the doorway into the adjoining room.

Press day hadn't got any easier, and Siobhan hadn't found time to follow up on the leads Doherty had given her. Griffin had been on her case ever since he'd come out of conference in a foul humour, muttering about the editor's solitary habits. Heffernan had done a U-turn on the front end, insisting that the Emmet Byrne piece was no longer strong enough for a front-page splash.

'Stupid wanker, he's still pissed off with Lonergan and

the DPP,' Griffin grumbled. 'Doesn't want to give credit where credit is bloody well due.'

Then, about half an hour later, a story Griffin had been keeping an eye on all week, about a pensioner who'd been missing for days from a residential nursing home in Cork, came good when the old boy turned up dead in a clump of bushes just three hundred yards from the home itself. Ever the opportunist, Griffin saw a chance for sensation. So Siobhan had been glued to the newsdesk for hours, working up the material coming in from stringers, agencies and whatever she could muster herself on the phones, into a hectoring lead about the appalling state of Ireland's nursing homes. At least it would have her byline all over it.

She'd just about got all that under her belt and was taking a short break when, scrolling through the AP wire service on her monitor, she spotted something that made her cough into the lukewarm cup of coffee she was sipping.

'Jesus, Paddy, come here. Have you seen this?'

Griffin, who'd been berating one of his junior reporters down the phone for failing to follow up information about a rat-infested old-folks' home in Tubbercurry, slammed his handset down and strode over to Siobhan, his face etched with stress.

'What now?'

'Look at this.' She pointed at the agency feed she had frozen on her screen.

3.35 p.m. Dublin: Gardai are refusing to comment on uncon-firmed reports that a young woman was snatched from outside

a city centre nightclub in D'Olier Street last night, saying only
that they are 'investigating all aspects' of the incident.

'What about it?' Griffin said.

She could see from the way his eyebrows were narrowing that he knew exactly what she was getting at, but he wasn't willing to play ball.

'Oh, come on, Paddy. What if it *really* wasn't Byrne?'

'And what if this is some Associated Press arsehole trying to make a great big heap out of fuck all,' he countered. 'We all know what "outside a nightclub" means. Some gobshite off his face on coke, and too thick to read the papers, sees some fella cutting up rough with his girlfriend and calls in the guards. And as for "unconfirmed reports", you know that puts it in the bullshit tray straight away.'

'And what if it's not? There might be some kid out there in trouble.'

Griffin stared at her and shook his head slowly. 'You're going to crucify me if I'm wrong, aren't you?'

'For the next year, minimum, no let-up.' She smiled, then stuck in the knife. 'And I'll tell everyone else, as well. It'd be a sad end to a great career.'

'Fuck you, too,' he growled, then looked over at Heffernan's door. 'But fuck him even more. Go on, hit the phones and see what you can dig up. It might be worth a few inches. Make sure you get on to that Garda contact of yours. I want to know if Lonergan and his crew are even aware of it. If they're not, screw them over good and proper.'

'Thanks, Paddy, I love you – sometimes.'

'Yeah, bollocks you do,' he said, turning away so she wouldn't see him grinning.

Mulcahy had assumed they'd be going into a bedroom. He had expected Jesica would be too unwell still to be up and about. So it was with a rush of relief that he realised the room set aside for the interview was a normal, comfortable sitting room. And that now, only a few weeks on from her ordeal, Jesica Salazar was recovered enough to be back on her feet again. Perched on a small sofa, in baggy grey joggers, matching hoodie and immaculate white trainers, she looked like a girl who was making an effort to appear like a normal teenager. But nothing, not the long strands of hair she tugged at to hide behind, or the huge cushion she clasped protectively to her chest, could conceal the bruising that still mottled and distorted her face in places, or the deep black bags splayed like ink stains beneath her eyes. Everything about her seemed wary, coiled tighter than a spring.

The psychiatrist asked Jesica if she recognised Mulcahy. The girl studied him anxiously, as if she had done something wrong, and then said, no, she didn't.

'We met in the hospital in Dublin,' Mulcahy said. 'My colleagues wanted to ask you some questions. I translated.'

Jesica put her hand up to her neck. If the red weal around her throat was still there it was hidden now by the high neckline of her tightly zipped hoodie. But his words clearly meant something to her because she nodded then with a simple '*Sí*' and bowed her head.

'As we discussed earlier, Jesica,' the psychiatrist said, 'the inspector needs to ask you some questions. If you feel well enough, okay?'

Jesica ignored her and, lifting her head, addressed Mulcahy from the side of her mouth.

'Did you find my cross and chain?'

'No. We're still looking for it.'

'It was my mother's,' she said indignantly.

'We'll do everything we can to find it.'

Again her head came up, this time looking at him straight, anger in her voice. 'He has it, doesn't he?'

In her eyes he could see pain, fear and, more than anything else, humiliation. But before he could reply the psychiatrist intervened again.

'Perhaps we should focus on something more constructive initially.' She spoke quickly, her accent unfamiliar to him, so he had to concentrate hard to get it all. 'I was told, Inspector, that you wanted Jesica to tell you in her own words what happened that night. Perhaps we should just stick to that, for now.'

'I told you before, I don't remember anything,' Jesica insisted. 'I've already told you everything I know.'

The girl's anger seemed directed at the psychiatrist rather than at him, so he said nothing for a few seconds. When the tension had dissipated a little, he sat forward and caught Jesica's eye.

'I know this is difficult for you, Jesica,' he said. 'But if you can't tell me yourself, perhaps you would let me put some questions to you.'

The girl relented. So slowly, gently, he started on the list of questions he had prepared, asking again about her time in the GaGa Club, who she had gone there with, who she had left with and at what time. But whether unwilling or unable, Jesica now seemed even less capable of answering his questions than she had been on the day she was attacked. What few answers she could give were slow, self-conscious and uncertain, her recollections hesitant and painful. Mulcahy could only feel pity for her, since she was obviously doing her best but was clearly also mortified that what had happened to her should be the focus of their attention. Just keep plugging away, he thought, so long as she can cope. Something might come of it. But he could see it was going to be a long and painful process.

The breakthrough came at around four-thirty p.m. Not thanks to anything Jesica or he himself said, but rather a remark the psychiatrist made while walking out of the room with Mulcahy after forty minutes of little or no progress. The low point had come when he presented the mugshots of Byrne to Jesica, and she had barely even glanced at them before shaking her head. 'I don't know what he looks like, I told you,' was all she said.

That was when Dr Mendizabal suggested taking time out. 'Sometimes, you know, in cases such as this,' she observed, once they were outside, 'the mind will protect itself from a pain that is unbearable. Only by finding a way round its internal defences can we hope to get to a place where we can address the trauma.'

'And how do you do that?' Mulcahy asked.

'Well, in a clinical situation, by hypnosis or hypnotherapy, for instance. That would be an obvious route in a case like this. You instruct the mind to lower its defences, and in such a state of relaxation it is remarkable what can emerge and begin to heal.'

'Do you think that would work with Jesica?'

'It is a therapeutic course that I fully intend to pursue.'

'So would it work if we tried it now?'

The psychiatrist frowned. 'It would be of no benefit to you. I don't know what the situation is in your country, but here in Spain it has long been established that testimony obtained under hypnosis is not admissible in a court of law. There are many precedents.'

'I'm sure it is the same in Ireland, Doctor, but if we're not going to get anything useful by any other means maybe admissibility doesn't matter. If we could uncover something that put our suspect's involvement beyond doubt, then our investigators might find another route back to proving it. Do you see what I mean?'

Dr Mendizabal was considering this when Mulcahy's phone beeped with a message alert. He excused himself and stepped aside to open it, noting with surprise that it was from Siobhan:

Another kid snatched last night, still missing. Lonergan, Brogan all in full-scale denial. Call me!

The shock hit him like a sneaky left hook. Rinn's face immediately leaped up, snarling, to fill the vacuum in his thoughts. The night before he'd considered the possibility that Rinn and Byrne might have been working together as some kind of team, but he'd dismissed it. There had never been any sign or indication that The Priest's attacks were the work of more than one man. Mulcahy was still thinking it through again when Dr Mendizabal approached him.

'*Lo siento*, Inspector, but are you alright? You look a little disconcerted.'

'Yes,' was all he said, before he remembered who he was talking to. 'Doctor, did you ever get any sense from Jesica that she was attacked by more than one person?'

Even as he was saying it, he thought of how the girl herself had always only referred to her attacker in the singular.

'No, never,' the psychiatrist said. 'In fact, I would think it would be unlikely, given what was actually done to Jesica. You know, sometimes sexual predators can operate in pairs but this is comparatively rare. And virtually impossible when you consider the severity of the psychosis manifested in the attack on Jesica. This is not pleasure that is being taken by the perpetrator, but a compulsion that is being acted out. It is not something that, at a psychological level, it is possible to share. It is only for the person who does it, him alone, do you understand?'

Mulcahy nodded, trying to recall what Siobhan said

440

her psychologist contact had told her the night before. 'Yes, that makes sense.'

'Why did you ask?'

'I've just been informed that another girl's gone missing in Dublin.'

'But you already have a man in custody, yes?'

'Yes, Doctor,' Mulcahy said, his voice lower now. 'But is he the right man? At this moment, the only one of his victims who can possibly help us with that question is Jesica.'

'But she says she did not see him.'

Mulcahy rubbed his forehead in frustration and, suddenly, the memory flashed up again of Jesica in the hospital bed in Dublin, rubbing the red weal on her neck, her voice filled with confusion and pain:

Hizo la señal del Cristo.

That was it, of course. Mulcahy turned to Dr Mendizabal again, looked her straight in the eye and felt sure she would understand.

'When I spoke to Jesica on the day of the assault, she told me that she'd seen her attacker make the sign of the cross.'

'And?'

'Don't you see?' Mulcahy said, demonstrating the gesture for her, exaggerating the motion of his hand as he drew it down across his face from his forehead to his chest and up to each shoulder in turn. 'She must have seen his face if she saw him do that. Even if she doesn't remember it now.'

As the psychiatrist took his words on board, her right hand smoothed the white cotton of her shirt on the left shoulder. Mulcahy wondered if she was aware of the habit, which he'd noticed her do repeatedly at tricky moments in the interview, earlier.

'Of course, I must put my patient's therapeutic needs first, Inspector,' she said at last. 'And we would also require Don Alfonso's permission, and Jesica's consent. But I think, in the circumstances, a case can be made for trying hypnosis. Jesica really does want to assist you, and you can see she is distressed by her inability to do so. It is arguable that if we enable her to help you now, it may contribute to her emotional recovery in the longer term.'

To Mulcahy's surprise, Dr Mendizabal even offered to go and propose this course of action to Salazar, and seek his permission. As soon as she was gone, Mulcahy started dialling Siobhan's number but stopped, wondering what the hell he thought he was doing. Was he suddenly in league with her? Instead, he clicked on Brogan's number and waited as it rang and went straight through to her voicemail. He cursed and hung up. What was the point of calling her, anyway, when he didn't even have a crumb of evidence for her yet. He sat down on a chair in the corridor, breathing heavily, wondering what to do next. All going well, he might be forced to make that call, and soon. But, for the moment, he was damned if he was going to entrust his future to an answering machine.

It didn't take long for Jesica to go under. In the room's dim light, Mulcahy looked on, absorbed, as the doctor took her

442

through the lead-in, getting her to lie on the sofa, asking her first to look up at a fixed point on the ceiling, then to relax, to feel her eyelids grow heavy, then her body, limb by limb, get warm and weighty, to relax, to go down into warmth and stillness, to relax, push away the demands and pains of the world around her, to forget the clamour and needs of other people, to feel only the warmth and heaviness in her limbs, her neck, her head, to relax . . .

It couldn't have taken more than two or three minutes before the girl was still and quiet, the only sign of life being her chest heaving low and slow, and her eyes, which seemed to flicker with a life of their own beneath closed lids. Mulcahy was amazed that Jesica had consented so readily to undergo this procedure. Perhaps with her physical healing under way, she felt a need to take on the mental trauma too.

Mulcahy watched as the psychiatrist did a few quick checks to make sure Jesica was fully under, asking her to raise the index finger on her right hand if she understood, which she did, then telling her she had nothing to fear, that there would be two voices talking to her from now until the session was over – her own and that of Señor Inspector Mulcahy – and that if at any time Jesica encountered something that was too painful to recall, she could lift her index finger again, and they would either move on to another subject or bring her back to a waking state.

Mulcahy had discussed a list of prompts and questions with Dr Mendizabal beforehand, and this list she now consulted in tandem with a series of her own notes on a clipboard. Mulcahy noted that her approach wasn't all that different from his own interview technique, first asking Jesica some general questions as a lead-in: about when she first arrived in Ireland, what the school was like and who her friends had been. At this stage Dr Mendizabal focused only on the positive, and steered away from anything that Jesica might find uncomfortable. Throughout this time, Mulcahy was struck by how mobile the girl's facial features had become, taking on an expressiveness rarely seen on people's faces in waking life, the muscles making subtle little smiles, tics and frowns of concentration that seemed to mirror her emotions and interior mental processes. Yet in her answers her voice rarely varied from a flat nasal monotone that reminded him, somehow, of the few occasions when he'd heard Gracia talking in her sleep.

Slowly the psychiatrist led a smiling Jesica on from friends to dancing, to dancing with friends in nightclubs, to dancing with boys, and then to dancing in Dublin on the night in question. Again Mulcahy noted how Mendizabal never said anything jarring like 'the night of the attack' or even 'that night', or anything that might foreshadow what had happened to Jesica later. As a result, he felt he could see her living in the moment as she described the club, the lights, the music and the grin of satisfaction reproduced on her lips when she started to describe how one boy, hand-some and blond 'like David Beck-ham', had approached her so confidently and swept her away from her friends.

Mulcahy only knew Patrick Scully from the video grabs

taken from the GaGa Club cameras but he was struck by the immediacy and accuracy of Jesica's description. He wondered if people under hypnosis were always so transparent. Although Scully was no longer a suspect, he felt they would never have pursued him at all if they could have heard this response from Jesica earlier. But that was now academic: no point in dwelling on opportunities missed. Not when Jesica was now talking about how happy she'd been when Scully suggested he walk her home, and how she had left the club on a high. But it wasn't long before she started feeling uncomfortable, when, leaning against a wall near the shopping centre in Stillorgan, he'd started putting his hands on her and she'd liked it at first, even when he put his hands down *there*, but then his hand became rougher and she didn't want him to do that, and she told him not to, but he tried it again and she pushed him away and he became angry.

Again Mulcahy noticed a distinct change in Jesica's facial expressions, the muscles dancing on her face. Dr Mendizabal caught his eye and pointed to the index finger on Jesica's right hand, which was wavering now, hovering just above the level of its fellows. Mulcahy raised an eyebrow but the psychiatrist shook her head, indicating with the flat of her hand that everything was okay. He realised that she was using the finger like a needle-gauge to monitor Jesica's anxiety level.

That anxiety stayed fairly stable as the girl described how Scully had finally stormed off, then it slackened as righteous anger and disappointment took over. She described then how she'd looked for a taxi. Mulcahy's hopes flared up then faded as she said she couldn't see one and had decided to walk on. And so Jesica continued, crossing road junctions, cursing Scully, passing the video hire shop and the 7-Eleven, and the walls and gates of what Mulcahy realised was Mount Anville primary school. Suddenly he saw her body stiffen, muscles shifting like riptides across her face now, in fear or pain, and her index finger was rigidly pointing up again, higher than before.

'No . . . no!' she moaned, her voice cracking, terrified.

Knowing this had to be the result of her first contact with her attacker, Mulcahy looked over at Mendizabal, who was herself looking concerned. The psychiatrist told Jesica to relax, to be calm, that nothing could hurt her here and now, and the girl responded, calming slightly. Then she told her to not be afraid but to look around her, to describe what she was seeing and feeling. Jesica began to speak again. Beyond the school, a car had passed and pulled in up ahead. Mulcahy was already feeling the tension, but then Jesica paused, her chin jutting out a little, as if she were looking again, harder, and then said: 'No, not a car, a van.'

'What colour van is it?' Mulcahy asked, not really expecting an answer, but he got one.

'White,' the girl said.

'You're sure?'

Yes, she nodded emphatically, white with black windows at the back, the streetlights from across the road burning orange reflections in them.

446

Mulcahy felt a kind of relief run through him, knowing this pushed things back towards Byrne, and, thinking of her earlier clarity, he wondered if she might be able to come up with something more specific, a model name or plate number.

'Can you see any writing on the van, on the back or the sides?'

'No,' she said definitely. 'There is a sign on the roof, across the top, but it's too dark to read.'

All Mulcahy's relief drained away, instantly replaced by puzzlement. Byrne's van had nothing on the roof. But something else in him was shifting, clawing at recollection until, in a flash of memory so powerful it was all but physical, he felt himself being pulled back from danger by Martinez at the roadside in the airport again. That taxi! Why hadn't he thought of it before? An MPV, a taxi *van*. What if Rinn had his fake taxi sign on a people carrier? He desperately tried to recall the vehicle mentioned in Rinn's traffic offence, but it wouldn't come. He was about to jump in and ask Jesica more about the sign but Mendizabal signalled him to wait, pointing at the girl's eyes which were now moving round like marbles under the tightly closed lids.

Suddenly, Jesica snapped her head back and her shoulders raised a couple of inches off the sofa, as if she had been struck in the face.

'He hit me, he hit me,' she gasped, the words so familiar to Mulcahy from her earlier interview. Her bottom lip was quivering and tears slipped from beneath her eyelids. Still Mendizabal did not intervene. Instead, calmly and steadily, she told Jesica to relax again, to take herself out of the scene, to rise above it and look down on it. The girl nodded and immediately went on.

'He is hitting me,' Jesica said again, her voice much more distant now. 'It's dark, he put something over my head, and it smells so much I want to choke. I can't breathe because he's hitting me, again and again.'

Mulcahy's heart went out to Jesica as he listened to her describe falling over in the darkness, the sharp pain in her legs and the back of her head when she hit the floor of the van as she was pushed inside. He remembered now what she had said, in the hospital room, about the attacker throwing something over her. It must have been to cover her face, to prevent her from seeing him properly. But that couldn't be right. She'd said he'd made the sign of the cross. *Like a priest.* It had been so vivid, so visual. She must have *seen* him.

'The sign of the cross, Jesica,' Mulcahy whispered. 'You said he made the—'

He was about to ask the question when Dr Mendizabal shot a hand in front of his face, shooting him a glare full of concern. She pointed to the girl's middle finger: it was rising and falling slowly.

'It's stopped,' the girl said, an echo of the terror she was reliving trembling in her voice. 'I hear nothing but the pain in my head. Am I dead? No, I hear him moving, crawling around me, like a snake, like a . . . aaaah.' Breath rushed from Jesica like she'd been physically punched again and her hands leaped to her neck as if she were being strangled. 'No, no, Mama, no don't let him hurt me . . .'

Mulcahy had to look away. He couldn't bear to see the pain and fear playing out on her face, all nerves and tics and terror as she relived her struggle, told how the chain around her neck gave way, snapped, and she could breathe again, great whooping gulps of air filling her starved lungs. And how she must have passed out for a moment then, because all she could describe was becoming aware, distantly, of violation, of crude fingers parting her thighs, cutting her clothes off, and how she began to struggle again, harder, so hard that the sack over her face slipped and . . .

Mulcahy's gaze snapped back to Jesica's face in an instant, expectation rising, checking from the corner of his eye that Dr Mendizabal wasn't going to stop her now.

'He is leaning over me, and I can breathe again, feel the air on my face, and hear again . . . yes, I can hear the words on his lips are prayers. "Our Father, who art in heaven, hallowed be Thy name . . ." He is blessing himself, and staring down at me, and making the sign of the cross . . . like a priest. And he's holding a burning sword in his hands and it is red with fire, there's so much heat, and he is praying over me, praying and touching me with the cro . . .' The girl gasped, her body rigid, snapping up from the waist for just a second, like a clasp-knife buckling, and she let out a low and terrible moan.

He saw the concern on the psychiatrist's face, heard her try to calm the girl and ask her if she wanted to come back, telling her she could come back any time if it got too much. And Mulcahy just couldn't let that happen, not now, when they were so close.

'Tell us about his face, Jesica. Tell us about the priest's face,' he pleaded.

He saw a flash of panic cross the psychiatrist's features, followed by anger. She glared at him again, warning him to stop. But she didn't interrupt, because Jesica, brave Jesica, had already begun to answer.

'No priest,' she gasped, through teeth clenched in fearful realisation, confusion and fear contorting the muscles on her face, her body twitching like it was possessed. 'A devil,' she gasped, as if she'd wrenched something up from her very soul. 'A devil's face, thin and red, and his eyes are burning fire, and the flames of hell are climbing up around him, on his face, on his skin. Burning!'

Jesica's entire body was shuddering with fear now, and Dr Mendizabal was slashing the air with her hands, warning Mulcahy not to say another word.

'Enough,' she said. 'That's enough, Jesica, that's good, very good. Now relax again, good girl, you have nothing to fear. Come away from that place, relax, take a deep breath . . . and relax.'

When the psychiatrist looked across at Mulcahy again, it wasn't with anger but relief, something he now felt washing over himself in a great wave as he realised what it was the girl had said. Something must have changed in him, in his expression, because Dr Mendizabal was now quizzing him with her eyes, as if to say: *Are you alright?*

'One more question?' he mouthed at her. 'An easy one, I promise. The last.'

She mouthed the words 'easy' back at him, a sternness in her gaze, and he nodded again.

'Good,' she said. 'Jesica, you're doing so well, so amazingly well. The inspector has just one more question for you, then it will be time to come back to us.'

The girl nodded imperceptibly, still breathing hard but in every other respect apparently calm again.

'Jesica,' he said, as gently as he could, 'those flames you saw climbing up this man, this devil, tell me, were they on his face or were they only on his neck?'

Mulcahy already knew the answer. But he wanted to hear it from Jesica's lips. So that later he could tell her honestly that it was her, and only her, who had put beyond doubt who it was that had caused her so much pain.

He didn't notice that he was actually shaking with emotion until he left the room and saw Martinez and Salazar waiting in the anteroom outside. Salazar creaked to his feet, looking anxiously towards the door behind Mulcahy rather than at him.

'How is she, Inspector? Is my daughter alright?'

'Yes, Jesica is fine. Dr Mendizabal is helping her settle again.'

Salazar exhaled a heavy sigh of relief, so much so he seemed to deflate physically. 'And did you gain any useful information?'

Mulcahy breathed out hard himself, trying to get a grip on what he'd discovered, knowing he'd have to be discreet if he was going to be able to put it to good use.

'Your daughter was very courageous, Señor Salazar, and you should be proud of her. I think we now have a partial description, but the event was, clearly, so very traumatic . . .' He broke off, unsure of how much more he should say.

'Does it match the suspect you have in custody?'

'That's hard to say, sir, as I have not met the man,' Mulcahy said, side-stepping the question as best he could. 'I'll pass the information on to my colleagues, and they will take it forward. Perhaps you would like to go in to your daughter now, as she was asking for you.'

Salazar grunted and made straight for the door. Mulcahy was relieved not to have to explain further. He fished his mobile out of his pocket and turned it on. It beeped immediately. A voice message left for him: Siobhan, going nineteen to the dozen, the whump and rush of Dublin traffic in the background.

'Jesus, Mulcahy, what a bloody day for you to be out of reach. Why haven't you called me back? Didn't you get my text? Look, it looks like another girl was snatched last night, right in the city centre, just up from the Twentyone Club on D'Olier Street. Same MO, everything – and all Brogan and Lonergan will do is tell me to go stuff myself, that it's an unrelated enquiry. I really need you to get in touch with them and tell them to take this seriously. There could be another girl's life at risk here, and they're just pissing about. Call me back, will you? Soon!'

Mulcahy clicked off and looked around him, the grandeur of his surroundings beginning to feel a bit surreal. What influence could she imagine he still had over Brogan, or Lonergan who he'd never even met? Who was to say this new disappearance was in any way connected? And what the hell could he do from Madrid? But the thought of another young woman going through what Jesica had just described was simply too horrible to be ignored. And he knew that now it came down to it he was just faffing about, putting himself before the safety of a missing kid. Even if that was only a possibility.

He picked the phone up and dialled Brogan's number again, expecting to go straight through to voicemail as usual. Amazingly, she answered within two rings.

'I just heard another girl's been taken,' he said.

'For fuck's sake, Mulcahy.' Brogan cursed beneath her breath. Like she thought she was dealing with a half-wit. 'Look, forget about that, will you? Some drunk says he saw a girl being dragged into a van in D'Olier Street. Someone else says it was a taxi. That's it. End of story. No body's been dumped, no kid has turned up laced with crosses. Not even a missing person's report. It's a non-event that's being whipped up into a story by the press – and especially your pal Fallon.'

'Maybe this girl just hasn't been found yet,' Mulcahy objected. 'He hid the last one pretty carefully, didn't he?'

'Yeah, so carefully that we found her within hours. And then we went out and caught him and put him in a cell, where he still was last time we looked – just an hour or so ago. Okay?' She gave a sigh of exasperation. 'Anyway, I thought Lonergan said something about you being in Madrid today, taking a statement? Didn't you go in the end?'

'I did, that's where I'm calling from now.'

Another long pause.

'So have you spoken to Jesica yet? Did you get an ID or not? Come on, Mike, get a grip.'

'I showed her Byrne's mugs. She didn't recognise him.'

'Fuck,' she said. 'We had pretty high hopes on that score. Lonergan wasn't so keen initially, but I persuaded him it was worth a shot.'

'Look, the thing is, Claire, I think I may have got a partial ID of someone else.'

'Someone else?' She sounded startled. 'What someone else? What the fuck are you talking about?'

'The guy I was telling you about the other night.'

'The taxi driver?'

'Well, he's not a taxi driver, really, but—'

'No, Mike, hang on a second now. Let me stop you right there, because I need you to get something into your head. There is *no* someone else. Do you understand me?'

'But, Claire, look, with this other kid missing, you need to see—'

'No, I don't *need* to see anything.' Brogan was really angry now. 'Other than that you are no longer a member of this

454

investigation team, so back off. Look, I don't know why you're doing this but I'm going to give you the benefit of the doubt and say honestly – and I'm telling you this as a friend and colleague – that you're being led up the garden path by Fallon. All she wants is a sleazy story to splash across the front page of that rag of hers, and she doesn't care who she uses or how she gets it. She's been hassling me and Lonergan all afternoon, and now she can't get any further she thinks she can use you to get to us instead. Well, it's not going to work, Mike, because we charged Emmet Byrne this morning on three counts: murder, aggravated sexual assault and kidnap. And do you know why? Because he put up his hand for it himself. He coughed for it. I was there in the room myself when he did.'

'But Siobhan says he has a history—'

'For Christ's sake!' Brogan shouted at him. 'It's "Siobhan" now, is it? What is she, your own personal fucking oracle? Listen to me, Mulcahy – Emmet Byrne is our man, he's our only man. Now I'm going to put the phone down and do you the biggest favour in your life and forget we ever had this conversation. Alright?'

'No, Claire, don't hang up, listen to me. I'm telling you, Byrne is *not* The Priest. This is all—'

But all he was left with was silence. Brogan hadn't listened to a word.

'What about the statement? What about Gracia?' Martinez was shouting as he ran down the wide stone staircase after Mulcahy.

'It doesn't matter, we can sort that out later. You've got to take me to the airport, right now. I have to get back to Dublin tonight.'

'What can you do there that you can't do from Madrid? Call your colleagues and let them take care of it.'

Mulcahy's glare was evidence enough of his seriousness. 'What the hell do you think I've been trying to do?'

'Okay, but there must be another solution. Dublin is hours away.'

'No, Jav, they're absolutely convinced they've got the right man. They just can't see how wrong they are.'

Martinez looked sceptical but Mulcahy gave him another sharp look. 'Come on, Jav, don't give me that. You know how it is. If I could think of any other way, I would. But I can't. I've got to get back there. Now, will you please find out what time I can get a flight?'

Martinez made the call as they hurried to his car.

'The last flight to Dublin is at seven p.m.,' he said, getting into the Mercedes. He looked at his watch. 'We can just make it if we're lucky. You are sure?'

'I'm sure.'

Martinez barked instructions into the phone, then snapped it shut. As he started the engine there was a hydraulic whish and the car's folding metal roof began to close over them. Martinez reached into the small space behind his seat and handed Mulcahy a blue lamp unit.

'You better put that on top, my friend. We are going to need it.'

*

456

'C'mon, Siobhan, that's it. You have to file it, *now*.'

Siobhan looked up from her screen and saw the clock strike five forty-five: copy deadline for the first edition. She uttered a stream of oaths, then pressed the send key.

'Fine, take the fucking thing,' she shouted back at Griffin. 'It's a pile of shite anyway.'

She hadn't been able to make any of it stand up. All she'd done was vent her spleen into a stupid little piece about Garda irresponsibility in ignoring the reported kidnap of a young woman and refusing to connect it with the Priest case. And she was lucky to get that in. She knew in every aching inch of her gut that she was right, but she had nothing concrete. No evidence even that there had been a kidnapping, apart from that one eyewitness who she'd tracked down and got some quotes from – becoming more convinced than ever he was telling the truth after he told her he was that rarest of Dublin creatures, a teetotaller. And all she could think of, while she bashed out her words onto the screen, was that another girl was in danger and she could do nothing about it. She felt sick in a way she'd never felt before, deep inside her. This was more than a story, it was somebody's life and – she looked around at the buzzing busy newsroom – nobody was willing to do a bloody thing about it.

Not even Mulcahy, it seemed. Some great collaborator he'd been. He hadn't even returned her call. Well, who needed him? She'd done the hard graft, scoured the obits and the death notices and the electoral register. She'd burrowed it out during every spare second that Griffin hadn't

457

been on her back. And now she had what she needed, and she sure as damnation wasn't going to waste that. But how to go about it?

She glanced around the office again and there, like he'd materialised out of nowhere, was Franny Stoppard, her old pal and absolute favourite photographer – or, at least, that would be how she'd approach him now, anyway – lumbering into the newsroom. A big bear of a man, he knew how to handle himself after years of fending off paparazzi-hating celebs. He'd be safe to go with, and she wouldn't even have to tell him why. Grabbing her bag and stopping only to tell Griffin she was done and would be back in an hour to sign off her subbed copy, she ran over to Stoppard and seized him by the elbow.

'Oh, thank God it's you, love. I've got one last job and you're the only one to do it.' She beamed him a dazzling smile despite his obvious lack of enthusiasm. 'C'mon, maybe we can get the scoop of the year for the late edition.'

If it had been a weekday, they'd never have made it. As it was, the roads were fairly clear for that time of evening and the siren and lights cleaved a path through what traffic there was, as Martinez's car surged like an earthbound missile out of Madrid. Mulcahy spent part of the journey trying to make himself heard on the phone to the Garda Transport Division in Dublin Castle. Rinn, they eventually confirmed, had two vehicles registered to his home address: a grey 03 Toyota Corolla and a white 05 Volkswagen Transporter. The rest of the time, Mulcahy spent berating himself for not having checked this out before.

As they turned off the autoroute onto the airport spur, Martinez looked at his watch and cursed. 'Only fifteen minutes to departure.'

He grabbed his phone from the dashboard and asked to be patched through to airport security, ordering whoever answered to get a car over to the diplomat's gate, and to instruct the control tower to hold the plane until a VIP passenger got on board. Minutes later, Martinez pulled onto a slip road leading to a gate in the chainlink perimeter fence. Inside, a car with an amber emergency light flashing on the roof was waiting, a policeman already holding the door open.

'God knows what sort of trouble I'll get in when they discover you're not the Foreign Minister,' he laughed.

'I'm sure you'll talk your way out of it,' Mulcahy said. 'You always do.'

Martinez pushed him forward. 'Show them your passport. I am not *that* powerful.'

Mulcahy did as he was told, and felt himself being propelled towards the waiting security car and into it, a hand pushing down on the crown of his head. The door slammed and instantly the vehicle screeched away. All he knew was he wanted to be in the air and on his way back to Ireland. His wish was granted faster than he could have imagined, as the car sped across the tarmac and pulled to an abrupt halt beside an Aer Lingus plane. There another security guy stood gesturing towards the gantry steps and the open door above, where a steward was waving him up.

Mulcahy hurried aboard and was shown to a seat just a couple of rows in. Even before he sat down, the plane had started to taxi out onto the runway. He remembered then that he hadn't called Siobhan back. But as soon as he pulled the phone from his pocket, the steward was in his face, telling him he had to switch it off. It was only then that he saw the little yellow envelope at the top of the screen, indicating that he'd received another text message. He clicked on read, knowing it was from Siobhan, waving the protesting steward away.

You prick – I've got it anyway. Rinn, Palmerston Park, right?

For the first time in his life, he felt like throwing up on a plane.

20

By the time they landed in Dublin, Mulcahy had put a lot of it together in his head. Not just about the scars on Sean Rinn's neck but also the fibres, and the path Byrne had been laying for Rinn. Then there was the van and the false taxi licence – the method must've been much the same for all his victims. As for Byrne's so-called confession, Mulcahy knew how scared and confused a man could get in police custody, especially a man like Byrne, who clearly wasn't the full shilling to start with. The rest of the details he could figure out later but, for now, he was sure he had the basics right and his priority had to be getting off the plane and ensuring Siobhan was safe and Rinn was taken off the streets.

He did not wait, as instructed, until he got into the terminal building at Dublin Airport to use his phone. He was dialling even as he pushed to be first off the plane, and clattered down the steps, running towards the terminal. But it was only once he was well inside, in the comparative quiet of the arrivals hall, that he finally accepted, after repeated attempts, that all he was going to get from Siobhan's number was a dead tone, followed by a message saying the person he was calling did not have their phone switched on. That wasn't good. If there was one thing Siobhan Fallon, chief reporter, would never do, he felt sure, it was turn her phone off. At passport control he flipped his warrant card open and was waved straight through. He looked at his watch: 10.05 p.m. Where the hell could she be? He rang directory enquiries and asked to be put through to the *Sunday Herald,* and then the newsdesk.

'Is Siobhan Fallon there?'

'No, she isn't,' a harsh male voice barked back at him.

'Do you know where I might find her?'

'Not a fuckin' clue,' the man said angrily. 'I've been trying for hours myself. On bloody press night, too. So if you do track her down, my man, be sure and tell her Paddy Griffin says not to bother coming back to work at all, if that's her attitude. Do you hear me? Tell her she's not to bloody come back here again unless she has the best excuse on the planet.'

The phone line went dead and Mulcahy's gut began to churn again. He remembered Griffin's name from the *Herald*'s front page. What was he again, news editor? If he'd been expecting to hear from Siobhan but hadn't, that really wasn't good. The best excuse on the planet? Christ, he hoped not. Mulcahy tried to think it through. Siobhan had texted him Rinn's address – so she must have intended going there, following up her lead. But why hadn't she told anyone else? And why, three hours later, hadn't she turned up again? Most worrying of all was her phone. Why the hell was it not on? He didn't want to think the worst, but it was the only option that kept on screaming in his head.

He was exiting the terminal now, half walking, half running, heading for the multi-storey car park. When he reached the Saab he put his forehead against the cool black leather of the steering wheel, closed his eyes and willed himself to calm down. It would be pointless going over to check her flat. He barely remembered which block it was in, never mind what number. And if she was there she'd be alright anyway, so no urgency there. In fact, if she was anywhere but Rinn's house it wouldn't make a blind bit of difference – because she'd be safe. That left him with just one option: head over to Palmerston Park, check the place out, and get Rinn arrested and into a pair of handcuffs. If Siobhan was still there, so much the better. If not, no harm done.

He was halfway into the city on the M1, the speedometer tipping into the red zone, when it dawned on him that it might be as well to have some back-up. Despite everything, he tried Brogan again but predictably the call went straight to voicemail. He left another message but didn't hold out much hope. There was no way she was going to phone him back. Not now. So he tried Liam Ford, a friend in need and all that, but got exactly the same response – voicemail. Shit. Saturday night, Liam was probably out on the piss. Was it worth leaving a message? Why not?

'Liam, it's Mike here, I need your help. Can you get back to me as soon as possible?'

Which was when he thought of another option. *As soon as possible*. It would be a payback of sorts, just not the sort he had envisaged. The anger hit him even at the thought of doing it. But what other choice did he have? It was the one and only bit of leverage he had left. He took his foot off the gas and, as soon as he came to a straight stretch, he glanced down at the phone and scrolled a few days back through his call log, stabbing at a number with his thumb. It was as good a time as any to settle that score now.

Palmerston Park was dark, empty and deathly quiet. Mulcahy roared up the road in the Saab and screeched to a halt behind a filthy blue Golf GTI. As he jumped out, the Golf's occupant got out too and walked back to stare at the minimal gap left between their two cars.

'Christ almighty, another couple of millimetres and you'd have had my back bumper off. What the fuck is going on? I thought you were off the case?'

Sergeant Cassidy wasn't looking at all happy about having his Saturday night disrupted. And Mulcahy wasn't in any mood to placate him.

'Shut up, Sergeant. I don't want any crap from you. Just your attention, alright?'

Cassidy scowled angrily at him. On the phone, Mulcahy had been nothing if not abrupt, only dictating Rinn's address to him and telling him to meet him there, *asap* – if he still wanted to have his job on Monday. It was a risk, he knew, but having Cassidy at his back was better than

464

nobody at all, especially now he had a hold on him. The explanations could wait till later.

Mulcahy looked up and down the road and saw exactly what he'd hoped not to see: the red open-top Alfa Spider was parked by the railings, about thirty yards further down the road. He pointed it out to Cassidy.

'Don't you recognise it?'

Cassidy looked blankly at it, then a slow glimmer of realisation lit up his features.

'That's right, Sergeant. It's your paymaster's car, and she's in big trouble here.'

Cassidy looked totally stumped by that, as if he didn't know whether to protest or not, let alone how to go about it.

'I don't know what you're on about, Inspector, but you're making a big—'

'You wouldn't be here if I wasn't right, so just shut the fuck up,' Mulcahy hissed at him. He turned away and pointed at the house. 'A guy by the name of Rinn lives in there. He likes to play at being a taxi driver, but you know him better as The Priest.'

'What are you bleedin' talking about, we've—'

'I think this guy's got Siobhan Fallon, but I don't want to spook him if I'm wrong. He already knows me, so just back me up, okay? That way, maybe I won't tell Superintendent Healy who was behind the leaks to the *Herald*. Maybe you'll even get to keep your job.'

Pushing Cassidy ahead of him, they went through the

open gates of Rinn's house. The place appeared to be in complete darkness.

'Bloody madness,' Cassidy grumbled. 'There's nobody in there.'

'Just go knock on the front door,' Mulcahy said. 'We need to get in if he's here. Tell him somebody reported a disturbance and see if you can get yourself inside. I'll come straight after you, as soon I've checked out the garage.'

Mulcahy headed for the old coach house, hoping the sound of Cassidy crunching across the gravel would mask the sound of his own footsteps. He stopped at the garage door and listened, hearing knocking at the front door, then the jangle of the old-fashioned bell from inside, then louder knocking as Cassidy upped his efforts to raise the household. Mulcahy looked back. There were no lights going on, or any other signs of life. He pulled the wooden garage door open and in the gloom inside saw a grey saloon car with a taxi sign on top. Not out on the hunt, then. But there was an empty space for another vehicle, big enough for a van. And another, larger, taxi sign was leaning against the garage wall beside it.

Locating a light switch by the door, Mulcahy flicked it on. Almost the first thing he saw made him stop. A pile of red plastic sacking lay in a corner, exactly the colour and texture of the fibres they'd found on all the victims' clothing. A couple of layers of full sacks were sitting on a wooden pallet beside the empties, shreds of opaque bulk-wrapping still stapled to the base of the pallet. Coconut husks, he read, for laying garden paths. He saw now how Byrne must have

466

ordered them and brought them over to use in the garden, only for Rinn to put the empty sacks and wrapping to less innocent use. Before he could investigate further, he heard Cassidy come in the garage door behind him, looking fit to kill someone.

'Like I told you, there's nobody bloody in there.'

Mulcahy shook his head and pointed at the taxi. Cassidy shrugged but then stooped down and scooped something out from beneath the car.

'Looks like he's incommunicado, too,' he said, turning over the find in the palm of his hand and showing it to Mulcahy. A smashed-up mobile phone that looked like it had been stamped on. With a lurch of his stomach, Mulcahy recognised the flashy Motorola handset immediately.

'No, that's Siobhan's.'

For the first time, Cassidy looked like he might actually credit Mulcahy with some belief. 'You're sure about this?'

Mulcahy nodded. 'Her car, her phone – what do you think? And you know there's another kid missing, right?'

'Fuckin' hell,' Cassidy gasped. He looked at the handset in his palm again, then quickly around the garage, reason getting the better of his scepticism.

'This guy, Rinn, uses taxis to pick up his victims. One's a van. And look at those sacks,' Mulcahy said pointing to the corner. 'Remind you of any fibres you've seen recently?'

Cassidy's eyes narrowed as he looked at the pile, then he suddenly cursed and dashed across the garage. 'What the fuck is that?' he shouted.

But he had already answered his own question, pulling away some of the empty sacks to reveal first a man's foot, then a leg, then an entire body. Mulcahy ran over beside him. Lying there was a big bear of a bearded man, showing no signs of life. Mulcahy knelt down to check his airways.

'He's still breathing. Give me a hand, quick.'

Together they dragged the man into the recovery position. An oozing head wound gave graphic testimony as to how he'd been struck from behind with something sharp and heavy. Some time ago, too, to judge by the amount of blood that had already congealed on the floor.

'A press photographer?' Cassidy suggested, pointing to the professional-looking cameras lying by the man's side. 'They must have come here together and both been caught on the hop.'

'Yeah,' Mulcahy said, trying to visualise the scene in the garage. 'But what the hell's happened to Siobhan?'

'I'll call an ambulance,' Cassidy said, getting up. But something else caught his eye and he walked over to the empty parking space and bent down to examine an oil stain on the ground. 'This must be where he kept the van. Something's been parked here fairly recently. Do you think he's taken her somewhere else? Knowing he's been rumbled?'

'That's what I'm worried about,' Mulcahy said. 'That van is his mobile torture chamber. But we've got to check this place out properly first. With this other girl missing as well, they could just as easily both be inside in the house somewhere.'

Mulcahy stood up and went to the door, desperately trying to come up with a plan of action. By the time Cassidy finished on the phone, he had the beginnings of one. 'You'd better give Brogan a call, too, and get the cavalry over here double quick. I'm going back to the house to see if I can find anything.'

Mulcahy grabbed a torch from a shelf and ran out shouting Siobhan's name. He banged furiously on the front door again, and peered through the downstairs windows. But the only response he got was lights flicking on in the house next door. He ran around to the passageway leading between the garage and the house. The wooden gate was locked but he just tilted at it with his shoulder and it sprang open with a crash against the wall and he ran into the back garden, still calling out Siobhan's name at the top of his voice.

The world was as black as pitch and everything but the electric dread of the pain felt dull and far way. Only the pain mattered, like a blade of white light, stalking her, seeking her out where she lay curled in the corner, desperately trying to hide from it, crying from the fear of it, praying to be dead rather than that it should find her out again. And then a bang. And a bell. And another bang, still louder. And every muscle in her tensed in the effort to make herself still smaller so that whatever new agony this was, it wouldn't come her way.

Then the noises stopped and she drifted in and out of the nothing, overwhelmed. It could have been an hour that passed, it could have been a minute. She'd already been there for ever. The banging came again, and a crash that seemed to tremble like thunder in the air around her. She tried to shrink further, felt her heart hammer, her ribs hurt, her breathing quick and low. Then she heard the voice. Not *the* voice. Not *his* voice. Not the voice she feared as much as the pain, the voice that *was* the pain. But a new voice. And it was shouting her name. So distant, so like it, she was sure it was her name. From somewhere in the mire of dead emotion inside her, a bubble of hope broke loose and drifted to the surface.

She tried to hang on to it, to make herself rise with it. She tried to answer, to call out to the voice. Her sole fear now was that it would go away and leave her as she'd been before. But no sound came from her throat. She tried again and gagged on the effort, realising too late there was something in her mouth, blocking not only her voice but her breath, too. She remembered her arms and legs, like forgotten territories, found she could move them. And, through a tide of pain, she forced herself to roll over on her back and there, above her, saw a glass pane high on a wall, a pale yellow light washing across it, so close it all but touched her.

Now she heard her name again, so loud, so clear she had to call out, although she knew she couldn't, knew the panic would rise against the gag, push the breath back inside her, make her lungs feel like they would burst. And she knew too, now, that it was too late, that her own cries were strangling her, that she was gagging and puking and choking and she was going to die like a rat in this hole. A spasm of desperation took hold of her and without even knowing, without even thinking, her limbs lashed out and as she fought for one last breath she felt her arm crack against a hard edge, then her ankle with a shuddering stab of agony in the bone and there was a creaking and a popping and the whole world collapsed on her and she knew that it was all over, that this was what death was like.

Mulcahy's first thought was that Cassidy had taken matters into his own hands and smashed one of the front windows. But then the crashing continued, popping and bursting, and he realised it was coming from inside the house. But from where? He was about to run round to the front when a last smash rang out and his eye was drawn downwards. There was a tiny window, barely more than a couple of feet square, in the wall at ground level. He bent for a closer look but the glass just bounced the glare of the torch back into his eyes.

'Are you okay?' Cassidy said, coming down the side passage and seeing him doubled over.

'Yeah, I'm sure I heard something from down there after I called Siobhan's name. There has to be a basement but I can't see any way into it.'

He shone his torch along the base of the wall again and for the first time noticed the shallow slope running towards the back of the house. Then he recalled the steps leading down from the living room to the garden. He said nothing further but bolted round the back of the house again,

Cassidy hard on his heels. Seconds later, he shone his torch on one side of the flight of steps and saw a padlocked wooden door leading in under them. With one kick of his boot he staved the door in and leaped inside, the beam of the torch picking up mostly dirt, grime and gardening equipment, but no sign of Siobhan or anyone else. Cassidy came in behind him and found a light switch. Only then did they spot the other door at the back. Mulcahy barrelled though it, the light from the outer room following him into this much larger space in which stood a crude wire cage, a huge table that looked like a metal workbench, and around the walls the accumulated detritus of generations. Over in one corner, beneath a small window, enveloped in a rising cloud of dust, he saw what looked like a collapsed dresser. Everywhere around it lay tipped-open boxes, their contents strewn about, broken bottles and glass and what looked like a vast dinner service smashed to smithereens on the cold concrete floor. And out from beneath this mess poked another leg, this one naked, and female.

'Siobhan!' He ran over, pulling panels and shelves of rotten wood away as fast as his hands could get to them. They dragged the worst of it off her quickly, the gall rising in him as they exposed the lower half of her body and, through the dust and dirt that clung to her, he saw the horror of the wounds that had been inflicted on her belly and groin. But even as his stomach heaved at the thought of the pain she'd suffered, he realised something wasn't right. Something about the shape of the hips, the length of the arms. Then the hair, it wasn't dark enough. As he pushed the last shards of crockery away from her face he saw clearly now: it wasn't her. It wasn't Siobhan. And a blind panic swept over him, which he had to kill while the cop in him yanked away the duct tape from her mouth, pulled back an eyelid for any hint of life, cleared the puke, dust and grit from her mouth with a crooked finger, and pressed his lips to hers, desperate to breathe life back into this girl, this woman who wasn't Siobhan but who had to be saved, had to be brought back, even as the hope in his own heart faded and guttered but refused to go out.

They found her name on a student card in a worn pink purse on the workbench: Shauna Gleeson, a second-year arts student at UCD. Beside it was a bag Mulcahy thought he recognised as Siobhan Fallon's, inside it a voice recorder, then, confirming his fears, her wallet complete with press cards and ID. By then he'd already taken a mallet from the rack beside the bench, and he ran up the steps outside, smashing his way in through the French windows to Rinn's living room. Cassidy came behind, the girl covered by his jacket, shivering in his arms. They had to find something warmer, a blanket, a fire, to get some heat and life back into her. Mulcahy checked out the other rooms on the ground floor, found a soft wool picnic rug draped over a kitchen chair, threw it back in to Cassidy who was settling the girl on the sofa, then he galloped up the stairs. Within a couple of minutes he'd been in and out of every room in the huge three-storey house. No sign of Siobhan Fallon, or of Rinn.

On the top floor, though, he found a small room, what looked to be a private chapel of sorts. On one side he could see a narrow table serving as an altar, covered in embroidered linens, candles and what appeared to be a large gold tabernacle. On the wall above it a thin finger of wavering red light illuminated a yellowing picture of the Sacred Heart. On another wall hung a faded silk banner, its six-inch letters in an embroidered arc spelling out SODALITY OF THE MOST PRECIOUS BLOOD. Which creeped Mulcahy out but meant nothing to him. If this was Rinn's hideaway, his hidden place, then here, he knew, he might find what he needed. Mulcahy approached the makeshift altar, its linen crisp, white and bare apart from the candle sconces and a small plain wooden cross with a grey spelter figure of Christ attached to it with jagged-looking pins. The tabernacle, on the other hand, was extraordinarily extravagant: large, at least eighteen inches square, and highly decorated in chased gold and silver. The mere sight of it tempted Mulcahy to bless himself, summoning intense memories of his own brief period as an altar boy. At the front, an ornate gold sunburst splashed across double doors, flanked on either side by ghostly silver saints, one holding a book, the other wielding a sword. On a frieze above and all round the upper rim was a motto bearing the words *Sanctus, Sanctus*, etched repeatedly.

Mulcahy used his handkerchief to turn, cautiously, the

small key protruding from the lock at the centre of the sun, then levered each of the doors open with a pen. Inside, a silver chalice, with a burnished gold interior, glinted out. What took his breath away, what made him lean further in and stare with disbelief, was what was crowded in behind the chalice. Six wooden crosses, identical to the one outside on the altar, but each of these had another crucifix hanging by a chain from the arms and draped across the figure of the Christ. One was as tall as the wooden cross from which it hung, all flaking gold paint and blobs of coloured glass; he guessed immediately it had to be Grainne Mullins's 'Versace' cross. Another, not quite as big but brassy and plain, was probably the 'vicar's' cross Caroline Coyle had lost. Towards the front he saw a glittering chain holding a delicately wrought figure of Christ on a gold cross tipped at each extremity with a large brilliant-cut diamond and knew it had to be Jesica Salazar's. The others, he guessed, would be Catriona Plunkett's, Paula Halpin's and, perhaps, Shauna Gleeson's.

But none yet for the other crucifix standing bare outside on the altar linen. Waiting. He swallowed hard.

He looked around the room again. It was telling him everything he needed to know about Rinn except the one thing he wanted more than anything: where the hell had he taken Siobhan? Outside he heard a faint wail of sirens, then a shout from below. He ran out of the room and by the time he reached the bottom of the stairs, Cassidy was already standing by the open door, a blaze of blue emergency lights reflecting into the hall, directing one paramedic in green and yellow overalls into the back room, telling another to see immediately to the man out in the garage.

'How's the girl?' Mulcahy asked him.

'Not good, poor kid,' Cassidy said, looking a bit pale himself now. They both stepped back as another paramedic bustled past them, a walkie-talkie squawking on her epaulette.

'Did you find anything up there?' Cassidy asked him.

Mulcahy nodded. 'Like his own private monastery. All sorts of religious stuff. It was him, no question. All the girls' crosses are up there. Trophies. But I'm damned if I can find anything about where he might have taken Siobhan.'

'Did you see this stuff in here?' Cassidy opened the heavy panelled door into the dining room at the front of the house. Mulcahy had stuck his head in earlier but, seeing no sign of his goal, he had moved quickly on. Cassidy pointed towards the long mahogany dining table, which had a mass of papers spread out across its surface. One of the dining chairs was pushed away from the table as if someone had stood up suddenly and left.

'I thought maybe this was what he was doing when Fallon and her photographer pal turned up,' Cassidy said. 'He'd have seen them coming in the gate, from here.'

Sure enough, most of the front garden, the gate and part of the garage were visible from that angle through the large bay window. Cassidy's mobile rang and he went straight back into the hall. The only words Mulcahy caught were, 'Yeah, boss, that's right' as he went out. He went over to the

476

table, tried to make out what it was Rinn had been doing there. Some sheets of paper were fanned out on the polished surface, along with a large-format book and a fold-out map of the Phoenix Park. Mulcahy glanced over the map, saw nothing out of the ordinary. Most of the paper sheets were photocopies. Turning a couple of them towards him, he saw that they were blow-ups of lines from religious texts. *They that are Christ's have crucified the flesh with its passions and lusts. (Gal 5:24)* and *Put to death, therefore, whatever belongs to your earthly nature . . . the wrath of God is coming. (Col 3:5–6)* He turned them away, repelled, and drew the book towards him. It was a glossy picture book commemorating the Papal visit to Ireland in 1979. On the cover was a picture familiar to Mulcahy, a head-and-shoulders shot of Pope John Paul II, resplendent in vestments of green, white and gold, holding aloft his crozier. Mulcahy opened the book at a place bookmarked by an old photo. The image on the large double-page spread inside was equally familiar to him: a high crane shot of the vast sea of people surrounding the huge raised altar in the Phoenix Park, flags on tall standards fluttering in the breeze, everything dwarfed by the massive cross behind.

Mulcahy glanced at the photograph that had been used as a bookmark, its poorly fixed Polaroid colours faded by the years. It was of a group of boys and girls, all ten or eleven years old, all staring at the lens awkwardly. The kids looked like they were on a day trip from a disaster zone. Some were in wheelchairs, others on crutches, their limbs encased in plaster. At one end of the group, Mulcahy thought he recognised the face of a much younger Sean Rinn, a sad-looking boy with buzz-cut hair and a forced smile splayed across his mouth. Beneath a gaping shirt and cardigan, the whole of his torso, from his chin down to the waistband of his smartly pressed trousers, was swaddled in bandages. In the background was the same vast crowd and altar he'd seen in the book. He flipped the photo over. Scrawled in ink on the back was a caption: *Sodality of the Most Precious Blood, Phoenix Park, Sept 29, 1979.*

He heard footsteps behind him and turned.

'Brogan's on her way,' Cassidy said. 'Says some of the others will probably get here first. She has to come in from Tallaght.'

Mulcahy nodded. 'Any idea what a sodality is?'

Cassidy squinted uncomprehendingly. Mulcahy held up the photo, pointed at Rinn, then showed him what was written on the back. 'I saw it upstairs on some kind of a banner, too.'

'It's like a kind of association,' Cassidy said, 'set up for people to offer special devotions, prayers and masses on feast days and special times of the year. That one would be to commemorate the "precious blood" Jesus spilled on the cross for the salvation of mankind.'

'How do you know that?'

'I was schooled by the Presentation Brothers. They made us learn all that stuff about feast days and sodalities by rote. Beat the stuff into us. The Feast of the Most Precious Blood *is sort of movable, if I remember right. The first Sunday of July each year. Around now, in fact.'*

Mulcahy didn't need to check the date on his watch, but he did so automatically. 'It's tomorrow,' he said, and somehow that piece of information didn't make him feel any easier.

Cassidy held his hands up, moving past him to the table.

'What are you bothering with all that stuff for?' he said, sharply. 'This is what I thought you'd be interested in. I know the boss will.' He pushed away the book and sheets of paper, clearing space around the map of the Phoenix Park. It was an old Ordnance Survey map, exquisitely etched and printed. Cassidy was stabbing his finger towards the left hand side, where a circle had been drawn in pencil around the Y of the Furry Glen and the crowded contour lines marking out the hollow where Paula Halpin's body had been found.

'Bang to fuckin' rights,' Cassidy was saying, but Mulcahy's eye had snagged on another part of the map, an area of empty parkland where there was no pencil circle, just a broad expanse of green with its name, the Fifteen Acres, printed across it. Beneath the name, hardly distinguishable from the print above it, something had been added in a tiny script: *Deus non irridetur.* His heart stalled. It was the same message Siobhan had been sent: God will not be mocked.

Mulcahy's mind was swirling now, arching up, reaching towards understanding but swamped by too much information to process it quickly. Fractured images of Siobhan

479

on the television, of places and dates, of crowns of thorns, jagged pins and the blood of Christ. Too many possibilities, none of them good.

'He must've had a plan for Paula Halpin,' Mulcahy said. 'But it didn't work out. You said she had heart trouble, didn't you? Maybe she had a coronary when he was assaulting her but he didn't realise until it was too late. So he stashed the body near to where he needed it to be, but it was discovered. Then he went out and got another girl, but at the last moment fate intervened and got him someone even better, even more appropriate.'

'What're you on about?' Cassidy said, looking up.

'It must've seemed like a miracle to him: Siobhan Fallon just walking in his gate like that.' Mulcahy paused, breathing hard, making sure it pieced together right in his mind. 'What do you make of that?' he said, pointing to the Fifteen Acres on the map.

'There's nothing there,' Cassidy said, 'just grass.'

'But it's an old map, isn't it,' Mulcahy said. 'What's there now? What's been there since thirty years ago? Since 1979. What's there that ties in with all this other shite around here?'

Then it dawned on Cassidy too, and for a second all he did was yawp and utter a low, breathy, 'Shit!'

But Mulcahy was already halfway out the door, in far too much of a panic to care if Cassidy was following him or not.

Mulcahy barely registered the great sweep of grand old Dublin he sped through as he negotiated the last clumps of

480

late traffic in Rathmines, jumped the bridge over the Grand Canal and onwards, past the arc-lit spires of St Patrick's Cathedral, tilting down beneath the gothic arches of Christchurch into Winetavern Street until, with a cater-wauling of abused tyres, he swung the car hard left onto the riverside at Merchant's Quay. From there he put his foot to the floor and kept his hand on the horn as they sped past bridge after bridge, leaving it to fate and sobriety to stop any other traffic straying into his path. Cassidy, who'd only just made it into the passenger seat before Mulcahy gunned the Saab and roared away, spent most of the journey in silence, one hand lodged like a shock absorber between the car ceiling and his head, cursing every time a wheel slammed into a pothole, watching the road ahead with the fixed focus of a man who's been in many a chase at speed and never once enjoyed the experience. Mulcahy barely noticed him or, if he did, he didn't care. His focus was on beating the Irish land speed record. Up the quays he sped, from Merchant's to Usher's to Victoria until finally, at Heuston Station, he ripped a few more millimetres off his tyres swinging north across the bridge to hare up Parkgate Street and in through the monumental stone pillars guarding the entrance to the Phoenix Park.

'Are you not even going to ask me why?' Cassidy finally said, as they plunged headlong into the darkness of the Park itself. Mulcahy switched on his main beams then glanced quickly over at him, as much time as he could spare before he had to twist the car into and out of a roundabout.

'No,' he said coldly. 'You shafted me. Why would a reason, good or bad, make any difference to me?'

'Maybe now's not the time,' Cassidy said. And Mulcahy just grunted as he floored the accelerator again, blazing a full mile up the rule-straight carriageway until, at the Phoenix Monument, he swung the wheel hard left and sped down into the still deeper darkness of Acres Road. Without any warning, he killed the headlights, and his speed, and let the car coast on into the black stillness. Mulcahy hushed Cassidy's gasp with a peremptory 'Shush!' He strained forward, trying to make out the way ahead, then steered the car onto a narrow slip road. He slowed to a snail's pace. Around them a thinly wooded copse of silver birch loomed like the endlessly mirrored bars of a cage, blocking their line of sight both ahead and to the right. To their left, spread out beyond the broad grass plain stretching away to the south, the lights of the suburbs twinkled on the skyline like a galaxy of earth-bound stars. Mulcahy brought the car to a halt in front of a low red-and-white metal barrier that blocked any further progress.

At just that moment, as if some higher power had decided to lend a hand, the thick cloud cover split apart and a huge moon lit up the landscape all around them. Finding themselves staring ahead across a vast expanse of lonely car park, both men seemed awestruck by what was revealed in the distance ahead: the steep grassy mound rising up from the flat land all around, the high sweep of stone steps cut into its side, the vast metal cross rising fifty, maybe sixty metres

482

into the night sky, its twin arms spread in glory, its cold, hard steel blazing white in the moonlight. And below it, even more exposed than they were, a lone white van was parked at the bottom of the steps – the only vehicle in sight.

'It's him.' Mulcahy turned to Cassidy, the tension cracking his voice.

'What the fuck is he up to?' Cassidy whispered. But neither of their imaginations wanted to go there.

'Can you see anybody over there?' Mulcahy asked. But he knew it was too far away. From this distance, the base of the cross merged into the darkness of the park beyond. 'They could still be in the van, but either way, we've got to get over there now. And on foot, so we don't spook him and get ourselves into a hostage situation.'

Mulcahy opened his door but Cassidy put a restraining hand on his arm.

'Wait, I'll call for back up, then we'll go.'

They skirted around the south side of the car park, keeping low, as good as invisible against the dark grass now that the cloud had come over again. For a while, every rustling footstep, every breath, seemed to scream out their presence to the emptiness around them, but they got used to that. And as the cross loomed ever closer, the stiff wind began to carry sounds other than their own towards them. Strange sounds, an irregular metal-on-metal hammering and a faint clanking that reminded Mulcahy of a sea breeze whipping through rigging. As they approached the base of

483

the mound, he waved Cassidy down with the flat of his hand and they crouched on the grass, eyes fixed on the van parked only twenty metres away now. There was no sign of life from it. Above them, the hammering stopped and the sound of something heavy being dragged across a concrete surface reached them briefly before being snatched away again by the wind.

'Whatever he's at, it's all going on up there,' Mulcahy whispered, pointing to the top of the steps. 'I'll go up the grass bank on this side and have a look, you head to the van and look after Siobhan if she's in there. If not, come by the steps to back me up. If he bolts he'll be coming your way. Okay?'

Mulcahy watched for a moment as Cassidy headed towards the van, then started making his way up the side of the mound. The wind was picking up, and the slope was steeper than it appeared from below. He felt the grass cold and moist against his hands, getting slipperier the more he sought purchase. As he neared the top, he looked up. All the weight and majesty of the towering steel cross seemed to bear down on him. Then he saw something strange. Swinging against the night sky, two long loops of rope were whipping in the wind, one hanging down from each of the great steel arms. And then he understood what the clanking sound he'd heard had been. But before he could figure out their purpose, he saw the ropes suddenly go taut, and what appeared to be a long, dark bundle began rising in a jerking motion against the upright column of the cross. As the bank of cloud above broke once more, the moon again illuminated the scene. And Mulcahy's worst fears were realised. Above him, a grotesque crucifixion was being enacted. The naked, lifeless body of Siobhan Fallon hung from a crude timber cross, which in turn was suspended by the ropes from the great steel arms above. Her hands and feet were dark with blood where they met the timber. Beneath her right breast a horizontal gash bled profusely down her belly. Her head, slumped forward, bore what could only be a barbed crown.

For a split second Mulcahy was paralysed by what he was seeing, fear and exhaustion threatening to overcome him. But there was no time to think, and something in his training, or in his heart, willed him up the last few feet and out on to the wide concrete platform at the top. Six or seven metres away at the base of the cross, dwarfed by it, Sean Rinn stood, hauling, hand over hand, his obscene crucifixion higher and higher. He was dressed in what appeared to be climbing gear, metal clips and fastenings dangling from a belt across his chest. But it was what he had in his hands that Mulcahy cared about: a loop of steel-tight rope that stretched up into the night and down, via a complicated-looking belay system, to a hook embedded in the concrete at his feet.

Could he take him by surprise? Mulcahy wondered where Cassidy had got to, but there was no time to wait. He stepped out onto the exposed platform, trying to keep behind his man. But before he'd even got halfway there,

485

Rinn sensed his presence and turned, panic and recognition seizing his face.

'Stop, you – keep back,' he snarled at Mulcahy. 'If I let go she'll fall. She'll die.'

Mulcahy didn't move a muscle, but the flicker of hope in his chest flared up like a gas main. She was alive.

'Come on, man, don't be a fool,' Mulcahy shouted into the wind. 'Don't make it any worse for yourself. Let her down. It's not too late.'

'Shut your mouth,' Rinn screamed at him. 'Shut up or I'll drop her. It'll be on your conscience, not mine.'

Mulcahy risked one more step forward, but even that was a step too far. Screaming at him again, Rinn let go of the rope. As it ran through his hands, Siobhan plummeted with sickening speed. Then, just as quickly, Rinn jerked the rope to a stop again, the thump of the abrupt halt eliciting a long, low groan of pain from above. Mulcahy froze as a shower of blood spattered down around them.

'Okay, Sean, I'm stopped, see,' Mulcahy said to him, as calm as he could despite the fear clawing at his brain, desperate to find something to say to make Rinn keep hold of that rope. 'I'm just trying to help you do the right thing here. I know you didn't mean to kill that girl, Paula. And you don't want to do that to Siobhan up there, either. She didn't do anything to deserve this, did she?'

'Deserve it?' Rinn roared. 'She's the worst whore of them all, wearing the sign of Christ's sacrifice round her neck even as she spews her filth to all and sundry. I told her, I told them all that God would not be mocked. But did anyone listen? Well, they'll listen now—'

Something in Mulcahy's face must have betrayed him, a flicker of his eye, perhaps, because Rinn suddenly whirled around then and saw Cassidy, advancing towards him from the top of the steps on the other side of the platform.

'Stay back or she dies,' Rinn howled, his eyes ping-ponging from Cassidy to Mulcahy, all but popping out from panic. Mulcahy knew he wouldn't have such a strong chance again, and he lunged towards him. But he wasn't fast enough to cover the ground. Rinn let go of the rope and ran.

For Mulcahy there was never any question: he was always going for the rope and not the man. The rush of its terrible burden falling, the shriek of the line streaking through the belay filled his ears. But his mind saw himself catching it, and his hand closed round something thin and hard and pliable, and he felt his palm scorched raw and his wrist snap back with a vicious crack. The force of it almost ripped his arm from its socket – but he had it. He had her. Both hands now. And through the pain he was holding on, and Cassidy was beside him, telling him that he, too, had a hold on it, and if they just paid it out slowly together they could lower Siobhan safely the last few feet to the ground.

It was all a blur to Mulcahy. His wrist kept shooting fusillades of pain up his arm and his shoulder felt like it had been torn apart. As the wooden cross finally touched the ground they laid it out as gently as they could until it settled flat on its back with a soft thud. Siobhan was in an awful mess, far beyond anywhere he could reach her, from the shock and the loss of blood, moaning and whimpering but still, just, alive. He went to try and lift her to him, to comfort her somehow, but Cassidy held him back, pointing to the ropes binding her wrists and ankles to the cross, and to the crude iron nails driven through her palms and the arches of her feet. He took off his jacket and covered her as best he could. On the wind, just then, they both heard the distant clunk of a van door closing and looked up together.

'Don't worry about him,' Cassidy said, phone in his hand, already dialling. 'I made sure that van's going nowhere, and back up should be here any minute.'

But Mulcahy's head was addled by pain and full of a black rage. He stood up and stumbled towards the steps, all his focus now on the van and the murderous madman inside it, who was still trying to get the engine to turn over. As he ran down each step another jolt of pain rasped through him like a bandsaw. He could hear a low wail of sirens and see the blue scatter of emergency lights through the trees, but he had to be the one who got there first. He was the one enflamed by righteous anger now. He was the one determined to exact revenge.

It was only when he reached the van that he realised he was in no condition to act as anyone's avenging angel. Light-headed already, when he pulled the handle on the driver's door a crippling torrent of agony flamed back up his arm and into his shoulder. Still behind the wheel of the van, Rinn was leaning away from him, desperately pulling something from the glovebox and at the same time kicking out with all the might in his legs. The van door shot out and smacked Mulcahy square on the chest and chin, sending him sprawling backwards on the grass. Lying there, everything became clearer and slower as a fresh agony pulsed from his shoulder into every individual nerve-cell in his body.

He saw Rinn jump from the van and loom above him, a gun cradled in his hands – a rust-mottled ancient old Webley revolver that must've been his grandfather's – a look of maniacal triumph on his face, screaming the Lord's Prayer at him.

'Our Father, who art in heaven,
hallowed be Thy name . . .'

The long barrel was aimed right at Mulcahy's eyes, and he couldn't even raise an arm to shield himself.

'Thy Kingdom come . . .'

Instinctively Mulcahy tried to roll away from him but couldn't and then, like a vision from above, he saw a dark shadow rushing up behind Rinn. It was Cassidy, with something big and black and glinting in his hand – it looked for all the world like a big metal cross – and he was swinging it.

'Thy Will be done . . .'

The last thing Mulcahy saw was Rinn going down like a dynamited chimney, the last sounds a sickening crunch of skull, the song of sirens and the screech of brakes and Cassidy cursing above him.

'Jesus Christ almighty, some gobshites just can't leave well enough alone.'

Epilogue

Mulcahy lay back in the stern of *Seaspray*, his wrist cast resting on a cushion, his left shoulder tight, snug and comparatively pain-free in the compression brace he'd been wearing every day for the best part of a fortnight. A dislocated shoulder, torn ligaments and a radial fracture of the wrist should really have cost him a lot more pain, he thought, but most of the repair work had been done while he was under sedation, and they'd got him up and out of hospital the following day. Now, so long as he was careful not to move suddenly and kept taking the anti-inflammatories, the worst he suffered was the occasional vicious twinge. Despite the threat of torturous physio to come, as far as he was concerned his injuries looked a lot worse than they actually were. Even beneath the baggiest T-shirt he could find, the Kevlar-like brace and wrist restraints made him look like an extra from a sci-fi movie – a fact that hadn't escaped his shipmate for the day.

'Ahoy, Robocop, get that down your neck and maybe then you'll loosen up enough to show me how to get this

491

yoke moving,' Liam Ford said, handing him another Bud and sitting down so heavily the keel threatened to break water on the port side.

Mulcahy let a disdainful grunt be his answer to that. There was no way they could take the boat out. He couldn't so much as man the rudder with this brace on, and Ford wouldn't know one end of a boat from the other. But, even tied up at the marina in Dun Laoghaire, just lying there in the cool air, with the sun on his face and a cold beer in his one useful hand, was enough for him. He closed his eyes and let the heat and alcohol lull him away until a curse, a rustle of newspaper and Ford's booming Cork basso forced him back to consciousness.

'I see your woman's been at it again,' he said, pointing at the wide red banner splashed across the top of the *Sunday Herald*'s front page. MY CRUCIFIXION HELL, PART II by Siobhan Fallon, with a photograph to match. Not that it was the main story any more, two weeks on: that honour going to some politician who'd been snapped snorting coke in a Leeson Street nightclub. 'Jaysus, will she ever shut up about it, do you think?'

'Not until they've milked every last drop from it,' Mulcahy said, smiling at Ford's pathetic effort to wind him up.

He'd already read the piece, as well as her first instalment the week before, and thought it was pretty good overall. How she'd done it from her hospital bed was beyond him. She must've had to dictate it to someone, he guessed. And although it was all hyped up too much for his taste, it was amazingly atmospheric. Oddly enough, though, both of Siobhan's articles, and the rest of the *Herald*'s coverage, were comparatively restrained by the standards of the rest of the press, who had proceeded to fall upon Rinn like a pack of ravenous wolves. Especially when word came back from on high that it was unlikely Rinn would ever see the inside of a courtroom, as he'd been sectioned within hours of his arrest and was now detained indefinitely at the Central Mental Hospital in Dundrum. His court-appointed counsel had already indicated that any attempt by the DPP to take the case to trial would be met with a motion to declare Rinn unfit to stand. And the consensus of opinion on that was that it would almost certainly be upheld, not least when Interpol enquiries regarding the years he'd spent teaching abroad revealed a long history of schizophrenia and abuse.

Thus unconstrained by any judicial threat of contempt, the press had gone to town on Rinn – by way of the butchers. Every unearthable fact of his life was pulled out, torn apart and pontificated upon by as many half-cocked pundits as had opinions to peddle. No one seemed even to notice, let alone care, that Emmet Byrne had been released, his reputation intact, or that Catriona Plunkett and Shauna Gleeson, Rinn's two surviving victims, were both still fighting for their lives in hospital. A couple of papers had given them a paragraph or two but the rest just trampled right over them in the easy stampede to heap judgement on Rinn.

Mulcahy silently cursed the lot of them. Few in the media

had any real interest in the truth, as far as he could see, only in making their voices heard above the throng.

Of course, Mulcahy had his own ideas about Rinn. He tracked them through in his head as he lay awake in the night, unable to find comfort enough for sleep. But few of them led anywhere definite. All the psychiatrists in the world could say Rinn was a paranoid schizophrenic acting in the belief that he was getting instruction directly from St Paul. It would never make any difference to Mulcahy. Only one piece of evidence struck him as having anything like the ring of truth to it. Something that he hadn't seen in any of the newspapers. It had been posted to him by an anonymous well-wisher in Kerry, a fellow cop, obviously, as it came wrapped in a Garda file folder – a photocopy of the 1974 accident report, dug out from the Killarney District archives, into the tragic car crash in which Sean Rinn's parents had died, and he'd been so badly burned. The contents included typed-up notes from the attending officers, who'd been the first to arrive at the scene some ten to fifteen minutes after the collision. Rinn's parents had been killed straight off, they recorded. Young Sean, just six years old, had been thrown by the impact out of the back seat into the front, where he'd lain in his mother's lifeless lap as the car caught fire and everything in it burst into flame around him. Only the gallantry of one Garda John Reynolds, attending, had saved the lad's life – risking his own by plunging into the fire, to pull the boy free despite the child's reluctance to let go of his mother, to whom he was clinging for protection even at this grim pass. So fierce was the heat, added a footnote at the bottom of the page, that a small silver crucifix, which the boy had pulled from round his dead mother's neck in the struggle to drag him free, had became fused to the palm of his tiny left hand and could only be removed days later by surgery, when the doctors at Killarney District Hospital deemed his condition stable enough to cope with an operation of that nature.

This was the kind of detail Mulcahy understood: something he could latch onto and let his imagination run with as far as it wanted to go. It was as much as he needed. What really mattered, in the end, was that Rinn had killed one young woman and ruined the lives of six others. And, of course, that he'd been caught. That's what got Mulcahy through the bad dreams and the night sweats – knowing for certain, when he woke, that he'd stopped Rinn.

It was that, too, which made his current human resources status of 'suspended pending disciplinary hearing' bearable too. At least he'd get to argue his case in front of a panel, and not just Brendan Healy. Of course, the obvious fly in the ointment there was Cassidy. The sergeant had turned up in the hospital the day after, pleading with Mulcahy not to grass him up to Internal Affairs over the leaks. If pleading was the right word, that is, for the grudging, wheedling bullshit he'd offered by way of justification, about how he'd never taken the money from Siobhan and even some bollocks about Mulcahy's father spiking his chances of promotion years back – for no good reason at all, he'd

495

whined. But Mulcahy knew his father had always been a good judge of men; he'd probably sniffed the rottenness in Cassidy straight off.

Still, Mulcahy did feel he couldn't just drop the sergeant in the shit now. After all, the man had saved his life. Yet neither was he sure he'd be happy to let it lie entirely. That something he'd have to weigh up carefully. But not now. There'd be plenty of time for that later.

The one thing he couldn't shake off was the memory of Siobhan Fallon hanging from the cross. She loomed there above him every night as he lay in bed, her naked body nailed to the rough planks, her blood showering down all round him, like an agonised spectre perpetually haunting his mind. Even going to see her in the hospital hadn't managed to dispel the memory or even dim it slightly. It had only made it worse, if anything. There had been something so awkward, so unsettling, between them in that room. She'd seemed so hesitant, so reluctant to meet his eye or smile. It was like they'd never known each other before. And then, after just five minutes, some other guy had come in, an older, odd-looking fella – Vincent something or other, he'd said – with a huge bunch of flowers, and Mulcahy had made his excuses and left. Rinn, it seemed, had succeeded in killing something that night, after all.

Mulcahy felt a stab of pain in his shoulder as he shifted his position to look around the harbour and out at the calm waters of the wide bay beyond. There wasn't much traffic going in and out just now and he longed to let a keen sea breeze wash across his face and body and cleanse him of this land and all the pain that inhabited it. Maybe Liam was right. Maybe he did need to loosen up a bit.

'Do you think you could handle her if we stuck to the motor and took her out beyond the harbour wall a bit?'

'Jaysus, he lives!' Ford laughed. 'Just tell me where to point the feckin' thing, and let's be on our way.'

Acknowledgements

Special thanks to my agent Broo Doherty for believing, to David Shelley, Daniel Mallory, Thalia Proctor and all at Little, Brown in London for their generosity, enthusiasm and support and also to Breda Purdue at Hachette Ireland.

Thanks also to my fellow writers at Criminal Classes: Kathryn Skoyles, Richard Holt, Elena Forbes, Keith Mullins, Cass Bonner and Nicola Williams, and our wise friends Margaret Kinsman and Chris Sykes; to Neil Midgley, Andrew Pettie and all the team at the *Telegraph*; to David Headley; to Lisanne Radice; to Dr Emma Norris; to the Bristol Writers Group; to Mark Bolton; to Noel Monaghan; to the staff at the Garda Press Office and all other members of the Garda Siochana who aided and abetted me in writing this book.

Finally, enormous gratitude to my mother, Jo; to Noelle, Carmel, Billy, Tony, Clare, Gill and Alison; and above all, to my beautiful wife, Angela, for her faith, hope and clarity.